LOTTE

MARTIN RAYMOND

indie
NOVELLA

First published in Great Britain in 2024
by Indie Novella Ltd.

INDIE NOVELLA www.indienovella.co.uk

Editor: Damien Mosley
Book design & typesetting: InsideStudio26.com
Cover Design: Charlotte Daniels

Editorial Support from Gina Adams,
Rachel Brook and Hanine Kadi

A CIP catalogue record for this title is available
from the British Library

Paperback ISBN 978 1 738 44211 9

Printed and bound by TJ Books in the United Kingdom.

Indie Novella is committed to a sustainable future for our readers
and the world in which we live. All paper used are natural,
renewable and sustainable products.

Indie Novella is grateful that our work is supported using
public funding by Arts Council England.

I.M.
Charlotte Agnes Candow 1896-1933

PROLOGUE

MARTIN

2pm Saturday 26th February 2017

Round our kitchen table, in the early gloaming of a late winter afternoon, the dead were casually introduced.

'You know about your grandmother?'

'Yes,' I said. It wasn't altogether a lie. But not entirely true either. Her death had been tragic, early, maybe a sudden illness, something once incurable, now trivial. That's what I knew. To be honest, I hadn't been that interested. What was the point? You couldn't change anything. What's gone is gone. Or so I thought.

'And the asylum?'

'Yes,' I said. That was entirely a lie.

'It's all there.' His pale eyes were level with mine. I often put his directness down to his Danish background – an un-British impatience with the tentative – and attributed his openness to his big teeming family. He went on. 'All the names are on the archive website. Terrible stories. Some photographs too, of the earlier cases, the Victorian ones. But

Charlotte Raymond is there.' In the silence he stroked his neat beard. We all sat there, me, him, Molly my wife, and Yvonne his partner – our daughter. We all considered the news from 1933.

One evening I was on an aircraft hit by lightning. During take-off. It was a commuter flight – tired men and women in suits going home at the end of a long day. There was a flash, a thud, our climb faltered and for a moment we were all weightless. But we didn't drop out of the sky. As we rose again, the pilot explained that systems had been checked and we would continue to Edinburgh as scheduled. What was remarkable was not one person reacted. It wasn't that no one squealed, prayed, clutched at strangers – it was that no one acknowledged what had happened at all. A raised eyebrow in row 12, maybe. We continued to read our Evening Standards. Checked watches. This is how the world ends. Not screaming but frowning.

Back at the kitchen table, I ate my home-grown runner beans. I nodded. Smiled, agreed completely with everything that was said and the conversation moved on as if nothing had happened.

1.

LOTTE

Thursday 16th March 1933

She closed the heavy door behind her, shutting all of them in: Sam, the boys, the baby and Grace too. Lotte sensed their sleeping bodies in their rooms, imagined their breathing, the tiny disturbances in the quiet house. She pulled on her gloves. Embracing the dark, she let herself be collected up by the night.

On the pavement, she paused, inhaled the cold air, sharp with smoke and dampness. As distinctive in its way as the smell of her baby's hair. This was what she needed.

She strode down the wide, familiar street that curved past the high villas, their towers and gables, round the crouching mass of the dark church on the corner. Her boots clicked on the stone. She felt no need to think about how she might be seen by others – perhaps a fellow insomniac, reading or smoking near a window.

The road was straight. Above to the right, the bulk of Stirling Castle floated between the rock and the inkier black of the sky. Three pinpoints of light up there, always. Lotte marched on. Her heart beat faster as she concentrated on the soothing mechanics of walking, finding a pace that would take her the maximum distance in the time she had. An apple and a crumbling scone in one pocket. In the other, her purse.

The last few villas were the biggest, back from the street, only the steep roofs catching the gaslight above big stone walls. She was on the edge of town now where paths ran down through the woods from behind the Castle rock. She did not want to run into a group of working men, emboldened by drink and the dark. Not that she feared working men, how could she? But she was wary of drink and wanted no intrusion into her solitude.

A parked car lay ahead, one red light glowing against the immense dark of the open country beyond. As she approached she quietened her step, ghosting as she went past. A daring lovers' tryst? Very modern. Or was it a commercial traveller sleeping here to avoid costs? Perhaps one that served the shop. She did not want an awkward conversation in the dark.

Then a junction. North or west? She sniffed the air like an animal. Already it was clear of the smoke that gathered under the lights on cold nights. There was a suggestion of a frost but, if anything, she was too warm inside her tweed coat. She turned to the west, the long level road along the Gargunnock Hills, the flat fields of the Forth stretching away on her right. A road so straight there were no surprises in the daylight. But in the depths of the night it was adventure itself. She felt the space around her, the inverse of the locked room and of Sam and Grace in the hallway, deciding what was best for her.

Occasional lamps gleamed from cottages and farms, in the distance the ochre clusters of lit villages. The still air amplified her steps on the road. She kept well out from the hedgerows and ditches, clipping along briskly on the gravelly centre. As her eyes adjusted, she distinguished different grades of darkness. The faint light of stars through scattered clouds picked out the dusty breadth of the road. Darkness pooled under trees and in the shadow of hedges. Out here, there was no smooth tarmac, and she could smell and feel the animal waste under her boots. No matter, they'd clean, and she couldn't always watch her step. She was out here because she did not want to watch her step. A gate to her right closed across the wider dark of a field and she jumped at the stumbling bulk of invisible cows. Her heart raced in the old, bad way. Calm, calm. She breathed slowly, taking her body in hand, settling it like a fidgety horse.

She forced herself over to the gate. Took in the sweet, silage smell of cow breath and the tearing sound of pulled grass. She ran her gloved fingers across the top bar of the gate, smooth from leaning farmers and stretching beasts.

'Just cows, just cows, just cows,' she said, breathing purposefully.

'Just fucken cows alright, lassie.'

Stepping back, the skin on her arms crackling with electricity, she felt her pulse in her fingertips. There was a peak of fear but then it was gone. There was no mystery here, she could make sense of this voice in the dark. And besides, there was a five-barred wooden gate.

'Good morning to you, missus.' The voice was Glasgow, of course, but not the roughest sort with notes of somewhere else, Ireland or Argyll. She could see his shape between the bars of the gate, sitting up, half under the hedge: hair, a beard, eyes white in the starlight. Over the smell of damp and dirt, the sharpness of spirits.

'Good morning.' She was breathing normally again, her heart at rest.

'A fine bright night to take the air.'

'Yes it is.' Politeness could get you through any encounter. 'Spring weather can be uncertain.'

'You don't need to tell me of that. The only warm air here is the breath of these beasts and that would stun an elephant.'

'The dawn can't be far off.' She slipped her father's watch out of her inside pocket. After three. She calculated the effect of the dull flash of gold on the man. But no, she knew there was no danger here.

'The dawn is earlier every day.' He coughed and in the dark field some cows made a short, thumping run.

'Are you travelling far?' She gestured back towards the streetlight glow. 'You're only a few miles from the town.'

These last few hard years had increased the traffic of men and women on the roads. Whether heading north or south, their quests funnelled them into Stirling where they beached in the vennels and the lodging houses.

'Town isn't the place for me. I am not partial to the company.'

'Are you going to a job?'

'Work isn't the cure.' He had made no attempt to rise, but his eyes never left her. 'It's the money that can put you right. Put you back to where you came from.'

'And where have you come from?'

'I had my business.' He paused, pulled on a bottle and the ether smell came through the dark again. 'I am an engineer. We were small, three men strong. The best axle brackets in Scotland.'

There was a rustle above in the trees. Birds beginning to move.

'But carts are going and there was nothing from the bank and then you'll do anything to stay afloat even if that sinks you quicker.'

She was leaning, listening as his voice dropped away. She reached into her pocket, into her purse. Without pulling it out she felt inside for a folded pound note.

'Please take this.' She bent and passed the note through the bars of the gate. His hand came into the dim half-light and touched her glossy gloves for a second. 'And please try to give up the alcohol. You know it will not help.'

'Thank you, madam.' She sensed he wanted to say the right thing. 'I would have been welcome in your house once. I will be again.' He was gathering himself as if to rise.

'Please, I've disturbed you long enough. I must move on. Goodnight, and I wish you well.'

She walked on quickly, not through fear of being followed, but to get away from what he embodied, a once comfortable life sprawled now under a hedge. How close they all were to having nothing. She glanced back. There were only black shadows where the gate lay between the hedge and the arching trees. But beyond the Ochils and the Castle rock, there was a lightness to the sky. She felt strong and clear. This was better than sleep and far better than a dark bedroom, the clock ticking and Sam restless in his own room.

At a crossroads she took a road to the right. As the sky became less dark, the black hills to the north began to form. The going was easy and level, her heart was steady and she turned to the fields and hedges. Sam, the house, the shop, Lily, the boys, her constant sense of anxiety were all soothed by the smells and sounds of the night. Even the words of the tramp could be worked away by the regular beat of her boots on the road, the ping and rattle of the odd stone she scuffed and sent rolling into the verge.

Then she saw the cottage. At first, she could not distinguish whether it was coming towards her or she towards it. She stopped. It continued. Square and dark with two small lights downstairs. Again, her heart broke into a run. Was it happening again? A live drunk behind a gate was something she could understand. But this vision was a real threat. She stood, tall and tense, quivering as she waited for her mind to make sense of the impossible.

As it approached in the dark, she heard the growl of the generator, a modern farm with its own electrical power. And then it was upon her. Towering, forcing her to step back onto the verge. The two men in the front, one old, one young, above the headlights and underlit by the dashboard, their brown coats and caps. Then as the float inched past not much faster than she could walk, she peered in through the slats. The huge liquid eyes of the calves, the delicate lashes and the sound of their breathing. Market day, of course. She watched the cattle truck sway into the dark till all that was left was a tiny red light.

A first bird sang. A blackbird, invisible in a tree as she passed below, its soaring treble filling the tree and the night. The single voice was joined by others as the sky lightened. She looked back over the hedge to the south and east. Blues and pinks in the sky, cloudier than she had imagined, hanging over the broad fields of the Carse. Her legs were tired now. She was hungry. She took out Grace's scone. It had crumbled away in her pocket to half its size, but she ate it anyway. The great hills to the north – Ben Ledi, Stùc a' Chroin, Vorlich – were fully formed now. Closer, she could see the lights of Thornhill, built on the slope above the Carse, like a coastal village.

She sang,

'I to the hills will lift mine eyes

From whence does come mine aid…'

Her voice rose above the road and mingled with the birds. The mist was thickening in the half-light when Peter appeared out of a lane, sauntering, swaggering even. He was wearing his helmet with the camouflage cloth, the one in the only picture she had of him in France. The only one not in a studio, no painted backcloth, but summer fields stretching away. This morning he had no rifle, but his pack was high over his shoulder, a cup or a canteen clanked. His face was pale but unmarked, tired around the eyes. Suddenly she noticed how gritty her own eyes felt.

'Hello, cousin.' He winked. 'You're early out.'

'Late. I'm not sleeping.'

'Over-rated, sleep.' He had a cigarette in his mouth now. The match flared in his face, warming it. She would have touched his cheek, felt the stubble that was still new to him. But that couldn't be.

'I'm better out here, in the open. You said in the open it's safe.' She drew closer to him, to the glow of his cigarette in the dawn.

He smiled in the shadow of the helmet. 'Little good it did me, in the open, out under the flares.'

'I can't do it. This life isn't working for me.'

'You're a woman now, Lotte. What did your mum say? You make your bed? My mum would have said the same. They were all great fatalists, the aunts.'

'Until they made things happen out of nothing.'

'You have your own family now.'

'I think I'd be better away from all of them. And then I think they would be lost. And I'd be lost too.'

'They need you, Lotte, more than you need them. Get some sleep, some peace.'

'I'm lost.'

'But you're not, Lotte. In your fine coat and collar.' He let out a thick screen of smoke. 'You're a woman of this town – of some standing. And the children. Keep on. This is nothing. Try a three-day bombardment.'

Two farm girls, a milk-churn between them, came out of a road-end in a giggle of gossip.

'Fine morning missus,' said one. The other rolled her eyes. What was this woman doing out in the dawn?

Lotte marched on. Peter usually cheered her, but it wasn't a lasting help. She walked on as the sun rose and the birds settled. She passed two cars and a motorbike trailing exhaust fumes before she came into the village to the chimes of the church bell. Six o'clock. At the inn she asked the maid for a pot of tea and if she could call a car to take her back to town. As she drank the tea from the floral cup, she looked out of the window across the ground she had crossed in the night, towards the Castle and the smoke rising above the town as fires were lit in a thousand grates.

The car took her back along the same roads she had walked in the night. In the gathering light and shifting mist the journey seemed shorter, prosaic. But the calm she had absorbed from the darkness stayed with her even though the ride in the back of the large car diminished the distance and the wildness. The night, the walking, had worked.

The road seemed so different now, in daylight, in the shell of the car, it was just scenery passing. She couldn't identify the gate and there was no sign of the tramp.

When they reached town she asked the driver to drop her

round the corner. As she walked from Melville Terrace into Snowdon Place, she saw Dr Campbell's car leave a plume of blue smoke in the roadway.

At the foot of the front steps she looked up to see Grace standing in the doorway. The two women said nothing. Grace turned her back and Lotte followed her into the sitting room. The house was silent.

'Where is Lily?' said Lotte.

'Sleeping upstairs. I called Dr Campbell.' Grace offered nothing more. She was going to drag this out, it seemed. Lotte pulled her hat off, ran her hand through her hair and made towards the doorway, the stairs. Grace stood in her way:

'Best to let her be. The child has suffered all night. As if she was choking. Breathing coming and going. I held off waking the house. Because I knew you were out again.'

'Let me see her.'

Grace stood square in the doorway.

'I waited till they'd all got up and breakfasted and were away to work and school. "Is Lotte not up yet?" Sleeping late, I said. And Lily too. Just let her sleep, I said. And expecting her to be up and running about at any minute. Imagine what it was like for me, waiting, holding off, hoping all was well.' She gathered up the corner of her apron to dab the corners of her eyes, one after the other.

'What did Dr Campbell say? Please tell me.' Lotte clung on to the night's peace even though the front room was flooded with light now, motes floating.

'He did a full examination, Dr Campbell. Colic, he said, and left a bottle.' She looked out from under her brows. 'Just colic. But that's not how it looked in the middle of the night.'

Lotte stood, walked into the light of the long window.

'Why? Where do you go? Leaving your family. What if something happens? There's men, there's all sorts.'

The two women faced each other. The rich red rug glowed between them in the morning sun.

'Because I need to. I need to walk.'

'I paid Dr Campbell out of the housekeeping – so he wouldn't send an invoice. I lied to your husband, your children. I can't lie for you always.'

'I know. You're like a sister, more than my own. This,' she swivelled on her heel, taking in the room, 'would be so much more difficult without you.'

Lotte turned away again, into the light. When she heard Grace's feet on the stairs she went over to the piano and lifted the lid gently.

The Journal of Dr John Fergusson:

Tuesday 18th April 1933

I start this journal in an unused casebook from the army. When I hold it up I can smell the life of another institution and it's just the place to record my own little war. Now I have the time, with Emily and the children in Buxton, I shall sit every evening and preserve fragments of the day and the memories they prompt– like ferns between these pages. Otherwise they will disappear. And if I ever face questions again, I will want more than my uncertain recollections. Here, back in Scotland, at this county asylum, I will have a proper testament.

This casebook with its scuffed leather and lingering air of damp– and worse – had lain in my desk at Rainhill, gathering more mildew in the Liverpool weather. And before then, it with me, unused, at Craiglockhart, another grand building with high windows, converted to contain the infinite variety of human misery. Our most infamous patient, Lieutenant Sassoon, would describe the vista over Edinburgh as more desolate than the Front, particularly on Sundays. In those days he was a subversive threat rather than a pacifist hero. Only his Military Cross saved him. I'd left before he met Owen and all that, but I regretted not making use of my journal at that time. I agreed with Sassoon on the view though.

Dr Andrews and I would stand at the Craiglockhart windows through that winter of 1916, watching the light die early in the afternoon, before the building shut down for the long terrifying night. In our three-month detachment we met Rivers twice. His focus was always the patients, not colleagues, but his presence was all over the hospital. A castle of damaged men.

'The old man's the future,' Andrews said.

'He has many to convince.'

'Look at the evidence here, man. Conclusive.'

'It's all a bit… anecdotal,' I said.

'It's better than any other treatment. And this could not be a bigger test. What these patients have been through isn't normal. And yet he cures them.'

'So they can go back to France and get a final cure out on the wire?'

'It's what they want. They're proper soldiers.' Andrews was an only son of the manse from up in Angus somewhere. He later lost his enthusiasm for psychiatry and retrained in anaesthetics– the coming thing. He was cut to bits by a long-range shell less than a year later, while assisting with a field amputation near Pozières.

'They'd be better with a poorer psychiatrist, don't you think? One that kept them mentally shattered but still in possession of intact flesh and bone. Our success is generally a death sentence,' I said as I watched the ships and Fife beyond disappear behind a drift of rain.

'Sometimes I don't think you understand soldiering one little bit.' His nail tapped the window for emphasis. For someone brought up in the Church, Andrews had a great appetite for the martial spirit. He was a better army doctor than I ever was because he understood that amid the shattering and tearing there was an excitement that couldn't be experienced anywhere but on the battlefield. Little good it did him.

We didn't see much of Dr Rivers. He was more interested in the patients than training juniors. But it didn't take much. A few stuttering words in the corridor, his wisdom left hanging in the air along with his pipe smoke. That was enough to make us acolytes. But under this remote influence and despite the dismay of seeing our greatest successes on subsequent casualty lists, we learned that physicians could not apply a simple cure to these sundered souls. All officers of course; private soldiers had to find their own solutions. Golf, fresh air, reasonable food, a tranquil choice of paint colour in the day room – these were all part of the treatment, but Rivers also knew that the source of recovery was inside the patient. You couldn't force them to come to talk about the unspeakable or force them to come to terms with the irreconcilable. You had to give them time to come to you. Patience. It wasn't the army way. So, we junior doctors were all swiftly shuffled through before the contagion could set in and we might be infected by these radical thoughts. But like a clever virus, Rivers' way would lock into your thoughts in a short time. Those of us who didn't end up like Andrews were carriers for life. Not that we ever mentioned it back at the Front. MOs were suspect enough, psychiatric training placed you firmly on the side of the shirkers and the cowards.

But Rivers brought me into this service – the asylums with their long corridors, their narrow, commanding windows. My future had been shaped by those four years just as much as many of the men and women who were our patients. Soldier or civilian, the sights they had seen when the smoke suddenly cleared out the trench or when they spotted the telegraph boy turning the corner into their street, these were the moments that ultimately led them to our admission rooms. We were alike in that respect – the patients, myself, even our bold, ambitious leader, Dr Alan Sneddon – all on a journey that had the same departure point.

Sneddon clattered into my office without knocking.

'Our doors are always open,' was his code. 'We can't have colleagues burrowing away in their own dens. We need collegiate sharing here. Professionals learning from each other. Communicating. Shut doors have no place.'

Difficult to argue with that – unless you had two closed doors and the formidable Mrs Nicholson as a defence outside your own inner sanctum. In addition, few of us chose to visit Sneddon.

'Doctor.' He stood in the doorway. I had one wooden chair, borrowed from the dayroom, to offer visitors. But he liked to stand.

'Doctor,' I said.

'The Councillors' visit. All in hand?'

'Selected patients for them to meet. Lunch in the medical staff dining hall. Round table discussion afterwards and tea with carefully selected nurses before they go. I'll draft an agenda. For your approval.'

'Perfect. Preparation is detail.' He caught my eye.

'Detail is preparation.' I completed the favoured homily of Professor Deacon and Sneddon's reminder of our shared training in Edinburgh. 'I'll have all the paperwork done by Wednesday.' And then I said nothing. He would have to get to the actual reason for his visitation without my help.

'Admission book up to date?'

'Dr Cunninghame has done precise work. Crystal clear notes.'

'A busy weekend I see. Dr Kidd of Slamannan sweeping his streets clean again.'

'He is doing his bit. He has an arrangement with the local police Sergeant.'

'And the Sheriff. We are not an alternative to gaol.' He was leaning against the door frame now, both hands now deep in his suit pockets. Casual. Dangerous. 'And a new private patient.'

'Yes,' I said. Let him come to me.

'And she's not a difficult sister or mother-in-law standing in the way of an inheritance?'

'She's a thirty-six-year-old mother of three. Her address is in Kings Park. Her husband is a shopkeeper.'

'Prosperous one?'

'Nimmo's, you'll know the shop,' I replied. It was a barb.

'I'm not a customer.' Sneddon deflected my thrust and we both smiled. When colleagues overheard our polite badinage, this habitual chit-chat, they assumed it was the ease of old colleagues, familiar since student days. How could they know of the abyss of frustration and resentment that divided us?

'I didn't think that for a second. Workwear. But not our work. And cheaper clothes for the people up in these streets,' I said.

'She'll meet plenty customers in here.' He closed the door and stood full square over my desk. I was always tempted to stand up at these times too. But that in itself would have been a sign of weakness. 'Diagnosis?'

'Probably our old friends – hysteria, environmental stresses, boredom, her children growing, a busy husband. Of course,' I said, taking the moral high ground from Sneddon, 'it would be professional to interview before diagnosis.' I got no response, so I went on. 'I suspect a few months shelter from all that will give her respite.'

'Let nature take its course?'

'With our help and guidance,' I said.

'And a little sewing. Perhaps some tennis as the weather picks up?'

'Cunninghame noted that she was a skilled musician. Plays piano and sings. Almost professional.'

'Excellent, a concert party or maybe a turn for the Councillors when they remember us again.' Sneddon was smiling.

'All tested solutions.' It was too early for a confrontation.

'Tested. Tested isn't research, Dr Fergusson. We are not warders, or games instructors. We're scientists.'

'Dr Rivers…' I couldn't help myself. Sneddon hated the fact I had the contact with the great man. His response was to discredit and dismiss. He cut me off:

'Dr Rivers' patients had a choice of languishing in a madhouse for ever, shooting themselves or going back to do their duty and lead their men. They weren't normal patients.'

'Our patients are never normal,' I said. Sneddon almost smiled again at this. But I could see he was on a serious mission.

'We are scientists. We need to develop treatments. Explore. We need to take risks. Push forward. It's what your man Rivers was doing, was he not? In his own way. With his – talking.' He paused. 'Your new woman, for example. She is all of the things you say. But she is also a surging mass of chemicals. All with their own capacity to bring joy or pain. It is our task to understand her chemistry.'

'There are the baths.'

'The baths. The baths? Are we a hydrotherapeutic hotel?'

'We are a therapeutic community.' I nodded sagely.

'You read the scientific papers. Chemicals are our future. And we should play our part in creating that future.'

I realised that was why he was here, standing over me.

'I think I need to interview her first. To build a proper picture of her situation and needs before we look at other options.'

'Don't get too attached, Dr Fergusson.' He turned, hand on the iron doorknob. 'You know, and I know, where that can lead.' Then he was gone.

He did not have to add that final threat, it was implicit in every conversation we had. I closed my hand round my paperweight, a curled ammonite I'd found on a beach in Skye, and in my mind sent it arcing into the panel of the door, into the space formerly occupied by Sneddon's head.

2.

LOTTE

Thursday 13th April 1933

Lotte looked down into the garden. She watched as Grace moved along the clothesline, the weak sun on her hair, red with flecks of white. Beside her, the three-year-old lifted the next wet bundle from the white circle of the basket, her silent babble constant as Grace dipped and stretched. Reflected in the window, Lotte ghosted against the brightness of the grass, the orchard beyond with its haze of green buds. Grace pinned Lily's clothes on the line. Identical white dresses, grouped together, almost holding hands.

She turned away from the window. The bedroom mirror, long, framed, was set at an angle that added to her height. Black skirt, white blouse, the tangle of hair and her face – insomnia pale. In the shadow of the room her brown eyes looked as black as her hair and skirt.

'No grey,' she said, softly. 'No grey.'

Out on the landing, light from the cupola overhead flared on the dark wood of the curved corner table. Downstairs a clock began to chime discreetly.

'Ten,' she said. 'Already.'

She took the stairs deliberately, as if counting, down its long curve. On the inside of the steps, as she always did, away from the mahogany banister with its brass studs, the iron rods. She thought of the stairs in her old home. This was not like the shared tenement stairs she had grown up with, spiralling down into the dark, past the sounds of rage and joy, muffled behind the blank doors on the gloomy landings. The smell of dust and cooking – and worse – as you descended. Here, all was sun and beeswax. She clicked the final brass fitting on the newel post with her rings. For luck.

Down in the hallway she took in the bright semi-circle of light above the front door. The hall table. The umbrellas, walking sticks in a tight bundle. For a second there was silence – Sam at work, the boys at school, Grace and Lily down the garden. The world was hers alone. This was when all was well. Content. Settled. She felt the urge to pause, put her foot on it, like trapping a leaf on a breezy day.

Grace and Lily were coming, their voices rising, through the back door, through the kitchen, up the back stairs, along the passage, their feet on the parquet and then on the tiled hall.

'Mummy! See me helping!'

'Of course, sweetheart. Are you feeling better now?'

Grace contemplated her. Lily nodded vigorously.

'She's the best helper, aren't you?' Grace put the girl's hair behind both ears. The curls sprang out straight away. 'She does more every day. All good things to learn.'

'There are plenty other things to learn than hanging out washing,' said Lotte.

Grace licked her finger and rubbed at an invisible mark on Lily's cheek. The girl made a face and ducked out from under her arm. She pushed into Lotte's side.

'Mummy save me!' she giggled, looking up at Grace.

Grace reached behind and retied her apron. The cotton draped white and spotless almost to the floor.

'I've bean soup for us at lunchtime.' Grace pursed her lips at Lily. 'Missy's favourite.'

'Ugh.' The girl shoved away from her mother, bounced off the hallway wall and leaned back against the housemaid.

'Careful. Careful,' Grace said, gathering the child in to her side. 'Bean soup?'

'Just for you and Lily,' said Lotte. 'I'm thinking of going out. It is such a fine day.'

'Me too,' Lily called.

'No. You and Grace will have lots to do here and you don't want to miss the bean soup. We can take a walk into town in the afternoon maybe.'

Lily was between smiles and tears, balancing with one shoe on top of the other as if deciding which way to go.

'Of course,' said Grace. 'It's helpful to give me warning.'

'I just need to get out. You know that.'

'Whatever you want, that will be fine for me. And Lily.'

'I'll be back after lunch and we can all go out before the boys get home from school.'

'Of course,' said Grace. 'You do as you think best.'

A little silence fell in the hallway. The three of them, gathered in the light of spring, the back door open, the house coming alive with the chill air from the garden, a smell of damp earth and trees.

'What would I do –'

'– without me? You'd be fine.'

Lotte leaned over Lily's head and touched Grace on the arm. Lightly, like a breath of wind. Grace picked up Lily and took her back to the kitchen.

Lotte stood tapping one foot on the polished floor. The black and white tiles with their changing perspectives and shifting shapes. Deep in winter nights she sometimes stood in the cold hall– her coat on, the house silent around her– searching these tiles for patterns, her walk almost forgotten.

But not today. Not with the spring sun. She took her coat, the one with the fur collar, for there was brightness but no heat in the sun, and her hat, pulled down over her wild hair.

'I'm away,' she shouted into the deep well of the house. There was a bubble of sound from the kitchen, far off. She buttoned her gloves, took an umbrella out of the stand – the black one, matching – and opened the door.

In the past week, as the seasons turned, the wide street had gone from photograph to painting, from monochrome to intense colours, the flowerbeds across the road in the Crescent vibrant with green, yellow and blue. She stood for a moment at the top of the steps. Wondering. She wasn't a visitor here. These were her steps, more or less. Her railings. The little front garden was kept finely clipped by Mr MacKenna. And there was Mr Dick's villa across the way. The hulking mass and tower of Mr McAree's house. She didn't know all the names, the distillery owner, the dentist, the accountant, the Inspector of Schools, the Medical Officer for Health, the architect, the shipmaster, the iron-founder. Her neighbours. 'They might have bigger houses, but ours is the oldest,' Sam would say. 'They're all show. Our house was the very first in the street. When the rest had cows grazing.' Sam made a joke out of the snobberies and insecurities of the neighbours, but there was a serious undertow, as if he were trying to push away his own insecurities and snobberies. And though their house was older, they were the recent arrivals.

It wasn't so much the houses for Lotte but the gardens.

The grounds. The huge open spaces between the buildings seemed a wild extravagance. 'Look,' said the proprietors, 'we've so much space we can squander it. We would rather have the beeches, the lawns, the bushes as big as trees. And even though you will never see us in these gardens, we can buy this land just for the pleasure of looking out at it.' She thought of the two rooms with six of them living there, the door onto the narrow stair and then out on to the street. Someone always in the shadowy hallways and stairs. Here the lavish garden, the wide pavements and wider road were usually empty. A gardener behind a wall, a housemaid, hardly ever a neighbour, and then a nod, no more. 'Not unfriendly,' said Sam. 'Just their way.'

In three years here the vertigo had never gone away.

She took the hill at a hard pace. Her heart beat faster, the blood pounding in her ears, she could sense the great channels through her body swelling. When that happened at night, in the dark, lying in bed, there was nothing she could do. Accelerating, racing, the more she panicked, the faster it got. But out on foot, when she was moving, she could take control, slow down, focus on the world and not the dark inside her head. Even on the flat she kept a fine rhythm, the sound of her heels on the stone always soothed, but she did not slow for hills. And here there were hills everywhere. This was her Stirling, the town of hills and cobbles and old streets.

The ancient streets, the streets of Kings, and Queens. On days she felt attuned to the world, she could smell the ages coming up between the cobbles, the history in the filth that collected between the stones. Some cars and vans rattled past, the pale blue coal fire smoke high above against the rapid spring sky. Past the County Buildings and the bulk of the Carnegie Library, the Athenaeum spire. Almost-grand buildings of a former capital.

Window shoppers peered at the sweeping bow front of McCulloch and Young. The new windows full of clothing, craft supplies, furniture. Everything and nothing. A man in a long brown coat and bunnet was very carefully examining a tastefully arranged cascade of long woollen underwear. She stopped and stood alongside him, following his intense eyeline. When he realised she was looking at underwear with him, she felt him flinch like one of his own beasts caught with a switch. She spoke before he could start away, back to the farm.

'They've the exact same, you know. Up the hill. At half the price.'

He looked at her, his clear outdoor eyes, not quite eye contact.

'Aye.'

'Just two minutes. Save yourself a shilling.'

She moved off before he would be crushed by embarrassment. The hussy speaking to him in the street. She knew the town men better, their bold hopeful eyes.

She turned into Baker Street. The cobbled hill narrowed away into the distance, into the haze of smoke and poverty. There were fewer vehicles up here, only delivery vans and the odd military car passing on its way to the Castle. A breeze came down the dark canyon. Old newspapers, bloody butcher's wrappings, rose up in the middle of the street. Women hurried past, all in dark clothes, the older women wrapped in shawls as if against Highland gales. There were plenty Gaelic speakers up here towards the Top of the Town.

When she lived here she would hear them through the walls sometimes. The songs, some surging with joy like waves on the shore, others a distilled essence of misery.

Outside the shop – their shop – she paused to take in the windows. Too many prices. Just a few to set the level were fine, but too many confused the customer. And more colour might help. She went through the double doors, both wide open despite the cold in the shadowy street. Everyone was busy with customers. Lotte hung back and noted how her arrival brought a tiny change of mood. Did Mrs Wilson increase the volume of her conversation with her customer? Her white hair as rigid as the cornicing around the shop, she was showing a linen nighty. The customer looked much more prosperous than their usual clientele. Someone fallen on hard times perhaps. Did the two sisters, Lolly and Lizzie, start to move just a bit faster? They were both serving a more typical pair of customers, an adult daughter, backed by her formidable mother, haggling over several pairs of overalls. One sister was talking to the customers, stroking the rough cloth of the overalls as if it were the softest, deepest velvet while the other balanced on the steps opening one of the hundreds of narrow, precisely labelled drawers that lined the walls.

They weren't twins, Lolly and Lizzie, one was the elder, but she was never sure enough of not mixing them up to use their names. One had a gladder eye, she knew that, and Sam thought she was responsible for a few extra customers. Probably Lolly, if she was the one who had once told her: 'You could join us, become a sister. Lolly, Lizzie and Lotte.'

She had not been that familiar again. Grace was one thing, but she had enough experience of shop assistants to know how to put them in their place.

Lotte organised a bowl of remaindered wool, turning it from a jumble into a careful pile, labels upwards, and marvelled at how everything– the boys, Lily, Grace, Snowdon Place, the MG and the Collard and Collard piano – all depended on whether customers would turn to this display and want to buy.

She turned as she heard the door open, up at the top of the stairs at the back of the shop. And there was Sam, so neat in his suit. Immaculate. Glints of gold at the cuffs and watch chain across his waistcoat. She walked past the customers–Mrs Down-on-her-luck now held an embroidered pale blue nighty up to the light– and followed Sam into his tiny office. He sat in his wooden seat back to his desk, a smell of duplicating paper filled the narrow room. Light fell from a distant skylight.

'Princess,' he said.

'Sam,' she said.

'Lily?'

'Grace.'

'Of course.' He reached over and pulled a spindly chair from under a table pilled with paper weighted by a huge adding machine, its handle cocked like a weapon. 'Sit down, talk to me.'

'Aren't you busy?'

'I'm never too busy to talk. You know that.'

She stood still, upright, and smiling because she did love Sam for his clever silliness, for his ability to have walked into all this, the shop, the paperwork, the adding up, and picked it up so fast, for his suit and his watch and his accent with only a mere trace of where he came from. Like her own, it was almost neutral, a better disguise than the smart clothes.

'McCulloch's windows are snaring them before they get round the corner.' She tapped her foot against the tall metal filing cabinet. 'Horrible windows, but they're stopping.'

'All that glass, all that square footage, all that overhead. They need to sell a lot more than us to pay it off. Looking isn't buying.'

'If they look long enough, then…'

'Then they'll come here.' He crossed his legs, pinching the crease of his trousers so they wouldn't stretch and bag. 'For what they want. For what they can afford. I know these people, they're no different from Birkenhead. They want value. They know what they can afford.'

'But I lived up that hill. I do know they want a bit more than we can offer.'

'Times are hard and not getting easier.' He could dig in quickly and she didn't want to leave an argument hanging until he came home and it spoiled everyone's dinner. You couldn't fault his determination. It was a great strength. Mostly.

'Times won't be hard for ever and we'll be left behind. Mrs Wilson's stock –'

'– is exactly what we need right now. Cheap and cheerful.'

'Cheap, it's true. But her foundations are pre-war. Start bringing in a little quality. Just a bit more expensive, a bit more lively, and see where it goes. Higher margins.'

'Lotte, Lotte.' He leant forward now, took her hands, his thumbs circling, soothing, irritating. 'You don't have to worry about this. We're safe.'

'We can't ever be safe.'

'As safe as we can be, then.' His hands gripped tighter now, pulled her towards him. 'There's no point in any of this if you fret and worry like—'

'Like my mother, my aunts?'

'They made all this possible, I know. And it wore them out.' Sam let her hands drop. 'But the shop is alive now like it never was before. And these are the hard times. Hardest times since the war. When people have more money again, anything is possible.'

'If we're prepared.'

'Just go back to the house and enjoy it. Enjoy the baby. Grace spends more time with her than you do.'

He broke off abruptly. She knew that he was searching, looking closely for any sign that she might be about to erupt, cause another scene in the shop. As had happened before. With the entire staff frozen behind their counters, eyes wide, no one able to act, waiting for Sam to come out of the office to bundle her away. And the customers all with a tale to tell. But when she knew it was coming, it didn't happen.

She pulled the belt of her coat, tightened the knot, put the confrontation away. 'Let's talk about it later.'

He stood and kissed her, just briefly, but he meant it, she could tell.

'OK, later.' He turned away, back to the invoices, the accounts, the tedium that connected all the strands, the ties that constantly needed to be adjusted and trimmed. She could do all of that and more. She wouldn't let Sam take all that her aunts had built.

Looking into the back shop, Government Surplus and Menswear, Mr Clark, the bachelor, was earnestly bent over the counter. Two pairs of long woollen underwear drooped over the glass front, flopping, headless wraiths. The farmer in his long coat had his back to Lotte, still as a carving. She didn't interrupt, but stepped lightly down the few stairs, nodded left and right – Mrs Wilson, Lolly and Lizzie – and was out again in the rattle of the street.

Lotte kept going uphill. As she pushed against gravity, she felt her body working, carrying her, responding. Her legs never tired. She'd always had strong legs. Good legs. These steep streets were her world.

It was busy. The rumble of vans and the thump of handcarts on the setts. Just before lunchtime, there were enough people about so that she had to step off the pavement. More men now. Before the economy collapsed, men were invisible here until Saturday nights. Now, they were about in daylight, running errands, real and imagined, filling their time. Until what? Until good times came back. The women never had that aimless look, they always had a destination, a mission. She passed the shops – chemist, grocer, household goods, brushes, wines and spirits, post office, grocer, furniture, more wines and spirits. And pubs. The Glengarry, The Forth Arms, The Caledonian, The Corn Exchange Tavern. More pubs than shops, it seemed. As she climbed the canyon narrowed, as if life were focused by the rising hill. The buildings leaned in, the awnings and the streetlights arcing above. People nodded and murmured as she passed. Older women who knew her when she was young, friends of her mother, her aunts' friends, neighbours and customers, younger women who knew her as someone who had left. Lucky. Not, good for her. Lucky her.

Before she got to the sharp elbow of Bow Street she paused and turned, looked back down the slope. The shop had once been in a perfect place, halfway up the liveliest street in town. But she could see how the economic life of the town was moving, sliding downhill towards the big new stores. And the buildings here were decaying. She looked up at the damp streaks, the small trees flourishing up in the high gables, the crow's steps with missing steps.

She strode on, into Broad Street, past her aunt's first shop– still a grocers. Then on uphill, steeper now. The Castle hidden by buildings but its hulking presence there all the same. Out of habit she went even faster here, past the few groups of men in uniform. Her age should protect her, but she was never sure. Underfoot she felt for the precise moment where the street took her downhill again, the sudden watershed when the ground shifted under you. And then she was in Upper Castlehill, another canyon, the great expanse of the Forth and the glare of open country down to the sea blocked by the dark buildings. She paused briefly at the passageway into number thirty-four. A black entry against the dark damp sandstone. They were scattered now. Her sister, her aunts, her mother. And Peter. They were all away. But she paused here, despite the chill she always felt, to note their presence in this place where they once all breathed the same air.

She was off again, downhill, turning back towards her home. Her home now. But as if to complete the tour of her past she cut along Wallace Street, the red sandstone terrace, facing south. Up there, its windows long and deep, was the first home they had bought after they got married. A fine flat, high and sunny. Proximity to the Auction Market kept it inside their price range. The street full of the great brown plates of manure that were never fully cleared between market days. Walking here with Peter on leave, he had called it a minefield. This grand terrace was full of cattle every Thursday. It sounded and smelt as if they were in a cottage in the middle of a lively field. Up there with the two boys,

James in her arms, Douglas by her side, looking down on the broad swaying hides of the beasts.

'Where are they going?' said Douglas.

'New homes,' she said. 'Nice new homes with deep grass and the sun on their backs.'

This walk was her own thirty-year-long journey through this town. House to house. She walked it nearly every day as a compulsion, an addiction. As she walked the iron that seemed to stiffen her body and tighten her mind into a dark hard knot was loosened. The barbed-wire tangles eased. By repeating she made a pattern, the weather, the people, the pace – every day the same but different, her steps created a rhythm. No, it wasn't an addiction, she had told Dr Campbell. She often missed days. It was healthy outdoor exercise. He had agreed. She dropped his pills through a grating as she walked home from the surgery.

The Journal of Dr John Fergusson

Tuesday 18th April 1933

The scream wasn't cut off completely when the cover was stretched tight, only muffled. It went on for as long as I was in the room. I had noticed Nurse Clark before, with her constantly untidy hair and huge eyes. The other I didn't know, but from her voice she was from the north. They were chatting about the dearth of hot water in the Nurses' Home. The screams went on, the canvas cover rippled and bulged at knee and fist level.

'You could have been more generous with the sedatives, Doctor,' said Nurse Clark, tucking a wayward strand of hair behind her ear. A bold one.

'She will quieten soon. Just keep an eye on the movements, Nurse Clark.' A little authority was my style. It is important not to be authoritarian. The more junior staff were the source of the real information about the patients, so it was wise to have a relationship.

'Of course, Dr Fergusson,' she said, with an additional adjustment of her hair.

'Keep an eye on the clock. And her movements. Make sure you record her disposition when she is finished.'

Nurse Clark provided me with a broad smile. The other one continued to stare down at the canvas cover. The movement was intermittent now. The sedative, the cold water and the pointlessness of struggle subdued patients quickly.

'I'll write it up immediately when she's back in her bed, Doctor.' It can be hard to distinguish ambition from mockery in our nursing staff. I took a sharper tone with Nurse Clark.

'It's not so much the immediate effect of the treatment that should concern us, Nurse, it is whether the patient is calmed and soothed by this therapy.'

Clark adopted a serious professional face and nodded.

'Long term, Nurse, long term. That is how we must work here. Our horizon is distant. There are no quick fixes.' Generally, we had few fixes at all.

The Highland nurse was watching the black canvas. There was no screaming now. Just a faint rhythmic panting, breath coming in short sharp grateful bursts, the patient under the required physical and mental pressures, pressures that would benefit her condition. Cold baths are the most humane response to hysteria.

'I shall leave her in your exemplary care,' I said. Nurse Clark dipped in what might have been a curtsey, a no man's land between deference and insolence. The other nurse looked up at me for the first time. Something bordering on judgement in her eyes. It was possible that she had recently come into our service, perhaps from general nursing, and was yet to realise that our form of medicine requires time, observation, patience.

That thought was in my mind as I prepared to interview our new patient. A private admission is a rare enough event in an asylum. But after what happened in Liverpool, I was both eager and anxious about our first meeting.

Her Certification was in itself unusual. In our community there are two groups. There are those whom you would immediately recognise as a danger to society. Then, there are patients who are so normal that visitors struggle to comprehend why they have been roughly, legally deprived of their liberty as if they were the worst of felons. Even the most depraved of criminals require more than the signature of two physicians and an officer of the court to place them behind walls.

This second group is, of course, much more interesting. And dangerous. Mrs Raymond, Charlotte, is remarkable even by the standards of a private patient.

As is my custom, I was first to arrive in the consulting room. A bare room with poor light. Table, two chairs. I was standing looking up at the high window when she was brought in. I love the mature trees at this time of year. The huge beeches, here for longer than any buildings on this estate. The massive buttresses of the trunks and the sprawling complex arches of the branches hazed all over with tiny green spots of new growth. The great iron tree dependent on the most delicate growth for its renewal.

Assistant Matron Kennedy suddenly acquired the airs of a lady's companion. 'Mrs Raymond for you, Dr Fergusson.'

You couldn't but notice her eyes. A dark brown that was close to black. And her black hair, curled, in a fashionable cut, exotic for Scotland, and her skin, so pale it seemed to glow.

'Please sit down.' I waved toward the plain wooden chair. There was nothing in this building that was not utilitarian. 'While Matron is still here, is there anything you need that we can provide?'

Mrs Raymond shook her head. She was a straight, narrow presence in this small room. Assistant Matron Kennedy pulled the door shut behind her. This was always an intimate moment.

'Please, sit.'

She maintained eye contact, a rare thing here, as I sat down opposite her.

'I'd say welcome to our hospital, but welcome always seems out of place in these circumstances.' It was an awkward way of putting it, I realise, but it doesn't help to be too assured, too professional. The patients need to know we are human.

She pointed towards the window.

'It's the bars. It's the thing I keep seeing.' She smiled. A fleeting, flashing thing in the grey room.

'You will get used to it. We're not a prison, but we are a hospital for unpredictable illnesses. We must make sure that the patients see the treatment through.'

She stared at the marked wood of the table. 'And what is my treatment?' When her eyes came up, I felt as if I had been smacked across my cheek. A remarkable woman. They often are here, of course, but she would have been remarkable anywhere. Those eyes! They had a confidence that was different from the frightened defiance I had often seen in these rooms. She was calm and contained. Though I held her gaze all I could see were the reflections of bold shapes, the pale walls and paler window.

'This is a place to rest. For illnesses of the body, convalescence follows treatment. Here convalescence is the treatment.'

She said nothing. I was forced to continue.

'And while you rest, we shall talk. We will discuss those things in your life that have been the cause of your...' I paused. It is important to find the right word, to show you understand the patient. 'Your complexities.'

She blinked. It was as if she had switched me off like a light and back on again. I went on: 'The things in your life that have caused you anxiety. That have changed your behaviour.'

'Things?'

'Pressures. We all have them. Sometimes there are just too many.'

'I don't believe my pressures are enough to keep me here.' She looked up and away to the window and the sky behind the bars.

'Few people think they should be here, Mrs Raymond.' She looked back at me. 'May I call you Charlotte?'

She hesitated, considering. 'If you wish.' Her voice was neutral, educated, with little trace of the local burr. There was nothing in Dr Cunninghame's notes to suggest that she'd had more than basic education, and although clearly well-off, 'she was not from the professional classes.' That was Dr Cunninghame's judgement. And, as Dr Sneddon regularly pointed out, Cunninghame would know, being an earnest young man from humble background in a hurry to jump social barriers. It was a condescending description that could have been applied to me at an early stage in my career. Sneddon is unimpressed by bright boys from small towns who have found their way to university and into this service. That is my background too. But Sneddon judges me by different criteria. Because of our shared experiences – and the power he believes he has over me. If I learned one thing in the war, it is that nothing is forever.

At this point in the admission process it is often difficult to either get patients to say a word or to let you say a word. Often there is little meaningful communication. Charlotte was different. And yet there was a hesitancy about her confidence. I do not mean the natural effect of being in this place. This seemed more of an uncertainty about how much of a private patient she was going to be. Some treated the staff, including the physicians, as if they were their own household servants. But most private patients were malleable, overwhelmed by shame, or perplexed by their apparent betrayal at the hands of their nearest and dearest.

'The bars are as much to keep these pressures away from you. Until you are strong again.'

'And talking to you is my treatment?'

'A discussion of your progress will be part of it. When possible.' It was important not to over promise. Even though I was already sure that I would schedule as many sessions with her as I could.

'And the rest of my time?' She was looking away from me now, at the window again.

'All of your time here is therapy. There is the kitchen, the laundry, a whole community here to be involved with. Once you have been assessed.'

'The kitchen? Laundry?'

'Therapy comes from work and from living. A rhythm and pattern to your life will help. We will assess you to see which occupation will suit you best.' I had said these words often. It seemed so banal, but I had seen the benefits of establishing a new, artificial life inside the walls. A reflected life perhaps, a flickering image of the real world, but one that was controlled, adjusted. 'And your music. We have a programme of concert parties here. For the staff as well as patients. If you have talent you are encouraged.' I looked down at Dr Cunninghame's notes – so neat, so precise – he will go far. 'You may have much to contribute.'

She ignored that. 'And when will I see visitors?'

'Visits are something that we discuss only after you've settled.' I was careful not to demoralise patients at this point. 'Jumping between one world and another is often unhelpful.'

She stared at me. 'We need you to focus on yourself,' I said. 'Not on others. Thinking about others all the time is often the root of problems. For our female patients.'

'My family?'

'Only after a period of time.'

'My children? And I help to run a business.'

There were three children in the notes, eleven, nine and three years old.

'We have to lift you from that responsibility. All responsibilities. For a short while.' It was difficult to explain the benefits of seclusion, isolation. Impossible even. But given what I had read in the notes of Certification, I was poised in case she flew at me across the table. That sort of thing wasn't unusual during admission interviews.

'Do you have children, Dr Fergusson?'

'Yes I do.'

'Then you know how painful this is.'

I agreed that it was painful. 'My two children are currently with their mother in England. She has had to look after her ailing mother,' I lied. 'So I understand the pain of separation.'

She stared. Her eyes huge.

'But often it is for the greater good. As it will be in your situation too.' She was calm so I was on edge. This was often the critical moment for patients, men as well as women, the point where they realised they might be a danger to their family, their own children.

There was no hint of manipulation in her gaze. I am familiar with the wiles of attractive patients. Too familiar. She sat upright in her chair, her fingers loosely tangled in front of her on the tabletop. No rings. That would have spoiled the effect.

'Who decides when I am well?'

'It's a decision taken by myself, in consultation with my medical and nursing colleagues.'

'And who decides when I see my children?'

'Again, it is a collective– a medical– decision.'

'What great power you have over me.' She let her fingers fall open on the table, like petals unfolding. It was a quiet gesture of mockery. Or challenge.

I decided to interpret her words as plain statement of fact.

'There's a great freedom from handing over decisions.' I smiled. But she was studying the table again.

'So, I am here until you decide I can leave, and I have no appeal?'

'You're a patient, my patient, not a prisoner. You are here for your own good.'

'My own good.' She had disengaged from me now. Her

eyes, half-lidded, focused on the ragged edge of the table. It was time to let this session come to an end.

'Shall I get Mrs Kennedy to take you back to your room?'

There was no reply.

I stood and knocked on the door. The key turned and Mrs Kennedy was there, serious and professional. Charlotte sat, motionless.

'I will look forward to seeing you again.' She did not look up.

LOTTE

Thursday 13th April 1933

She was out again that afternoon, in Murray Place, walking a pace or two in front of Grace and Lily.

'You could take account of those of us who are a wee bit slower,' said Grace. She was pushing the baby-chair and had Lily by the hand. Lotte paused. She took in the window of every shop they passed. Every detail, prices, products, displays. And not just the clothes shops. It was all the same business ultimately – responding to the customers, their needs, desires– wants fulfilled or frustrated.

Lotte stopped abruptly. She put her forehead to the cold plate-glass window. Lily stretched up to the glass and did the same.

'What do you think, these irons? The electric ones. Will they catch on?'

Grace stood behind, looked over their heads, Lotte leant back, looked up at the reflections.

'From my professional point of view?'

'As another opinion.'

'I hear there have been shocks. Burns are bad enough without shocks.'

Lotte turned, put her fingers through Lily's curls.

'I'm not suggesting you know more about ironing than I do,' said Lotte. 'I have done my share of ironing. And had my share of burns.'

Grace stared into the window. 'The ironing at Siggshill House took a whole day.' Grace adjusted her hat, tucked her hair under. 'And little thanks. That's why it's fine working for you.'

'A happy time, though,' said Lotte. 'Meeting Thomas.' She knew Grace's story. Her husband, Thomas Semple, had made the leap from chauffeur to garage owner.

'Three garages,' said Grace. 'He had vision. Mr Semple. Vison, but not so much luck.'

'I didn't suggest that. No one knows better than us the work it takes to build a business.'

'It came between us and a family.' She had both hands on Lily's shoulders. 'Then it was too late.'

'Mr Semple,' Lotte turned away from the window, 'was a hero.'

Grace looked away. 'A hero. And stupid. He was old enough. He didn't have to go.'

'Oh Grace.'

'Lotte!'

Both women turned, Lily squinting up into the glare.

'Mrs Semple, good afternoon, and Lily.'

'Frederick,' said Lotte.

'Mr Thornlee,' said Grace.

'You've escaped the printing machine?'

'I've put two thousand handbills through its jaws this morning. Including three hundred for your husband.'

'We are grateful, I'm sure.' Lotte gave a little bow of her head. Almost ironic.

If Frederick looked tall it was mainly due to his thinness and his dark suits and high collars rather than his height. Was it the same suit? Or did he have more than one identical outfit? The dash he hoped to cut was always slightly undermined by the inky marks on his cuffs.

'I'm out to buy some provisions, I'm not as fortunate as you, with Mrs Semple to help you out. But I'm glad I've seen you.' His attention was focused now on Lotte. The other two could have been in another street. 'I've something to discuss with you.'

'Nimmo's are always first to pay you, I'm sure.'

'No, no it's not money or invoices. It's something much more important. Let it wait until practice tomorrow.'

'Mr Thornlee. Don't tease.'

'It's not the place to discuss things.' He looked about theatrically. 'Out here, on the open pavement. I'll see you in church tomorrow evening.' He half-glanced at Grace. 'It will be worth it, I promise.'

His grin seemed guileless. He was not someone to tease, but he had the air of someone whose thoughts were not always spoken.

'Well then, I'll have to wait.' Lotte adjusted the fur collar of her coat.

'I shall leave you to your errands. Mrs Semple, Lily. Lotte.'

They watched his stiff gait as he hurried off and then was abruptly gone into MacEwan's.

'Don't say a word,' said Lotte.

'I haven't,' said Grace.

'Mum,' said Lily.

'He means well,' said Lotte. 'He's just a bit awkward.'

'Forward.'

'No, I don't think so, he just doesn't know how to talk sometimes.'

'You need to watch them. Single men,' said Grace, without a trace of humour.

'Not married ones?'

'All of them.'

'He's a brilliant musician. Brilliant.'

'Brilliance isn't everything.' Grace was still looking at the spot where he had disappeared into the grocers. She took Lily by the hand. 'It must be four, we should get on. Shouldn't we, sweetheart?'

Lily made a face. Lotte took her other hand.

'What is his great secret, do you think?' said Grace. She was setting a firm pace now, Lily running between them to keep up.

'He'll have found a new piece for me. I'm sure it's how he spends his evenings. Looking for obscure music. Like the version of *'Lead Kindly Light'* he found. It took the congregation two verses to recognise it.' She tightened her grip on Lily's hand.

'Maybe.' Grace wasn't amused.

'He's a church organist, not a Lothario,' Lotte said.

'Stop!' Both women looked down. Lily had been half-dragged for the last few steps, the toes of her white sandals scraped with fine dark lines.

That evening at seven they sat in the dining room. Sam at the head of the table, his back to the window, Lotte and Lily, wriggling, at one side of the table, the two boys at the other. The novelty of a spring evening meant there was no need for electric lights. But the light was pale and tentative. Grace had brought the six plates of broth up from the kitchen on the big tray. She served them all then placed her own plate at the end of the table and took her seat.

They bowed their heads, and Sam spoke.

'Be present at our table, Lord. Be here and ev'rywhere adored. These mercies bless, and grant that we may feast in paradise with thee.'

'Amen,' they all whispered.

'When does Grace say grace?' said James. There was the briefest of pauses, but when Sam laughed quietly there was a wider ripple.

'Very good,' said Lotte, 'although we might all have just possibly heard it before.'

'No, James, I've never heard that before,' said Grace. 'That's very funny.'

'Quietest Monday for a long time,' said Sam.

'There have been more pit lay-offs,' said Lotte. 'And one of Mr Drummond's men told Grace that two more seedsmen have been let go.'

'If the farmers aren't buying seeds then the outlook is never good,' Grace added. She was considered to be the expert on all things agricultural, and a great harvester of gossip.

'I'd already ordered handbills from Wingards. The less you take in, the more you have to put out. The Thornlee boy was straight round with them before we closed. Expecting the money in his hand.'

'He's hardly a boy,' said Lotte.

'He's sharp enough. You'd think it was his own business and he wasn't the hired help.' Sam tucked his chin into his stand-up collar and did a pitch perfect Frederick Thornlee. '"You understand the times we are in, Mr Raymond, we do need the payment before I can leave them with you. You don't let people pay for their clothes after they've worn them for a week."'

The boys giggled.

'He's a very good musician,' said Lotte. 'You should make allowances and be less cruel.'

Sam put his spoon down on the empty plate. Straightened it.

'He did say he'd met you and Grace.'

'And Lily,' said Grace. Sam looked up. 'Lily was there, too.'

'Yes, I know,' said Sam. 'He told me. He's a great lad for the detail.'

'He has some news for me. I've no idea what it is. He's discovered a new hymn maybe.'

Sam made further adjustment to the plate. 'Grace. I think we're all finished.'

Grace collected the plates, stacked the spoons on top, neat and silent. When he heard her safely on the stairs down to the kitchen, Sam said: 'I know he's harmless, Lotte, he'd make a good minister himself, he's got the air of one, but don't get yourself any deeper in that church.'

'It's not the church. It's the music. You know that.'

'I know. I know we don't have the fancy singing at the Methodists, but it's hardly a concert party in the Holy Rude, and he's not John Barbirolli.' He paused for a moment. 'It's not something to take too seriously. Not for a wife in your position.'

Lotte pinched the white tablecloth between her fingers. Two little white peaks of snow. The only sound was the faint swish of Lily swinging her legs under the table. The boys were silent, eyes down.

'Seriously?' The word crackled and hissed. Lotte worked at the tablecloth.

'I know it's important – your singing, your music. But you've had your time. Your moments. Everyone loved you – your voice. Don't spoil it.'

'Loved.' She said this as if interrogating the word.

'And there's nothing wrong with a few solos on a Sunday. People in the shop talk about it. Atheists sit through the sermons just to hear you. You've brought sinners to God.' Sam tried a smile. 'Just be sensible about what's… about what's appropriate.'

Lotte looked round her family. The betrayers. The fear and anger couldn't be separated, burning inside. She saw the flickering looks, one to the other, Douglas and James, Sam to both, Lily's big eyes staring up at the big brass light fitting.

She stood up, the solid silver salt cellar in her fist, like a grenade. They all turned to her, still, watching her hand.

'Don't speak about this again.' Lotte pronounced each word distinctly, addressing them all. Then smiled. 'I'm not so hungry now.' She placed the silverware delicately on the tablecloth. In the hall Lotte passed Grace. They said nothing.

MARTIN

8 pm Saturday 26th February 2017

When Mikkel and Yvonne left, Molly said: 'You've still got a choice. You can leave them all be. You can let the past stay in the past.'

'Or?'

'You can make sense of it. Find out all you can and maybe it will explain a lot.' She dropped the empty wine bottle into the recycling tub. 'You don't have the option of not knowing now. I mean, who does that? Researching someone else's family? Like it was a project.'

I was usually the one critiquing partners, testing their credentials. But I'd warmed to Mikkel. He'd been Yvonne's partner for five years. I was usually ready to defend him.

'I'm sure he meant well. His family is important to him. He talks about them all the time. He believes in it — the family. He feels we should respect where we've come from and know who we are. I don't think he'd consider the possibility that I wouldn't be interested in my family.'

Molly rattled the recycling tub. It was nearly full. She'd been a social worker and met lots of families.

'Families,' she said. 'Aye. Right.'

We were that statistical anomaly, Molly and I – a pair of only children. We were resourceful, imaginative and self-contained. Or alternatively, indulged, entitled and selfish. Possibly many of these things all at the same time. A Prince and Princess. As children we'd both known our hearts sink when friends from bigger families closed the door because they were having a family event. Just family. Over the years I'd found it difficult to separate my thoughts from Molly's. It's as if she was always working a second or two ahead of me, and had been for nearly forty years. I hadn't noticed so much when two children, then two teenagers, occupied so much of the airtime. But now the closeness was almost uncanny. It's why loss had such terror for me. Another reason not to turn away from another loss.

She turned back to me.

'He could have asked you. You know? Was it something you wanted to know. Would you like to hear how your gran died? Your face was grey. No one believed your lie – you had no idea what happened to her.'

'All I knew was she died young.'

'You can't ignore it now. It's not something trivial in your family history. It's a death in an asylum that no one talked about.'

I said nothing. We'd reached that stage, Molly and I, where you can say much without saying anything at all. I was stacking the dishwasher – meticulously, efficiently. Here we were, at a point in our lives where all the battles had been fought, the silly concerns of work put into context. The trajectories were all settled, predictable. Mikkel had tipped us out of that carefully constructed serene present tense. Here was a whole other story to own. To make decisions about. It just took his few words.

I knew all about words. I'd spent a lifetime working in communications for the NHS. Communications has its own place in the rigid hierarchy of medical professions. A long way below the catering staff. We'd retaliate by saying that our words could save more lives than vaccines or precision lasers. I can't remember anyone being much impressed. But it was true.

As I placed the plates in their proper slots, I thought about asylums, specifically the asylum at Larbert – the old Stirling Asylum. Also known as Bellsdyke. Change the name, but you can't change the purpose. Enough of a folk fear of the asylum lingered around until my childhood to make it part of playground culture – 'You escaped from Bellsdyke?' – was the sort of thing older boys said if you had no response to a spot of casual extortion.

Until they built the motorway, the long grey wall of the asylum ran alongside the main road from Stirling to Edinburgh. On rare family outings to the capital, my mother would point it out. 'Poor souls,' she'd say. My father said nothing, eyes ahead, hands on the wheel. Even with applied adult imagination, I can't recall a sense of discomfort or exaggerated composure about these moments in the Morris Oxford. But now it struck me that perhaps my mother didn't know that it might be better to keep quiet about the asylum. Maybe my father had never known about the asylum – been told that his mother had died in a hospital. An ordinary, non-stigmatised hospital. Already things were starting to turn upside down. I closed the dishwasher door.

'Perhaps they never told the children. Perhaps they meant well too,' I said.

'They weren't children for half a century.' She wasn't going to give up. 'It's part of your past. How can you understand yourself if you don't understand what happened to your grandmother?'

'What if I don't want to know? What if the thought that there might be a genetic link back to an asylum isn't exactly reassuring?'

Molly narrowed her eyes, leaned forward and peered into my face. 'It would explain a lot. The funny moods, that thing you do – the irritating teeth tapping thing.'

'I don't have funny moods. I'm a sensitive artist.'

'Anyway, I thought your family were fat cats? What with their cars when no one else had them.' Molly was doing her bit to recover the mood. It had been a good day. Up till that point. 'I was always waiting for the money to turn up. Still waiting.'

'We were. They were. Snowdon Place.' That had been the address. Pretty much the best street in town in those days. I'd passed along it many times without even stopping to speculate on which of the impressive villas had been theirs. 'Not bad for my grandfather. He'd done well for an apprentice grocer from Birkenhead. He got lucky by bumping into long-lost relatives in Stirling when he was demobbed, and then building up a business.' That was the family myth. The origin myth.

'It won't be like that.'

'How?'

My wife leant back against the pure white worksurface. 'It will be much more complicated than that. It always is. Rags to riches. It's the way men tell stories. It won't be like that.'

'Another reason not to poke about. The dead have their myths. And the dead have their reasons. It's not for me to question.' But as I said it I felt a thread beginning to tug.

But Molly wasn't going to let me bury this in my file of unresolved issues.

'What were they hiding? Was she one of these women who got sectioned because they got pushy or awkward? I've read about these cases. Your grandfather was capable of that.'

'No. I don't think he was. I can criticise my family, that's my job not yours. He was hard, and driven.' I thought of the tension that was always there between my father and his father. I was a child but I could tell there was something vibrating in the air. I batted Molly's line back at her. 'I'm sure it will be more complicated than that.'

She stuck her tongue out.

'Childish,' I said.

'Pathetic.' She put her thumbs in her ears and waggled her fingers.

'I was happy enough not knowing about this.'

'Were you?' she said.

My grandfather and my father were very different — but they both made the same shape in the world, a shape I see again when I pass a darkened shop window. I thought of the unlikely way they had prospered in the army — both ending up with sergeant's stripes. I thought of the strange, solemn decades between their world wars. And I thought of how there was always something left unsaid. At the centre of their lives was a huge loss – not just a death, but a denial of a death. Part of being an only child is never having enough family. It wouldn't be right to let one go. I felt the tick of curiosity that would become a beating, pounding obsession. Molly crossed her arms, a sure sign my argument was done.

'You can suit yourself. But you're going to be left with all these questions hanging. Maybe you owe it to your grandmother to tell her side of the story. Balance it up. Give her a voice.'

'But I can't find out everything,' I said. 'They're all dead now. All of them. James, Lily, my dad. No one has the story.'

'All the more reason to do it. And fill in the blanks, make the connections. Imagine.'

I could start to see it now. The past emerging like an old photographic print in a tray of emulsion. Molly wasn't finished. 'You better go and find out. If you don't your grandmother's going to be lost. She's already disappeared out of your family. You've said it yourself, she wasn't spoken about. That's the only thing that keeps us alive after we're dead. She's had a sort of double death. If you don't tell it, her story will be lost too.'

She left me alone in the kitchen. I locked the back door, switched off the lights. The dishwasher hummed and the tiny lights on the front of the cooker blinked. It felt safe. Lotte's home must have felt just as comforting, just as secure.

3.

LOTTE

Saturday 2nd May 1908

'Walls are for climbing.' Peter reached above his head, his fingers claws, shoved into the space between stone and stone. At thirteen he had two years on her, and an extra foot's reach. 'Don't tell me you don't want to know what's on the other side?'

With a shuffle and twitch and a small hail of dried mortar that Lotte brushed out of her hair, he was abruptly above ground, suspended above the earth by the toes of his plimsolls and his hooked hands.

'Don't fall,' Lotte said.

Above, Peter snorted and there was more debris.

'Watch there isn't glass.'

'It's a wall not a window.'

'Along the top. There's sometimes glass.' But Peter was beyond Lotte's advice. He was so high now she had to squint against the glare of the white sky to keep him in sight. He was a slow-moving blur. And then he was still. Straddling the top of the wall, impossibly high. He stared away into the hidden distance.

'Oh God.'

'What?'

'It's amazing. You won't believe this.'

'What?'

'What I'm seeing.'

'Tell me.'

'No, never. You'll have to come and look.'

'How?'

'Climb up. It's easy.'

She could imagine what it was like on the other side of the wall. That wasn't a problem. She could make things happen in her head, especially with Peter, she could create anything in there. But that was not the same as seeing it, living it. She could imagine what it might have been like before her father died, before she could talk. But that didn't help much. It didn't make the dark times disappear.

She had imagined what moving to a town unfamiliar and strange would be like, suddenly living with aunts and cousins, including Peter, whom she had never met before. It was terrifying. But the reality was that everything had worked out just fine. After a month or two, it was as if they had never lived anywhere else. So, imagining was all very well, but sometimes, quite often in fact, what you projected inside your head turned out to be completely wrong.

And this wall was a challenge, something to be overcome. This, said her mother, was life. One thing after another. What mattered was how you dealt with it. Did you run away, or did you take it on?

She approached the wall.

'Guide me.'

'Reach up, but not too high, so you can pull up.'

She felt the rough edges under her fingertips. Her toes scratched and scrabbled as her arms pulled up. The tips of her boots too big for the cracks between the stones, the old red stones.

'Now pull up with your hands and push down with your toes.'

And so she rose, determined. Not needing Peter's instructions now, but scaling the wall, moving in a new way.

'A real mountaineer.' Peter's face was close now, almost level. She reached long over the rounded coping stones, felt for a grip. She seemed to swing out for an instant, but though her other hand was pulled and rasped, she hung on. Her hand found an edge again, gripping and pulling, and there she was facing Peter, legs astride, high above everything. Strangely secure.

'It's just the same,' she said. 'The view. It's just what we see from home.'

Although the angle was different, it was what they saw from the kitchen window. The airy view over the smoke and jumble of the town, to the curves of the river, the way the bends almost curled back on themselves, the faraway hills and the chopped off finger of the Monument.

'No, it's not,' said Peter. 'We made it ourselves by climbing up here. Look, it's sharper, brighter. I'll draw this when we get home. No one else has seen this view.'

He swung round, swaying out over the drop, longer on the other side, falling away into a tangle of scrub, the backs of houses and yards for chickens and pigs. The graveyard, the village of the dead, was down to the left. Peter's sweeping hand took in the hills to the north, the traces of white on the tops, clouds going back all the way to the edge of the world. And familiar though it was, it did seem wilder, bigger, and now theirs. No one else was up here, seeing all this from the same spot.

'And then there's that.' He pointed, almost straight above. Lotte put a hand down to grip the rounded stone and looked.

The black cliff loomed over them, the rocks merging into the Castle, wall upon wall ending in the cut-out edge of the battlements against the glare of the sky. For the first time she felt the vertigo, a sense she was not on the wall, but projected high up there onto the battlements. Precarious. She gripped the stones between her knees with both hands.

'Looks taller from here.' Peter was looking at her, not at the view. She had no brother, but this must be what it was like. 'You're not a bit frightened, are you?'

'Course not.' And she wasn't. This was more than fun. This vertigo, the air under her boots, brought an intensity, living but more so. Her skirt and drawers were blackened by the damp soot that smeared the saddle of the wall. She could hear her mother already: 'Do you have any idea what it takes to buy these?' And when the man opened his window and shouted at them from one of the toy houses below and they climbed down, Lotte led the way, sliding the last few feet down the wall. Her hands and fingers were black and streaked with blood, her boots scuffed beyond polish. The looming row didn't matter, the damage was a badge of honour, tokens of a shared adventure.

LOTTE

Friday 14th April 1933

She hadn't slept properly since Lily was born. That is what she told everyone. But the truth was that she hadn't properly slept since they moved here, when Lily was tiny. She had moved into the bedroom at the back– thinking that sleeping alone might help. It wasn't quiet she needed. The rooms she had slept in all her life had high windows, suspended above streets full of life and noise, late and early. Broughton Street, when she was a child in Edinburgh, Upper Castlehill, even Wallace Street, were deep wells of activity where the last revellers merged with the first commercial activity, a relentless tapping of iron on stone, furtive conversations and the sudden shouts of men and women– joy and anguish.

Here, the clock ticked on the upstairs landing, a dog barked discreetly, the wind worked on the branches of the apple trees and nothing was louder than the pumping of her heart and the pulse of blood in her ears.

To lie still was to feel the night all around, life closing down. To get up, to feel the dressing gown against her legs, the polished boards under her feet, the cool of the stairs, was to stay alive. She wandered the rooms, the streetlight on the long wood of the dining room table, the fading fire in the sitting room, the lingering cooking smells down in the kitchen. Everywhere the closed doors, Grace and her family all asleep, all shut firmly out of her world for these dark hours. Every night she found herself drawn to the windows, to the streetlight, the wide road and the blank dark faces of the houses. It was as familiar as breathing, this steep town and its castle. And so, she walked.

She wanted nothing for these expeditions. Her boots were of fine soft leather, but handmade, robust. Her coats, hats, always suitable. Her father's watch, so she was never caught by the dawn, the home waking up.

At first, she had walked the streets round the King's Park. The villas, the high walls, the gravel drives. The trees, dripping or sighing or full of birds. She met no one. There might be an occasional light in an upstairs window for her to speculate about. Someone working over papers, fretting a business decision? An argument, a blighted bedroom? But there were no raised voices, no shrieks, whatever despair festered in these tall houses with their turrets and battlements, their long windows and high chimneys, it happened silently, politely.

Breaking out of the quiet residential streets to climb the hill felt like no risk at all. The route up past the empty municipal buildings, into the streets she'd grown up in, was such familiar ground that she could sometimes return home and be unsure if she'd dreamt it all, whether she'd imagined or experienced the journey. The mediaeval town held no fears for her. The vennels and doorways pitch black. It was like owning a dangerous dog, frightening to others, reassuring to her. She loved the cobbles, wet and deserted under the streetlights.

Tonight she took the turn onto Spittal Street – she didn't want to pass the shop, start to rearrange the window in her head at this time. These walks were to empty her mind not to fill it up. That was easy enough to do. At the top of Broad Street, she paused. The wide market street, the stone skeleton of Mar's Wark, its black eyeholes. The iron grills. This was always a haunt of the dispossessed and the dislocated. Of all the dark corners of the Old Town, this was the one her mother warned her about most often.

'No one will hear you away up there,' she said. 'Everywhere else, if you get in trouble just shout. Somebody will come. No one will leave you.'

She had never been sure of that, never reassured that amid the mayhem of some nights in these streets anyone would distinguish her genuine cry for help from all the other howls. Now, she leaned close to the wall, smelled decay, urine, the fruit smell of spirits. She peered into the absolute black of the graveyard beyond but could see nothing, hear nothing. Behind her, the perpendicular stone of the Church. The stained glass was black from this side, the glory of their light reserved for the inside, for the believers. Clouds passed behind the pointed spikes on the buttresses. The saints shadowy. She thought about the dark interior, the dry bible smell, the silence, the organ pipes. A dead building waiting to come to life.

She hurried past the wide mouth of the Castle parade ground. There were soldiers and movement at the gates to the Castle itself, even at this deep time of night. They worked to another timetable. She hurried past. Where there was a break between trees and houses, she paused to look out over the town. The lights of the new houses down in the Raploch. 'Too posh,' they said up here. As if the damp, the crumbling stairwells, rattling windows that kept you awake in even a light breeze were to be chosen over new houses with gardens and hot water. She looked beyond the town down the Forth, the lights of the villages, the mines, the shale works, the farms glittering off into the night all the way to the open sea. This was one of the things you missed, living below the rock, down on the flat ground beside the river, this sense of having the nation in your gaze. Behind her, over the endless walls, she could hear the slap and thump of the soldiers, their boots and their rifles. The secret codes, military rituals that had been part of the night sounds of this place for centuries. Lotte's world was up here on this ancient hill. The ancient, black church and closes, the cemeteries tumbling down the slopes, the derelict tenements, the life inside shaking the stones and slates from their walls and roofs, the wildness barely contained.

As she walked back downhill, the stones wet and slippery with rain and spit, Lotte sang in her head: hymns, musical hall songs, opera. Singing out loud would not be helpful. But she needed to express her joy, for this was when she was happy, when everything seemed possible, when it was all solved, her plans for the shop, for her music. By not thinking, by concentrating on the world around her– the feel of the stones, the smell of the coal smoke– she could sense a future, hidden still in mist, but out there. Even Peter could be resolved.

At breakfast she knew she looked tired, but her tiredness had been remarked on for so long, that walking all night was easily concealed. For Sam, breakfast was as much a symbol of family cohesion as dinner. And cohesion centred on his performance.

'My father was on the scaffolding, fitting plates by six am every day. We ate together only on public holidays. Christmas, Easter, Whitsun. And on the Twelfth, for those years in Belfast I suppose.'

'Did it make a difference?' she once asked. 'To the family?' It might have been before Lily, while they were in Wallace Street, when they would eat breakfast in the sunny bow window, the street far below.

'Families were different then,' he'd replied, waving towards the two boys. 'Fathers weren't expected to talk to their children. That was for mothers. Respect. That was the thing.' The two boys had sat, silently. Were they cowed by

Sam's booming personality, filling the room? Or did their sidelong glances suggest that she was their concern? Worried for her, or wary of her volatility? She had shaken her curls and winked at James. He'd smiled back, shyly.

Today, Grace brought the porridge in, plates steaming. Oddly, for someone born in Belfast and brought up in Birkenhead, Sam was a great believer in boiled oats for breakfast. Sometimes he was more Scottish than the Scots. The boys looked down at their plates.

'Eat up boys,' said Lotte. 'Grace is an expert with porridge. You're very lucky.'

'When I worked for Mr Ward, he was even more discriminating in his porridge tastes than Sam,' said Grace.

'You see. Breakfast of successful men,' said Sam.

'Particularly when we were in Sussex. We had to take a sack down with us. The local staff were amazed. They'd only read about it.'

'Dr Johnson said oats were for feeding horses in England, people in Scotland. Like potatoes in Ireland. Can't go past the basic foods.' Sam drained his tea.

Lotte looked on. She heard the talk, the spoons chinking, tea pouring. She watched the passing of teapot and sugar and salt, Grace making sure the boys ate up everything, fussing at Lily. She watched them swim about as if through the glass of an aquarium. Voices reached her. But in the same way as sounds reached her when she was walking at night – distant, unconnected noises.

'I have an idea,' said Sam.

Grace looked across the table. Lotte swam up to the surface: 'An idea?'

'Yes. The weather's so good, let's go for a run in the car on Wednesday.'

The boys rolled their eyes.

'I'm sorry, boys,' said Sam.

'Why early closing? Can't we wait till Sunday? Have a whole day?' said Lotte. 'For the boys.'

'I thought maybe just us.'

'I can look after Lily,' said Grace. 'And see to the boys when they come in.'

'No,' said Lotte. 'No, it should be a family outing.'

'But the boys shouldn't miss school,' said Grace as she tidied the plates.

'No.' Sam was adjusting his tie, his high collar. 'We can't have that, but the four of us can go. This weather might change and the car costs too much to sit in a garage.'

'I could do a picnic.' Grace smiled at Lotte. 'It will be good for you to get out in the open air. Help you sleep.'

Lotte passed her plate to Grace, collected the plates from the two boys.

'No picnic, we'll eat out. Where shall we go?' Sam brushed crumbs from his suit. 'Ladies? Where will we explore?'

'You choose,' said Grace.

'Lotte?' said Sam.

'Honestly, I don't mind.'

'Up into the country,' said Grace. 'The lochs. The hills.'

'Yes,' said Sam. 'The hills, the mountain air. Just the thing. What do you think Lotte? The Trossachs?'

'That would be wonderful,' said Grace. 'Or what about the Lake, over to the island?'

'Excellent idea. Lotte?'

Lotte glanced up. It was Grace who responded: 'Where would you like to go?

'I don't mind,' she said. Lotte felt as if she was returning to them, their voices becoming sharp again.

'Drink more.' Grace leaned over with the teapot. 'You need to find a way to sleep more.'

Lotte felt a twist of anger begin to swell in her chest, but she inhaled deeply and gestured the teapot away.

'Sorry, I'm just a bit wearied,' she said. 'A trip to the island would be perfect. If the boat is running.'

'I'll ask,' said Grace.

The two boys were silent.

'Boys,' said Lotte. 'We will go and take a look. On your behalf. Then we will go back later, in the summer. Promise.'

Douglas and James looked only slightly less disappointed.

'But what if we can't?' said James. 'What if something happens and we can't go back? This might be our only chance.'

'Don't be silly,' said Grace. 'If your mother says we will go back, we will.'

'Exactly,' said Sam. 'Time to get ready.'

'Come,' said Grace. 'Let's get you organised and out the door.'

'I promise,' said Lotte.

The Journal of Dr Fergusson

Tuesday 18th April 1933

Sneddon liked to move the time of the weekly medical briefing. Other Medical Superintendents I worked under had taken great pride in the immovability of these meetings. At Rainhill the medical meeting was at eight-thirty every

Monday morning, and had been since 1864. Sneddon would change the time and day via memorandum. We were expected to cancel whatever other commitments we had. It was a demonstration of power.

'Doctor Cunninghame. We will start with admissions.' Sneddon sat at the top of the table with his back to the glare of the window. We arranged ourselves in roughly hierarchical order, though Mrs Nicholson was placed at Sneddon's right hand with her open notebook and a large stack of minutes and papers.

Cunninghame briefly described the admissions. Sneddon pursed his lips at Charlotte's name but said nothing.

'Which room has the private patient been allocated?' said Dr MacKenzie. She adjusted her glasses. Cunninghame looked down. We were all in awe of Dr MacKenzie. She was the best psychiatrist in the building. Even Sneddon recognised that. 'Someday,' he had told me once, after one of these meetings, 'she will be Superintendent.' It wasn't clear whether that was a prediction or a threat to put me in my place.

Meanwhile, Cunninghame searched his papers. Sneddon let him suffer for a few moments before stepping in to rescue him: 'Matron will have that detail.'

Meanwhile, Dr Harris carefully studied the admissions list and kept his pen poised over an open notebook. Our senior by a decade or so, Harris' role was to provide historical context to any issue. Other than that, I could not remember a single contribution. He was an attentive attendee, however. Both Sneddon and I had attempted to catch him out on recall of previous decisions and his responses were always sharp.

We worked briskly through the short agenda. Finally, Sneddon came to the last item.

'Any other,' he paused here, always, 'competent business?'

We looked at each other.

'No? Then perhaps you will indulge me,' he said. 'I'd like you all to look at this paper. Mrs Nicholson has two copies. We will circulate by seniority. I'd very much welcome your views.'

Mrs Nicholson placed a scientific paper in front of me. '*Drugs, hysteria and the establishment of a positive progression to recovery.*'

'When would you like our views?' Dr MacKenzie was squinting through her horn-rimmed glasses at her copy. Harris and Cunninghame, excluded by their lowly place in our short but steep pecking order, studied their own notes.

'Is this not,' I tapped my copy of the paper, 'rather a distraction, when we have so much to do?'

There was a silence, so that the hum of the whole community seemed to fill up the room. Our colleagues waited.

Sneddon leaned back in his chair.

'I admire, Doctor Fergusson, your commitment to the…' he paused here '… to the practicalities, of our profession.' He let that settle. 'But we are all agreed, are we not, that we are scientists first and physicians second?'

Dr MacKenzie flicked the few pages of the paper. I placed my copy flat on the table so Sneddon could not see my hands shake. He went on:

'There's no hurry, I appreciate the demands we face.' I felt his eyes on me as he said this. I didn't rise to it. Around the table heads nodded sagely.

'I'll have this with you tomorrow,' I said to Cunninghame, fighting to keep my voice even as I felt Sneddon pass behind me. I adjusted the lapels of my coat, mantling my rage.

LOTTE

Friday 14th April 1933

It had been more than six months before, September last year, but she could still feel the electricity all through her body as she stood on the top step of the nave. Just a few feet of elevation but it raised her over the seated congregation. Far bigger than the usual Sunday morning gathering, this evening concert. No, not a concert, the Minister was clear about that. But despite his prayer of welcome and the hymn they would all finish with, it was a concert, a recital. Lotte stood alone. Frederick was half-hidden, hunched over the keyboard and tucked away behind the brass lectern. Her recital. The faces along the pews, the hats, the suits, dressed up and here because they wanted to hear her. Not out of duty or habit, but preference. They had come out on a beautiful Sunday evening, just hours away from the start of the working week. Some she knew, faces jumping into focus in the crowd. Sam and Grace were a few rows back, the boys refusing to sit in the front pew. Sam winking, she was sure, but she let her gaze sweep past him. Letting them all down was her greatest anxiety. And she could do without anxiety for breathing was everything – keeping control of her lungs, her diaphragm.

She looked over her shoulder, saw Frederick's eyes fixed on her, framed in the mirror above the wall of stops. He nodded, she nodded and he began, the chords rolling towards her. She filled her lungs, and then her voice joined the organ and out it went, like a great bird flapping lazily into the stone spaces of the old church. From the tiny place in her chest, a few pints of air swelling and opening and blossoming as the sound grew and filled the space above the heads, the hats, the tight perms, the collars of the best coats, rubbing against the old pillars, the lost corners and pushing on past the back row to the great beech doors with their brass studs, and on, upwards, the sound, her sound, her voice, reached into the great arched spaces of the mediaeval roof, a gentle airburst of purity and emotion.

There were no nerves now. She followed the contours of the song like a map, simultaneously in the moment of the note and looking ahead to where the music led. She stepped along the intricate path of the notes, the bass drone of the organ under Frederick's feet pacing out the steady rhythm. As she sang, the words – 'shepherds watchful' and 'peace abiding' – were transformed, became strands of feeling to snake and twist among a hundred people.

There was no rush. There might have been a time she wanted this over as fast as possible. When to have done it, was to be preferred to the doing. She thought back to the concert parties in 1918, during that winter fifteen years ago. That had been a real test. She was twenty-one. Her mother and her aunts had no illusions about her audience.

'We live within a shout of a barracks, we know fine the ways of soldiers,' said her mother.

'And a filthy, dirty shout it is too,' said Aunt Jessie.

That crowd in that camp shed was so much bigger. All angry men who wanted to get home, for it to be over, the army life that had enveloped them, harmed them. Now they were adrift in camps, waiting. She felt she was thin compensation for those long empty months. She had rushed her songs the first time, uncertain. But they cheered at the end for long minutes. And they listened. They were all under army discipline, so, despite the family warnings, she didn't have to fear shouts, comments. There was plenty noise when she went on, in her demure Sunday best. But when she could feel their silence, their attention as she sang, she almost lost the rhythm of her breathing. That had been a bigger event, more people in the echoing tin shed, more things to go wrong. It had changed her life.

But that night in the Holy Rude, affected her more deeply. Perhaps it was the ancient place, the stones, their weight pressing down on the rock, on the whole town. Perhaps it was the deeper silence here, beneath her voice and beneath the organ, the quiet of concentration and total attention. She felt their focus all the way through her flesh down into her bones. It galvanised in a way that pregnancy and motherhood never had. She was absorbed in the music-time, lifted out of normal time. And yet this wasn't conceit.

'Look after yourself, no one else will,' said her grandfather. His advice was always given to her alone – not to her sister, Marguerite.

'Rise above,' said her mother. Mary's own story was one of reinvention.

'Be yourself,' said Peter.

This was her, and there was no conceit. If anything, she felt humbled that something as natural as her voice, given direction by the music and sharpened by hours of practice, could touch so many people. They would go home and remember this, remember moments that she had created. Years from now, at good moments and terrible moments in their lives, they would remember the way she phrased a line, the way she left the note hanging there in the cool evening air of the stone space. Even out in the street, on her way to the Golden Lion dining room and the waiting, meaningless chatter, the shadow of the old church was enough to bring back that feeling. It was modest and infinite at the same time, this difference she had made to the way that others saw the world. And in these hanging, transcendent moments she had been truly herself.

The noise in the dining room of the Golden Lion Hotel always made her uncomfortable. It was hard to believe that gossip and cutlery could combine to make such a din. Even on a weekday, even in these difficult times, the clatter was constant. It meant there was always a much greater chance of picking someone up the wrong way. Or being picked up the wrong way.

Mrs Dorothy Wingard was there first. The printing business was just round the corner. They hugged, Lotte took her coat off and sat. They were close to the window and the glare was painful.

'I've had to listen to John telling me to make sure I mention the invoice at some point and then I've had to listen to Frederick telling me how he has exciting news that he's not going to tell you until practice tomorrow night. You are the main topic of conversation in that works.'

Lotte laughed. 'You can take it as done that you've told me about the invoice. John knows there is no question about it. Unless you buy a new coat on the way home and never say a word.'

'That is an idea. We could start a whole new trading system.'

'And as for Frederick, I'm just as sure his news isn't as spectacular as he is trying to suggest.'

Dorothy looked down at the card menu.

'No, Frederick is very talented.' She paused, squinted at the card. 'With his music anyway. He has a touch of artistic flamboyance about him. And he is too much on his own. As a bachelor.'

'He's just a bit frustrated by his situation,' said Lotte.

'He has a very good situation with us.' There was a sharpness about Dorothy that sometimes verged on the spiky, but Lotte felt a real warmth for her. It was always clear with Dorothy – when you had overstepped a mark you knew about it. With others you could snag a tripwire and never know. Not at the time anyway.

'I know that, he speaks so well of you all at his work, but he's stuck with me and other amateurs. He should be involved in music full time, a professional, working with professionals.'

Dorothy looked directly at her. What had she said?

'Don't say that. He is lucky to be able to play for you. Your voice is unique. I'm not an expert, but your concert at the Holy Rude was magical. People were crying.'

'Was it that grim?'

'You know what I mean. You moved them.'

'It's just for fun.' Lotte picked up her own menu now.

'But it isn't really, is it?' Dorothy was serious.

'It could have been more. Once. But it is too late now. It's just silly now.'

'That's ridiculous.' Dorothy leant towards her. 'If you have a gift, you use it as fully as you can.' There was a pause, a beat. 'Just don't rely on Frederick.'

At other tables the diners looked up as a mild commotion simmered at the doorway. Mrs Arbuthnot and Mrs Jenkins arrived and emerged from their fur coats, passed to a waiter who bundled the furs high like a trapper's sled and carried them off to the cloakroom.

'Late as always,' said Jane Arbuthnot, taking a seat at the head of the table. She started to un-pin her hat, velvet with a collection of game-bird feathers, when she saw that Mrs Jenkins had sat down with her own hat still on. The removal quickly became an adjustment. 'I met Elizabeth outside the shop and we just lost track. Talking, you know.'

Elizabeth Jenkins smiled thinly. Like Dorothy she was in her early forties. Her husband was a partner in the oldest solicitors in the town, and so she was the discreet holder of all their secrets.

Mrs Arbuthnot made the first conversational move by reminding the group that her son was about to graduate in medicine from Glasgow University that summer.

'A difficult outfit choice, I'm sure you'd agree, Elizabeth.' Mrs Jenkins' sons were both lawyers in Edinburgh. 'I shall prod you for advice later. Children are such a gift.'

Dorothy was childless. This was a game she sat out.

'And Charlotte, both your boys show promise, do they not?'

'They're good boys at school,' said Lotte. 'Douglas shows real promise at music.'

'You must be proud. Taking after his mother.'

'He has a real passion for it.'

'He plays beautifully,' said Dorothy. 'Very mature.'

'So important for them to have an interest,' said Mrs Jenkins.

'Just like my two.' Mrs Arbuthnot was tackling her grapefruit half. 'Andrew just loves his books, and John would rather play golf than make money. Almost.'

'It's not like a…' Mrs Jenkins paused to put down her spoon. 'Profession, though? Is it? Music?'

'It…' Lotte felt the rushing in her veins. The deep twist round her heart. There was no point in saying it. They wouldn't understand. 'It's a calling.'

There were smirks over the white tablecloth. Except for Dorothy: 'Any of us who have heard Lotte sing know that it's more than a hobby.'

'Of course.' Mrs Jenkins almost touched her lips with her linen napkin. 'But a profession is so important for young people. To set them on their way.'

'That's what I told my two.' Mrs Arbuthnot had decided where she was going to side on the question. 'I told them retail is all very well, but you need choices. A profession gives you that. You will not have to serve behind a counter at ten o'clock at night. You can leave that to your father.' They all laughed quietly.

Mrs Arbuthnot was safe in the knowledge that everyone here would be aware that her husband's days of late-night shopkeeping were over. As the owner of the biggest furniture emporium in the town, he had plenty of minions to face the customers late on a Saturday night.

'Let us hope none of them have to go off to fight again,' said Lotte. She did not want to deliberately darken the tone, but she hated their air of comfortable certainty. Had they no experience of malevolent fate? Dorothy had been pregnant twice and had no children. She understood.

'I know my boys would do their bit,' said Mrs Jenkins.

'And mine,' said Mrs Arbuthnot.

'I hope mine don't have to,' said Lotte.

'Hear hear,' said Dorothy.

'We all hope that it won't come to anything, of course.' Mrs Arbuthnot was always alert to any potential unpleasantness around the table. Any unpleasantness was for later, never across the table.

'It may not come to that,' said Mrs Jenkins. 'I heard that the High School debate voted against fighting for King and Country. Was your oldest involved?' She gave Lotte her full attention for the first time.

'He is much too young,' said Lotte. 'But I hope he knows what horrors are involved and appreciates that everything has to be done to avoid conflict.'

Mrs Jenkins nodded sympathetically: 'There is no question we would prefer peace, but we must, all of us,' she paused again to glance round the table, 'high and low, do our duty if it comes to it.'

'My husband did his duty in Greece.' Lotte knew she was on solid ground. Mr Jenkins' special skills had placed him well out of harm's way as a contract lawyer for the army.

'We all did our duty,' said Mrs Jenkins.

'And my two boys will be first to sign up again,' said Mrs Arbuthnot, parking her knife and fork neatly across her almost empty plate. 'They will, I'm sure, be in high demand in the military.'

'Doctors will be needed,' said Lotte. She didn't look up.

'But did you also hear, Lotte, of the exchange visit being cancelled?' said Dorothy, pointing to a way out.

'Douglas wouldn't tell me anything of what goes on in school if I paid him,' said Lotte.

'I did hear something,' said Mrs Arbuthnot, but sadly it didn't seem to be enough to be able to lead with this particular piece of gossip.

'We had the school call to cancel a handbill for a concert they were hoping to have. A concert with their exchange school in Dresden.' Dorothy was much better informed.

'Why?' said Mrs Jenkins.

'The school didn't say.'

'It will be because of the situation there,' said Mrs Arbuthnot. 'Herr Hitler and the new government.'

'Yes,' said Mrs Jenkins, 'they have much to do there, probably not time for frivolities. School exchanges.'

'There's a country to sort out, over there,' said Mrs Arbuthnot. 'We could learn a few things. The National Government.' She snorted, politely.

Mrs Jenkins pointed to an imaginary spot on the tablecloth:

'Precisely, inflation, communists. And…' she lowered her voice, but not that much, '…our Hebrew friends.'

'You can criticise their methods, a bit rough and tumble, and his supporters are the very worst sort,' Mrs Arbuthnot lowered her voice too, glad of a chance to conspire with Mrs Jenkins. 'But their heart is in the right place.'

'They would take over any profession.' Mrs Jenkins was animated now. 'Law. Medicine. It will happen here if we aren't careful.'

Lotte and Dorothy were silent.

'I suppose in business you are used to their malign networks?' Mrs Jenkins sat back in her chair.

Lotte felt her shin tapped under the table, she looked up to see Dorothy raise her right eyebrow a fraction.

'My goodness yes.' Mrs Arbuthnot moved quickly to avoid a silence. 'It's almost an accepted part of the furniture trade, you can't compete with one big family all looking out for each other's interests.'

Then, for fear of further unfortunate pauses in the conversation, Mrs Arbuthnot abruptly moved them on. To a reliable subject for small-town gossip: an abandoned baby.

'Dreadful!' said Mrs Arbuthnot, diverted. 'What sort of mother? Left out on the coldest night of the year.'

'Where?' said Mrs Jenkins, who had clearly been kept from such distasteful news by Mr Jenkins. It was inconceivable that he was unaware.

'Ballengeich Cemetery,' said Dorothy.

'Did you not live up there, Lotte?' Mrs Jenkins said this quietly, smiling.

Lotte felt the shoe on her shin again, a gentle rub, so she said:

'I did, and Mrs Arbuthnot is right, there are good and bad in every place, every part of town.'

'Good and bad everywhere. And there are always those with the gumption and hard work to pull ourselves up.' Mrs Arbuthnot nodded meaningfully.

'Amen to that,' said Dorothy. 'And what do we have planned for these lovely spring days?'

As the conversation meandered on, Lotte found herself drifting away. Dorothy would pull her back in at moments, but she felt as if she were listening to the wireless, with the signal growing faint, the static crackling.

'Are you feeling well?' said Mrs Arbuthnot while the coffee was being poured into the tiny cups. 'You are quiet.'

'Perhaps rehearsing songs in your head?' said Mrs Jenkins, with a thin smile.

Later, there was intense debate over the bill. 'Us independent women, we are worse than the men. Are we not like the National Council of Women?' said Mrs Arbuthnot. They laughed. Coats on, they moved out into the keen air,

Mrs Arbuthnot hesitating long enough to be able to work out the direction Mrs Jenkins was taking. Dorothy and Lotte walked together.

'Sorry about bumping your leg. I'm so clumsy,' said Dorothy. They smiled together.

'You're a good friend,' said Lotte, taking her arm. 'It's just, these women.'

'I know. But this is a small place, if we only spoke to the people we agreed with we would have no one to talk to. Or hardly any.'

'If I could work round them like you do, all would be easier.'

'You have to bite it down. We all depend on each other, and not just in business. It's not worth the battles.' They walked in silence for a few steps, paused to let a barrow come out of a pub. 'It is difficult though.' Mr Wingard was Jewish. Dorothy had once confided in Lotte. But he was converted to the Baptists and well disguised.

'I feel on the fringes of all of it,' said Lotte.

'You've as much right to be there as any. You earned it.' Dorothy stopped. Two women side by side in a busy late afternoon street. 'I know it has been difficult. I know you have Grace, she must be a great help, but you have me too.' She kissed Lotte on both cheeks. And she was gone, round the corner to the print works. Lotte stood for a while, watching the traffic, the people, as if from a great distance.

LOTTE

Friday 19th February 1915

Lotte ran up the stairs at Upper Castlehill, the four, spiralling flights, lifting her skirts. She had been dawdling home from the milliners - such a fine October afternoon, the low sun, the shadows sharp -when in Bow Street she passed Maggie Tulloch.

'I'd not bother going home this evening,' she said, 'there's a huge row at your place.'

When she got to the top landing all was quiet. The hallway silent. When she opened the kitchen door it was as still as a photograph, everyone frozen, waiting. She stood, breathless.

Peter, head high under the oil lamp. His mother, Lotte's Aunt Margaret, with her hands flat on the table leaning right across, her eyes flashing. Lotte's mother sat at the table, the fingers of her hands locked together in front of her as if handcuffed, or praying. Aunt Jessie, was over by the fire, sewing, stabbing, pulling, her own rhythm.

Lotte said nothing. No one had registered that she was there. She didn't need to ask. It was clear what had happened.

'Lotte, you tell them,' said Peter. He didn't look at her, his eyes were fixed on his mother. 'Tell them what it's like to be around here, with all these uniforms on the streets and me in my work clothes.'

Lotte said nothing.

'You don't have to go,' said Lotte's mother, staring down at her hands as if they might suddenly become dangerous.

'But I will have to go sooner or later. They can't rely on volunteers forever.'

'I'm not going to say you're wrong there,' said his mother, 'but stop and think for a minute why they need so many.'

'Aye,' said Lotte's mother, 'ask Mrs MacKay, or Mrs Wills, or Mrs MacDonald, or Mrs O'Hare, or Mrs Smith, or Mrs Reilly or Mrs Caitlin.'

'Or Mrs Laing,' Peter's mother joined in. 'Ask her. Two she lost, on the same ship. The same day. Two letters. The same post.'

Peter shook his head. 'I'm going.'

'Lotte speak to him,' said Jessie from the corner. Her spectacles flashed in the firelight. 'He'll listen to you.'

Lotte took her hat off, put her bag on the chair. She stepped over to Peter and held his arm.

'Don't treat him like a boy. He is going. He can't stay.'

Her mother made a noise between threat and exasperation.

'Lotte understands,' said Peter. 'Listen to her.'

'We can't persuade him to change his mind. It's going to be better if he goes with our blessing, surely?'

'You know nothing at all of what this is like,' said her mother. 'Are you giving him your blessing to be blown to bits? Or come back here half a man? No legs or burnt with gas?'

Lotte started to speak. Her mother cut her down. 'That's the blessing you're giving him.'

Aunt Margaret was still motionless over the table. Tears fell on to the oil cloth.

'It's only Lotte wants you to go,' her mother said. 'Only her thinks you'd be better off with your face cut away.'

Lotte clung on to Peter's arm like a spar.

'He's brave but he's clever too. No one is as quick and clever at keeping out of trouble. Most come back and he'll be one of them.'

'It's about six months since this started,' said Peter. 'In early, out early. I'll be back before you've missed me.'

'You'll be back before you know it, right enough,' said Lotte's mother.

Peter's mother said nothing. Something had been settled without being settled. The three sisters, who could fix anything, who could persuade anyone, had been thwarted by Peter, and Lotte. It was a kind of victory for them both. It was up to Peter, his life. And she would always support his freedom, long beyond the point where it was sensible.

4.

The Journal of Dr Fergusson

Wednesday 19th April 1933

'I thought this would be a more pleasant place for us to talk,' I said.

We settled down on a bench at the far end of the garden, where it looked out over the rest of the estate. She was in a long dark skirt and a fitted white blouse, with a plaid blanket over her shoulders. It put me in mind of refugees in France, the dislocated, the comfortable suddenly put out on to the roads. Although we sat at each end of the bench, meeting patients outdoors was not normal practice. But if Sneddon wanted us to innovate, I was prepared to do my bit.

She looked out over the bare trees against the white sky. 'This is beautiful.'

Her eyes were the darkest I have ever seen. I found myself staring at the curve of her eyelashes. Her eyes were tired. Asylum eye, common to staff and patients, but at this stage in her stay they still had some sparkle.

'Not what you expected?'

'I expected a straight-waistcoat.'

'We try to avoid restraint at all costs.' It was one of Dr Sneddon's proudest achievements, a continuation of our long policy of minimal restraint. We didn't count threats and drugs as restraint. 'It's a tradition here. Before the war, they rewarded the staff with grand outings after a long period without the use of restraints.'

'Outings?' She half turned. It is interesting to me, a student of the human condition, that the conventions of polite conversations survive in these unconventional situations. It is how we cope with the unthinkable. We thank the physician for the death sentence.

'Yes, to Rothsay, the entire staff. In two batches one July day. Train, steamer, meals.'

'While the other half looked after the patients?'

'Indeed. Without restraint.'

She pointed to a tree at the bottom of the slope. 'Look at the leaves on that one. There's always one that's ahead of the rest.'

The tree was vivid with the green stubble of new growth. 'What kind is it?' I asked.

'No idea.' There was a faint smile. 'I am a town girl. Born in Edinburgh.'

'I was a student there. And worked there during the war. At Craiglockhart Hospital.'

'With the officers there? Sassoon the conchie?'

'It was a bit more complicated than that. I was back at the front by the time he was there. But I worked with his doctor – Doctor Rivers.'

'They could afford to object. People like Sassoon. Not many had the choice.'

'Lieutenant Sassoon was a hero. MC. That helped. And he wasn't one to shirk his duty.' I didn't want to end up giving her a lecture about what we had all learned in that place. 'You grew up in Edinburgh?'

'I wasn't there for long. Then I moved with my mother to live with her sisters. To Stirling. The Top of the Town.'

'Notorious.'

For the briefest moment I saw what lay behind the admission report, what the GP and the Officers had seen. Her eyes flashed with a sudden, unlikely ferocity. 'None of it's true.'

Her voice had a quiet intensity. I wasn't alarmed, there were plenty staff around, but I did not want this session to end prematurely. And an accent was suddenly there, behind her educated voice. 'There are good people and bad people everywhere.'

'In Snowdon Place?'

'*Especially* Snowdon Place.' Her anger was gone. These flashes of lightning, gone as soon as they came, must have been a test for her family.

'But it must be more pleasant?' It was a much better street than I could aspire to. .

She didn't reply immediately. 'My husband has worked very hard. So have I.'

'It is a lovely street. I'm sure a lovely house.' She said nothing, so I went on. 'And yet you ran away.'

She turned on me again. 'Ran? Away?'

'The walking.'

'Am I here because I like to go for a walk?'

'Walking is a healthy, wholesome pursuit. I am an enthusiast. Love to walk. I shoot. But at night? A woman?'

'It's not allowed?' She furrowed her brow. 'Or is it showing some dark weakness I have? I'm running from my family? Is that your diagnosis, Doctor? I have had these conversations with my GP. With Dr Campbell.'

'Your family were concerned for you. It is dangerous. A woman at night on her own. I know this is 1933, but they were worried that you put yourself in harm's way.'

She was quiet. This is our work. Things happen in these swirling silences. We don't normally record this level of detail, in case notes, but this is how insights are gained. This was the moment where relaxation, secluded surroundings, and the gentle probing of a concerned professional brought about self-awareness and reflection. This is the future of my profession.

'I wanted to be on my own. That is all. I didn't have to think when I was alone in the night.'

'I understand that, but the danger?'

'I never felt afraid.' She paused again, more useful reflection. 'No, never afraid.'

'You were brought up in a poor household?'

'In a slum do you mean?' I had broken the moment. Poor practice. I had allowed her to convert reflection into anger.

'I meant you'd be aware of what men can get up to in the darkness.'

'That I'd be seen as street walker because I walked the streets? I never felt at risk. It was a comfort to me to walk. In the town and out in the country.'

'What did you think about as you walked?' She was instantly calm again. So unpredictable, inconstant.

'I sang. Out loud. And in my head. I watched the world grow light. I felt the ground under my feet and sensed the miles dropping behind me. Do you need more?' She looked towards me again; was this mischief? Mockery? Intelligent patients were always more of a challenge. 'Or do you want to ask me about my marital relations? That is what Dr Campbell was most interested in. And if I'd taken to motherhood.'

'We can talk about all of these things,' I said. 'We can have many more conversations like this.'

'And that's my treatment?'

'Yes. This is, I believe, the best way. Better than.' I paused. I would have to make her a conspirator at some point, but I didn't want to frighten her too soon. 'Better than other treatments.'

'What are these men doing?' She pointed, hands still under her blanket, towards a group of six men wrestling with the grass roller. They struggled, not with the weight – they were all big men – but with the coordination of their forces against an inanimate object. We were too far to hear, but the staff member was gesticulating wildly, as if he was the crazy one.

'It's the cricket pitch. Preparing for the season. We are quite good.'

'Do you play?'

'No,' I said, 'it's not my game. I never learned. Dr Sneddon is very keen. He is the Medical Superintendent. He went to a school where they played a lot.'

'The staff is the team?'

'No, mainly patients.'

She was silent as the dumb show continued at the end of the grounds.

'Will I be employed? Everyone seems to be.'

'Private patients are special. We can discuss.'

'I'd like somewhere away from the day-room.' She said it without expression.

'You are not at risk there.' I said. 'The staff are always alert.'

She turned towards me again. I felt her presence, the narrow space she took up on the bench. 'I'm not frightened of anger. I've dealt with customers all my life.' It wasn't clear if she was joking. She went on: 'I'd like to work in the garden.'

'Women patients work in the kitchen, laundry or in the sewing room.'

'Not the office? I have skills.'

'The asylum office doesn't meet the criteria for recuperative occupation. It can be too stressful an environment I believe.'

'I'd like the garden.'

'I shall see,' I said. 'We should go back in. It's much colder now.'

The cloud had thickened and the light was lower. In truth there had been no warmth in the brightness, a spring day of sunshine and cold, an illusion. I walked Lotte back along the paths through the immaculate flower beds.

Nearly three months ago Sneddon had ordered me to the treatment room. Not for the first time. The patient, a woman in her thirties was sedated on the bed. I didn't know her. Sneddon had to maintain his own case-load, so I assumed it was one of his. A nurse was fussing, adjusting the pillow, the gown and sheet. The restraints.

'That is all we need for now, Nurse. Dr Fergusson and I can manage from here.'

A final tightening and she left. The light, this late on a December afternoon, gave the room a gloomy chill, appropriate for our mission.

'Cheer up John.' Sneddon was always at his most dangerous when he used my first name. 'It's not the lab of

Dr Frankenstein.' He tightened a wrist strap by a notch. 'Or the cabinet of Dr Caligari.'

'You know where I stand here.' What did I loathe more? The vileness of Sneddon's methods, his ambition, or the fact that he could compel me to collude?

'You're standing there as the Depute Medical Superintendent of one of the biggest and best asylums in the country. And we are advancing medical science by taking forward an important exploratory procedure.' He looked over his glasses at me. 'Have I missed anything?'

I said nothing. Sneddon smiled, another danger sign: 'And you're my oldest friend. I'll add that to the brew. It is fitting we do this together. Both our names will be on the paper.'

Friend! Was it mockery or did he really believe it? We seemed destined to be locked together, smiling and pretending, drawn back even when we tried to escape. The charade even when we were alone. What boiling emotions we conceal under our white coats, our professional courtesies. But he was right, he couldn't do this on his own, without collaboration. And maybe it was appropriate it was me. We had known each other through momentous times. From perching together in anatomy lectures, all the way through the war. Sneddon's good war – his glittering war. My university prizes leading nowhere. Even my presence here in this hospital was due to him. Some days it seemed like destiny.

'This poor girl,' he gestured, 'has tried to kill herself four times. Should we do nothing, she will without doubt try again.'

He turned her limp wrist under the strap, her eyes were open, but she barely acknowledged his touch.

'See?' Her wrists were criss-crossed with blue scars.

Sneddon turned to the drug trolley.

'Water, hanging, cutting, she's been inventive in her methods. Imagination is so often part of this pattern.' Sneddon selected a syringe. 'What should we do? Keep her here till one day she gives staff the slip? Steals a needle to swallow or some carbolic acid from the laundry?'

He stepped over to the corner and opened his own leather bag. 'Send her back to her family and let them have the guilt and horror of finding her hanging in an outhouse somewhere?'

'Difficult cases will always be with us,' I said. I had no appetite for another debate. I had had them in this room in similar situations. I wanted it to be over. Until the next time.

'Difficult. But they shouldn't be impossible. There's only so much we can do with our lawns and our laundry and the garden.' He turned and looked over his shoulder at me. 'And your talking.'

'If we don't listen and don't understand, we can help no-one,' I said, lamely.

'I know that,' he said. 'I don't dispute it either. But it's not enough.' He was all focus and business. A man intent. 'My problem with my work, with our project, is the absence of subjective patient insights. I cannot get them to report what the experience is like. The moment where they move from one state to the next. They can't articulate how it feels from the inside.'

He was filling a syringe now. His white coat glowed bright against the grey wall.

'I can only observe the process and measure the outcome, not how we got there.'

He turned, the syringe was full, the liquid a dull yellow. At that moment, he looked so much the figure of the mad scientist I could have laughed. Perhaps I should have. Perhaps that would have changed everything. I was silent.

'There should be no such thing as an impossible case. We should be prepared to treat. Intervene. Develop the tools that will help us to cure. In this place,' he waved the syringe in a tight arc. 'We have too much patience, always waiting. Until what? No one ever leaves here. No one gets better. We're stuck. It's time to open a new file, calibrate differently. Shall we move the story forward. Doctor?'

He indicated that I should help him find a vein. This was the closest he could get me to place my thumb on the plunger itself. He administered the drug with no suggestion of doubt.

He caught my eye. 'He who hesitates,' he said, smiling, and started his stopwatch.

I was always quite shocked at how quickly the drug started to work. No matter what variation of dose Sneddon used, it began to affect the patient almost immediately. She showed signs of agitation. Sweating. Her brow was smooth and shiny. She seemed to come out of the sedative, breathing faster, her eyes open, moving rapidly, but with no acknowledgement that we were in the room.

'Just a moment,' said Sneddon and tied a robust bandage round her open mouth, lifting her pretty head gently, like a proper doctor. 'Protect the tongue.' He then stood back and we both watched carefully as the drug took hold.

The rapid eye movement settled to a staring and while she never focused on us, there was no lack of consciousness. Her mouth was open on the gag, gnawing. Her limbs shuddering.

But then her body went rigid, the convulsive movement stopped, her eyes opened even further, with a look of total and complete terror. It was as if she were looking at all of her worst nightmares gathered in this bare room.

Sneddon leaned forward over the bed. His face was pale with concentration. He drew closer and closer to the patient's face. I'd seen this obsessive reaction before with Sneddon – 'Our first rule. Observe' – but his attention was now as intense as if she were a lover. This time I noted that the crotch of his suit, through his open coat, was pressed hard against the side of the bed.

'Look at her,' he whispered. 'What is going on inside her head?'

'How much longer?'

'Only a few more minutes, it's a medium dose.'

The patient now closed her eyes, tight as if in extreme pain. Sneddon leaned in even closer, he was inches from her face.

Then she stopped breathing.

We did what we could. The two of us. But it was no use. The loss did not seem to register with Sneddon.

'I suspect she'd have been another inarticulate one,' he said.

The Italians had only been able to go so far. Sneddon was convinced they had had casualties too. It wasn't something you put in a journal article.

I had been in this room before, of course I had. But this time I felt unable to quell my revulsion with any soothing scientific outcomes. The absolute terror in the young woman's eyes disturbed me in a new way. It was like nothing I had seen before. Not even in France. And it hadn't been caused by the threat of having limbs ripped off by high explosives or the prospect to dying alone in agony in a hole under the open sky. No, it had been caused by some liquid that Sneddon had cooked up. A chemical. That disturbed me almost as much the sparkle I saw in his eye as he leaned over the patient while she died.

LOTTE

Friday 14th April 1933

When Lotte returned to Snowdon Place she went upstairs. She washed and changed her clothes. It was her way of moving between worlds. Even when she had been out walking at night, when she washed and changed it brought her back into the domestic life.

She crossed the hallway into Lily's bedroom. The child was asleep. High points of red on her cheeks, but breathing in that effortless, invisible way of children. Lotte knelt down, stroked the child's soft curls, felt the faintness of her breath on her cheek. She pulled the covers up over the chubby bare arms and kissed her lightly on the head.

Downstairs she stood at the sitting-room window, one knee on the long stool. The day was almost gone. She wasn't going to hide, in her own house.

Grace was in the kitchen. The marble top of the centre table was covered with a rolled out biscuit mix. Grace had cut into it, the perfect circles clustering at one end. She pushed the cut raw biscuits out onto a baking tray with a shove of her thumb. They dropped onto the tray one after the other. But for a faint click as the cutter went through and the flop of the pastry onto the tray, the operation was almost silent. Grace's head remained bent over the work.

'She's fast asleep now,' said Lotte. She leaned back against the working surface. She looked down at Grace's tightly pinned hair as she worked.

'She will need it,' said Grace, and paused to place the edge of the next circle as close to that of the previous cutting as she could manage. 'The lamb.'

'It is not easy for me to explain why I need to go out. To walk.' Lotte said. 'I don't expect you to understand. I know it seems odd. Strange.'

Grace put the cutter down on the marble top. Leaned the heel of her hand on it and looked at Lotte for the first time.

'I'm not judging you. That isn't my place.' She looked down again. 'I count you as a friend, and I couldn't be more worried about you.'

'I'm perfectly safe.' Lotte kept her voice steady. 'I don't want to be a worry to anyone. Which is why...'

'Why you don't tell your husband?'

'Which is why I slip out and back without anyone noticing.'

'Except for me? I don't count?'

'I'm totally safe. Honestly. There is no-one out at that time.'

'But I know you're out. I can hear you. Your footsteps overhead. The door.'

Lotte could see Grace's eyes were wet.

'I'm the one lying and listening. Waiting for you to come back. That's how I heard Lily. Crying for her mum.'

'I don't want you awake too.' Lotte pushed herself upright, her back and legs muscles felt strong. She knew what the reference to Lily meant. Grace the childless mother. 'One of us awake is enough.' She smiled. 'Grace, please help me with this, please try to understand.'

'I do help. I lie.'

'I don't ask you to lie for me.'

'But I do lie for you. And that isn't easy.' Grace started to cut into the mix randomly, the circles overlapping, the doughy mix flopping back down in semi circles, crescents. 'But I do it because the thing I don't want is an unhappy house and unhappy children.' She chopped on at the mix.

'It's like a medicine for me.' Lotte leant forward now her hands on the wide table, the cool marble under her palms. 'It helps me get through the next day.'

'But on no sleep?'

'In bed without sleep is the worst thing there is.'

'If I'm your friend,' said Grace, her hands still now, 'then you must try to stop this leaving the house. Come down to talk to me in the kitchen. Or let's both of us take a turn around the Park. Together. At dead of night. That will be the same, but safe.'

'No, no,' said Lotte moving round the kitchen now, taking the pots off the range hanging them in their place. 'No. That would not be the same. It isn't company I need.' She stopped and smiled across. 'Not even your company. It's being alone.'

There was no resolution. Grace took the mangled biscuit mix mashed it into an oval lump and began to roll it back out, smooth and thin.

Lotte walked round to the dresser. *The Stirling Observer* was lying, sharply folded into four at an inside page, right in the middle, with the headline –

ABANDONED BABY FOUND AT BALLENGEICH

The paper had been carefully left to expose the headline. Grace didn't look up. 'That's the sort of people out and about with you in the night.'

'I heard when I was out yesterday.' She read quickly down the column. 'It's not a part of town I'd walk to,' she lied.

'A bad woman. Or a bad man, did that. The very worst.' Grace lent into the mix with the rolling pin.

'That was the view in the Golden Lion, too.'

Under the pressure of the rolling pin the mix opened into long gaps. Grace scooped the strips together and started again.

'Women who'd leave their baby out. In April, frost the night before. Out in a graveyard. They are the dregs.'

Lotte said nothing. She pretended to keep reading. Grace wasn't finished:

'Who would do that? Women crave a child, would give anything for a child. And others have one and throw it away. Like rubbish out in a bin.' She let the words hang in the floury air.

'It was well cared for. The baby. It says here it was well-dressed and properly wrapped up.'

'Cared for.' Grace stopped rolling.

'This,' said Lotte, 'is a terrible thing. For everyone. I don't believe a mother does that out of badness.'

'What do they do it out of then?' Grace held the rolling pin in one hand. 'Kindness?'

Lotte tapped the newspaper with her fingernail.

'It will come out. There will be more to the story. The newspapers only tell you what it looks like, not how it actually is.' Lotte turned back to the paper. 'The poor woman.'

'The bad mother,' said Grace.

Lotte kept her back to her. She felt Grace's fury between her shoulders. They knitted together and she let her arms sag where she lent on the dresser. The tension flowed down to bunch in her fists.

'No real mother,' said Grace.

When Lotte turned round, Grace had the full baking tray in her hands, glaring at the pale biscuits. She opened the oven door, slid it in and banged the heavy door shut.

'Prison is too good.'

'It will all out in court, I dare say.'

'It will,' said Grace, bent over the controls. 'What was Frederick's news?' Hunched down, she looked up suddenly at Lotte.

Lotte hesitated. 'Nothing really. It was just a new setting he'd discovered. From his old tutor.'

Grace turned back to the cooker. 'He's a bit of a dramatist is he not, your Mr Thornlee?'

'He is young and takes his music very seriously. He has a passion for it.'

'As you do.'

'What do you mean?' Lotte kept her eyes on the folded newspaper.

'I know your relationship with Mr Thornlee is very professional. That is exactly what I meant, that you share an interest. An enthusiasm.' She paused. 'Not everyone has that understanding though.'

'What have you heard?'

'Nothing. Nothing at all. I would alert you if I had. You know that. And I'd swiftly put a stop to any gossip I heard too.' Grace was at the tap now, washing her hands. 'But not everyone knows how deep your shared interests run.'

'Please tell me what you are suggesting.'

Grace took two steps towards her. Her hands were in her apron pocket.

'I'm suggesting nothing at all other than I have such regard for you, for Sam, for the children. It would break my heart if there was talk in this place about you.' She wiped her eye with the edge of the apron. 'And you, so fragile.'

'Oh Grace, I'm not that fragile. There have been bad times. You know that better than anyone. But I'm getting better.' She picked up the paper, rolled it into a baton, smacked the back of one of the chairs lightly. 'I am better. And the walking is what helps me. And the music.' She pointed with the paper. 'And I'm not like this poor woman.'

Grace smiled. 'If you see how Lily is then we can maybe all have some lunch. If you're in for lunch.'

'The Golden Lion was unusual for me. Dorothy is a friend I suppose. But the rest.' Lotte ran her nail down a stack of side plates. They made a flat little scale. 'They're not friends. They're not for me Grace. I just don't fit. I've never felt part of them.'

'So why meet them? Why not spend more time here? With us.' Grace let the question hang. The baking smell had started. There was a tick from the oven.

'I just need to be out. In the air.' Lotte unrolled the newspaper in her fist, carefully flattened it and smoothed it on the surface by the dresser and left the kitchen.

LOTTE

Sunday 21st May 1916

'Do they really use this?'

Lotte reached down between her boots and pulled at the bright green moss. When she squeezed the intricate miniature forest flat it sprang up again, apparently bigger than it had been before.

Peter picked up his own piece of turf, rubbed it between thumb and finger, sniffed.

'They say it's better than cotton. Better than bandages. And it cleans the wounds.'

'I'm glad you haven't had first-hand experience of that,' said Lotte

Peter took another sniff.

'Some of the lads say that it smells of a woman.' He inhaled deeply. 'I can't say I'm experiencing that myself.'

Lotte threw the sphagnum at his head. He ducked, and for a moment the vivid green of the moss was held suspended black in the sun, against the whole of the central plain of Scotland, the tiny winding-gear, the towns, the bings, the chimneys, the flash of greenhouses, the blue haze over the factories, the coiling rope of the river, a suggestion of the faraway rail bridge and the naval ships on the Forth. Then it dropped out of sight.

'I've heard this said. It coarsens lads. The army.' Lotte shaded her eyes, looked straight at him.

'I learned more swear words among the nice boys at the Art School.'

'This will change you,' said Lotte. 'It's bound to.'

'Says the expert.' Peter lay back. 'Doctor Charlotte Candow, the eminent and distinguished lady physician, outstanding in her field.'

'Like a scarecrow,' said Lotte.

'Outstanding lady physician. Indeed, the only lady physician, today pronounced that young gentlemen exposed to the rough ways of the lower orders may find that their time in His Majesty's forces will extend their vocabulary in previously unrecorded ways.'

'You know what I mean.'

'Doctor Candow also conceded that close exposure to the decapitation by high explosives of said lad's best mates may induce the odd bad dream in future years.'

'Have you?' Lotte squinted at him.

'No, of course not.' Peter chewed a piece of dry skin from his thumb. 'I told you. We gunners are so far from the front that we only hear a far-off rumble. Flashes at night.'

He rolled on to his elbow. Behind him Lotte could see the distant Wallace Monument, the Castle beyond. Just below the outline of the Castle, clinging to the steep slope, she could make out their home.

'The flashes at night. The flares. It's like nothing else. Impossible to capture. I tried in my sketchbook. Hopeless. I saw photographs in training, nothing like being there. So much material for the future. Honestly, I wouldn't want to miss it. There aren't many artists out there.'

Lotte pulled up another clump of sphagnum. She studied the detail. A tiny landscape, a forest in her hand, against the sweep of the land at their feet.

'How far is far?'

'Miles, honestly. The best billet by a long shot. I'd only be safer in the stores.'

'But if you can reach them, they can reach you.'

'It's all about making them keep their heads down.' He sat up now. 'Trying to get us is like trying to hit the Castle from here.'

They both looked out across the sun-lit land, the great hills away to the north. Lotte closed her eyes. She saw the Castle, flames shooting through the old roof, stones raining down, men shattered like the rubble that lay along the edge of the castle rock, a tall black column of smoke reaching up through the white passing clouds and beyond.

'It could happen though?'

Peter reached into his battledress pocket, took out a tin of cigarettes, a box of matches, cupped his hands as he lit up.

'They'd have to get lucky. We'd have to get lucky. Or unlucky. The country boys who look after the nags say the odds are longer than a three-legged horse. They couldn't hit a barn-door or whatever that is in Hun.' He drew the smoke down deep. 'And if we're honest, we couldn't hit the whole barn. You know how good I was at maths at school and yet they said I was chosen because I was good at numbers.'

Lotte pulled her knees up, pushed round so she was facing him squarely.

'Peter. Do not get killed.'

He tipped his head back, blew smoke straight up, into the breeze.

'I am serious,' said Lotte. 'I supported you. Against the aunts. Do not get killed.'

'We don't have that choice,' said Peter, serious now too. 'No one wants to.'

'But don't volunteer. Don't make it worse than it is.'

'It's the first thing you're told. Never volunteer. Always stand at the back. Don't draw attention to yourself.'

'Just don't.' Lotte picked at the sphagnum again.

'Don't think I don't know that.' He shuffled across the grass and moss. He mirrored her position, hands round his knees, cigarette thrown down on the grass. The soles of his boots against the soles of Lotte's.

'People say we're worse than sweethearts,' said Lotte.

'Worse?' Said Peter.

'Just like.'

'Better.'

'How?'

'Because.' Peter rubbed the knuckles of his clasped hands softly up and down the knuckles of her clasped hands. 'Because we're friends. As close as any couple. We don't need more than that. .' He smiled. 'There's lots of new words I've learned, Dr Candow, but you know what I mean.'

'I can't tell if you're right,' said Lotte. 'I can't tell what others feel, certainly not my sister. Who knows what's going on in Marguerite's mind when she's flirting with boys. And all those other lassies with their sweethearts away.'

'Can't compare feelings.' Peter took his hand away, leant back. 'They're unique to you. I just know you are the most important person in my world. And we can't spoil that.'

Lotte felt something well within her. It was like the moment before you laugh out loud or burst into sobs. But it went on without resolution.

'Don't die,' she said.

'I'll try,' he said.

'Peter.'

Over his shoulder, where he had thrown his cigarette, smoke was curling around the dried grass. There were flames too, hidden in the sunlight, but the heat turned Stirling, the Castle, the Gargunnock Hills into rippling distortions.

'Your cigarette.'

Laughing in the smoke and the ash, they stamped the fire back into the ground.

Friday 14th April 1933

The town at night drew her. The familiar was recognisable but also mysterious. Shadows and pooled light. With collar up and hat pulled down tight, it gave her a sense of anonymity she never had during the day. At any other time, she felt totally exposed by her lifetime in this place. The women in her social circle, the congregation, the customers and the people who knew her as a child and young woman. All had, she supposed, their own version of her. All these fragments, joined together like the sort of paintings Peter admired, created a community version of her that sometimes seemed as real to her as the version of herself she held inside her head. As she walked the streets she carried their stories with her. Gossip was what held this town together. She had always been around shops, those community crossroads of tales told and tales transformed. She knew how little it took to become a character in that story.

As she walked the pavements in daylight, with Grace and Lily or with Sam, she pulled her story along behind. For better or for worse, they all knew everything. She was the lucky wee bissum from the Top of the Town who got what she deserved, or otherwise.

At night, the coat, the poor streetlights brought invisibility. She was generally alone. Only once had she passed a policeman. 'Good evening Madame,' as he tapped the front of his helmet. She was certain she was marked down as a strange woman, no accounting for what notions they had. Out at all hours walking the street. No actual streetwalker would have a coat like hers. The police were well acquainted with any women who sold sex in this small town. Even the part-time amateurs who, through daring or desperation, now found that an act they had grown to devalue was given a different sort of value. She had noted the women her mother and aunts had whispered about. Or not even whispered, no words were required. There was a look they exchanged when names came up, when furtive men were met on the stairs.

There was judgement but not condemnation. Better shame than a dead child because doctor's bills could not be paid. And better that luxuries came out of side earnings than the household budget. Respectability was precious because it offered a chance to escape. Her mother, her aunts, always had an eye on the longer journey. But pragmatically, who knew what you needed to do to survive in the short term, to keep out of Orchard House?

The policeman would know all this as well as she did. As would any men who watched her from the vennels, from the doorways. She was not a woman to approach. Too much risk. This was the security of the small town. An irony, that it was the surveillance that protected her. These quiet night-time streets were safe in their emptiness, their silence. Drink was different. Drink she had always feared. The unpredictability of character. The cheerful old boy from the top floor, slipping her and her sister a penny on Saturdays, who squeezed the front of his trousers and lunged at you if you forgot about his regular outing on the third Friday of each month when his ferocious wife let him off the leash for a night. It was as if nothing had happened the next time you saw him. Everyone too frightened of his wife to say anything. Or maybe sorry for her. 'Harmless really.'

Maybe.

Drunks were easy to see or hear. Their cunning had drained out of them in the vennels. Hand against the wall, steadying, as the dark stream ran back between their legs and down the steep slopes. She avoided paydays, avoided the few hours between ecstasy and oblivion, the clockwork pattern where the screams and howls of closing-time faded down to the midnight solitary song, the uncertain footfall, the huddled heaps in the shop doorways reeking of sick and urine. She

understood of all this. Sometimes she imagined explaining it
in detail to Mrs Jenkins.

She walked on. She took in the shops at night. The
windows that she knew well, dark now, drained of colour. The
ghostly shapes of mannequins, the outlines of furniture, the
sinister cutlery. These huge dark windows seemed to be the
limits of the night world, the goods looking out rather than
being looked at, the window-shopper becoming the display.
She had once asked if she could stay in the shop overnight.
Sam had looked at her as if she had asked to join a circus.
She loved the idea of being in there with the goods, the tall
walls of drawers, the counters and tills. And out there in the
streets the few night dwellers, walking, staggering. Perhaps
one would stop, stare in, and she would stare out. A spectre.

Sam refused. And he held the keys.

She stood on the pavement outside the Golden Lion. The
carved beasts above the door. She imagined her hand on
the damp mane. Cupping an ear. She looked out across the
breadth of King Street. Above the level of the yellow haze
of the streetlights William Wallace shouldered his sword. She
remembered the cannon displayed here in 1915. It was only
a month or two after Peter had signed up. There were regular
letters from his training camp. Funny and self-deprecating to
his mother. They sat round the oilcloth as she read them out.
The ones he sent to her, addressed to her at work, to the
millinery shop, were darker. Reading between the censor's
black lines she sensed Peter's shock at he grinding brutality
of the language of the soldiers, terror held at bay by hard,
unfeeling words and behaviour. . His drawings for his mother
were full of fun, caricatures of his comrades. For her there
were dark abstract images in the margins. They suggested
hanging sacks, impaled on bayonets. Straw spilling on to the

ground. Then, one rainy lunchtime, she and Marguerite had come upon the cannons – the chalk sign:

CAPTURED AT LOOS
BY THE 7TH DIVISION SEPT 25TH 1915

Huge wheels, angular metal: it was as if Peter's sketches had come to life. Her sister flirted with the young private. 'No, I wasn't there when they captured them. We were further up the line. But I talked to a lad who did. The Huns ran so fast they left their dinner cooking by the guns...' As the soldier prattled on, Lotte walked up to the rope stretched across poles pushed between the cobbles. She was as close as she could get to the wheels, the vicious simplicity of the barrel, the oiled complexity of the levers and the breech. It was as powerful and beautiful as a steam engine. She thought of Peter's love of the intricate and functional, how he loved to draw down at the station – the precise detail of moving parts.

'How it fits together. How it works. That is the purpose of art. What else is drawing for? To show that everything is all joined up.'

She thought of the purpose of this machine. It functioned solely to kill the enemy as efficiently and as surely as possible. It was what Peter would be facing. Perhaps was facing.

'These Hun howitzers can lob at you from miles away.'

'Do you hear them coming, do you get any warning?' Her sister was wide-eyed now.

'If you hear them, then you know it's not for you, sweetheart. You know some other poor bas... pardon me, comrade, has bought it.' The soldier glanced across to the sergeant, stiffly at ease beside the guns, cap low over his eyes, raindrops on the bright visor.

Lotte thought of death coming out the sky, oblivion without warning. Without time to consider, to contemplate, or to even create a last image to have in your head before the darkness.

'The Huns also use them at lower trajectory. Four feet across the ground. Hundreds of miles an hour. Until it hits something. Or someone.'

Her sister was entranced.

'What is your name my dear, if I might ask?' His voice was quieter now. This was going beyond his superiors' idea of boosting civilian morale, she was sure. It looked as if it was a moment when he regretted not having a moustache to curl.

'Marguerite.'

'French?' he said. 'Here?'

'No, my mother and father liked it. Thought it was different and would do well for me. Make me stand out. And Charlotte too.' She made a graceful gesture towards her sister. 'Your name is important, our mother says.'

The soldier glanced towards Lotte, caught her eye, nodded curtly to ensure she didn't have an opening into their conversation.

'Your older sister?'

'No.' There was hardly any hesitation. 'No, she's my younger sister, but likes to look after me.'

'Well, Marguerite,' he rolled the name like a man who was familiar with the language. 'I should like to find out more about your exotic life.'

The image of a shell as wide as the barrel of the gun screaming though the smoky air of a battlefield, skimming the mud, and of Peter, walking towards it, his eye taking in the intricate, tangled beauty of the wires, the vivid colours overhead, filled Lotte's mind. She shook it away and fixed her sister with her dark eyes.

'Flattered I'm sure,' said Marguerite. 'But my little sister is anxious to be gone. I wish you the best of luck and I hope you capture more of these.'

'I shall do my best always to engage with the enemy.' He lowered his voice, leaned into Marguerite's pink ear. 'Up close, bayonet length. Safer that way. Not like the poor fellows who operate our guns. On the receiving end of these lovelies,' he patted the barrel, wet with rain. 'Shells dropping in on them without warning all hours of the day and night. Out there on the open. Nowhere to hide. Poor devils. With my rifle and bayonet, I've more chance.'

Lotte took her sister by the arm.

'No need to bring comfort to our lads single-handed,' she said, pulling her away.

'Oh honestly. It's just fun.' Marguerite looked back over her shoulder.

'Fun?' They were down at the bottom of the street by now. Lotte half turned and pointed up. The black full stop of the barrel pointed straight at them, the soldier now chatting to another girl in a light coat.

'Nothing serious.'

'Fun. With Peter out there. You heard what he said. How can you say this…these machines are fun?'

'Trust me, I know when boys are showing off. He was just trying to impress. Peter wants us to be positive. Chin up.' Marguerite tucked her face into her scarf. She could sulk for Scotland. 'Least that's what he told me. Being miserable is not his way.'

'No,' said Lotte.

'Remember what he said, "If the War Office letter comes then that…"'

'Then that's the time to pull down the blinds. But not

before.' Peter finished the sentence. She was back in the dark street and it was 1933 again. Peter was standing behind her now, wearing his army cape. His reflection on the wet cobbles looked like a blackbird testing its wings, or drying them. 'What was the point in wasting all that time anticipating what might not happen?'

She spoke to the shadow on the road, she did not want to see his face in the streetlight glare.

'You knew we wouldn't listen to you. We spoke about you every night round the table. I thought about you every hour of every day, at least.'

'That was just a waste then. All these hours you could have been thinking about something more interesting. Or you could have been singing, playing the piano, the things that made you smile.' He was looking for a light under his cape. As it caught the wind its reflection rippled on the wet street. Preparing for flight.

'No. It wasn't time wasted. When I thought about you, I was with you.'

'But I came back.' There was a brief cupped glow above the cape in the roadway, and then it was gone. He was gone.

Lotte looked at the broad slope of the street. It had changed since 1915. The world had turned and people wanted more. She readjusted her eyes to the gloomy pools of light. To the silence. 'Gateway to Baker Street, the road into the town.' That was Sam's view. She looked at the hotel, the plate-glass of the bigger shops. No. This was now the town. It had slid down the hill. Their shop was marooned in the past. She walked on along Barton Street. Heading home. This was where the future was, in these wide streets, not the narrow trenches of the old town.

Now she had one last chance to fly, to let her voice take

flight through the room, touch all the people. Frederick had given her that. Something to grasp. That would be a fitting end to this part of her life. Then she could focus on Sam and the shop, and the boys and Lily. Grace would help too.

And Peter was always there to guide her. Lift her. He didn't have to point the way directly. She just had to listen hard to herself.

5.

The Journal of Dr Fergusson

Wednesday 19th April 1933

'I love these trees.' Charlotte stood still and put her head all the way back as she spoke. The great black branches and the finest twigs overlapped all the way to the light grey sky. 'It's like a cathedral.' She walked on a few steps through the wet grass. The hem of her asylum dress was dark where it hung down below her thick coat – her own. Private patients were allowed their own clothes, but Charlotte had chosen to wear the institutional uniform. She stopped again where one of the big branches swoped down almost to the ground.

'Your dress. It's wet from the grass,' I said.

She didn't look down. 'It will dry.' She was examining a vivid green bud.

'You don't wear your own clothes?'

'I don't want them to spoil.' She was flicking the budding leaf with her thumb. 'Look how tiny this is. But it supports all of this.' She gestured up at the towering tree.

We walked on to the bench. It was beaded with rain. I made to wipe the water away with my hand but Charlotte was quicker. She flicked the wet from her fingers. We sat side-by-side and looked back towards the main building. In the sun it became a grand country house again.

'Someone once sat here and looked at their home,' I said. I wanted to hear about her home, her origins.

'It took a small army to run a place like this. Grace told me. Indoors and outdoors.' She unbuttoned her coat. 'Grace, our housekeeper.'

'I don't have experience of servants,' I said. On the edge of my vision I could see Charlotte's mouth purse in irritation. She ignored the bait.

'My mother was on her own from when I was very small,' she said. 'When my father died, we had to move in with my grandfather. In Edinburgh. He wasn't wealthy but he wasn't poor. He had a business to pass on to his own sons, the ones that were left. But he said that an education was necessary if you had nothing to fall back on.'

'Very enlightened.'

'For a tradesman?'

'No, I meant very enlightened for his time.'

'He wasn't so forward-thinking. He thought we'd make better marriages if we could play the piano, speak properly.'

'Better yourselves?'

'Pass ourselves off.'

'Did you? Do you, feel that's what you did?'

'I married a grocer's apprentice who had learned how to keep books and track money as a quartermaster in the army, I wasn't marrying out of my class.'

'What about your sister?'

'The same. But we married ambitious men. We could speak well, so we were helpful. It isn't that complicated, I don't think.'

'Your grandfather paid for the music lessons?'

'Initially. And for the elocution lessons.'

I said. 'The way we speak is the great indicator. I understand that myself. The judgements made…'

'…every time we speak.' She was eager now. 'I see good women, and men, caught by their voices. Not what they say but how they say it.'

'But expensive, relatively.'

'An investment.'

'For your grandfather?'

'Not for that long. There was.' She hesitated. 'A falling out. And we left Edinburgh to stay with my mother's sisters, two sisters, here, or Stirling anyway. But they found new teachers for us here. They were in business, my aunts. They understood investment.'

'You said a falling out?'

'I think so.' The hesitation returned. 'I was very young.'

'And your aunts?'

'What?'

'They took you in, the three of you? Did they not have children too?'

'My Aunt Margaret did, a son Peter. But Jessie, my other aunt, wasn't married.'

'And were you close to your sister?' I said. Siblings are often the key to mental distress.

'I suppose I was – then. Later I was closer to my cousin, Peter. We just got on better. Marguerite seemed to always know what she wanted, where she was going, the sort of man she was going to marry.' She tailed off, wary still. There was plenty there to return to in a future session.

'Was it not crowded. Up there?'

'At the Top of the Town? In the slums?'

'I'm sure it wasn't a slum.'

'People say it will all be pulled down someday soon.'

'The rehousing programme is much admired.'

'By those who don't live there.' There was anger again, gathering under her dark level brows. 'We lived well, we weren't poor. They ran a business. The house was owned and they didn't see any point in having extra overheads.' She had calmed down now, back to Kings Park. 'There's a community up there. There was business to be done and we were at the centre of it.'

'I know,' I said. 'Forgive me, you will appreciate that many of the people here are from that area. It distorts my perceptions.'

'There are people here from everywhere.' The anger had gone. She smiled. I felt it again. Her warmth. Her family must miss her very much.

'Quite.' I said. 'Do not think for a moment I am a snob, Charlotte.' I had decided early to use her first name. Unless she objected. 'Anything but. As I said, I have no airs and graces about my origins.'

'You don't have to. You're a doctor!' I was on the receiving end of her gentle mockery. Before I could tell if she was smiling, she was up and moving on, restless.

'What is this?' she said. 'A wall within the walls?' Our walk took us across the deserted lawns, behind the walled garden.

'That,' I said, 'is Miss Brown's domain. She's not officially one of the troops. A volunteer. She comes in to run the walled garden where she irritates the gardening staff and soothes the souls of our most disturbed patients.'

'Is that why you suggested I might want to work there?

'No. I thought you'd value the outdoors. And enjoy Miss Brown's company. She's a bit different. She's not regimental, as we'd say in the army.'

'No one talks much of the war. Not even in here.'

'We've plenty casualties. It didn't stop in 1918,' I said. Charlotte was striding through the grass. I had to keep up. Then suddenly she stopped. We were in the centre of the lawn. I was conscious of all the eyes from all the windows.

'You didn't have to kill , did you? As a doctor, you at least knew that you'd done your best.'

I couldn't see her eyes as she spoke, the light was behind her, her face shaded, but I could still feel her gaze.

'I did my best,' I said. 'It was never easy. By candlelight in the Regimental Aid Post I had to choose. There were never enough stretcher bearers, so it was a choice who you saved.'

'Men were changed. Peter, my cousin. He couldn't walk away from what he saw.'

'I did do my best.' Was I convincing her or myself? 'I made mistakes. We all did. In the dark you'd miss entry wounds. The men were beyond telling you anything. In fear and pain they made no sense. I had minutes, less, to decide whether I gave them the chance of living on for forty years with a story to tell. Or left them to a final hour in a dark dripping dugout.' She was still looking at me, out there on the lawn. I felt I could tell her everything. Almost. 'I wasn't convinced that the ones we sent down to Casualty Clearing, the saved, were the lucky ones. We could fish out the debris, sew them up, pour on antiseptic, but we couldn't pull out the things they'd seen and heard.' She looked down now, there was cut grass stuck to the toes of her boots. 'Albert Stoneleigh,' I said. 'An apprentice chemist from Nottingham. My orderly. My partner in being God. He stood by me all those terrible nights. He was cool and thorough, never complained. Had two beers with the lads in a bar in Amiens and went out back and opened a carotid artery with an army-issue scalpel.'

I looked up. Charlotte was away, across the lawn towards the high buildings. Her feet left a trace through the grass. 'Charlotte,' I said, 'I'm sorry.' I ran after her.

When I caught up with her, I nearly grabbed her by her arm. Instead, I moved in front of her. 'I forgot myself. I didn't mean to be so graphic. Forgive me.'

'No. No,' she said. 'It's not that. I didn't want to hear any more. I'm sorry. I'm sorry you all had to go.'

'You shouldn't have to listen to me. I'm supposed to do that for you.' And yet it felt good to confide, if not to confess. We were standing facing each other again. 'You now know me almost as well as I know you.'

She smiled. Marvellously. 'It's better to share, is it not?'

I could think of nothing to say. We walked in silence back to the side entrance.

Will this diary end up in a damp box in some loft? Maybe this scribbling is more about the here and now? My own therapy in the absence of anyone I can talk to. Better get it out on to paper than let all this rage around in your head. This morning I decided to make a move on Sneddon's position.

In his outer office Mrs Nicholson gave me that thin-lipped smile which makes me wonder what Sneddon says about me. I can see her stifling amusement as he repeats something I've said. A tiny, shared confidence to reinforce her absolute loyalty. See how I trust you? But tittle-tattle about me with the administrative staff would show just how seriously he takes my views, takes me. At least it goes no further. I cannot imagine Mrs Nicholson gossiping with Mr Nicholson. Indeed, I cannot imagine Mr Nicholson at all.

'Please just go in, Dr Fergusson.'

Sneddon had his head down over his papers. It was satisfying to note that the area of skin towards the rear of his skull flared through his greying hair more prominently than I remembered from my last visit. The sun came through the big windows to the left. There was an intensity to it, almost warm. In our business this season is a busy time. This is when the world quickens but leaves our people behind. In Spring sunlight they have to face the fact that darkness comes from inside.

'Just bear with me John.' He wasn't going to look up. Yet. 'I don't want to break my delicate train of thought.'

'Indeed,' I said.

His papers were arranged parallel to the edge of the desk, overlapped precisely to reveal the titles. His pipe, tobacco tin, pen tray, all present. A full Lee-Enfield bullet clip weighted a batch of read papers to his right. He was nearing the end of a substantial file only just constrained by a powerful bulldog clip. You can't work in this service without learning how to read upside down. Typed across the top of each page was – ARRANGEMENTS FOR THE LONG-TERM NUTRITIONAL WELFARE OF PATIENTS. This was a new level of tedium even for Sneddon. I tapped my fingers gently on the edge of his desk. Walnut. I imagined Charlotte's dining room table was like that. When I listened to her I found myself picturing her house in great detail, a table with rich burrs, polished daily. And in my mind, and in this journal, she had already become Charlotte, no longer Mrs Raymond. I thought about the ravaged wood of the dining area tables. Bristling with skelves. Absorbing decades of rage. We had cut her adrift from a world she could recognise under her fingers. Rough wood, rough clothing. I felt the urgency again.

'My new patient. When you're ready, of course.'

He raised an eyebrow. 'Settling in?'

'No one settles here.'

'True. It isn't really the point is it? I meant that she may have more…' He waved vaguely with his hand, two fingers together, a casual gesture as if inviting an invisible guest to pull up a chair. 'Difficulties. In transition. She's a paying guest and we're not the Ritz of London.'

'You mean those poor wretches who come here from off the streets or Orchard House. Do they have less difficulty?'

He smiled, warmly. 'Most of them are positively grateful. There is only beneficial work here. Therapy, not hard labour. And better food.' He tapped the file.

'I'm not convinced that ironing or scrubbing floors is therapeutic.'

He smiled. 'Your sceptical nature did you no harm in the anatomy hall. And I cannot pretend that a questioning demeanour isn't at the heart of our science. But.' He paused and began to pack his pipe. 'You could just let some of the little things go. Concentrate on what matters.' His fingers worked at the tobacco with the same intensity as I had seen them searching for a vein in a female patient's arm. It is the details that tip us into irrational hatred as much as the ones that are life-defining.

He stared out into the well-kept garden. There were buds on the bushes. He usually waited a few more minutes before looking beyond me. One of his games to remind me where I stood in the hierarchy. I had a strategy for this. I simply followed his gaze out through the window and waited for him to make the next move.

Miss Brown was clipping at a bush with her secateurs. She was as thin as the adolescent cherry trees beyond the lawns. In her puttees and with her short hair, she had the air of an officer examining the other ranks as she snipped silently. Beyond her, two inmates were working toward each other across the small lawn both spearing the turf with forks. Step, step, push.

'Your garden.' Sneddon was on his feet now. He walked over to the window, tapped the glass lightly with the end of his pipe. Miss Brown looked across, waved as if disturbed by a fly, and turned back to the bush. The patients continued to bayonet the lawn. 'Is a different matter. Something worth bringing back from the old days.'

'It is a connection with natural life. So many of our people are from the country but farm labour is beyond them.'

'Good honest work, too.' Sneddon had a trusting belief in work.

'For many here, good honest work is what has helped to break them in the first place.' I didn't disguise the edge in my voice here. Sneddon had an Edwardian view of the lower orders which the war had done nothing to dispel.

Sneddon kept his back to me, blue clouds floated above his head. He let my comment drift past.

'That, however, is decidedly not the case with our latest admission,' he said.

'She is from a very comfortable background.' I had to pick my way onto a more favourable position before I mounted an attack.

'She may be paying a fee, but our treatment here is not based on favouritism or fortune. If it is good enough for one, it is good enough for all. As the Politburo might say.'

I wasn't sure if he meant the Commissioners or Stalin's

henchmen. His back was still firmly set against me, so I walked over and joined him at the window.

'Your initial diagnosis and treatment plan? I assume that's why you're here.' Sneddon adopted a brisk Superintendent tone.

'I'd like time,' I said.

'We'd all like time. Come with me to Edinburgh and see how much the Commissioners like to jaw about time. And the Councillors. They are all with me. All looking for faster...' He paused. 'Better treatments.'

'You've discussed *your* treatments?' I was certain Sneddon was acting outwith official approval.

'Not in detail. The Commissioners will need more proof. And the Councillors would never understand. But in time. When I...' He paused again. Pipe again. 'When *we* have more evidence.'

I was keen to separate Charlotte from this strand of the conversation: 'Her hysteria is due to her life. Her life outside. I think what she needs most is respite, sanctuary. A sanctuary.'

'Asylum, you mean.' Sneddon puffed.

'I think if we give her time and listen then there is every chance she will go back to her family, and soon.'

'Exactly that. Getting back to her family is what she wants and needs. You know we have the means to shock her out of her state and back on an even keel.' He took the pipe out of his mouth now and glanced in my direction. 'I've seen the Sheriff's report and the medical reports. I'm not sure talking is the answer.' He looked down sadly at the extinguished bowl.

Show no weakness. Persevere. Force him to make the arguments.

'A week, that is all that I'm asking for. Then we will speak again. Review.'

'She was a danger to herself. Her family deserve more.'

'Do you mean the walking?' I said.

'A woman out in the dead of night. Alone.' His pipe stem was jabbing in my direction, although he continued to look out at the garden. 'It's not right.'

'It brings her peace.'

'It's not normal. Not safe.'

Outside, the two patients had surely long since vanquished the lawn, but they continued to jab, soundless behind the glass. The symmetry of their motion seemed broken. While one continued to step, place his fork then kick down on it with his right foot, the other was burying his fork deep in the turf with one powerful arched movement. He was a gaunt fellow, but his powerful arms were raising and stabbing the heavy fork with vicious purpose.

We watched carefully, Dr Sneddon and I. This is what we were here for, observing, interpreting, making sense of the unusual, the perplexing.

'You can talk for a day or so more, Doctor, and then we shall treat her. 'It's for the best,' said Sneddon.

A day. Or so. Not enough. I was about to defend my position for a final time when the white-faced man raised his fork high over his head and brought it down on to his foot. He fell like a tree on to his back. I could see the gleam of a tine through the sole of his shoes. It wasn't silent through the glass now, but all was muffled as if in an aquarium. The injured man bellowed, Miss Brown and the other inmate stood open-mouthed. When Miss Brown finally got around the box hedges, she held the man by the shoulders and kept his torso upright, the fork lying awkwardly along his leg. The patient's face was now the colour of the sundial.

'Mrs Nicholson,' Sneddon shouted, 'telephone the sick bay, will you, tell them to get a couple of chaps and stretcher round to the garden.'

Outside, the casualty was now hidden by a kneeling Miss Brown, the soles of her neat little boots wet and muddy. There was no roaring now.

'I expect you should take a look too.' This wasn't for discussion. Events had given him the edge on me. This was how it had been between us for decades, he was always quick to take advantage of circumstances – great and small. There was no going back to our argument now. Sneddon had the initiative: 'Plenty iodine onto the wound, do you think? It's not High Wood but I can't imagine the lawn affects a high standard of hygiene. We don't want an amputation on our hands.'

He was back at his desk. He fingered the edge of his papers.

'The end of the week. I shall book the treatment room for Sunday.' A sudden shriek came from outside.

In the outer office Mrs Nicholson was on the telephone and in her element, 'Yes, I did say emergency, and I did say Dr Sneddon insists…' A moment later and I was in the dispensary filling a syringe with morphine. When I got out on to the lawn Miss Brown was still kneeling on the grass in the sunshine, supporting the injured man. It was like a religious painting.

There was no sign of a stretcher party and the other patient was hunkered down at the far end of the lawn, staring at the grass between his feet.

Miss Brown glared up at me. 'Thank God you are here. This man is in great pain.'

'I think I have seen enough bayonet wounds, Miss Brown, to have established that.'

The man was so pale now he was almost blue. He was breathing fast, but perfectly composed. I pulled his arm out of his canvas jacket and unbuttoned a ragged cuff. He didn't flinch as I injected the morphine.

'You know this routine, soldier? Just try to breathe and let this do its work.'

His lips were thin with white matter at each corner, but his voice was strong.

'Thank you, Doctor. It was an accident.'

'Poor fellow.' Miss Brown held his other hand.

'We'll get you patched up,' I said, but by now, having made him comfortable, I was happy to leave it to the nurses to remove the fork and clean the wound. My days of this sort of work were behind me.

'Doctor.' His brows were down now, I could see the pupils had narrowed already, but it wouldn't have made much impact on the pain yet. 'Doctor. This will get me home now, won't it?' And then he added, 'I'm no coward.'

'Lie still soldier, we'll have you sorted in no time at all.'

'It was an accident, Doctor, she saw it.' His eyes moved to Miss Brown. 'An accident. Enough to get me back home to Scotland though?'

When the two orderlies eventually arrived, I left them to it. Miss Brown and I were walking back to the main entrance and so were cushioned by distance from the shrieks as they lifted him.

'That poor man,' said Miss Brown. As always, I had to pick up my pace to match hers. 'To inflict such pain. What agonies he must have.'

'For some it never ended. We can only do what we can to provide some safety.' I was aware of the criticism inadequately concealed in almost all of Miss Brown's observations. As a volunteer, she felt herself separate from our hierarchies. As a second cousin or some-such of Lord Drummond, she was always confident enough to challenge professional men. With her almost military hairstyle and masculine clothing, she was unique in our community. She needed careful handling at all times. We were nearing the front entrance and I knew she was never keen to enter the main building if she could avoid it.

'We cannot cure the incurable Miss Brown, we can only offer some comfort. Perhaps we shall think twice about who we expose to potentially dangerous garden tools.'

A life lived outdoors meant it was difficult to put an age to Miss Brown, but her eyes were the palest and purest of blues.

'Dr Fergusson, I have a firm belief that the smell of the earth and the sound of the birds calms and soothes their demons.'

'I could not disagree.' I was keen to leave her on a positive note.

We were standing by the doorway now. I put a hopeful foot on the first step, a sign of how busy I was. I did not want a long debate with Miss Brown. She was a modern woman, a woman who viewed men with open suspicion, if not hostility – she was an unpredictable and unconventional ally in this tiny theatre of conflict. I was always wary.

I was ready to disengage and sprint up the steps, but I turned back.

'I wonder, Miss Brown, if you might find a task for my new patient. She is not a self-mutilator, but a troubled woman. Dr Sneddon sees only one route for the very troubled, but I feel you and I, between us, could help her more.'

'Is she the private patient?'

'Yes, but that's not why I'm asking. She is a lover of the open fields and hedges. A compulsive walker.'

'My garden – our garden – may give her more distress. We have an estate wall that is nine feet high.'

'The smell of the earth. The sound of the birds,' I said.

'I will do what I can to help.'

Later that afternoon, with my office door shut firmly, I settled to complete my paperwork. Some things about the army I had hated. The playground hierarchies that allowed people like Sneddon to prosper. The petty cruelties and the lack of common sense. These were daily torments for me. But the rigorous focus on order, a place for everything and everything in its place, was the thing that I loved. It was what gave me comfort, security. The routine, the ordered filing cabinets, the ability to find exactly what I needed at any given moment. The absence of my wife and children and spaniel allowed me to extend that precision into what life I had outside these walls.

The alternative to order was set out clearly in France. Chaos is death. And I also observed, among the best officers – the top units, that discipline and form could be imposed at the very extremes of human experience. Bombed-out trenches were turned into training-standard defences in a matter of hours, working field-hospitals rose out of a waste of mud and rotting horses.

It is my belief that our mission – our calling – as physicians of the mind, is the imposition of an ordered understanding of the chaos that raged inside all our heads. The patterns of memories, experiences, sensations, interactions contending with each other like waves in a disturbed sea and occasionally joining into a mighty swell that overwhelmed the breakwaters. Our task is to explore, to examine, to look and listen long and hard enough to make sense of the maelstrom, find a pattern which will enable our patients to build defences that might break the surge, still the waters. Our emotions bring us joy. Even my beautifully ordered files have value to me because I have an inner surge of positive emotion when I lay my hands directly on the memo I need. But I am careful that those emotions do not get out of hand, that my pleasure I take from order does not get out of control. In France, fear was the only emotion that mattered. It preserved men and broke men. In equal measure. What made the difference was whether you understood your fear and created some order around it, or let it overwhelm. For the self-mutilator on the lawn this afternoon, the fear had never been contained.

I started to work through my paperwork systematically. But I was conscious I was hurrying through the pile of nurses' reports on my patients. As the nursing staff have become more professional, we have found it valuable to make use of their more sustained contact with the patients. Their written reports are a great help to us physicians charged with making decisions. We do not have time to sit for hours with patients, and in any case the observations of their unguarded moments provide us with insights that we would not extract from formal interviews. I intended to favour Charlotte with a disproportionate amount of my time, and not just because she was a private patient. But I was still anxious to see if there was a report on her first day with other patients.

I therefore abandoned my systematic appraisal of the reports and dug down until I saw her name at the top of the observations form.

I took in Nurse Clark's 's report on Charlotte in one gulp:

I collected Mrs Raymond from her room at 7 a.m. She was dressed in her asylum clothes and washed and I would also say had fixed her hair, but her hair is a great mass of dark curls so does not need fixing. I took her to the dining hall for breakfast. She sat alone but interacted politely with the women she was sat with. She showed no great nervousness and replied to all who asked her questions. After breakfast I took her to the dayroom and sat her beside a group that I thought she would get on with. It included Alice Ogilvie who is a bit older than Mrs Raymond but I thought would be of interest as she was a singer in the past and so they would have things to talk about. There were a couple of other quieter and more respectable ladies in the group too. I went round the groups in the dayroom, keeping an eye on my women as I generally do at this time, but I kept one eye and one ear on Mrs Raymond due to this report, and her being new. It is often a difficult time for them when first exposed to the dayroom, especially private patients. I saw that Mrs Raymond and Mrs Ogilvie were talking amicably on operas and arias and composers. Mrs Raymond did not even seem upset when Mrs Ogilvie began her story about the time she had met Mozart. She asked lots of questions about the experience and seemed amused rather than astonished. Those of us who have heard the story a few times are not usually as indulgent, but it suggested that Mrs Raymond might not be as shocked at some of our patients as I might have feared. And we have no one else with Mrs Ogilvie's knowledge of music. After a while I took Mrs Raymond to Nurse Warriston who took her to her second induction interview with Dr Fergusson.

I read the report again, slowly. How close you can feel to someone when seeing them through another's eyes. Particularly Nurse Clark's sharp little eyes. Mrs Raymond wasn't our normal private patient. Not a bored wife of the type Professor Freud specialises in, although there will be sexual undercurrents to investigate – there always are. She's not a troublesome relative to be parked away from the family for a while. Or a victim of a vendetta. As far as we know. The circumstances of her arrival will be interesting to explore in due course.

6.

LOTTE

Friday 6th March 1914

How did Peter get the tickets? He told her the long, complicated story. His tutor at the College of Art had known someone who was a member of the Royal Society of Edinburgh. But then he and his wife had a falling-out related in some way to a female student. And so, the tutor had not felt able to go. He was heartbroken.

'He could have thought about that before the female student,' Lotte said.

But, unable to explain to his colleagues why he might now be able to give away two of the most difficult to obtain tickets in Scotland, he had announced that he would give both tickets to deserving young people. The next generation. Pass on the cultural torch.

Which is why Peter, in his best suit, and Lotte in a dress and hat that cost a month's wages, found themselves walking up Lothian Road to the Grand Opening Concert of the Usher Hall.

'Is that the Provost?' Up ahead, outside the new building, there was a carriage, with matching black horses like a funeral. A gold chain flashing in the low evening sun.

'A pillar of the community. An upstanding citizen.' Peter curled his lip. Around them the good burghers of the city were beginning to notice his attitude as much as their youth in this white-haired crowd.

'Peter.' Lotte whacked him on the shoulder with her clutch bag. Drawing even more attention. 'Enough.'

'Oh Lotte,' he said, as they shuffled up the steps toward the uniformed doormen, 'what on earth are we doing here?'

It was mild for early March, but the ladies of Edinburgh and some of the men were fully protected by their mink and musquash.

'More furs than an Eskimo wedding,' said Peter.

Lotte elbowed him discreetly. Or so she thought. There was muttering. She cast a critical professional eye on the hats as they shuffled along with the crowd .

'Our luck we will be sat behind that one.' Peter nodded towards a particularly extravagant creation.

The brass and the woodwork flickered in the lights. There were gasps of excitement as each audience group entered the hall. Lotte and Peter had many flights of stairs to ascend behind the slow-moving crowd before they reached their level.

'I mean, thoughtless really, he could have got us the Grand Circle. Typical. We're going to have to rough it with the riff-raff away up here.'

Lotte put her elbow to use again, but in truth she didn't care one bit, Peter's commentary on the crowd and the action was part of the excitement of being here. Peter took a programme sheet from the usherette, passed it to Lotte.

'This is your department.'

She looked down as they stood there at the top a steep

flight of steps that seemed to lead right to the edge of the void.

6ᵀʰ March 1914
Grand Opening Concert
Usher Hall

She skimmed the first few lines, the dedication by the Moderator, the speech by the Provost, the formal opening by Mr Usher's widow. Then the music. Bach, Handel, Beethoven, Wagner. A new piece by Hamish MacCunn.

Peter looked over her shoulder.

'All your Teutonic favourites are there. And only one Scot.' Peter had picked up lots of political views at the College, including a leaning towards Home Rule. She wasn't sure where that fitted with his socialism – 'Aren't countries old-fashioned now?' – but Peter could always find a way to resolve contradictions.

They moved down the stairway towards their seats. With each step the enormity of the space seemed to unfold. A vertigo, like approaching a cliff you couldn't see when descending a hill. They were two rows back from the edge of the precipice. Below, in the distance, the orchestra. Above, much closer , the huge circular ceiling. All around, and from the great open well of the auditorium, there was a low roar. It was unlike anything Lotte had heard before. She was familiar with concerts in the Albert Hall back in Stirling, but this was of a different scale of space and excitement.

She remembered nothing of the speeches. Not even Peter's muttered commentary. But the music stayed with her forever. The precision and passion, the mounting cadences appropriate to the space. And just as moving, the small, quiet notes, the soloists, players and singers and the way they harnessed the attention of so many people and commanded the space with a single note just as powerfully as the full orchestra and the great machine of the organ. She felt the notes deep in her chest, her whole body resonated, became part of the sound.

Afterwards came the rush for the train. They were impatient with the crowd, moving slowly as if everyone wanted to hang on to this moment of history. Faces glowed in the cool air. A few overheard complaints about the 'Hun programme.' Running down the stairs at Haymarket, then the journey through the dark, the dismal stations. She said nothing, and Peter, sensitive as always, slept, or pretended to sleep. Lotte gripped the harsh fabric of the seats behind her knees and with fierce concentration imagined her way through the five pieces she had heard. The uniqueness of the event, the tension in the audience had all registered with her, of course. But the music was the thing. And especially the Wagner, the *Liebestod*, pure emotion, rising and falling as waves through that enormous space. Over and over in her head she replayed the last note, falling into silence that was held, on and on, gaining in substance until the audience finally broke it with wild enthusiasm. Wild for Edinburgh, anyway. How much better to have left the silence. Much more appreciative to have the audience stunned into complete, quiet contemplation of the huge truth of love and death.

Her mother and her sister, Marguerite, were up, her mother working on her accounts book, moving invoices and receipts around multiple separate piles on the yellow oilcloth. Marguerite was flicking through a fashion magazine. Margaret and Jessie were in bed already. Her mother asked politely about the programme, the new hall.

'How many were there?' said Marguerite. 'Anyone famous?'

'Do they have catering?' said her mother. 'Does the Council get the profits?'

Lotte and Peter told their stories. The furs, the Provost, the great drop over the edge, the brass-work. But Lotte couldn't tell the proper tale– of what that music on that night, in that place – had meant to her. How it had lit something inside her. She sat with it burning there, her coat still on, round that table where the aunts cooked their plans, took on the world. Burning with a deep joy and sadness. The everyday, the work, couldn't give her this. To be at the centre of silence as the last note ended. To be the cause of such deep emotional response. But there was a harsh truth too, that despite her voice and skills she could only ever have this experience sitting in the audience, not out under the lights. Her aunts had worked miracles on this table. The sort of economic miracles that might allow her to buy tickets, perhaps put her own mink casually across the back of a front row seat. As she looked down at the programme, she knew the front row of the audience was the closest she could hope for.

LOTTE

Saturday 15th April 1933

Sometimes there was a beadle around. He would find jobs to do at the back of the church among the musty piles of Bibles, tracts and hymn books. Other times he would slip off and return at nine to lock up, smelling slightly of beer and tobacco.

Tonight, he was in the vestry, mopping the tiles.

'Fine night.' He was a man so thin that the handle of the mop seemed a natural extension of his arms, his figure in the boiler suit something that a child might make out of pipe-cleaners. And yet, Dr Macleod had told her that the beadle was Mentioned in Dispatches. One night at Ancre he had crawled close to a machine gun post and killed all the crew by throwing a bomb into their midst, allowing most of his unit to retreat. He now lived with his aged mother on a pension and his beadle wages.

'I can forgive him his indiscretions,' said Dr Macleod. 'Or at least tolerate them.'

There was a faint rushing noise as she went into the high vaults of the church proper. There only if you listened hard. It was the sound of the organ filling with air, the electric motor that had finally dispensed with the manual pump. And it rendered obsolete the two youths who pulled the long wooden handles in the gloom among the pipes and valves. No longer would wisps of blue smoke waft out between the long pipes on a Sunday morning as they enjoyed a contemplative cigarette during the sermon.

As she walked between the rows of pews towards the raised altar, Frederick played with the bass notes, in slow march time, the Arrival of the Queen of Sheba. It was a joke. He looked over his shoulder. 'All hail,' he said.

'Don't be silly,' said Lotte taking off her coat and placing it over the front pew. It wasn't clear at this point if it was going to be warm enough to do without it.

'I'm not being silly.' Frederick swung his legs over the long bench and came over the carpeted altar area towards her.

His black shoes caught the lights, for someone who had never been in the military he had extremely well-tended footwear.

Lotte opened her music case and took out the Handel.

'I've gone over this a few times on the piano.' She opened the manuscript book, 'since Sunday. It isn't any less tricky.'

He took the manuscript from her. They stood there, slim in front of the tall dark windows. Where couples stood as they were taking their vows.

'We will come to this in a moment.' He closed the book, looked down at its buff cover – *Saul. Handel.* In black gothic script. 'In fact, we will be spending much time with this composer, and one or two of his countrymen.'

'What is this?'

'You,' he said, 'have a concert to prepare.'

'Please don't tease. Just tell me what this is.'

'The Festival of Sacred Music. In August. We, you, will have a place on the programme.'

'How?' Lotte didn't let herself respond, held back. It was too unlikely.

'Last winter, I told you, I asked my old teacher from Edinburgh, Herbert Jones, to come to your recital. He came. But had to slip off to get his train. I didn't want you to think that he had left early because he wasn't impressed, so I said nothing.'

'He came all that way?'

'I had told him you were remarkable. Worth an hour on the train on a winter's night. There didn't seem to be any reason to add to all to the anxiety by telling you he might be there.'

'But you didn't tell me after either?'

'No. And because I hadn't heard from him, I thought perhaps he'd been caught up in other work, his teaching, his Ensemble. But.'

'But what?'

'He sent me a letter this week. He has organised the Festival almost single-handed. Choirs and soloists from all over the country, Birmingham, Cardiff, Leeds. And,' Frederick gestured with the Handel, 'he hopes from Germany too.'

'So, what is our role?' Lotte felt her excitement rising.

'You, he said, will appear in the closing concert. On the Sunday evening. He wanted the best of local talent, and not just the people he knows in Edinburgh.'

'But I'm not exactly fresh talent.'

'It's not about fresh talent. It is about talent. He loved your voice. He says in his letter – mature, strong, unique. Look,' he reached into his dark jacket, 'read for yourself.'

'No.' She stepped back down the three steps and sat in the front pew. 'No, I don't need to see it. I'm just not sure.'

'Not sure?' He followed her down the stairs. Sat beside her on the pew, twisted round to face her, his eyes took on a life she hadn't seen there before. She saw how young he was. The mask of maturity he normally exuded had dropped. She saw the, what, twenty-eight-year-old? The nervous printer's salesman, uncertain about closing a deal, rather than the maestro she usually saw.

'Where will it be?'

He paused; he couldn't stop a smile breaking out. The effort of containing his excitement almost made him mispronounce: 'The Usher Hall.'

She looked up where the yellowy lights failed to penetrate in the old church, the high arches. But in her imagination this pace was lost suddenly in the vertiginous stairs and hanging balconies of the Usher Hall. The musicians, tiny, their noise swelling up towards her. The soloists alone, distant and commanding, their voices penetrating space.

'I couldn't. I can't do that.'

'It's just like here. But bigger.'

'My voice isn't big enough. I'm not trained.'

There was something in the way she said that, a hesitancy, that encouraged Frederick to push on, with greater confidence.

'We will practice. The pieces will be second nature. And,' he paused again, she found herself leaning forward. 'They will be listening. Straining for the next note.'

'Now,' she said, 'you're exaggerating.' She looked up towards the distant ceiling again. 'Will you be there?'

'Of course. Professor Jones, Herbert, has said that I can have access to practice on the Usher Hall organ.' He said it with hushed reverence. 'And we will have time to rehearse in the Hall itself.'

'It's hard to contemplate,' said Lotte. 'Hard to envisage, in my head.' Which wasn't true. She could see and hear it all – looking out into the darkness, her voice filling the space. 'I need time to think about this. Discuss it. At home.'

'No.' Frederick had shuffled along the shiny smooth wood of the pew now. 'No, don't think about it too much. Just say yes.'

Frederick was an unusual man, his talent and his ambition tucked away here. He had talent beyond a part-time post and a day-job in sales. Now his eyes were wide, alive with a vision of opportunity. And she too saw a resolution to the huge yearning for something more. All her time and commitment to music would have a fitting pinnacle. This would give it all a point and purpose.

'Yes,' she said. 'Yes. We will do this.'

She was surprised to look down and see that Fredrick had both her gloved hands in his. She looked up. He saw the glitter in her eye. But he put her hands down.

'Lotte, you will be marvellous. You deserve that stage.'

'And you do too.' She hesitated. 'I don't need it to go further than that one night. That performance.'

'Of course. It will be up to you.'

'I know this is an opportunity for you. I won't let you down.'

'I know that. You are so sensible.' He blushed like a boy. 'Sorry, that makes you sound very … mature.'

She smiled, she felt two decades older than him, not one.

'I know what you meant.'

'I meant you'll work and take it in your stride.' They were turned together now on the narrow pew. In the excitement of their shared mission they had drawn closer. He reached across the short distance and laid the back of two fingers on her cheek. They were church-cold. She didn't move. Her heart began to race. She looked away towards the frenzy of colour in the stained glass.

'Lotte.' His hand touched her hair. Her curls ran through his fingers as she moved away, slowly but deliberately. 'Lotte?'

She didn't look back. She closed her coat, fingers working the big buttons. Then she pulled on her hat.

'I'll work very hard. I'm not so sure about taking it in my stride.' Her tone dismissed the intimacy, the fingers in her hair. She picked up the Handel manuscript. 'We must deal with Sunday first.'

'We will,' said Frederick, getting to his feet stiffly, 'and then we have concert pieces to choose.'

Lotte was at the big, dark side-door, she turned back, her eyes shadowed by her hat. Frederick stood there in his black suit, Lotte could still feel the cold of his fingers on her face, could sense the presence of a different life hanging there. But she said firmly, 'I have some ideas for that,' and closed the big door behind her.

The Journal of Dr John Fergusson

Thursday 20th April 1933

When I had been in the Asylum for a month or two, Sneddon sent for me. He looked up from his desk. I was in his debt, but he had made no reference to the reasons for my rapid move.

'Thought I'd just have a quick chat. I'm impressed at how well you've settled in.'

'It's a welcoming team here.'

'Good. Can't have been easy. People gossip in these places, you know that.'

'What else is there to talk about, but colleagues and patients? It will pass.' I said. If only that were the case.

'Exactly! That is the attitude. Silly nurses.'

'We should give them more faith in their abilities, their professionalism,' I said. And I believed it. 'They'd gossip less if they felt more part of the decision-making.'

'Precisely. Lots of ways they can feel part of it.'

'Some places have involved them in deciding on patient treatment.'

'No. That interferes with our clinical judgement. We can't make these decisions by committee, John, that's what we're trained for.' He tapped the pile of papers on his desk. 'Ultimately that's my responsibility. Of course, we can consult with the nursing staff, but they wouldn't want that level of responsibility.'

'The matrons here are very committed.'

'To a fault,' he said. 'Anyway, I wanted to say that your garden concept is a very good one. We have always had the farm. Self-sufficiency, income. All good news for the Commissioners. But the garden has been a bit of plaything till now.'

'Miss Brown has been the driving force.'

'No, no. She's all very well for weeding the borders and what not, but only you can recognise the therapeutic value.'

'Well,' I began.

'Take the compliment.'

'Thank you,' I said

'Precious few in this job.'

'Indeed.'

'And you need them, don't you?'

'We all need reinforcement. It's basic isn't it?'

'No. I meant *you* need it. From the Gold Medal onward. You need the pat on the back.'

I wasn't at all sure where he was going. I smiled anyway in the hope it was a light badinage. I was wrong, of course.

'That's why, if I may make an observation, you are the Deputy.' He leaned back, the letter-opener under his hand. 'You can't advance if you need someone to tell you the work is fine. You need self-belief.' He looked at me, his eyes narrowed, searching for a reaction. I wasn't going to provide that. 'Self-belief.'

'It's a point of view,' I said.

'It's true,' he said. He had made his point, pinned me in my place.

We chatted on but he had done his bit.

'What were you looking for? On your walks?' I said. We were in the interview room. It was a bare and bleak place to talk about the open road.

'Looking?'

'Yes, you kept walking. Didn't you? It wasn't an occasional thing.'

She looked at me steadily. Her black eyes. Such a curious mix of confidence and anxiety. Not that inconsistency was a surprise. Sudden deviations from the normal defined most of our patients.

'I loved to walk.' She shrugged, her shoulders seemed so delicate and fragile in her plain dress. 'It was my time.'

'To think?'

'To not think.' She smiled. Quite rare in here. A proper smile. 'It made me part of the world, I suppose.'

'Didn't you normally feel part of it?' I was conscious that I was leading too much. Poor professional practice. I was over eager. Too keen to help her. I had to take my time. This was still an early conversation, and it was going to get more difficult. But the talking cure, as Rivers would insist, only works if it comes from deep inside the patient, not suggested by the physician. The intensity of his relationship with patients like Sassoon and Owen took time and commitment.

She waited before replying. I didn't sense that she wanted to second guess which answer might be expected, or even attempt to deceive. Lies are part of our daily practice, but patients who carefully formulated the truth before they spoke were more of a challenge. Honesty and directness can be disarming in real life. Here, they are subversive.

Finally, she looked up and said, 'I felt like I was watching the world. Commenting on it in my head. But not part of it.'

'Commenting?'

'Should I say there were voices?'

It was almost as if we were sharing a joke. I was thrilled.

'Voices in our heads are what we all do to make sense of life as we live it. There is no harm in it. Unless it is a different voice. Someone else.'

'No, it was all me. My voice. But there was no commentary when I was walking. I was living.' She looked up at the barred window. 'For that time, when I was out walking, I didn't need to comment in my head because it was all there in front of me. I didn't need to think much.' She looked back at me again. 'If that makes any sense?'

'When you felt fully alive?'

She frowned. 'No, I was alive all the time. I'm not, I wasn't, in some kind of coma. But I felt as if I was at the centre of this huge world swirling overhead. And connected to it. I hadn't felt that since I was small.'

'Is that why you walked at night?'

'You do think this is a problem, don't you?' She made this completely unconfrontational. It was a genuine question.

'In medicine we often suggest walking as a cure.'

'Prescribe it?'

I felt a growing intimacy. Or was this just charm she could switch on to manage situations?

'Well, I wouldn't go as far as to say that. But there are clear advantages in outdoor exercise, clearing the mind, getting a perspective. But we would never suggest in the middle of the night. Not for ladies.'

She moved on the hard chair.

I didn't want to get stuck on this topic again. I had more serious things to discuss: 'We might come back to the walking.'

'The music is different.' She said this suddenly. I was going to devote a whole session to the music. It had intrigued

Cunninghame in the notes as much as me. But if she wanted to talk about it now that was fine.

'Different?'

'It is when I do, did, feel alive. Totally involved.'

'Of course. Intense moments of performance will give us deep emotions. Emotions that are rare in normal life.' It seemed such an obvious thing to say. But I found my concentration drifting. Perhaps because I knew what Dr Sneddon had in store for her. Perhaps just because I was sitting in the same room as her. The professional boundaries. Again. I was as convinced as I had ever been that closeness to a patient doesn't harm them. In fact, with someone sensitive and intelligent, it could make a positive contribution to their recovery. But it wasn't an argument that would convince many of my peers. In fact, best not to have to make the argument at all.

'No,' she said. 'It's not that.' Confidence, not bravado or aggression or confidence trickery, is so rare in this place that it often has the look of recovery about it. I knew that wasn't the case here. But she was so sure of her feelings. Perhaps that was the problem. Friends and family aren't usually ready for direct communication about feelings. I said nothing, let her tell me.

'No. It's not about my intense emotion. It's about what it meant to people listening. Even a little bit, even changing them slightly for a very short while. But multiplied up by everyone in the hall...' She let this all trail off.

'Is that what you feel as a performer?'

She looked up again.

'I'm not a performer. I couldn't say that. But I've experienced it, the moment, just enough.'

She was not going to say anything more on that, so I let the subject drop. There was the glimmering of a narcissistic complex tucked into her words. There would be plenty more time to explore that. I hoped.

The morning light in this room drained it of even more colour than usual. She looked like a photograph. I suppose I did too. A gaunt, tired man in the middle of middle age with the slightly ragged look of a man living without wife or housekeeper. My cuffs not quite a crisp as they should be, collar not exactly symmetrical. But I was on her side. She had given me a reason to take on Sneddon, finally.

'I would like to talk to you about your music in detail in a future conversation. Is it something that's been part of your life for a long time?'

'Since I was ten.'

'Did that mean sacrifices?'

'Do you mean how did my family afford lessons?'

'It is a luxury. Some would say frivolous. My background is not privileged, that is why I said sacrifices. I am from a mining village.'

'Like Mrs Arbuthnot?'

'Who?'

'A friend. An acquaintance of mine from the town. She makes much of her humble roots.'

Mrs Arbuthnot and the question of roots and origins would be another avenue to explore. I didn't take notes as we talked. I find recalling conversations in this way to be just as accurate. The distraction of scribbling puts up barriers. I didn't want that, and besides, I could remember everything she said perfectly.

'We are all from somewhere, it doesn't have to define us,' I lied.

'My grandfather was ambitious for us all. The music, the elocution lessons. he was always thinking of the future. But we didn't stay with him for long. There was,' she hesitated, 'a falling out. And we left Edinburgh to stay with my mother's sisters, two sisters, here, or Stirling anyway. But they found new teachers for us here. They were in business, my aunts. They understood investment.'

'You said a falling out?'

'I think so.' The hesitation returned. 'I was very young.'

'And your aunts?'

'What?'

'They took you in, the three of you? Did they not have children too?'

'My Aunt Margaret did, a son Peter. But Jessie, my other aunt wasn't married.'

'Was it not crowded. Up there?'

'At the Top of the Town? In the slums?'

'I'm sure it wasn't a slum.'

'People say it will all be pulled down someday soon.'

'The rehousing programme is much admired.'

'By those who don't live there.' There was anger again, gathering under her dark level brows. 'We lived well -we weren't poor. They ran a business. The house was owned and they didn't see any point in having extra overheads.' She had calmed down now, back to Kings Park. 'There's a community up there. There was business to be done and we were at the centre of it.'

'I know,' I said. 'Forgive me, you will appreciate that many of the people here are from that area. It distorts my perceptions.'

'There are people here from everywhere,' she said. 'Some are poor, some are rich.' The anger had gone. She smiled and I felt it again, her warmth. Her family must have been unmoored by her sudden episodes. And they must miss her very much. I caught myself staring at her again. I moved on quickly.

'I don't know if Miss Brown has approached you. She is in charge of our garden. She is not strictly speaking a member of staff, but we convinced the Medical Superintendent of the benefits of gardening therapy for all. Not just men.'

'No one has spoken to me.'

'Would that be suitable for you?'

'A suitable position?'

'You did express that preference.'

'Yes, of course,' she said. She was staring towards the window. 'Is it deliberate that you can't see out these windows unless you stand up?'

'I thought we could focus more on you, and your difficulties if we had less distractions. Rather than meeting outdoors.' We were nearly out of time, so I continued: 'Doctor Sneddon is the Medical Superintendent here.' She must have heard the name. In her social circles. Or perhaps Sneddon was above trade. 'He is a very eminent scientist. He has great ambitions to revolutionise our medical practice. To make it more…' I wasn't sure what the correct word was here. 'More modern. More effective.'

She was looking puzzled for the first time, perhaps because she had noticed my nervousness.

'He is conducting a trial. An important trial of a new treatment. It shows some promise overseas and he would like to develop it further here.'

'A positive treatment?'

'Yes. But in my clinical judgement it is not suitable for you. I wanted you to know that in case Dr Sneddon approaches you himself and with a view to your volunteering for his programme.'

'Volunteering. You make this sound like the army.'

'We are both ex-military men, Dr Sneddon and I. And this institution is not unlike the army.'

'Because there is danger?'

'There are always dangers in experimental medical research. Dr Sneddon will explain that. But like the army, there is a structure here, discipline. And we reserve the right to do what we think is best for patients. In the end,' I hesitated, 'we decide.'

'So why will he ask me to volunteer?'

'Dr Sneddon prefers enthusiastic participants.'

She shook her head, as if shaking bees or flies out of her glorious hair, as if she were already in the garden, or out on one of her walks.

'But why are you telling me this, Doctor Fergusson? If you don't think this is for me then you are my doctor and that's it. My cousin, Peter, was in the army. He told me never to volunteer. He came back blinded.'

'The point is,' I leant across the table, the morning was now coming in through the bars in such a way that she was striped with light, one eye highlighted, sparking, the other in shadow. 'Charlotte, Dr Sneddon can be persuasive, and he also makes the final decision on when you are cured, when you can leave. And when you can see visitors.'

Both eyes were in light now. She blinked and I could see they were wet.

I went on, I had committed myself now: 'Ultimately he can insist on the treatment. It is very unpleasant. And the outcomes are uncertain.'

I let that sink in a bit. I didn't want to frighten her too much. I hoped she wouldn't ask for details.

'But what sort of treatment doesn't work? I don't understand.'

'All medicine starts with uncertain outcomes. But we vow,' I said, 'not to do any harm.'

'So I can volunteer or I can be treated against my will? Is that what you're telling me?'

By saying nothing, I answered her question.

She didn't cry but her face paled – paled more than it was already in this bare room.

'But,' I said, 'it won't be like that. I have spoken to Dr Sneddon. He agrees that you and I can continue our programme. And assuming that goes well, then he will hold off on,' I floundered a little, 'your treatment.'

And there I left it. Left her. It was cruel, I know, to leave her in that room waiting for a nurse to take her back to the dayroom. But necessary. I wanted her to have time to think a bit more about Dr Sneddon's plans. I could have shocked her to the core with what happens in the treatment room. I have learned, over the years, that with sensitive patients like Charlotte, imagination will work more effectively than anything. I felt that by our next conversation, and at this stage I was planning on daily sessions, she would put her absolute trust in me. If by saving her I would also defeat Sneddon, then all to the good.

I was caught by Assistant Matron Kennedy. She had an air of importance about her which made me worry that she had some bad news to give me, to bring me up short.

'A visitor is in the entrance hall. They are asking for someone they can talk to. About Mrs Raymond.'

'Is it a relative?'

'No.' She was now the one with the information and was going to make the most of it. 'Normally.' She adjusted the bib of her uniform. 'Normally, the duty Matron would deal with unannounced visitors.' She made me wait. 'And that, of course, this morning, is myself. But I felt.' I crossed my arms, she was drawing this out all the way. 'I felt, Doctor, in view of your particular interest in the case, that you, yourself might want to deal with the enquiry.'

'Thank you, Nurse,' I said. 'I will. And the relationship with the patient is?'

'A friend. Is what she said.'

'Friends cannot make enquires about patients.' I was sharp now. But intrigued.

'This I told her, Doctor. But she was determined to see someone.' She looked down at her shiny shoes, then up. 'In Authority.'

'Very well,' I said, 'Thank you, Nurse.'

I took a long walk along the central corridor, past patients, staff, the complex patterns made on the floor by the light through the window. I walked at speed, breathing in the curious mix of bleach, polish and human beings, a constant in every institution. No matter how many summer windows were open, it never dispersed.

As I walked down the left-hand branch of the main staircase, I saw her sitting alone opposite the reception office. A woman of early middle age. Slight, in a dark coat that seemed too warm for the day. Her hair must have once been a startling red. There was a small bag between her boots which were dusty from the driveway. Public transport only came directly to the house on specified open days or for events. Casual visitors were discouraged. She looked up as I came across the wooden floor towards her. She had that air of curiosity and fear all civilians have when they step into our world. Normally, I would have sent her packing. Or rather I would have had her sent packing. But I was keen to talk to anyone who had a connection with Charlotte.

'Good morning,' I said, 'I am Depute Medical Super-intendent here.'

She stood as I approached. Curiously, she gazed beyond me, her eyes moving round the panelled walls, the stairs, the distant cupola.

'This was a lovely house,' she said. 'I've been sitting here thinking, it's a shame it has been reduced to this.'

She was clearly not the little tawny mouse she had appeared from further up the stairs.

She gestured back towards the doorway, the drive and the trees:

'And a lovely park. Situation. I'm sure it's appreciated.'

'Oh, I can assure you it is.' I was on the brink of being defensive. 'In what way can I help you?'

'Doctor…'

'Fergusson.'

'Sorry. Yes. I work for Mrs Raymond, who was admitted here two days ago. I'd like to ask about her condition.' She looked above me again. The chandelier. 'If that is in order.'

'In principle, no, it is not at all in order,' I said. 'We communicate, if at all, with close relatives. A spouse. A parent.'

'In principle?' she said.'

'You are neither. Being,' I said, 'an employee.'

She lost her poise. I had a vision of long miles to get here, on the train then the omnibus, speculating on what might confront her when she arrived, and the prospect of a fruitless journey.

'I am Charlotte's, Mrs Raymond's, housekeeper. And her friend. If you ask her, she will wish to see me.'

Nurses, office staff were passing through as we spoke. Visitors were rare enough to attract attention. I was conscious of steps slowing, heads turned.

'This,' I said, 'is irregular. But we cannot discuss patients in an open area. Wait.'

I went through to the general office and collected a key. I led the visitor to the empty Depute Accountant's office.

It was a tiny corner office with a narrow faux-medieval slit for a window. Atmospheric but gloomy. She put her bag down and sat in the only chair, apart from the Depute Accountant's wooden swivel chair. I occupied it. Precisely in the centre of the desk was a document I thought I recognised. ARRANGEMENTS FOR THE LONG-TERM NUTRITIONAL WEFARE OF PATIENTS. But further down the cover in smaller type I read– COSTINGS AND FEASABILITY.

I was behind a desk. Immediately back in control. 'I'm sorry I don't think you've told me your name?'

'I'm Mrs Semple. Mrs Grace Semple.'

'And you are close to Charlotte– Mrs Raymond?'

'Very.' Behind her nervousness, there was determination about her. 'She is like a sister to me.'

'And you to her?'

'She has her family. And her own sister.'

'Not to mention her husband and children.'

Her brows narrowed. 'I can assure you I'm here after long discussions with her family. They are beside themselves with worry.'

'But thought it better that you enquired rather than they did?'

She leant forward. 'I am here to report back and let them know when they can visit themselves.'

'That won't be possible for the children.' I said it kindly. 'Not appropriate.'

'I – we – understand that Dr Fergusson. Mr Raymond, Samuel, is also very anxious to visit.'

'That is natural,' I said, building the bridges. 'And it is thoughtful of you to make the journey on his behalf.' I smiled. 'With the possibility that you may not have been able to speak to anyone about the case.'

She met me half-way. 'I'm grateful that you have the time to sit and talk to me.' She half smiled. 'You must be very busy.'

'We have much to do here. The building is full of problems that cannot be resolved out there.' I indicated the tiny slit window.

'Will her problems be resolved? Will she be cured?'

I had the conversation back into my own territory now. A matter of expertise. Professional judgement.

'That depends.' I said. 'On the nature of her problem. We can only act when we understand.'

'But you can treat her? You can make a difference to her?'

'We can do our best.'

'Is that all?' It wasn't a criticism, I realised. She was emotional.

'If we cannot resolve, we can provide a life. Here.'

I caught some of her perfume, over the stale essence of stacked paper. Not perfume, something more, the smell of Charlotte's home.

'She is under our protection now, Mrs Semple. It isn't really up to you. Or her family.'

'Who, then?' She was emboldened by her nervousness. 'We wanted to do the right thing. Sending her here.' The relatives needed that reassurance. They always felt they had done too much or too little. Rarely the right thing.

'We will decide how much progress she makes.'

'We?'

'Her physicians.'

She had been with us for a couple of days. I had had only a few hours with her, but I already at that moment I could project to a time in the future when I would feel an empty void in my life. I imagined Mrs Semple ushering Charlotte into a quiet back room at home, hanging up her travelling coat, drawing the curtains, settling her into a leather armchair, asking about what she needed. Keeping the children shushed downstairs. While at the same time I would be here, managing the nurses, battling Sneddon with increasing viciousness on both sides, with only evening walks, the wireless and writing this journal to look forward to. On into the darkening nights of autumn. The thought unnerved me.

I wanted to hear what she could tell me about Charlotte: 'She strikes me as a remarkable woman.'

Mrs Semple's green eyes met mine briefly.

'She is. Very. A great friend.' She fiddled with her gloves, which I noticed she kept bunched in her left hand all this time. They looked to be kidskin, but so fine they could be balled into her small fist. 'Talented, too. People wept when she sang.'

'Yes,' I said, 'the gifted can be over…' I paused. 'Sensitive?'

She looked down at the gloves, opened them out, smoothed the fingers of first one then the other against her leg as she spoke.

'Her turns came out of the blue. We'd get no warnings. Suddenly she'd be angry.'

'We all get angry,' I said. 'Usually it is suddenly.'

'But this was more than anger. She would suddenly become a different person. Then back again as if nothing had happened.'

'And upset?'

'Very. So regretful.' She left the gloves be for a moment.

'Hysteria isn't uncommon.'

'I have seen hysteria,' she said. 'I was in service for over ten years. I have seen how life can overwhelm people. Men too. But this was more.' She went back to the gloves. 'We had to lock her in her room. Sometimes.'

'We?'

'Her husband and I.' She stroked the glove. 'We had to. For the sake of the children.'

'Did you think they were in danger?'

She looked straight at me again.

'Of course not. But it's not right they would see her. Like that.' The gloves again. 'So upset.'

There was so much to interest me here I almost started to make notes on the Depute Accountant's paperwork.

'And this had gone on for some time?'

'Since her first born really. Since we stayed in Wallace Street and through the birth of the other two children. But it only became so bad when we moved.'

'To Snowdon Place.'

'Such a lovely house.'

'But not good for her?'

'I couldn't say it was the house.'

'No, that is our job.' We smiled. Almost conspiratorially.

'I thought– we thought– that the quiet would help.'

'But it didn't?

'No, that was when the walking started. Daytime first. Then night.'

This was turning into a treatment session one step removed from the patient. And yet it was difficult for me to bring it to an end.

'These are things we will talk about with the patient herself. As part of her treatment.'

'Can Sam and the children visit? Soon?' She was alert, she sensed that the conversation was coming to an end. Working in service breeds an acute awareness of others, their likely reactions. It was the same with soldiers. It could lead to hyper-sensitivity, of course, danger in every hedgerow. I had seen the same in ex-military men and former servants alike. We were over-subscribed with both groups in this institution.

'Our treatment only works by separating patients from the familiar— home and family. It wouldn't be suitable.'

'Then can you give her these.' She lifted the bag. 'It's some of her things. I thought she'd need them.'

'All clothing is provided here. The clothes she came in will be carefully kept aside till she's ready to go home.' She put the bag down again. 'Whenever that is.'

'Not even these?' She laid the kidskin gloves across both her palm as if they were an offering. 'These are her favourite gloves and they will keep us in mind. Her family.'

'You were wearing them?'

'Yes.' She held the gloves out.

I took the gloves, although I was not going to give them to Charlotte.

'I will see that she gets them.'

'Thank you,' she said. 'May I come back?'

'We have your address, of course,' I rose. 'We will keep her family appraised.'

'I am her family.'

I folded the gloves, and put them carefully in my pocket before I showed her back to the main entrance and the long drive under the trees.

MARTIN

Monday 13th March 2017

Nothing much can go wrong in a university library. The smell of old books and unturned pages, soothes the spirits, dampens despair.

The Archives and Special Collections were in a glass office, boxed away from the urgent whispers of students. I was shown into a room of organized calm, a white table, some khaki boxes and, covering half the table, a huge leather book, closed like an un-sprung trap.

'The entries for admissions are in the book.' The librarian was bearded, reserved in his tone, like the technicians you find in the acute areas of hospitals, focused on the process rather than the possible outcomes. 'And they also recorded deaths in the same volume.' He paused. 'I've marked both pages.' He gestured towards two torn pieces of paper and retreated to his section of the glass box, pulling the glass door behind him.

I looked out at the students, sat down and opened the past. Long columns of meticulous handwritten facts. Who, what, when. Names, reasons, dates. A ledger of double-entry misery. The admissions for 1933 ran on over several pages. Legal enforcement was less common than I'd anticipated. I flipped over a few pages to the discharge columns. There were very few recoveries.

I ran my eye down the column for admissions in 1933. And there she was, Charlotte Agnes Raymond, aged thirty-six, a private patient, so a cut above the bulk of the admissions. Her address too – 5 Snowdon Place. Lost grandeur. Here the address leapt out from a column full of Orchard House – the Stirling poorhouse.

I resisted the urge to take it all in at one gulp. Just words, but my heart was beating hard. I bent down into my bag, took out notebook and pencil. I read on. Her Bodily Condition: Indifferent. I stumbled a bit here. I looked up and caught the librarian looking at me through the glass. Was this the normal response of relatives? Should he have left a box of tissues in the room?

I plunged on, back into the awful past. Form of Mental Disorder: Simple Mania. The attacks had lasted 'several days.' Drs Frazer and McFarlan had provided medical advice for Sheriff Substitute Alex Nimmo Hoon which allowed him to have my grandmother taken to the asylum against her will on the 6th of April 1933.

I turned over a few pages to the second marker. There she was again, half-way down a full page of the dead. So many different ways to die. Charlotte died of Exhaustion from Acute Mania, the result of a long-term heart problem.

'Did you find what you wanted?' The librarian appeared across the desk. 'Is everything OK?'

'It's all here,' I said. 'Thank you.'

'You might want to look at the annual reports for the asylums.' He lifted a brick-wide book out of the document box. 'It's context.'

Context is what I needed. How else could I make sense of the words — 'several days of attacks' — in a family with three children under twelve. Was the sudden intervention of Sherriff Substitute Hoon and the doctors a terror beyond imagination? Or a relief? I had little sense of what 'exhaustion from acute mania' might mean. And I wasn't sure if it was something I wanted to explore any further. The only context I had so far had been its inverse, a death alluded to but never spoken off. When I was a child, these allusions sailed high beyond me. When I was a teenager and young adult, I had other things to worry about. It wasn't a question I was ever going to ask and no matter how hard I tried I couldn't imagine my father ever raising the subject of his dead mother.

The context I got in the library was an 800-page annual report for all the asylums in Scotland prepared and published by the General Board of Control for Scotland — previously the General Board of Lunacy. A beautifully bound record of every aspect of every institution in the land, these sprawling village-states with their own economies and social life and culture. Every meal was detailed and costed, every escape – rare and always unsuccessful, every suicide – rare and describe in excruciating detail, every apple from the many orchards, every admission, and every discharge. All set out without emotion and in tiny font and crisp tables. The effect was to distance. To render my grandmother into a statistic. I made my notes.

'There's also this.' The librarian was beside the desk again. 'You might be interested.' He placed a slim document on the table. It hadn't been in the box. The clear plastic cover was buckled and had turned a sickly yellow. The front page had one line title. 'The 1933 Journal of Dr J Fergusson RAMC.' Typewritten. I flicked the pages. Page two was a dark photocopy of inky handwriting. The rest of the pages were photocopies of a typescript. It was pre-computer copying, blotchy and uneven.

'I hesitate to give you this.' He pushed his glasses up his nose. 'We don't have any way to verify its authenticity. It was given to us by a distant relative of Doctor Fergusson. The donor said he'd found the original document when clearing out his great-uncle's house. It had been damp, so he dried it out. But did that too fast and the pages just crumbled away.' There was a hint of professional distain. 'So the original isn't available. We've only got the photocopy of one original handwritten page. The rest is what the relative typed up himself before the original...' He made a disappearing movement between thumb and fingers.

I looked down at the handwriting. Looking at the whole page it was neat, in that schooled way of the old times. But closer up, word for word, it was difficult to read, rushed, as if it hadn't had any audience in mind. I flicked to the rest of the photocopied typescript. It had an unfinished look about it too. There were pen alterations down every page. Words cancelled out and illegible scribbles above or in the margin. Sometimes the replacement words were completely obliterated and corrected too. And at the back an official document, just as blurred.

'I think you'll find it interesting. But I'm just saying that we can't verify it as a document. Any of it.'

At this point it would have been impossible not to read it. I nodded and thanked him.

· LOTTE ·

When I got out into the car park, the March afternoon was dimming into evening. The outlines of the Ochils beyond the wire-frame trees, were dark blue against a sky that still held some light. The air was cold with a smell of wet leaves and soil. As soon as I got into the car the reek of the big asylum ledger came back. And its relentless columns. I drove out of the campus down the hill and the town lights stretched off in front of me. Away to the West, the Castle stood out against the darkening sky, a single light at the highest point.

7.

LOTTE

Saturday 15th April 1933

'No.'

Lotte didn't respond. Her heart was racing. Sam was on his feet, pacing the rug in front of the fireplace. Behind him, on the corner table, the lamp held by the dancing, arching woman, shook enough to catch the light. Lotte sat on the sofa, leaning forward, her hand clasped in her lap. Calm, calm – let him rage till he was done.

'We've come all this way.' His fists bulged in his pockets. 'All this way. Both of us. And people say – his wife still works. They can't be doing that well.'

'What people say…'

'Does matter. We're a business, it matters what people think.' He had stopped now, she didn't look up but sensed him close, leaning forward. 'And now this. On a stage in a public place. In Edinburgh.' His speech stumbled, his anger ran ahead of his words.

'It's for one night, it will be less than half an hour.' He didn't interrupt but hung there, above her. 'Just a final moment for me, to launch my teaching.'

'There won't be any music teaching.' He turned away then. He wasn't a violent man. She had never feared him physically, but knew his long moody withdrawals, his back turned, his moving to a separate bedroom. 'It's not appropriate. We aren't struggling.'

'Sam, it's not about money, it's what I want. To help you and to have something that's mine.'

'I'm not sure you know what you want.' Sam hesitated, and his voice softened. 'You put us through so much. All of us.'

'I have got better.' She said.

'I don't need your help in the shop. I want you to have a life that's away from all that. I've built the shop up so far, I can manage, I think.'

She pulled her patience around her like a shawl. 'But my aunts…'

'The aunts did well. But that was the war. And now they're all gone, scattered. I took on that responsibility remember.' He stopped abruptly, sat down opposite her. 'Lotte, don't take these things on. I don't want to argue. You know the last thing I want– we want– is another episode.'

She kept her rage locked down. She had no answer to that. The street was darkening outside, lights coming on in the dark evening shapes of the villas. There was that deep silence again in the house. The boys busy with homework, Grace and Lily down in the kitchen. She felt her heart settle, there was a better way than meeting rage with rage. Sam was backing away too.

'I need to look at some invoices before tea. Let's not come back to this.'

She said nothing and he left her to the big room and the gathering dusk.

LOTTE

Tuesday 21st November 1916

She wasn't the only one on the platform. With wartime restrictions, there were few people waiting for trains or arriving passengers in the normal, peacetime way. They tended to be men in long overcoats, bored and badgering the shrugging porters about delays. But Lotte belonged to a different gathering on the platform.

Her people were the women, maybe the odd brother or father, but this was essentially a female tribe who were too anxious to be bored. They were here at all times of the day and night. The trains were late, the day of arrival as vague as the hour. But they had to be here. They rarely spoke to each other, the air of fretful introspection didn't encourage enquiries about the weather, let alone who they were waiting for. Any joy in welcoming a returnee on leave was tempered by a trepidation. Wounds were never discussed in letters. How could you reassure in a few lines of smudged pencil?

Sometimes there was the briefest acknowledgement of the reason for their waiting. Tiny signs, signals of membership of this sisterhood. Mothers, sweethearts, sisters, they recognised a tension in the shoulders, a stance that pushed them on to the balls of their feet as if straining forward to see down the track, round the curves that caught the last of the evening light, down through England to a busy port, men shoving and jostling on a stone dock, iron bollards, high clouds over a restless sea, and then France, more rail lines stretching to a faraway point. And beyond that imaginations either failed, or projected images of unbearable horror. You could see that entire journey in their eyes as they waited.

Lotte knew some of these women. But even then, talk was reduced to a word or two.

'Billy?'

'Yes. Today. I hope. But I thought that yesterday.'

'Is he…?'

'As far as we know. God willing.'

And to converse further was to risk the train arriving in the middle of it all. The most intense emotion on these wartime platforms was relief. It never went beyond that. Relief tempered with the sure knowledge that in a few days you would be back to begin the cycle all over again. Unless you were faced with such devastating wreckage that they were home for good. Lotte had witnessed those moments. The shattered faces, the truncated bodies, the shaking hollow men. And they were the ones whole enough to arrive back unaided.

Each stood alone with their terrors as the evening darkened, as hopes and anxiety rose and fell with each arriving train. The smell of coal smoke trapped by the cold night air. Steam swirling. Oily air. White faces leaning forward. People came and went, but the scattered line of dark coats, hats pulled low over faces half covered in collars and scarves remained the same.

Until finally – though they would have waited for ever, perhaps would have preferred to wait forever, suspended always in expectation – it was resolved. The train doors opened, lurching figures in greatcoats, kitbags. A movement forward from the ragged line of women, each giving the others space to scan the opening doors. The search in the gloom for faces, the hope that it was one they could recognise easily.

Peter was never large. But his coat and bag diminished him further. She knew he was changed from the moment she hugged him. There was an unyielding steel to his back and shoulders; narrow, bony and rejecting.

'How was the trip?' she said. Foolish question.

He said nothing. All around the awkwardness of the moment was as palpable as the steam and grit. Hugging over, pairs stood, almost as if there were a reluctance to take this strangeness, this otherness indoors, into the domestic world. Enough to ensure all was well, more or less, in this brief contact and send them back on the next train without having to dig deeper, uncover hard little truths that would torture the spirit and blacken the brightest day for months, maybe years, ahead. The few mumbled words from another world beyond the experience of these wives and sweethearts and sisters.

'Are you hungry? You must be?'

This time a smile. But Peter's mouth seemed different too. A thinness to the lips, a paleness. His eyes, all watercolour.

'Have you eaten anything today? Or longer? When did you leave France?'

'France?' He spoke the word as if it were a Pacific island, lost to the world.

'When did you leave?'

'Leave?' he said. 'That will be right.'

'You're home now.' She took his arm and, as they left the steam and smoke behind, she caught a smell, a trace of Hades. His was his best uniform, kept good for the journey, but it still reeked of damp soil, of clothes buried and washed and buried again. A smell she had known before. One day, Peter had dared her to go into a small stone structure built into the corner of the wall around the Snowdon Cemetery. She had edged into the gloom– tiny windows, Peter watching from the slim iron gates. A heugh, a chisel, a small hammer laid on a rough table, spades and scythes propped against the wall, clay pots. A chill of accumulated dank days and nights. Earth and worse. She hadn't lingered, not for fear of a bearded figure looming in the doorway, but because of the smell. This is what being buried is like, she thought.

There it was again as she gripped Peter's arm, clung on as if the arm were a stout rope. Under the streetlights outside, the greatcoat looked spotless, but still, in the cold autumn air, the scent of underground. She decided that if Peter wanted to be silent as he re-entered this strange world then she would leave him be. But the uniform attracted attention. Men nodded and muttered as they passed on the long walk up the hill.

'Welcome back, son.'

'Thank you. Well done.'

Bunnets touched, stepping out of the way. She could see a different reaction, though, from the women they passed. None of the undisguised contempt that had upset him in the year before he volunteered, but a wariness, as if he carried a contagion, the possibility of grief.

'Here's where they had the cannon,' she said as they reached the top of King Street. There were no cars and few people now, the cobbles glistened.

'Cannon?' he said.

'German guns that had been captured.'

He said nothing.

'The soldier there was chatting up Marguerite. You know what she's like.'

He didn't respond.

'He said you were safer, with the guns. You were a long way back.'

His steps seemed to falter at this point, as if his hobnails were sliding on the stone. He stumbled to a stop.

'Is that what he said?'

They were standing side by side. She still had his arm. He didn't turn to face her, just stared up the narrowing street, towards their home.

'He didn't say how we fire for as long as we can. Dropping death miles away.'

'He didn't really know anything,' she said. 'He wasn't a gunner. He was just talking. Showing off.' She was keen to get him home, up the hill. The damp was condensing out of the air now. His coat had a mizzle of wet round the shoulders and stood-up collar.

'We're the most hated people on earth at that moment. Demons. All the effort is in finding us. Locating the flashes. Drawing the triangles. Then stamping on us like we were insects.' His feet were moving now but he wasn't walking. Stamping and twisting his boots, rasping on the pavement. 'Crushing.'

'Let's get home, it's wet now. They're all waiting.'

He started to walk.

'Lotte.'

'Yes?'

'Say nothing. To them.'

'I know. I won't.'

'You can't.' He stopped again. 'I'm not asking you to help,' he said. 'But if I need you to help. Will you?'

She tugged his arm.

'Of course I will.'

'I don't mean now. I mean later.' He looked at the street ahead. 'Just help when I ask. Not when I don't.'

'I won't ever abandon you Peter. But…'

He turned to her for the first time since the station. He put his hand to her lips. The nails clean but ragged. The smell.

'Shh.'

It was the same gesture he made at the station two days later. Just he and Lotte again— it was too much for his mother, his aunts. Fingers to her lips.

'Shh.'

LOTTE

Saturday 15th April 1933

'If that gets painful at all, just let me know.'

The hairdresser wasn't the one she normally saw. Her trips here were fairly pointless. Taming her hair was beyond any advance of modern science. The usual girl, though she was by far the youngest here, seemed to understand that this was a fortnightly ritual that had symbolic rather than practical significance for Lotte. She and Lotte had an easy conspiracy that accommodated the fact that Lotte's hair never looked much different when she left compared to when she arrived. It was a fair exchange they made, complex and satisfying on both sides.

But this new woman today, older, her hair disciplined into tight furrows and coils, with a sheen that projected light rather than reflecting it, didn't understand the nature of the transaction. She took no hints from Lotte's short answers to the technical questions. A bit of heat was all that was required she had suggested, to fix the curls. Lotte knew it was a forlorn exercise but was willing to go along for some peace under the hot air.

'Magazine?'

The options weren't exciting. *Women's Own, Picture Goer* or *The Listener*. She took *The Listener*, flicked through to the classical music section towards the back. The hot air stroked at the back of her neck.

She stopped abruptly. The photograph wasn't dramatic. A cluster of men, so close their dark suits made a deep continuous black border. In the centre, an older man, hard sharp features. And, with his back turned half away from the camera, and closer, so he seemed to tower above all the faces, the most famous profile in the world. She read the caption –

Maestro Karl Muck talking with Adolph Hitler during his visit to the Leipzig Gewandhaus for a concert commemorating the 50th anniversary of the death of Richard Wagner.

She gasped.

'Shall I turn this down, madame?'

Lotte did not answer. She felt a physical pain in her breast. It was as if one of the pairs of stiletto scissors that lay around the room had been pushed through her skin and muscle, past bone into her vital organs. She couldn't have articulated this deep sense of wrong. This affront. She didn't follow politics, she had skimmed articles and absorbed headlines. She didn't need to know the detail. She recognised a bully. What hurt her was evil associating itself with music. That the conductor, the embodiment of goodness, was surrounded by the hard, gloating faces, his head bowed as he paid homage to a street tough. And all in the cause of the memory of a musical genius. The soaring voice in the Usher Hall drowned out the hot air rushing past her ears.

If all that was good and pure could be absorbed by all that was evil, then war was closer than she thought. She had read little about Wagner, only what Frederick had told her when they'd looked at scores, scores they knew were beyond them. But he represented creative genius, something beyond politics, broken windows and bloody faces in the street. The shock was followed by a wave of fear. Fear for Douglas, that she would be waiting again at the station on another autumn night.

She stood up. Pushed the dryer away.

'Madam?'

Faces under dryers and above oilcloth capes turned. Scissors were poised, mid-cut.

She opened her purse. A girl brought her coat.

'Is there a problem?' The manageress appeared.

Lotte couldn't speak. She pushed coins into cupped hands. She was on the street before she had both arms into the coat. The past was coming again, pursuing her. She hummed the 'Liebestod.' People were turning in the street. She hummed louder, the stately march, growing in her chest. And then she was singing. Not loud, but loud enough. Later, from the look on Grace's face it was clear that word of her singing had reached home before her.

The Journal of Dr John Fergusson

Thursday 20th April 1933

Sleep was beyond me. Increasingly that was the case when I spent a night in the building. I needed the natural night noises of the farmhouse to soothe me. Here I was under the same roof as the treatment room. Sneddon was long gone, back to the family home, on the slope above the river. The villas of Bridge of Allan matched his aspirations. But although my room was well insulated from the night noises of the asylum, doctors can visualise suffering without being exposed to it for twenty-four hours.

I sat up, smoking and reading *The Scotsman*. So many war memoirs. British and German, all in the last few years. I read the reviews, not the books. If you had been anywhere near the front the descriptions seemed so insipid. Distorted through the consciousness of the writers and the words they used. Once, when I was out on a shoot, walking up partridge in September, I noticed some tiny blue flowers growing among the dying grasses in a field. I had a solicitor, from Cupar Angus or some such, on my right. I said, 'What's these blue flowers we're walking over?' I pointed down with my gun.

'Not a clue,' he said, pausing and rubbing the toe of his boot over the grass and peering down.

'I'll look it up when I get home,' I said, 'got a book.'

'Good luck,' he said, 'I'd rather not know.' He stopped and looked down again. 'They're beautiful and delicate and knowing what they're called, all that Latin stuff, will just spoil it.'

I felt the same way regarding books about the war, but in reverse. All these words just diminished the horror, the overwhelming putrid, pus-filled, poison of it all. These public-school boys showing off. The great roaring wastelands reduced to neat little black words marching across the page. It was a sort of sacrilege.

When I was first commissioned, I didn't have the experience to cure anyone. I could train officers in how to lance blisters, instruct soldiers in the correct use of first aid packs. That was when the planners anticipated a few hundred deaths based on engagements in the Zulu Wars. It wasn't long before those of us fresh from having to overcome the sights and smells of Professor Deacon's anatomy class were exposed to a different level of horror.

The barely competent recent graduates, too green to be given a proper surgical role, were allocated the most forward positions. The fewest skills to offer were the most expendable. I can't shape the tumble of sensations I felt then into sentences for this journal. It is impossible to separate out the different positions our battalion was in, the orders, the different sectors. The big shows, the names on battle honours, were often less terrifying than the limited sorties, the raids in the dead of night when a hundred men would be caught out by the wire, lit by flares and cut down.

The wounded were all brought to me, the officer in charge of the Regimental Aid Post, just off the line, in range of the enemy's heavy weapons. My job was as triage. I hate that word. I hear it slip into civilian chatter and flinch. I have to breathe deeply and resist the urge to take the speaker by the lapels and tell them exactly what it meant.

Those awful nights. Rain running off the canvas, oil lamps turned as high as we dared, the distant pounding and chattering. They were brought in, those ragged men, feeling their hearts fading with every beat, too fearful to look at their wounds under the flares. These were the lucky ones, hauled out of the earth and taken for judgement. The medical orderlies moved along the line with the lamp, calm, so that I, God, could look down from above and assess, choose.

Solomon's judgements. Few bullet wounds, for they were usually not worth the stretcher bearers' time. The bearers, mainly pacifists who balked at taking lives, had been sent out to the most dangerous job of all. The choices they had to make were hard too. But a bullet did such damage. The entry points were at such unlikely angles, for no one walks upright under fire. A crouching man, a man bent in terror would take a bullet in one shoulder, then exit through the other hip and then on through his comrade following behind. That pitiful illusion of shelter – keeping in the lee of the man in front. Bullets hitting equipment or bone became small explosions, the water-bottle, the shattered pelvis became their own projectiles. The bullet wounds rarely got as far as treatment.

We were usually presented with the outcome of shrapnel. Lumps of metal, jagged or blunt, tiny or the size of a head, always accompanied with filth. These were the wounds we saw in the Aid Post. There was no third part to our triage. The walking wounded were bundled away by the NCOs. We didn't have the time for near misses. The orderlies and I were only concerned with life and death. Black and white. After a moment's examination we gifted one soldier a future of children, grandchildren, a drink in the pub on a Friday at six, a gold watch on retirement, a knee-trembler with a prostitute, companionable decades in bed with a wife, an afternoon on the beach. To the other, we gave an hour or less in a dripping tent, some opiates if we had them, perhaps even someone to hold your hand. Then dark.

On a bad night we had thirty seconds to decide. Appearances could be deceptive. Men with half a face gone and their uniforms and bodies torn, who would live on for forty hard years. But there were times when the orderly and I would hunt with the light to finally find a hole low in an intact soldier's back. A hole a quarter of an inch long, but they would be dead by the time we turned them back over. Physicians should learn from their mistakes but not dwell on them. In France there was no time for either. We took comfort that even if we made mistakes that was better than the alternative– to be left out there to die alone.

I had many orderlies in that time. Comrades in judgement. Life. Death. The best was Albert Stoneleigh. An apprentice chemist from Nottingham. No one was cooler, more thorough, his touch on the ravaged bodies, delicate and kind. He cut his throat in the jakes of a bar in Amiens. We could send the living to Casualty Clearing, perhaps all the way home, but I was never convinced they were the lucky ones. For as they sat out their years in offices or shipyards or on a tractor, they carried with them the scenes they had witnessed out there by the wire. We could fish for the debris, sew them up, pour on antiseptic, but we couldn't extract the things they had seen and heard.

On these sleepless nights there was no escape from the past. As I contemplated how I could help Charlotte, they were there, in front of me. Boys. They may have been trained to kill, but they weren't men yet. This boy had been marched in front of the Court Martial. I had a vivid memory of the Major sitting upright behind the table, his leather and brass glowing in the evening sun that slanted through the farmhouse windows. A makeshift courtroom. Probably 1917 sometime, the days and dates slipped away, but all the other details were always there as soon as I closed my eyes. I sat at one side. There was no real need for me to be there. It made no difference, and no one cared. Particularly the Private under guard. My written report was enough. But I thought it was another sort of cowardice to stay away. There was a brief discussion between the Major and the army lawyer. The Major was from the Private's own Division, it seemed. Most irregular. A Field Punishment should be presided over by a senior officer from outwith the Division.

'For God's sake, man,' said the Major. 'This Private has been held for over a week. Don't you think it is in everyone's best interests to bring this to a conclusion?'

The lawyer was out ranked and out manoeuvred. He concurred.

'Private,' said the Major. 'At ease.'

As if.

He was young, early twenties, fair, from the East Staffordshires. It was easy to imagine him in five years with a wife and a baby, in a village in the low hills out there, repairing tractors and quite the modern man in the ancient landscape, or in a pub in the Potteries, white from the clay on pay-day, one more light ale before home to the wife. You could imagine anyway.

'I have here Second Lieutenant Harvey's testimony. You were ordered to remain in support of the Lewis gun crew during a night operation, covering a raiding party on no-man's land. You twice asked the Corporal in charge of the crew to stand down to relieve yourself. When that was refused the Corporal noted that you had slipped away. He sent another man to report this to the officer in charge of the sector – Second Lieutenant Harvey. He found you in a dugout and ordered you back to your position. This order you obeyed. But less than an hour later Second Lieutenant Harvey found you again in the same dugout and ordered you back down the line to face charges of desertion.'

The Major put down the buff sheet of typed paper. He took a drink of water. The Private had kept his eyes fixed on the edge of the table throughout. It was a beautiful old wood table. At some point it had been the pride of this prosperous farm. Elbows had rested here, Sunday lunches, a tall bottle of wine, laughter.

'Is this an accurate account?' The Major looked up under bushy brows already speckled with white though he would have been in his thirties.

'Yessir.' It was a mumble.

'Second Lieutenant Harvey is unable to provide his own testimony here today as he went missing in action five nights ago. You are aware of that, Private?'

The Private nodded.

'A brave officer who put himself in danger for the good of his men.'

The Major took another drink.

'I will not lecture you soldier. You understand that you put your comrades at risk on that night. During an action every man depends on his fellow. Any weak link in the chain risks everyone.'

'It was the flares.' He said it all as if one word. 'Sir,' he added.

'Yes,' said the Major. 'So I understand. Captain?'

He raised his left hand off the table. The lawyer shuffled his papers.

'The defendant has been a loyal and effective soldier since enlistment early in 1916. He has an exemplary record, but in recent months has found his nerves under stress, particularly during night operations. He put it down to seeing two comrades badly injured while on a night raid on the enemy trench system. He has associated the images to the particular light thrown by flares. Since then he has felt himself to be unreliable during night operations.'

'Flares, Private?' The Major would not survive the year. I recalled seeing his name on a casualty list. He had a DSO by then. I could imagine that he would be a brave man, an officer who would rather die than display caution in front of his men. 'Flares are harmless. You learn that in week one of basic training. And night operations are operations. When do you think we should go out on no man's land? When the sun is blazing down and birds singing? Have you learned nothing?'

The defendant was silent. In fact, I never heard him speak another word.

'Medical report,' said the Major without looking up.

'I have a written testimony and Captain Fergusson is here in person.'

He looked at me for the first time.

'Not that you are unwelcome Captain, but your report would do.'

'The RAMC believes in good service,' I said. No place for humour I know, but I didn't want a tongue lashing.

The Major looked down at my handwritten sheet. I'd had less than ten minutes with the defendant earlier that afternoon. I had asked him if he felt that he was fit for service. He said he had never felt fit for service. He worked his thumb with his other fingers as if he could wear it down to nothing. I asked him the standard question:

'Did you seek help, from your superior officer, from the medical orderlies?'

There was a faint smile at that.

'No.'

'This is a very serious charge,' I said, unnecessarily.

He nodded.

'Do you wish to tell me anything more.'

He took an intake of breath. But just exhaled and shook his head.

'Thank you Private.' I said, foolishly. He was one of the first I had seen.

I left him there working his thumb on the deal table.

The Major handed the paper to the lawyer. He cleared his throat and read: 'I have today examined No 4242 Pte Thomas and find that he is physically fit.'

'Anything to add to that, Captain?' The Major put a curl to my rank which suggested that doctors in uniform had no right to pronounce on matter of army discipline. Even less than the lawyer in uniform to his left.

'No,' I said.

'And you, Private Thomas?'

There was a deep silence in the farmhouse. Dust floated in the sun.

'Private Thomas you deserted your post in the middle of action, putting all lives at risk. You will be held overnight here and will be shot at six hundred hours tomorrow morning.'

In the quiet there might have been a sob, but the Sergeant marched Thomas out of the room before anything unseemly could develop.

'Thank you, gentlemen,' said the Major. 'Beastly business.' He stood and straightened his cap on his close-cropped head. 'Beastly. I'd rather they shot themselves in a comms trench.' He turned to me as he got to the door, or the curtain, doors were too valuable around here to remain on hinges.

'Captain, speak to Lieutenant More about arrangements.' He semi-saluted, his swagger stick clicked against his cap.

Once they began, the images couldn't be kept at bay. A firing range. Behind the lines, but not so far as to be out of earshot of the rolling boom of the heavy guns. The sandbag horizon, grasses and wildflowers along the edge, the white morning sky above. I stood with the officer. Once I'd been joined by a priest. But generally, it was just a young officer. It was felt in some quarters that this was a fine experience for an ambitious subaltern, to see discipline through to its extremity.

No one spoke beyond what was essential. Eye contact avoided. Touches of humanity made this all the more difficult. A nod, a swagger stick touching a cap visor was enough. Words would have somehow made it all more real. And the lack of reality was what made it possible to go through with the act. To turn a comrade into a target.

'Cigarette?' said the officer. He was a green second lieutenant. They were all young. He had a faint Welsh burr to his accent. We were late in the war by now, public school officers had been harvested already, and I came across more and more grammar schoolboys. Smarter usually, but with too much imagination for the terrible occupation they had been given.

'Thanks.' We lit up and blew smoke out over the wall of the range. The two of us standing and the third prone and still.

'Not one of mine,' he said.

'Of course not.' I said. It was a mark of failed leadership. Another reason for shame.

There were orders, the rattle of wood on metal preparation of rifles, no great ceremony, no time wasted, and the finality of the shot. I stared at a ripped sandbag while this went on, the contents crumbling out into the mud.

Moments later the officer and I were approaching a body hanging on a pole like something in a butcher's shop. Cut down by the Sergeant, not a job for a commissioned officer, before he marched the traumatised squad back for breakfast and rum. As if that would repair them. The corpse was left to the officer and me. The wounds round the heart, five ragged holes. Sometimes it was a neat single hole. Too small to kill, you might think. All depending on the ratio of blanks to live. Either way there was never any doubt. No need for a physician really. But process. Process.

'Always see the best marksmanship here,' said the officer. 'None of these fellows wants to make it last. Wish they'd take as much care on the front.'

We waited till the orderlies came with the stretcher. Blood soaked into the sand. The guns boomed on in the distance.

'Were you at the Court?' Asked the officer.

I had spoken to the boy twice. Once to pronounce him fit to stand trial and once to pronounce him fit to be shot. I wasn't counting my third professional pronouncement.

'Yes. Poor lad.'

The Court, where I testified that he was fit to stand trial, wasn't the last time I saw Thomas before the firing range. I had to certify that he was fit to face the squad. Men often collapsed in these moments. There was a close guard over the men the night before. Attempted suicide, being able to make a last decision, was common. So too were seizures, heart failure, all the expected results of putting a human under extreme pressure.

It was my duty. I did it all to the letter. Pronouncing a man dead by firing squad was not a task I imagined carrying out. Not when training. Not when learning compassion from Dr Rivers. Not when I had first imagined I might put on a white coat, dissecting mice at school. Nor did I expect to pronounce a man fit to face a firing squad. There was a purity about the decisions I made there. Mistakes are made all the time, but in chaos and disorder, they are acceptable. When terrified, it was easy to misdiagnose. It was more difficult to be complicit.

Friday 21st April 1933

I sat at my desk, working down through the layers of my in-tray. Process. Again. I spotted Sneddon's Italian paper an inch or two down. Or at least I spotted a large buff envelope with a yellow tag. The type we use for confidential reports. I yanked it out from the pile and unwound the string closure.

The margin of the paper was marked with long broad fountain pen strokes. So many it was almost a continuous line down the side of the paper. There were two exclamation marks, and a question mark. A double question-mark.

On top, paper-clipped neatly to the original paper was a large sheet of lined foolscap. There were two lines –

Do you condone this nonsense?

This dangerous nonsense?

Then the initials, EM. Elisabeth MacKenzie. I was not alone then in my caution. Cunninghame was too early in his career to risk a confrontation. And Harris would not care to question too much either. Too disruptive to his lifestyle. But now I knew I had a potential ally in the medical staff, even if Dr MacKenzie had her own agenda.

There was a knock on the door, so I put the paper back in

the envelope and placed it in the bottom drawer of my desk.
I tore up the covering note and dropped it in my bin.

'Yes?' I said.

It was Assistant Matron Kennedy.

'Doctor.'

'Come in, sit down,' I said. She closed the door behind
her and stood behind the chair.

'I won't Doctor. I am just going off shift. But before I do, I
thought I should come and see you rather than send a nurse.'

'Is there a problem?'

'I hope not.' She put a hand on the back of the chair.

'Your patient, Mrs Raymond, is in great distress. And
is demanding to see you. We would normally sedate. But.'
She put both hands on the chair back and moved it closer
to my desk. 'But I wondered.' Did she almost look over her
shoulder? 'Whether you might want to speak to her.' She left
that hanging.

If there was discussion about the amount of attention
Charlotte was getting, even if that was among the senior
nurses, then my safest course of action was to approve
sedation.

'Thank you, Matron. Please send word that I will meet
the patient in the consultation room in five minutes.'

She nodded but didn't immediately leave. She expected
more. I would have liked to dismiss her curtly. But I said:
'It is a very complex case. And at a sensitive moment. I feel
that time invested now will pay off as her treatment develops
later.'

'The nurses say that she has settled surprisingly well. Up
till now.'

'I'm pleased to hear it. However, this is an unstable case.
And.' I said, rearranging papers needlessly to bring this

conversation to an end, 'I cannot discuss a case in any more detail with you.'

She couldn't really challenge me any further.

When she left, I settled myself in the empty office for a moment. This would be a vital encounter. Composed, I set off down the corridor at a brisk pace.

Charlotte was already in the room. She was seated at the table, a nurse standing behind her. The electric light, a high overhead bulb in a yellowed shade, was on already, although the brightness of the day lingered out beyond the bars.

She didn't turn round when I entered, ignored my words with the departing nurse. I knew she would be right outside the door, standard practice with a disturbed patient.

When I took my place at the far side of the table I was opposite a changed woman. Her black hair, exotic and romantic, now seemed wild and uncontrolled. Her eyes were in shadow.

'Charlotte…' I began.

'Mrs Raymond,' she said. Her arms were folded under her breasts, her shoulder hunched forward. I could see the outline of her collar bones through the thin uniform.

'Of course…' I said.

'I need to go home.'

'And you will.'

'No,' she said. Her eyes had been moving around the room, up to the light, the window. They now settled on me. They burned with hatred. I understood so much more from that one look – about her condition, about the events that brought her here – than from all of our previous conversations. Connecting with emotion, with passion, is so vital.

'No,' she said again. 'No. No. No. I have to go now.'

'But we have discussed your treatment. The process. It will take time.'

'I must go.'

'I understand how you feel.' Did I? 'I know how unnatural this place seems in the first few days. But it will get better.'

'It won't, though, will it?'

'I promise that I will look after you.' I said it casually. Neither Charlotte, nor the nurse with her ear pressed against the door, would guess what a step it was to say that. These words took me over a professional boundary. Like the lines painted around temporary military prisons in France. Step across the mark and your sentence was doubled. Just a line across an abandoned farmyard. A promise made.

'Will your promise save me from the room?'

'The room?'

'Where the experiments happen.'

'Rumours are not to be given weight here,' I said. Wondering suddenly if she had picked up other gossip. About me.

'The things he does to women. With drugs.' There was real fear now in her eyes. 'People die of terror.'

I leant back. Body language can be a denial as much as words. No one knew that better than I did.

'We are physicians here. Do not believe the things you hear. The patients in the dayroom are not known for their honestly. Or their moderation. We would never put patients at risk.' I leant even further back.

When she stood up, I felt no anxiety. The tables here are wide. Deliberately so. It is hard to reach across them; even the most potentially violent patient has to make a long reach.

But she didn't reach. She put her hands down to her side of the table and with the force of her pelvis, her hips, she pushed the table across the floor and right into my body.

It struck me below my rib cage. Adrenaline flashed into my system. My hands went to my ribs, instinctive protection for the part of me that hurt most. If she had gone for my face, my eyes, I'd have been at a disadvantage. But she made no move. She was still, all the rage seemed to be within her. Her breath came in short sharp pants that sounded like a machine drawing in air. Her face was flushed. Hyperventilation in its classic form. She sat down and so mirrored my posture, her hands cupping her rib cage on both sides. By the time the nurse came through the door she saw two people holding their own bodies, the table between them.

'Shall I get more help, Doctor?' I could tell she could not work out what had transpired. I wasn't sure myself.

'No,' I said, gasping slightly. 'We just had an accident with the table.' I put my hand down to the edge of the table, to demonstrate. It was unexpectedly heavy. 'Unsteady,' I said.

The nurse was unconvinced but had no real cause to say anything more. This was not how incidents in consultation rooms usually ended. They could involve up to ten nurses and orderlies. We hated restraint. Unless there was no option.

'All is fine now, Nurse. I will call you if I need to.'

Charlotte's breathing was still loud and shallow.

'Would you like some water?'

She didn't answer.

'Or would you like to end the interview now and resume when you've calmed down?' This was not my preferred option. But she didn't move. 'Or we can continue.' She looked up, there were sharp red points on her otherwise pale cheeks. Her breathing was still rapid. I could only imagine what her heart rate was like. She nodded. I could only hear her breathing in the bare room, her frailty after the huge energy that had filled this room. My ribs ached.

'I will protect you.'

'I must go home,' she said again.

'You will,' I said. 'When you are better.'

'Has no one called for me? From home?'

'No,' I said. I fingered the gloves folded carefully in my pocket. 'But we explicitly tell relatives that they must leave patients alone until they are settled.' The gloves were soft as skin. 'And that can take many weeks. Months.'

She wasn't going to cry. She was as strong as she was vulnerable.

'I won't be drugged. Like the other women.'

'Not all are women,' I corrected. 'And the treatment is at the edge of science. Dr Sneddon is highly regarded in his field. He believes that he is on the verge of an important breakthrough.' I spoke the lies as if I believed them. Soon I wouldn't have to.

'They say there is screaming like no one has heard.'

'Who says this?'

'Nurses.' This was more than gossip – putting us all at risk because they thought Charlotte was someone with connections, outside influences.

'Staff will always talk. Exaggerate.' I smiled. 'You must know that.'

'I won't be drugged.'

I hesitated for a moment. I wanted her to understand how much she was going to have to depend on me.

'Treatment here is at the discretion of the medical staff. Ultimately the Medical Superintendent.' I let that hang in the air a little. 'What would be the point of patients choosing their treatment.' Her eyes were wide now. Huge and black. I found myself sitting back further from the edge of the table. 'We will decide.'

'Please,' She said. 'They say the drugs involve creating visions. In your head.'

'Research has shown that trauma induced by drugs can obliterate memories which may be inhibiting the progress that patients can make. Should make.'

'No.'

'Charlotte,' I said, leaning across the table. 'Trust me. Dr Sneddon's treatment is not for all cases. I believe it will not help you. Dr Sneddon disagrees. I will persuade him.'

'Persuade?' Her eyes were enormous now.

'Yes, I can change his mind. I know him very well, we have been colleagues since we were boys, since we trained together.'

'No, I want to go home.'

'That will not be possible.' She thought about standing up, I saw her cheeks begin to redden. But she was an intelligent woman. There was no real option but to trust me. To cling to me.

'Nurse,' I called and the door opened almost before I had finished the word. We have substantial doors here; you have to put your ear very close to hope to hear anything.

As I passed Charlotte, I almost touched her shoulder. But I have learned something over the years.

'Let's speak again the day after tomorrow. I have a rare day off,' I said. 'We'll continue the programme when you've had time to rest.'

I had my gun to oil and my shooting kit to look out. But first I had the paperwork I hadn't been able to finish at the Asylum. I opened my briefcase. On top of the pile was a bundle of mail that had arrived late in the day. All official mail was opened and sorted. Only personal mail was left in the envelope. There were very few of those for me. Especially since Emily had stopped writing.

I was surprised to see a plain white envelope, address in a hand I didn't recognise, Liverpool postmark. I looked at the envelope for some time. Envelopes cannot be unopened. The contents unseen. Over such trivial actions, lives are changed. Taking a deep breath, I took my letter opener – a spent Mauser cartridge soldered on to a brass blade – and carefully slit the envelope.

I turned the page over. It was from Dr Claremont. He had been the only colleague to speak to me when I had returned to take what remained of my personal effects from my office. Effects I would have cheerfully abandoned, but my pride, and a desire to supress gossip, meant that I was determined to show face. It was in no one's interests to have widespread discussion of my departure for Stirling. Certainly not the rest of my medical colleagues.

Dr Claremont was a brusque Ulsterman. Dedicated to the craft. No less horrified than the rest by what had happened, but someone not given to moral judgements. Perhaps because he was certain his God would deal with me ultimately in ways that were more imaginative and decisive than merely pretending you were invisible in a corridor. Or perhaps we were both members of that wide and diverse club – ex-combatants and their families – a freemasonry of misery. One day at lunch he had indicated my regimental cuff links. Pointing with his fork: 'Military man?'

'Yes, nearly the full four years,' I said.

'I lost my older brother,' he said. 'That first day. With the Ulster Division.' He didn't need to say more.

Whatever the reason, he shook me by the hand when he met me on that last day. Now he was writing to tell me that I might be interested to learn that Hazel Burton had been found dead at an address in Formby. Neighbours had smelled gas, police called, all too late. No one else involved. Because of her relatively recent release she was still classified as an out-patient and so the Asylum had been informed. He added, reassuringly, that her husband had written to the Medical Superintendent to thank all the staff for their work with her over the years she had spent with us. Clearly, the husband had said, nothing more could be done.

Indeed.

I tried to remember her husband's name. She must have spoken of him. But all I could remember was the smell of her auburn hair. The way it caught the afternoon light through the gap in her bedroom curtains. Her husband at work, the children at school. Was that the room she had been found in? Unlikely. If it was gas it would have been the kitchen, the brass pots hanging, the range with the Dutch tiling and the view out to the back garden, the wooden table where we'd drunk her husband's red wine.

Claremont said that because she was one of my patients, I would surely wish to know what had happened. It is not an outcome we are unfamiliar with. We cannot succeed always. There is no blame attached. In normal circumstances.

Evidence and gossip are two different things. For Emily it was enough. That there should be gossip, that my reputation had any tarnish attached to it, took her and the boys away from me.

There was no question that our relationship brought Hazel back from the edge of the abyss. While what I did was wrong, it was also right. And no one would have known. No one did know. Only nurses with too much time, too little to do in the nurses' home but chatter and speculate. And allow Matrons to overhear. But Hazel had been ready to return home. Others examined her too.

How lucky I had been that Sneddon had a vacancy. And how unlucky I was that Sneddon was asked to examine her by Taylor. If he hadn't been in Liverpool that week for the Royal College seminar. Luck, fate, the delicate, pattering fall of coincidence and consequence.

What you know, and what you can prove, are different categories in science. The letter shook very slightly in my hand. This changed everything. Sneddon's generosity, his rescue was balanced by what he heard in his interview with Hazel. The great lever of power that it gave him over me. The reason I stood in my white coat and watched him torture women. His regular airy enquiries about whether I had heard from that woman in Formby. He couldn't ethically refer publicly to confidential patient consultations. At any moment, however, he could have asked the BMA to investigate, to question the patient. Now there was no one to investigate.

I took the letter over to the black fireplace. I lit a match, touched the edge and watched the words disappear. Back at the table I turned to the other correspondence. As I slipped the matchbox into my jacket pocket, I felt Lotte's gloves. I took them out, smoothed them on the table. I picked one up, the right hand, and brought it up to my face. I inhaled her deeply. Now I was one step closer to saving her.

LOTTE

Saturday 15th April 1933

'Sit yourself,' said Grace, pulling out a chair at the head of the kitchen table. She rattled kettle and teapot, looking back over her shoulder. Lotte's head was down on her forearms, her hair a tangled mess. Her head came up suddenly.

'Where's Lily?'

'In her bed,' said Grace. 'She gets excited some days.' She fussed over the tea. 'So excited, over nothing. Then she seems to just collapse.' She brought the tea across to the table. 'All or nothing. Like her mother.'

Lotte's head went down again.

'I'm fine. I just saw something that gave me a shock and I had to clear my head.'

'Saw? In the street?'

'No, I was in the hairdressers. It was in a magazine.' Calm now, she realised how ridiculous her reaction would seem to Grace. 'There was talk of war in it. I worry about the boys.'

'They've talked of it for years.' Grace poured into the two cups. 'We'll never make the same mistake twice. No one wants it again.' She looked solemn.

'Sorry,' said Lotte. 'I don't mean to bring it up.'

They sat in silence for a moment. The kettle ticked.

'No. I don't mean to dismiss it. And I know you must be worried. As a mother.'

'We're all worried. Not just mothers.'

'If you're not a mother you haven't anything to lose.'

'Grace,' Lotte leaned forward. She was going to touch Grace's hand, but something about the way it lay on the table, so still, made her think it might be like touching marble. 'You lost your husband. It's not just mothers.'

'Mothers are different.' She brought both hands together, clasped tight. 'A mother's loss is beyond anything. It's why you can't take it for granted.' She looked Lotte full in the face. The depth of Grace's judgement was plain in her eyes. Lotte bowed her head for a second, gathering herself. But when she looked up Grace was the housekeeper again, and smiling. 'I know you take none of it for granted. Your ones. And it's why I will always be here for you.'

'I know that. And it is a comfort, it really is. To know you are there.' She was going to reach for her hands again, but again she hesitated. 'And I'm sorry that you have lied for me. To Sam. About the walking.'

'A fib is a little thing.'

'Not always.'

'Oh, there's worse. Much worse than a lie.'

'I don't doubt that,' said Lotte. Relaxing now. 'Please don't worry about me. It's been difficult I know, but you have protected the children when I wasn't able to.'

'It's not the same,' said Grace. 'They need you. I am not a mother.'

'You're as good as.'

'But that's not the same. I'm not a mother. I'm not family.'

'But Grace, you are family.'

Grace hesitated, as if she were gathering something inside her, then she said:

'I'm not sure you understand family. Appreciate it. You have a sister that you never see. I'd have given a lot for a sister.' The fire rose in her voice and died away almost as quickly. 'I'm sorry, you have been ill. That was unfair.'

Lotte tapped the kitchen tiles once with the toe of her

boot. 'No Grace, I'm the one that's sorry. You had your own family. Mr Semple.'

'Until that was taken.'

'The war…'

'Took from us all.' There were bright red patches on Grace's cheeks now.

'You have us, said Lotte. 'We are your family. We, I, won't let you down.'

'I know,' said Grace. 'But you're not family.' And she began to talk. It wasn't a conversation anymore, Grace's voice took on an urgent tone, she wasn't to be interrupted. It was a story that needed to be told to the end. 'We were at the Sussex house. The Wards weren't gentry. They were above that. He was a famous man, an important man. Politicians, other writers, grand people from overseas, they were the summer guests. They all ate at our table. I was so young, but I was in charge of ten — men too. Just that lunchtime I overheard Mr Ward telling an uncle down from London how his Scots housekeeper could beat any butler for household management. It gave me such a glow. I thought of where I'd come from. I looked down at the jet pin that I always kept at the neck of my uniform. It was all my mother had passed on to me.' Grace paused. 'Not that I'm saying it was better than here. Just different.'

Lotte nodded. But she said nothing.

'I was in the kitchen. I remember it was so hot in there. July. I was there alone, the outdoor staff were busy in the garden, Cook and kitchen staff with an hour after lunch before they were back to set up afternoon tea on the South lawn. I ran a tight ship.' She smiled. 'It was a quiet moment, but there I was, still looking out for cut corners, crumbs swept into corners.'

Grace let the silence gather for a moment in this, another, kitchen. Lotte imagined a Grace a quarter of a century younger, at the peak of her profession, at the heart of the great service apparatus of the house. This must seem such a diminished space.

'He'd been there at lunch, young Mr Ward, down from Oxford. Bored. And now he was in the doorway asking for the keys to the cellar. For a bottle of fizz to take down to the riverside. I warned him that he'd have to square a missing bottle with his father. But I couldn't refuse. When I went over to the key-safe he was right behind me. I could smell him. Alcohol and soap. As I reached up for the key his hands were over me. Here.' Grace touched her breast with one hand. Her eyes were focussed on a spot on the tiled floor.

'I wasn't unfamiliar with men,' she said, picking up words like she tided rooms, precisely, methodically. 'I was a virgin but knew about men. You lived close to boys, and men, in service, and with a lax housekeeper or butler all sorts went on. But even in the good places it was chance whether you were believed, or they were. Chance who was let go without a reference.'

Lotte watched her carefully, but there were no tears from Grace, just a story unfolding as if it had happened the day before.

'If I'd screamed, broken some plates, there was a possibility the outdoor staff might have heard. But these houses were designed to keep the kitchen unseen and unheard. I wasn't even angry, just confused. But when he tore at my blouse and my mother's pin disappeared across the kitchen it was as if I suddenly knew what he was doing.' Grace's hand came to the corner of her mouth. The briefest of gestures.

'That place was full of knives, skewers, hooks,' she smiled again. 'Cook called it the torture chamber. They were all to hand. But anything I did would only have made it worse.'

'Grace.' Lotte made to reach out, but Grace resisted.

'I fought him hard in my mind for years after. But in that moment I knew I couldn't do it. I became one of the girls we'd all heard about, someone's sister or cousin. It was all over fast, like a function. Then he took the key to cellar, the bottle to the river. "Thank you, Grace," he said. That was almost the worst bit, using my name. He was back at his mother's home in London by evening. But for me it was a rush. To cover up. To be back in charge before the rest returned. Wash it away in three inches of bathwater.'

A hardness came back into Grace's face. 'Mr Ward told me that evening that his son had asked him to apologise for the inconvenience that afternoon. "He speaks highly of you," is what he said. And I thanked him. Imagine. I couldn't hide my condition for long. And I wasn't going to make up a story about a village boy or a visiting footman. And Mr Ward believed me. Of course he did. I was trusted with his houses. With the keys. Mr Ward wasn't unkind. He sorted me financially. And he was a modern man. I ended up at an address, a posh doctors in London. A beautiful house. It didn't make the pain any less or the emptiness after. Or the complications.'

Lotte felt the weight of Grace's story pile up, word after word, as if it were another presence in the kitchen, heavy as the zinc-topped table.

'But Mr Ward, was also a family man. Family was everything. You'd know that from his novels and the articles he wrote for the London papers. How could he sit with his son and have me serve, be there in the same house. He'd discussed my situation with a very good friend, a good man and a better employer, he had a place for me. Mr Ward told me he was sad for me. I'd been like a member of the family. Then I met Thomas. He didn't mind that children were now out of the question. Without the money from Mr Ward a chauffeur couldn't have started a garage business. I was lucky, really.'

'Oh Grace. I had no idea. You never said.'

'No, I didn't. I'm more than that,' Grace said softly. 'I've other stories.' She looked up for the first time, her eyes fierce. 'I've had other lives.'

They sat there in a quiet so deep it was only after some time they both, at the same instant, registered Lily, calling down through the house, a rising wail.

'Gr-aaaa-ce?'

LOTTE

Thursday 23rd March 1911

She must have been at high school, just before she left to start work at the milliners, so maybe thirteen or fourteen. She had been in the shop with Aunt Margaret. Groceries, then. Hard work. Everything heavy, packaging filthy from the delivery journey. Even then they made their plans to move into clothing. So much cleaner.

They shut at ten. Everything brought in off the street, everything settled in the shop for the night. Slicer cleaned. Bags and boxes up off the floor. Her aunt moving round, not a wasted movement, quick, neat. The counter, the till and the shelves like an extension of her limbs. They'd had this property for over a year, but there was always one eye out for something else. They had plans, the aunts. Always have a next shop, a next project, or more than one. Things changed, times changed, people changed.

'Won't you be sad to leave here?' she had asked.

'Sad? Why?' said her aunt. No sentiment. It was a shop, a means to an end. Moving on, getting out. Orchard House, lying at the bottom of the town, across the river, was another motivator.

'People like us get stuck,' Aunt Jessie had told her once. 'They get worried about dropping back, it all going wrong. They get buried in this order, that invoice, and can't see where they're going, can't get their heads up to look at the future.'

Margaret turned the lights out. The street was gloomy, a drizzly mist hanging around the lights. Few people, as it wasn't a paynight. The four pubs they passed in the first few minutes were quiet. The men had plenty appetite for the warmth and light of the pub. Lotte had never been inside, obviously, but the orange glow, the warm yeasty reek from the open doors was so much more inviting than the dank stairs in the older tenement blocks.

As they walked up the narrow curve of Bow Street, a noise came down the hill towards them, like the sound of the sea as you approached through the dunes. At the mouth of a vennel there was a small crowd. No more than eight, mostly men, a strange excitement animating their faces under their bunnets, a glitter in their eyes. In the middle of the ragged crowd two women, young, twenties, one barefoot, both bent at waist, both black-haired, wild, white knuckles catching the light as both fists flexed and tightened buried deep in each other's hair, scrabbling for a tighter grip. They seemed silent, but between the occasional shouts from the men there was a breathing that Lotte hadn't heard before. It was a deep, compressed rage, an anger too big to be solely for the other girl but a rage that rolled and expanded over the people watching, the street, the town, their lives, the universe. As they moved under the light, she saw the wet faces, spit and snot, the ripped blouse and exposed breast, a dark nipple at the centre of the men's attention, a bloody scratch all the way along a forearm. They were locked together, turning, feet slipping, oblivious to the watchers.

Aunt Margaret shoved her with her hip, off the pavement and across the cobbles to the opposite side of the road. 'Don't stare.'

They picked up their pace. There were faces at windows above, but this was a small commotion. The two women had not changed position, immobile with hatred, fused with a diabolical energy. No one, male or female, made a move to intervene.

'Come,' said Margaret. 'Leave them to it.'

When they were further round the curve of the street the sound receded.

'Fighting like beasts,' said Margaret, her lips a single dark line. 'What lives.'

Lotte nodded. But she could feel her body tingle with an excitement. It wasn't just the primate violence, the unexpected flesh exposed on a damp night. There was something about the fierce energy concentrated in those fists, the indifference to the eyes, the judgements. There was something in the intense struggle – futile, pointless, though it was – that rejected a submission to fate. They might mock and judge, but there was something in the fury of the women that was bigger, grander, than the staring men and indifferent women. She could never say it, but it felt close to the determination, something close to rage, that she saw in her mother and her aunts when someone tried to thwart them. She pulled herself away and had to run to catch her aunt.

And as Lotte grew older, she began to see how it was done, the application of energy and will needed to build the business. She had in her mind a defining image of the household. At night, the tea washed and away. She would have a book, Marguerite her *Woman and Beauty* magazine, Peter sketching down at the living end of the big room, and Jessie, Margaret and her mother would be at the kitchen table, gathered around accounts books, piles of receipts, invoices. The sharp tang of carbon paper. Scraps of pages with tall lists of figures – compared, recounted, checked, discarded and a new set of figures added and subtracted.

A low murmuring. The sisters all dark-haired, with the same sharp look across their deep-set eyes. Voices were never raised, but there was plenty of debate. Consensus was a destination. And not always reached on one night. They would come back, harry the problem, worry at it till they had agreement. A majority never enough, Lotte had seen many vetoes. Jessie the spinster, the youngest and the most severe. But in business the risk taker, the goader, the one who suggested new territories. And the one everyone was wary of, with her Council of Women meetings and her ideas about housing. She was the one who had taken the fire and focus of the family to other, bigger enterprises, other aims.

'The places people live in make them. Live like an animal, behave like an animal. Better housing is the start of a better society.'

When Jessie's glasses and notebook came out of the fine handbag she had made for her by the saddler, and she unscrewed her Conway Stewart pen, there was a quiet, determined excitement in the room.

Her mother was always cautious, always looking for the downside, the hidden risk. Her maternal influence went beyond Lotte and Marguerite. She looked out for her sisters, saving them from the pain of over-extended expectations, and restoring morale when they had to regroup. She had no time for the indulgencies – handbags, coats, meant nothing. Security was everything. Something to fall back on was always more important than looking the part.

And Margaret, pragmatic – 'Let's get on, let's make a start and see where it goes.' Always the one to take the lead. Tall and thin with her angular haircut and beautiful long coats, Lotte sometimes fancied she saw something of the riverside bird about Aunt Margaret, studying the flow before she stabbed at a dozing fish. Decisive. But she could step back just as fast and let the whole family watch a threat rush past.

The overhead lamp pulled down low on its chain pulleys. Curtains undrawn, the night pressing up to the window. Out beyond the high window, the Forth far below, the yellow glow of the town, the clusters of light spreading away into the night. But at the centre of it all these three heads, so close they almost touched. The aunts. From this intense little circle came their food and their shelter, the fine clothes and the furniture. Lotte had felt the jealousy swirling around them from her first day at school. This was as good a property as any in the district. Big enough to take lodgers as an extra income to tide over hard times. And it was theirs, or Margaret's anyway. Her name on the deeds.

'You have to own,' she said. 'It has to be yours. Your name on the papers.'

She had been abandoned once, left with debts, a change of clothes and the next day's food. She wouldn't take that risk again.

'Not a man between us,' Mary, her mother would say. It was true; one dead, the other– who knew where. And Jessie– 'A man? What would I do with one?'

Lotte watched them over her Mazo de la Roche. Studied the alchemy of the aunts' planning. Scribbles on opened-out envelopes were the starting points, the calculations that could locate a new, cheaper supplier, define the value of a new shop or create a surplus that led to new dresses for them all. Opportunities conjured out of thin air.

'If you own one thing, it can let you own another.'

They got credit on the back of property, property on the back of trust. They never missed a payment and there was always a reserve of money in the Bank of Scotland at the foot of Baker Street. She had visited with her mother to deposit money. The manager, a man with all the self-importance of her school headmaster, came out of his office: 'Mrs Candow, so nice to see you. Who can I get to help you today?'

The black and white squares on the floor and the high ceiling of the bank, like a church.

'Why does money need so much room?' She had asked on the way back up the hill

'It needs to breathe,' her mother said. 'Breathe and grow.'

They had sat at a desk with carved legs as the bag of money was counted and pieces of paper were signed. There was a handshake and the next day her mother or one of her aunts was off to Glasgow to speak to the wholesaler. With two bags. A handbag and a leather bag that held a notebook, letters, a fountain pen. It was like a school bag but infinitely more important.

And the next night the bag was opened with new papers to discuss, to pass round, more calculations.

This was how they moved into clothing.

'Groceries are halfpenny profits.' Jessie said. 'We'll never get away on that. Not in a hundred years.'

'What do we know about clothes?' asked her mother.

'You've worked in a draper's shop, don't be ridiculous, of course you know about clothes.' Jessie wasn't used to losing arguments.

'That's not the same as running a clothes shop.'

'We can put it together,' said Margaret slowly. 'You know the stock, I know the books, Jessie can do anything she turns her hand to.'

'Lotte knows how to sell hats,' said Jessie. 'And Marguerite can decide if she wants to sew on ribbons for ever. We won't even have to hire.'

'What about Peter?' said her mother.

'Peter's going to college,' said Margaret. 'He has talent.'

Lotte, Marguerite and Peter weren't pretending to be deaf anymore.

Marguerite said. 'Don't include me in your plans. I've got prospects.'

Peter kept sketching. Lotte could see that it was the Castle, but distorted, bristling with modern looking weapons, an airship overhead.

'I will help in any way I can.' Lotte said.

'We won't get airs,' said Margaret. 'We will stick to the people we know. Up here there's been no quality to buy. They can't afford the shops in Barnton Street. We can give them good stuff at good prices.'

'They can't get a buyer for the Stirling Arms, you know.'

It was notorious. Perhaps no one was brave enough to take it on. It was the best building in Baker Street. A landmark.

'Pubs, now?' said her mother. 'No.'

'No. No,' said Jessie. 'It's the site, it's perfect. Halfway up, or down the street. Halfway to town, halfway to work and home.'

'Let's do the sums.'

They did, and with many meetings in the bank over that first winter of the war they bought the building. A shop and two flats. And so the aunts and the three grown children stood and watched at the doorway as the workmen tore out the stinking floor and the old wood of the bar fittings polished by a million elbows. A few hours later it was a shell. But in days there were counters, shelving, and it was a shop.

A miracle. The only other shops owned by women were small affairs, enough to keep a widow alive, or entertain a bored wife. But this was ambitious. A proper business.

In the same way, they made Peter's college place happen. The three sisters. More sums, options laid out and ticked off. They approved Marguerite's match, too, with just a faint whiff of disappointment.

'Your sister's the prettiest girl in the town,' said Peter.

Lotte stabbed him in the hand with a stick of charcoal. It left a black rash which he blew clean.

'It runs in the family, of course. But honestly, she could do better. Don't you think?'

And this was how the aunts built their business and ran the family.

LOTTE

Friday 9th May 1919

Why Sam? Why her? She could see all around the mystery of relationships. Marguerite, for instance. The curl of her finger was able to hook boys. She had settled on Morris, her eye on a bungalow on the Bannockburn Road. How did it happen? How did you know? Or did the music stop at a certain moment and you sat in whatever seat you could?

The mystery of finding someone was dramatized in the concert party. It was out at the barracks at Cambusbarron, a miniature town which had grown up on the edge of Stirling over the last four years. The war had been finished for six months, but long wooden sheds were still full of men waiting to be demobbed. Five hundred restless, bored men who just wanted to go home. Five hundred men and her. Not just her, there were other local girls who could sing, who had songs that excited the boys more than her safe selections. But of those five hundred it was Sam who asked if he might meet her before she went home.

What did Sam see from his seat in the long khaki rows? A nervous black-haired twenty-two year old woman in a white dress concentrating hard on the music, standing so straight on the stage that her back ached for days. He said it was her voice, that was how he knew. What made her connect with him? His intelligent gaze, his smile. And he had things to say. Peter apart, she grew up among men who had little to say and sometimes these few words were too much. Sam had plenty words. Usually they were the right ones.

He had stood in the corridor at the back of the hall. A

draught blew her hair over her eyes, she pushed it back, pulled her wrap around her. This was a novelty, almost like a stage door.

'Miss Candow, may I compliment you.' Accents from all round the country had been common in the town for the last four years. His was hard to place. Everywhere and nowhere. She noted his Sergeant's stripes.

'You have a wonderful voice.'

She'd taught herself to take the compliment, not bat it back, not to self-deprecate, to resist the search for the catch, the irony, but to take it in her two hands, feel its texture and put it in her bag to take out later when the doubts arrived.

'Thank you. It's difficult to pick songs for men who have been through so much and are still far from home.'

'They won't want to go home if you come back next week to sing again.'

She cracked a little at that.

'I think home has more to offer than a concert in a cold hall.'

He held up a finger for emphasis. It was a one of his little ticks. She didn't know then it was a gesture she would see almost every single day for the next fifteen years.

'I mean it, I'd cancel my de-mob for more of your voice.'

'Does that say more about your home than my voice?' He laughed at that. A big generous noise.

They were still standing awkwardly in the corridor, soldiers squeezing past.

'Home is always home,' he said. 'No matter what it's like.'

'Is it far?' she said. 'The home you're in no hurry to return to?'

'Birkenhead,' he said.

'Liverpool?' That was the undertow of his voice.

'Birkenhead,' he said again. 'Not the same.'

'What will you be returning to? When you get home?'

'I'm a grocer,' he said, 'or will be soon. I've been a quartermaster for three years. You're laughing. Is that a funny job to do?'

'No, no,' she said. 'It's not rude, it's just that I've worked there. In a grocers. My aunt had a grocer's shop, with my mother, and her sister, too. They've got a draper's shop now. Right in the middle of Baker Street, it used to be the Stirling Arms, but they bought it and converted it. That shook up the business people here. Three sisters doing something like that.'

'The three sisters?' She registered that he thought he had said something clever. 'You know?'

'Pardon?'

'Macbeth. The three witches. And here we are, in Scotland?' He tailed off.

She laughed again: 'They can be diabolical sometimes. But the aunts aren't witches. That is too much. You're the educated one, then.'

'Anyone can read a book, go to the theatre.'

'Well,' she said, shrugging her wrap on to her shoulders, in a deliberate way, as if she were putting on an overcoat. It was a mime for leaving. 'It has been nice to meet you.'

'Mister? Mister Raymond. I was just finishing your sentence.' He was staring intently now. 'Don't you want to know who I am?'

'I'm sorry, yes of course.'

'And what about the nature of my business, why I accosted you here? I play. The piano. And I wanted to suggest that rather than taking you out, that I might be able to accompany you, on the piano, when you practice.'

'I have an accompanist.' She stalled.

'I can see that. But extra practice is never wasted. I've got access to a piano at the Methodist church in town.'

'You're a Methodist?'

'In a way,' he said. 'Not devout, but yes. Don't look like that, we're not Hindus.'

'And we would just meet there, in a church hall, to sing?'

'Yes. Why not? You can bring a friend if you like.'

'I have my sister.'

'Perfect, bring her along.'

Marguerite sat right at the back of the plainest, coldest hall Lotte had ever been in. She'd read a magazine before stepping out for a cigarette, letting the sprung door slam as loud as she could. Sam chased after her the first time she did it to make sure she went behind the hall and didn't bring the religion into disrepute.

At first, she brought the music of her favourite songs. Then he brought his. She didn't know where he got the sheets from. The hymns came from the church, presumably, but had he carried these song manuscripts all through the war?

'Salonika,' he said when the inevitable question came up.

'That couldn't have been nice.' It was a reasonable thing to say but she couldn't recall having read or heard anything about it in the last four years.

'It was horrible. Disease kills you as easily as a bullet. But it wasn't France. And I'm glad of that.' His honesty was unusual.

'My cousin was in France. He was wounded.' She left it at that, and he didn't press her for more.

He told her of his early time in Belfast. Under the cranes, the mountains close by, the rain and the drums: 'Like something out of Kipling,' he said. 'The natives restless.'

He told her about Birkenhead. More cranes, terraces. The huge smoky city across the water, towers and steeples. The river full of ferries, great liners from America and Canada turning slowly with their black smoke rising all the way to the low clouds.

They were walking, Sunday afternoon, along the Back Walk, the stone bulk of the Castle rising above them, scrubby bushes sweeping away until the sheer rock took over. There were lots of other couples despite it being an overcast day, the hills like another band of cloud to the North.

'It's such a different place,' she said. 'You must miss it lots.'

'I miss the river. And the library. Maybe the park and the running ground.'

'That's quite a lot.'

'There's a river, library and parks here too.'

'But not your family?' She said, probing.

'No,' he said, swinging his umbrella at a straggly thistle. 'No. I don't not miss them. But they don't expect me to come back. Albert went long before the war. He's in the American Coastguard now. In Hawaii. Imagine.' He whacked another thistle. 'I don't want to get that far.'

'It gives people chances, the war,' she said. 'My aunts say they'd never have got on if there had been the usual men running the shops. Making the decisions. It was their chance and they took it. They had to learn how to do it from scratch.'

'Sometimes you need a shock, to do new things. It's a bright thing that comes out of dark times.' he said.

'When my father died,' said Lotte, 'it felt like we had to learn everything from scratch too. Especially when we came here from Edinburgh.'

'Why did you leave Edinburgh?' He put his umbrella over his shoulder. 'Sorry about all this talk about leaving.'

She laughed. She loved his effort, his pleasing her, engaging her. Not like the monosyllabic boys who expected you to do all the conversational work, who never listened, or even looked to see how you were responding to their grunts.

'My mother never really explained it,' she said. 'She just packed up one day and the next thing we were at the station on our way to her two sisters. There were lots of us back there in Edinburgh, lots of family. My uncle and his wife and their children. Three of them. The three of us. And my grandfather. It was his place.'

'I know about full houses. Never quiet. Never alone. I'd find corners to read and my brother would hunt me down.'

'I missed my cousins. But my mother said we would just have to forget them as we'd not be going back.'

'Did something happen?'

'Things always happen.'

'A fall out?'

'Maybe. No one said anything, but we were small. And then we had cousins here and that was that.'

They walked on. The damp glistened on gorse bushes, tiny drops on the thorns. Sam stopped, pointed with his umbrella towards the monochrome smear of cloud and hill.

'I love this,' he said.

'It's cold and wet.'

'It's cold and wet everywhere. But look at that.' He pointed to the walls above. 'It's all history. Hundreds of years.'

She rubbed her cheek on the collar of her coat, saw the glitter in his eye, how all this looked to him, who hadn't grown up here.

He said: 'I took *Kidnapped* out of the library over and over. The librarian would tip me off. "It's back in again." I'd read it upstairs, looking out into the street. The black bricks. I'd be here. Walking down over these hills.' He waved the umbrella again. 'To cross the bridge at Stirling at night. Out of the Highlands. It still seems more exciting and exotic than Greece ever did.'

'I've not read that.'

'You don't need to,' he said. 'You've got your music. Your voice. It's a gift. You don't need more than that.'

She wasn't sure what he meant. But he stopped now. And so had the rain, it was just damp condensing out of the air. She felt something was going to happen, the couples on the path, the dull sky didn't register with her anymore, they were clearing away for something. He was very serious.

'I don't want to go back.' His arms, his hands were around her shoulder, her back. 'I want to stay here. With you.'

He kissed her. It wasn't the first time she'd been kissed, nor the first time he'd kissed her. But it seemed different. As if setting something running. Setting something free. In the steep streets round her home boys loved to set balls going. Footballs, marbles, all types. See how far they would run by gravity alone. Some boasted they had reached the Forth. On the Back Walk between the Castle and the flat Carse and the far hills she felt something start to roll down the hill, something that would have enough momentum to carry all the way to the river.

LOTTE

Sunday 16th April 1933

She set the metronome ticking, on the lid of the piano, above both their heads. The weight set to *Animato*, the arm swung out beyond the wooden pyramid. They sat there on the piano stool, Lotte and Douglas, while James, Lily and Grace were down in the kitchen. There was morning light from the pearly grey sky and the smell of wax polish.

Douglas waited with hands poised above the keyboard as he absorbed the pace of the metronome. It wasn't a difficult piece if played at half the speed. Lotte watched his hands try to keep up with his brain. Watched the miraculous flow between notes on the pages, pinned back under the brass restraints, through the player's mind and fingers and into her head. It was never something to take for granted. The way Chopin, Douglas and she were complicit in this moment, the sounds rising, falling and combining, until they collapsed mid bar. Lotte flicked the page back.

'Let's try it again from the start. Just try to keep up the momentum.' She tucked the page in. 'You're making real progress with this. It's not easy.'

Douglas prepared to go again.

'Will you do this with others?' he said.

'Other pupils?'

'Yes,' he said. 'Become a piano teacher.'

'Would I be any good?'

He hesitated; it was a novelty to be asked an adult opinion. 'Yes, you would.'

'I'd like to. Piano and singing.' Sitting side by side, both focused on the manuscript in front, it was possible to talk in ways that they couldn't in normal circumstances. This early morning practice, before Douglas and James set off for their schools was a stolen time too, a slice of calm between breakfast, Sam's early departure for the shop, and the yawning day. After a night walking, it was when she felt at her most vibrant, most positive. Before it all closed in on her. This was the arc of her days, beginning in the brightness of the light on the red carpet, the flowers on the low table translucent even without sunshine, the noises below in the kitchen, the piano alive, and then the curving descent towards darkness before the night brought her the terror of absolute dark, and then the relief of the open street.

'You would be good,' said Douglas. 'Would that be your job?'

'Sort of. I've got work to do with the shop.'

'Is that not Dad's job?'

'It is his job. And mine. My mother and my two aunts started it. I've got things to offer.'

Douglas leaned forward as if he were about to start the piece.

'Will I work there too?'

'If you want. Or…'

His hands were poised. Lotte went on: 'Or there's your music.'

'Isn't that just for your spare time?' His hands were back in his lap now. 'Like Mr Thornlee.'

'Mr Thornlee is a very talented man,' said Lotte.

'But he works in the printers?'

'It isn't easy to make a living through music. Mr Thornlee wanted to be a teacher. But…' Lotte wasn't quite sure why that had not happened. Frederick explained it in terms of professional jealousy, colleagues taking against him, misunderstandings over references.

'But he has two jobs now. Choirmaster and printer.'

'Dad says he's not very good at either.'

Lotte took a breath. 'That's unfair. I don't think selling print is as exciting. As fulfilling. As making music. That's all.'

'Right,' said Douglas.

'But listen. It is better to try to make a life around music, than never to try. And you can try.'

'It's hard work.'

'But worth it. Look,' said Lotte. Her voice quickened and dropped. 'You must not tell anyone of this. This is between you and I.' She glanced down at him. Promises. Secrets. They opened doors and you couldn't be sure what shadows would enter. 'You and I, we're musicians. So, you must promise.'

Douglas nodded earnestly.

'Mr Thornlee and I are going to be involved in a concert.'

'Like at the church?'

'Yes. No. Yes, a concert like that, but not at the church. At the Usher Hall. In Edinburgh.'

'I know where it is.'

'It's a huge event organised by one of Mr Thornlee's old teachers. There will be thousands of people there.'

'Will we all be there?'

'Yes, of course. All of you. I just want it to be more of a surprise when it is closer to the time. But I'm going to be practising, so you can help me with that. Can't you?'

'Of course I can. And I can keep secrets too.'

'It will help,' she said, 'help with being a teacher. There's lots of competition here. But if I've sung in the Usher Hall, that will make a difference.'

'Won't you do it again?'

'No. That will be that. I'll be too old.'

'You aren't old!'

'I'm too old for singing.' Lotte collected herself. Focus on the task. 'Chopin one last time before you have to go.' Douglas's narrow shoulders were rigid and angular under his school blazer. His face, reflected in the angled keyboard lid, was white, his mouth a thin, blurred line.

'Mum?'

'What is it?'

'If there's a war will I have to fight?'

Lotte sat straight and still on the stool.

'Why? Why is that in your mind now?'

'The debate, the debate at school.'

'Wasn't that the older classes?'

'But we all got to hear about it.'

'How would you have voted?'

'I'd have said no, fighting isn't good. That's what Dad says. He says never again.'

Lotte found her hands working on the end of her leather belt, pulling twisting.

'He's right about that.'

'But you'd have to. When it came to it. When it's not just talking about it. Or voting about it. Then you would have to go. Wouldn't you?'

Lotte felt her heart start to run away again. Beating like a running horse.

'They can't make you. In the end. They can't. Anyway, you're only twelve, it will be a different world by the time you're eighteen, all that stuff in Germany will be sorted out by then.'

'But you'd have to.'

'It would be hard not to, but you can say no.' With each reassurance she felt a terror take hold inside her ribcage. Deep inside she saw Peter's face. And she saw Grace too. Powerless in that kitchen. Peter and Grace had been victims of overpowering forces that had placed them in danger and denied them escape or justice. The image of Douglas caught up in future madness, helpless and torn, blazed in her imagination.

'Dad went happily.'

'They all went happily. But it didn't last.'

'It will happen though, won't it? War? Everyone says.'

'Things can change.' She felt a sense of falling. 'But yes, it probably will.'

Douglas was silent. She thought of Peter. His face under the light falling through the glass roof of the station. The smell of smoke and steam, and something else. His eyes. She shoved Douglas with her shoulder. She had to overcome her fear.

'Don't worry. It might be soon and you'd be too young. Or years from now and you might be too old.'

He didn't say anything. They sat there, each inside their thoughts, until James appeared in the doorway, Grace and Lily behind.

'It's time to go,' said Grace.

LOTTE

Tuesday 22nd February 1920

She had to ask her mother. And her aunts. The three sisters, the aunts, would decide. Collectively. They would convene and work out what was best for the whole family. Sam too. If he was suitable.

And so he would have to be interrogated. Round the table. Sam in his suit. A thin sunlight coming in over the rooftops, over the Forth, the Ochils.

'How long have you been apprenticed?'

'Who with?'

'Quartermaster? How many men under you?'

'What sort of stock were you handling out there?'

'Local? Was it shipped all the way out?'

Sam, smiling, everything thrown at him was caught, was picked out of the air.

'Did you organise uniforms, too, for all those men?'

It was like an interview for a position, which indeed it was. Lotte watched them nod, almost smile, even scribble in the account book, for they were soon at the point of showing him what they had done – built over that hard half-decade. Woven a fine web of trust among tough, sceptical women, a delicate net, transaction after transaction, from customers who had no time for shoddy goods or sharp practice. The aunts had respect for hard work and tight budgeting, so never cut corners with customers. Suppliers were different, of course. There was no mercy there.

'We can find a space for you,' said her mother. 'Not a full role, but enough to help you and Lotte get started.'

'For now,' said Jessie. 'But we can't stand still either, we need to grow.'

'Time for that.' Her mother nodded.

'Let's see how you settle in,' said Margaret.

When Sam had left, they sat on for longer with Lotte. Required her to set out her plans.

'There's room for four of us in the business,' said Margaret. 'You and Sam will have one share of what we take between you. We need to look after Peter too, he is part of our calculations.'

Lotte looked out into the darkened hall and Peter's door.

'You best go and tell him now, too,' said her mother.

LOTTE

Sunday 16th April 1933

Lotte paced up and down the living room. The boys in bed,
Sam at the shop, working the books on a Sunday night. Grace
downstairs in her room. She switched the wireless off. The
clock ticked. The curtains were open. She had told Grace to
leave them. She wanted to see the light fade. The road was
shiny now under the streetlights. She paced. Her mind was
full of the Usher Hall. This was her future– the music lessons.
And music was an escape for Douglas too, away from the
shop, from working till 10 o'clock. A calling not a business.
He was as talented as Frederick and now they could afford
university. More or less. But it would take the business to grow
and flourish. She had so many ideas for that. Jessie's way,
keep looking forward, never look back, keep growing, keep
expanding. They were in the wrong place. It was all about
position, she could see that. She saw that every time she went
out. She could feel the disaster waiting, the streets themselves
could not last. In the depths of the night, when the streets were
empty of people, drained of energy, it was clear the buildings
were crumbling, nearly dead. Years ago, at Jessie's Council of
Women meetings, they had recognised that the area had to
change. But no one listened and the decline continued. They
still had customers because they were poor and didn't feel
comfortable in other shops, but that would not last for ever.

'Move now,' she said. Did she speak aloud?

She paced faster. That was it. Relocate. She could see. Her heart beat faster. She looked up at the mirror over the fire, Jessie's gift when they moved here.

'Don't over-use it,' she had said. 'But never go out looking like you don't care either.'

There were points of red on her cheeks. She put her hands to her face. Burning. As if the ideas racing in her head were boiling to the surface.

'Walk. Walk,' she said. Calm the runaway horse pounding in her chest.

She would walk up to the shop. Perhaps meet Sam, explain what she had worked out – for the shop, for Douglas, her music teaching. Perhaps even about the concert. There was so much. Her black times seemed remote now. This was a proper plan for the future. She looked at the room, the piano. The Collard and Collard was more than half the price of the car. But so much could come from it. This was a perfect room for students to learn and play. She imagined it filled with music and sunshine every day. And then at night she and Sam could discuss the business. Take the shop forward. New ideas, new lines. Lotte and Sam, heads together over the dining room table.

She went into the hall. The stair disappearing up into the gloom, the hallway through to the stairs to the kitchen. Should she call down to Grace? No. She would be back home very quickly, with Sam. She looked down the hallway to the dark stairwell to the kitchen. The kitchen that was Grace's world, where she must have spent so much time alone with her memories of that ordeal. Lotte shuddered at the thought of how Grace must have fought down images and feelings every time she handled kitchen implements. To have kept that within herself. All that time Lotte had felt they were so close, yet not one word.

Lotte closed the front door behind her and stepped out swiftly across the road and along the broad streets. No umbrella. Never mind, not so wet. It was whisper-quiet here, the misty night muffling, closing in on the pools of yellow around the streetlights.

As she climbed into the town there was more noise. It was early, not quite ten, so there were plenty of people in the streets, mainly men, collars up, caps down, clustering round the pubs, elbows on the window ledges. The pubs were dourly shuttered, but most of the men were drunk – there was always a way on the day or rest. Their gaze was like a touch on her back. She hunched into her coat. It wasn't a novelty, this feeling she'd got used to from girlhood. The stare that couldn't be challenged.

When she turned up the hill into Baker Street, there was much more activity. Vans delivering late, lights on, a brewer's dray, solid patient horses, the traffic pushing people onto the pavements. A few women went past. A different sort of look from them. What was she doing out? A woman like her. A mass of men was blocking the pavement outside the Star. She stepped off the pavement and crossed the cobbles, keeping one eye on the group, when she walked into the middle of another group of five men.

'Excuse me,' she said.

'How, what have you done?' There was laughter. They were crowded into a space between a van and a shop front.

'It's what she's going to do I'm interested in.' The accent wasn't Stirling.

She stayed calm. It was a busy street. She wasn't alone.

'Brass are you?'

'First we've seen.'

In the confined space the smell of alcohol was strong.

'Gentlemen,' she said. 'You've had a fine evening I can tell, please let me past.' Stay calm. The aunts' advice. Never look scared because that makes it worse. And get your shoes off to run hard. You can recover from cut feet.

'Gentlemen.' There was more laughter. And a hand on her waist. 'Not for you then Bertie.'

'Too expensive by far.'

'Not if there's a group discount.'

Another hand was on her right arm now, hard, insistent.

'Come.' It was Frederick. 'Come.'

'Oh, here's a lively one.'

'Don't you fucking barge in on us.'

'This was our find. Fuck you.'

There was a scuffle. A hand pulled at the front of her coat. Boots kicked out. One caught her shin. She gasped. Not so much pain as surprise. Frederick was kicking back and pushing her at the same time. Into the vennel. Frederick crashing the barred gate shut. Fingers caught.

'You fuck.'

'Fucking get him.'

Frederick pushing her away from the gate and shoving a bar through to secure it. Fists round the bars, spitting. Then they were gone, some laughter and the wave of energy and hate fell back into the natural swaying sound of the night-time town.

'Here.' Frederick gave her a folded linen handkerchief. She pressed it to her lips. It was dark in the vennel. When she looked up there was only one dimly lit window, hanging. The rest was a long narrow trench of black. He was almost invisible. She could smell his soap.

'Thank you,' she said.

'Why –' he started to say, but she cut over him.

'I'm on my way to the shop.'

'Of course.'

'I can't tell you how...'

'Lotte.' He moved round to face her. The vennel was so narrow that he was inches from her face. The only light reflected of the wetness of his face. 'Lotte. Don't say anything. It is fate. Providence.'

'Frederick.' She put two hands flat on his overcoat. It was damp. Slippery. 'It must be OK to go back now.'

'No, Lotte, don't you get it, this is fated.' His mouth was near hers.

She pushed but he put his hand behind her head and his mouth was over hers. His tongue like a wet live thing, moving. She could go no further back. There was a hard object behind her thighs. A bin. Bins.

'I've thought so much about this. All those hours.' His hands were pulling at the belt of her coat. The knot tightened and he abandoned that and pulled the top half of her coat apart. His hand slid under her blouse, pinching, pulling.

'I know you think it isn't right.' He was panting now. She twisted and turned but his weight crushed her. 'But I know you want this for us too?'

'Frederick, please.' It was like using a familiar name for a stranger.

His hand reached to push her skirt up, tugging as it caught on her boot hooks. He was breathing like a beast, Lotte was bent back over the bin, her legs kicking as he thrust his fingers, jabbing. She thought of his ink-stained hands.

'I told you this. I told you about our training. Under pressure is when you need to think most.' It was Peter. At the barred gate, framed by the streetlight at the end of the vennel. Peter.

'There's always something. A weapon. A spade, a stone. You or the Hun. It won't be you.'

Fredrick put both hands to his trousers. It was a moment. She started to fall to one side. She reached out her right hand to steady herself – the galvanised metal of the bin lid.

'You see, you see,' said Peter, calm. Slow. 'Always something.'

Her hand gripped the handle of the lid.

'Now,' said Peter. 'Vulnerable places only. You have to do this, I can't help. You get one chance. It has to tell. Face, balls are best. But quick, Lotte. Don't fuck about.'

She swung the bin lid. As it rose, she put her left hand behind the edge and drove it as hard as she could into Frederick's face. His head went back. She heard it against the other wall. The sound was like an overripe apple falling on the shop floor. He gasped. But quietly. She braced herself. Wasn't it enough?

'Go Lotte, run. For fuck's sake have you never listened to me?' Peter wasn't so calm now.

She slid off the bin. She had to step over Frederick. He was sitting upright against the wall, a dark presence, his legs on the wet flags. His hands held his face as if he were pushing it back into place and it weighed a great deal. Her instinct was to bend over him. To help.

'Lotte, are you listening to me?'

She clipped down the vennel. She paused at the iron gate. There was no noise behind her. She settled her coat. Where was her hat? Tucked into her collar. She tugged it out. The street was quiet. She pulled the gate shut. A hard, final clang. She didn't look back. She took out her watch. She had only left the house twenty minutes before. Twenty minutes. She'd fallen. If Sam was back before her that's what she'd say: She'd fallen on the wet cobbles.

But Sam wasn't back before her. The living room light was off. And as she closed the front door behind her, it was Grace, standing by the hall table who took her face between her hands.

Journal of Dr John Fergusson

Friday 21st April 1933

I returned to the rest of my in-tray, working down, relentlessly. I drafted a number of memoranda and put them in the typing file. I had letters to write to relatives, always the most difficult, covering letters for files being sent to other institutions with transferred patients, and finally some references for several of our staff hoping to be accepted on the College's training course.

It was late by the time I finished. On nights when I slept in the building, I enjoyed the walk from my office to my room along these silent corridors. The whole building had settled for the night. It felt like a breath going out, a stillness descending. Nurses, their white uniforms reflected in the polished floors, tended to float rather than bustle. At this time I could genuinely believe that we were making a difference, that we had offered peace and calm to so many.

Later, I knew well, when there was total silence, the presence or absence of sleep would bring out the demons of the dormitory, the private rooms. No doubt in the Nurses' Home too. The waking and the part-dead alike would find their heads full of terrors, the squeals and the sobs and the names called out, the breath caught and the screams swallowed back all the more awful because they are muffled, stifled, damped down by the power of the place to constrain and conform. Don't disturb, don't upset. Suffer, but quietly.

There is a direct way to my room, but of course I took a detour. It took me past Charlotte's room. 154. I looked at the panelled wood. The builders of the original building here had cut no corners with the fittings, it was only subsequently that we bought furniture cheaply and replaced it infrequently. The handle was brass, the keyhole too. My master-key was in my pocket. I felt the weight against my thigh.

I looked to right and to left, down the long poorly lit corridor. I put my forehead against the door, barely touching. Then hurried on to my room.

MARTIN

Monday 20th March 2017

I set out for Stronachie, along the Tillyrie road. That was the best route for 3am. As I'd put my boots on, my dog opened one eye then curled tighter against the radiator. They like their routines, dogs. I was wide awake in order to disrupt routine, my head full of the archives, the journal. I needed to follow Lotte, feel the night air around me, try and make sense of the void of all these years.

The door clicked quietly behind me. It was cold and dry. I couldn't see much of the sky because of the streetlights. The gravel crunched and I handled the gate gingerly opening it just enough to slip through before the point it started to squeak. Already, I was a stealthy nightwalker. Who wants to be spotted walking about at this time? No one has a good reason to be out at this time. Not a reason you can explain to reasonable people.

This is what they call a quiet village. In the middle of the night it was stone dead. There was a faint breeze somewhere high above, around the rooftop dishes and aerials, but along the two short streets that took me beyond the lights, all was calm.

Up past the church and graveyard, I balled my fists in my down jacket pockets and pushed on, out over the empty motorway and on into the dark. Proper dark. There was no moon and the stars were covered by high cloud. I was conscious of the noise my boots made on the roadway. To lessen the chances of tripping on vegetation or being smacked by the trailing arms of hedges, I took to the centre of the road. Just like Lotte. Up on the hillside lights blazed around new developments, little suburbias in the middle of an ancient grazing. Further out, farm security lighting made intense white clusters.

Lotte walked a more muted world, yellow oil lamps in farm windows, a few dim headlights. More shadows. I had the privilege of my phone, with its sharp white light. And my gender. Did she suppress her imagination, or use it to counter the terrors? At any rate it wasn't enough to keep her in her home. I heard the gurgle of water in the ditch. I was warm now, the road led uphill all the way, high enough now to see the villages clustered round the black levels of the loch, all the distances distorted by night. A few silent trucks, centred in their own light, appeared and disappeared down on the motorway. At a gate I disturbed a group of sheep. They thrashed through the dead bracken and grass, noisy ghosts.

I wasn't anxious out here. Where I grew up, I walked miles in the dark on country roads. Even when I wasn't full of cider and lager, I was comfortable with the shadows, the sudden field noises, old men on unlit bikes appearing out of the darkness. When I moved away, I never relaxed on city streets at night. But country roads were just fine.

Back then, what did terrify me was getting back to the family home. The final ten yards from the back door up the stairs to my bedroom to avoid an inquisition from my father. Interrogation and the disapproval. Disappointment. That I might be wasting opportunities. To be lax about schoolwork was a crime that required swift retribution. The smell of cider was the essence of failure – or missed chances that would never come again. The thrill of drinking cider in the dripping woods made no sense to him. All generations think they are uniquely distanced from their predecessors, but there can be few gaps wider than that between the 1930s and the 1970s. For him there was no teenage angst, no teenage wasteland. No teenage anything. His was a different time, away back, before the Second World War.

His anger, while it could be colossal and frightening, was a way of showing he cared. Other sorts of emotional engagement were not extended to me. Not that I expected anything. Dads didn't. That was a job for mothers.

We got on fine. When he didn't get a whiff of drink or if I hadn't collapsed in self-pity. For what is teen-life without booze or self-pity? He had no time for emotional indulgence. When I was in tears of frustration over nothing at all he'd say: 'You should try a time in the army. Then you'd learn what it means to be resourceful.' It wasn't said unkindly. That was his late teens, in the army in Germany. In 1945. Not shot at, I don't think. Though it's unlikely he'd have told me.

He told me one thing. That he'd driven his military truck into Cologne one grey afternoon and for miles and miles he'd driven along roadways cleared through rubble. Former suburbs and city streets. And away in the distance, constant and miraculous, the towers of the cathedral. Remnants. In adulthood I used to visit Cologne a lot. One early evening I went into the dark, terrifying cathedral while the organist was filling the vast space with some JS Bach. When I got home, I told my father all about the experience. I'd found it very moving. He didn't. At all. It was an attempt by me to close the distance. Music the great universal, across time and place. It didn't work. I supposed there would be other opportunities. Of course, there weren't.

I was out now, beyond the streetlights, out in the open countryside, on the hill road. The trees blocked the views over the other villages. Above, there was now some space between the clouds. An aircraft blinked silently. But there were plenty of noises in the verges and forest darkness. Disturbed birds and animals. The road was still rising under my feet. I thought of my grandmother walking the steep streets of Stirling. I thought of my father, eleven years old, adrift after she died, with his huddle of siblings. He was the oldest. After he died his sister said: 'Douglas always looked after us all.' I am an only child and unqualified to judge these relationships. But when aunts and uncles came to our house, they generated their own atmosphere. They didn't behave like a close family. There were no half-references to events only they shared. But there was a sense of omission, things unsaid. A distance from the rest of us, that they were survivors of something so big that they need never speak of it again. And anyway, no one else would ever understand, so why bring their story into the secure homes they'd worked so hard to create?

The forest had closed in on both sides of the road. I could smell the pine resin. The sky had narrowed to a lighter strip of darkness between the jagged treetops. The wind had picked up at that level, distant branches swayed. I walked on till I felt the road start to tend downhill. Time to turn round and head for home. I knew now what he'd lived through, what they'd all lived through. But I'm not sure I understood. The distance was too much for me. The way back seemed shorter, downhill of course, but not as long because it was more familiar. It's an illusion – like water running up hill. If you know the way, it seems less of a stretch.

It was grey when I got home. Too late to go back to bed, I settled down at the kitchen table and opened my archive notes.

8.

The Journal of Dr John Fergusson

Friday 21st April 1933

'Come,' I said.

We stepped onto the gravel at the front door. Again, I found myself reaching for her. But that wouldn't do. Not because I had learned a lesson or anything like that. Not because she wasn't attractive. Lord no. But I was beginning to see her in a different light. Charlotte was a way to redeem myself in my own eyes. I could help her, save her, it would be a sort of atonement for the past.

'Where are we going?' I sensed in her brightness, an adventurous spirit, open to the new and different. It wasn't a trait that fitted small town life.

I led the way across the lawn, passing the spot where we had our moment of near connection. 'I thought I would reveal the secrets of our inner wall. Introduce you to Miss Brown and her garden.'

'Is that a task for a senior physician?' I hadn't led the way for long, she had quickly overhauled me. And, as usual, she had pinned me down with her question. No, it wasn't a task for me, but I had an idea that a conversation with Miss Brown might be helpful for us both.

We walked past the orangery until we came to the walled garden. A party of four men was setting out wood and panes of glass along the wall. There is a piece of research, awaiting a keen junior, which will explore how we might diagnose our patients purely from the way they walk. The tentative-fearful, the tentative-watchful, the tentative-for-fear-of-standing-on-ordnance-or-body-parts, the tentative-trying-to-look-bold. A whole life in a walk.

'Gentlemen,' I said, 'can you direct us to Miss Brown? I believe she should be in the garden today.'

A tall, bearded man spoke from the back of the group. He raised his arm, pointed with its full length as he were a prophet consigning us to a wilderness journey.

'Yonder,' he said. 'She is yonder.' The hand fell like a railway signal and he went back to moving the planks.

He had pointed through the sun-worn door into the walled garden itself. The brass of the handle was green with use and weather. Where blistered green paint had broken away, a dark blue layer was revealed that probably pre-dated the Asylum. I pushed open the door and ducked into the sanctuary. The walled garden was the part of the Asylum that seemed to me most redolent of our purpose. It wasn't just the high wall, blocking out everything but the crowns of the tallest trees. It was the quiet that always nestled here. All but the loudest disruptions were held back by these old stone walls. The regular rows of vegetables, the flower beds in season, the canes painstakingly lashed together by patients to provide support for beans and peas, all set out the virtues of patience and order in a way that hours of indoor instruction could not manage. There was a delicate balance of discipline and freedom here.

Miss Brown was directing one of the gardeners. The Asylum staff resented her outsider status as much as her airs. But many of the patients, men who had spent their lives on big estates, idolized her, perhaps her patrician tones took them back to a time of security. There was never a shortage of patients keen to work in the garden.

She was bent over in her khaki jodhpurs, long laced-up boots and some sort of leather waistcoat with multiple pockets and straps. Delving among some wispy green shoots, she stood up straight as I approached, a long-handled fork in her hand like a trident. Her unruly, almost-white hair framed her face like smoke.

'Miss Brown, a damp morning. But good for the leeks, I'm sure.' I pointed at the neat row.

'The radishes, Dr Fergusson. The radishes respond to moisture not drenching. What brings you here? And your...' she studied Charlotte, '...colleague?'

'Mrs Raymond is a new patient, private patient. I think she might benefit from working alongside you.'

Miss Brown was now focussed on Charlotte. She excluded me completely. 'You have a garden?'

'I have a gardener.' Charlotte said.

Miss Brown beamed. Her manner was intimidating on first acquaintance. It was a test Charlotte had passed. Miss Brown turned on her muddy heels. 'Come!'

She led the way towards the cluster of sheds and greenhouses at the south-east corner of the walled square. We kept up with her long stride. She opened the door in the smallest shed. We all had to dip our heads to enter. There was a smell of earth, but all was neat and clean – a bright Persian rug, two wooden chairs, a desk. A military surplus stove. She indicated that Charlotte should sit on one of the chairs. 'Dr Fergusson you can perch.' There was a wooden crate that might have once held lawnmower parts. I dusted the edge with my sleeve and sat.

'You don't sound local,' Miss Brown said. She was focussed on Charlotte, I was out of her eyeline.

'I am,' said Charlotte. 'I'm from the Top of the Town. But live in King's Park.'

'Ah,' said Miss Brown.

Beside me there was a shelf of gardening books, so well used that some volumes appeared to have been recently dug from the earth. And on the shelf below, hundreds of brown envelopes, all the same size, arranged like books. I pulled out one of the envelopes. It was feather-light and rattled faintly. I had caught Miss Brown's peripheral vison.

'More important than my bookshelf. My seed-shelf. Make sure it goes back where you found it. There is a system.'

I slipped the envelope back more or less where it had come from. I hoped she wouldn't come over to check.

She was back to Charlotte. 'I brought it from home. And I won't be gifting it to the Asylum, much too valuable. What is it you do Mrs Raymond? When you are not here.'

'My husband and I run a shop.' Charlotte was in profile to me. I was excluded.

'Ah, that explains the gardener and King's Park. You women from the business classes were a great asset during the war.' Miss Brown had a directness which, for all that we were in charge here, my colleagues and I lacked. Perhaps it is why she seemed to connect with the patients. 'God knows you couldn't have left running a war to my people. Look at the hash they made of it.'

'I hadn't you down as a Bolshevik Miss Brown.' I was keen to reestablish myself in the conversation.

She didn't ignore me exactly, but she directed her reply to Charlotte. 'A revolution will come. It will take time because the British people are very polite. It might even take another war, but it will happen. In the meantime, we can start with the place of women. We're much less polite.' She smiled conspiratorially with Charlotte and began to re-fuel her pipe. 'You don't mind, do you?' That wasn't addressed to me. 'So, what other things interest you beyond business?'

'Music,' said Charlotte. 'I sing and play the piano.'

'Well?'

Charlotte hesitated, then said. 'Very well, yes.'

'Then steer clear of any suggestions you take part in anything musical in here. It will break your heart. And family?'

'Two boys and a little girl. And my husband of course.'

'You have help?'

'Yes, Grace my housekeeper.'

'It will be a bad day when they all go too. A woman needs time for interests. A family is never enough.'

I tried to regain some control. 'Mrs Raymond also likes to walk. It's one of the reasons she is here, and why I thought she might enjoy the garden.'

'Reasons? Is walking an affliction now Doctor?'

'It is if it becomes obsessive.' I was mildly irritated now.

'I hope I'm never here as a patient and I'm cross-examined on the things I enjoy doing.' She shared this with Charlotte. I didn't really want to consider what sort of patient Miss Brown would make. And we can all become patients.

'Come and join me here. I will keep a sharp eye on the degree of compulsion you exhibit through your walking around my garden.' Miss Brown was enjoying herself at my expense. 'You will, I hope, find that being in nature, your hands in the soil, will do more for your recovery than anything else on offer here.' She and Charlotte were now linked in mirth.

'As you are aware Miss Brown, we have a range of therapies, this,' I looked out at the garden, 'is one.'

'Troubled people need the opposite of walls Doctor. Unless it's pinning an apple tree to a south facing wall. Gardens, nature, will be the future of your work.' She turned to Charlotte once again. 'We shall start tomorrow. We shall get you back on your feet, so to speak, before they,' she indicated me with her pipe stem, grinning, of course, so I wouldn't take offence, 'trap you here.'

I stood up now. We had been here long enough. 'I will decide when Mrs Raymond is ready to begin her work here with you.'

'Very well.' She took Charlotte by both hands. 'We will see you when you are permitted. Stick with Dr Fergusson is my advice. He is a good man. I think. On the other hand, avoid Dr Sneddon and his projects.' She still had Charlotte by the hands. 'Understand?'

I took out my watch. It was time to go. 'We must get back to the main building,' I said. 'I only dropped by this morning to introduce you. I'm on a rare day off today. I'm shooting this afternoon.'

Miss Brown squeezed Charlotte's hands. We were finished. 'Where do you shoot?' She gave me her full attention now.

'Cromlix?'

'Ian Gibson's place. Surely he's in London now?'

'We've never met him,' I said. 'We deal with his factor.'

'You miss nothing by dealing with the factor. Gibson's the rudest man I know.' She stepped across to the seed library and selected an envelope. She pinched seeds from deep inside.

'Here,' she said, and pulled open the side pocket of my tweed. She dropped the seeds into the pocket. She patted the flap down three times. 'Leave some up at Cromlix.'

'What is it?'

'Field horsehair,' she said. 'Gibson's gardeners will be rooting it out a decade from now.'

We were quiet as we walked back, but it wasn't the companionable silence that I felt we had established after our last outing into the grounds. Our bond weakened slightly. Still, I saw no harm in Charlotte being with Miss Brown. If she had heard gossip about Dr Sneddon's work, then it would help convince her that there was a risk. But it was a concern if Miss Brown had more evidence than mere nurses' gossip. I disagreed with Sneddon's project on professional grounds, of course. But I was also aware of the consequences of discovery for my own career. Sneddon had a great gift for hiding failure. But I was wary of Miss Brown with her extensive network of connections. Who knew how far they might reach.

LOTTE

Monday 17th April 1933

Grace sat on the bed beside Lotte and put her hand over hers. They both stared at the muddy and torn stockings on the floor, the blouse, the boots. Her gloves were bunded together like a pair of fighting sea animals. Beyond, the window was full of green.

'Tell me what to do,' said Grace. Lotte was silent. Grace's hand felt cool and still. Lotte's bare feet were bruised above the toes, her left ankle was scuffed as if drawn across a rock. 'Dr Campbell?'

Lotte shook her head. Her hair fell forward round her face. Out on the landing the clock chimed. Ten. The chimes seemed to go on for longer, as if listening so intently added to the hours.

'Lily?' said Lotte.

'Sleeping,' said Grace. 'Boys at school, Sam left early for the shop. I said you'd slept badly again when he left.'

'And who was at the door?'

'Your friend Dorothy Wingard. She had news.'

Lotte let the silence grow into every corner of her room, the plain back-bedroom cornicing above the sombre standing wardrobe, the long mirror, the dark blue velvet curtains.

'News?'

'Mr Thornlee is in hospital.' Grace's hand tightened on the back of Lotte's. 'He was attacked last night at the bottom of Baker Street.'

Out, down through the window, the blossom in the orchard was shaking slightly in the breeze.

Grace went on: 'Thugs got him in a vennel and hit him in the face with something.' Grace touched her apron to her face. 'They say he might lose the sight of one of his eyes.'

Lotte was silent. The stillness of the room was a comfort that she did not want to lose. If they didn't move or say anything then the moment would stay like this forever. The furniture creaked, the house made the tiny wooden sounds she was familiar with in the dead of night when everything settled, creaked as the world turned.

'I will say nothing,' said Grace. 'Never.'

'What should I say?' Lotte let the future into the room, began the next phase.

'Nothing.'

'You fought back,' said Grace. Her hand relaxed.

'I didn't think,' said Lotte. 'If I'd thought, I wouldn't have.' She heard Peter laugh somewhere. Lotte wanted the silence to grow around them again. That bottomless silence she'd heard before. In the stairwell. 'I should tell…' Lotte gathered herself to move.

'No. Think of the conversations you'd have to have. All the words. Say nothing. No one knows,' said Grace.

'Frederick…'

'Will say nothing. How can he explain? And you.' She gathered up both of Lotte's hands and squeezed, 'Were here.'

They sat side by side on the bed. The morning light from the window made them both as pale as inmates.

'I always thought there was something wrong about him,' said Grace.

'I was going to sing with him, in Edinburgh.'

'Were you?'

'I'm not sure now. I think it was a lie.'

Grace pushed up from the bed. She started to gather the clothes. 'You go back to bed. I'll take Lily up to the shop and say that you are ill and can't go today.'

'Go where?'

'Up into the country – Sam's idea for a trip for you. And me, and Lily. It's today.'

'No. No, I don't want to be here alone.' There was a sudden panic in Lotte's wide eyes.

'You can't go on a merry jaunt in the car. Not today'

'If I can't do that, then I can't go on. Full stop.' She shook her black hair, dispersing the agitation like raindrops.

Grace stood over her. The light from the window curled around her, Lotte couldn't see her face, only the determined set of her shoulders.

'You need to recover. You need time.'

'I need to keep going.' Lotte looked up into the shadowy face.

'You need to do what you think is best. But I don't think this afternoon is wise.'

'I should tell the truth.'

Grace knelt down, took Lotte's hand in hers. 'He will say nothing. Dorothy said he has family. They will see to him. He will say nothing. He can't.'

'But I ...'

'He deserved it.'

Lotte was suddenly aware of birdsong from the garden. Had that been there all morning?

Grace's face was close to hers. 'Dorothy said the streets were full of drunks last night, and any one of them might have done it.' Grace shook her head. 'And you were out there. Walking about. Foolish.' Her voice had a different edge now.

'So, it was my fault?' Lotte's lips felt dry, hard.

'This is why I pleaded with you.'

'No, no. It could have happened anywhere. The church. This house. He's been here often.'

'But it didn't. It was out in the streets in the dark.' Grace's grip on her hands was painful. 'What were you thinking of? Wandering all these nights. In the streets.'

Lotte looked straight ahead, over Grace's neat hair.

'No,' she said.

'You put yourself in danger.'

'No. I walk because I need to, because I want to.'

'It has to end now. Before worse happens.'

'The worst has happened. It won't happen again.'

'Look,' said Grace. She leaned back on her heels, dropped Lotte's hands and stood again in the light. 'Look.' She waved her arm at the space of the room, the window, the door onto the bright landing. 'Look at what you have. A wonderful husband, the boys.' Her arm dropped. 'A baby.'

Lotte smiled. 'Oh Grace, I've let you all down.'

'What is wrong? You've had help before. Why not speak to Sam?'

'I can't. I don't want to trouble him.'

'Trouble? He won't think it trouble.'

'I'll sort myself, I'm the only one who can.'

'But Dr Campbell?'

'Can't help either. Only I can.'

Grace stood, her hands in front of her in the pocket of her apron.

'Help me,' said Lotte. 'Help me by saying and doing nothing. Let me see to myself. Please.'

Lotte could see Grace's hands moving together in the apron.

'Please.'

'I will never let you down,' she said. She dipped down and scooped up the clothes. 'Let me get these downstairs. If you are going, we have to get moving. Sam is going to be back at eleven.'

They waited to let a cattle float across the bridge at Doune. As it passed the driver waved. There was a smell of cow dung.

'Pooh,' said Lily.

'Poor beasts,' said Grace. They sat together in the narrow back seat.

'Pooh indeed.' Sam was not a countryman. He crunched the car into gear, and they lurched forward. Lotte looked out over the stone parapet. The river ran brown and white between the black stones, the trees on the far bank bent low over the water.

Over the narrow bridge and up a curving hill. Sam looked back over his shoulder.

'I agree, Lily, horrible cows. Great big smelly beasts.'

Lily giggled. Lotte looked back, too, and smiled. A large black beast, formless and oppressive, sat with her in the cramped interior as they rattled along. She shifted her feet on the metal floor and pulled her coat tighter. They were under an avenue of trees, the tracery of the branches like the Holy Rude roof. Lotte glanced down at the little mirror attached to the door. Peter was there. His helmet low over his eyes, everything in shadow. She couldn't make out his expression. But she was comforted that he was there. He had not abandoned her.

Sam steered round a pothole. 'Sorry ladies, didn't think you'd want to be shaken like that.'

'Please be careful,' said Lotte.

'Look at these wide empty roads. This is what we should be doing every week in the summer. What do you think?'

Lotte nodded.

'That sounds just the thing,' said Grace. 'What do you think, Lily?'

'Yes yes yes!'

'That's the vote carried then.' Sam coaxed a little more speed from the car as the road straightened. Lotte sat back in her seat, braced her feet against the metal in the footwell.

'Take the boys with us, of course. In the holidays. They will love it. We can all squeeze in. Even more fun.'

The distant hills were not so distant anymore. This wall of rounded hills had been a part of her life for as far back as she could remember. A remote hazy presence when viewed from high windows in Edinburgh. And in Stirling they seemed to be the furthest limits of her world. It always gave her a thrill to approach them on this road, to watch them grow and become distinct.

Sam was silent for a while then he said: 'I should tell you this before we get there.' Lotte and Grace stiffened at the same time. The car rattled and jostled. Sam looked straight ahead. 'Your friend, Mr Thornlee. He was attacked by a group of drunks last night. The devils nearly blinded him it seems. In Baker Street.'

Lotte and Grace said nothing.

'I don't know what was going on last night at all. There were gangs of men up and down the street. People saying none of them were local. All drunk.' The car shook over stones. No one else spoke. 'I thought about closing early, but it was a busy evening. I walked the whole staff down the street though. Seemed quiet by then.'

'Just awful,' said Grace.

Sam went on. 'Certainly is. Just the last thing we need for business. They weren't local, that's one thing.' They approached a slow-moving van. Sam shifted down a gear and the car shuddered in a new way. 'I'm sorry,' he said, glancing towards Lotte. 'I know he's your friend.'

Lotte glanced down at the mirror on the door.

'Absolute animals. Men and drink,' said Grace. 'Have they caught anyone?'

'You may well ask,' said Sam. 'No witnesses, they say.'

'So these vermin will get away with it?' Grace leaned forward; Lotte could feel her presence at her shoulder. She kept her eyes on the hills.

'It's the way of the world I'm afraid. Get away with murder. Almost.'

'Wicked people,' said Grace.

'I'm sorry,' said Sam. 'He was a lovely pianist.'

'Yes,' said Lotte.

'He might be able to continue,' said Sam. The van pulled over and let them past. Sam waved cheerfully out of the open window.

'Just dreadful,' said Grace.

'We'll be there shortly.' Sam was egging the car on again. 'I know it's a shock, Lotte. News like that. But you can have tea. Or water. When we get there.'

'Does he have family?' Grace was almost between them, leaning forward between the front seats.

'In Glasgow. Mrs Wilson says they want to take him home soon as they can. So that must be the facts. She's never mistaken.' Sam shook his head: 'Terrible, terrible.'

To Lotte it was like listening to a drama on the wireless. The voices talking of imaginary events. Far away problems. She felt no need to participate.

'Are you alright? Shall I stop?' Sam asked.

Grace squeezed her arm in a new way – a prompt. You're on now, Lotte. Your turn.

'I'm fine. I'm fine,' she said. It was her new voice. Before last night and after. Two worlds.

'We've plenty time.'

'No. I'm fine. Just a shock.'

'Can't walk the streets in safety.' Sam licked his lips. 'It always comes back to drink.'

'Not like the Methodist way,' said Grace. It was almost a tease. A way back to a cheerful day out.

'Religion isn't all superstition,' Sam said. 'There are practical things in there too.' Sam the pragmatic, Sam the sensible. Lotte felt a surge of affection for him. And sadness for everything that sat in the car beside them.

'Well, I hope they get them anyway,' said Grace, with feeling.

'Me, too,' said Sam. 'Trading is tough enough without people being attacked in the street.'

Vennel, thought Lotte, not street. But she kept that and everything else within her tightly buttoned coat. Grace shuffled back into the bench seat in the rear. Lily was looking out the side window.

'Look,' said Grace. 'Lambs.'

The Journal of Dr John Fergusson

Friday 21st April 1933

The Wolseley was near the front of Gibson's house. I parked a distance away where the drive started to curve back out towards the gates. I didn't want to make it easier for Sneddon to engage me when we were leaving, after I'd made my stand. There was no one in the entrance hall. Stags heads glared down at me, reproachfully. The game book lay open on a circular table in the centre of the hall. Sneddon had already written his name in it, but his was the only one under the date. Gibson ancestors frowned from the stairway. Unlucky stags and lucky great-uncles in Indian robes apart and although I'd been brought up in a four roomed cottage, I felt quite at home here. This was a more comfortable version of the entrance to the Asylum. A grand building that was designed to impress or perhaps intimidate.

I followed the rumble of masculine voices through the hallway and down a short flight of stairs. I passed the kitchens: a smell of meat, flashes of copper, iron-work and white tiles. Sneddon and another man in tweeds were in the meat still. They were silhouetted against the light that came in the open back door, the courtyard beyond.

'Dr Fergusson, I presume.' Sneddon liked to deploy his sarcasm against me in front of an audience. Even an audience of one.

'Alan,' I said. We weren't at work now. 'We did say two o'clock, didn't we?'

'And you are bang on time as per. I am the early one. Couldn't stand the house any longer. You know what it's like with the boys home from school.'

He knew that I was a very long way from my own boys.

'I can imagine.'

'This is Strang, the keeper.' He waved towards the man at his side.

'You haven't been here long then?' I shook Strang by the hand and moved round the room slightly to get a better look at him. His eyes were shaded by his cap but he had the cautious air of a proud man who had spent a life under the direction of capricious masters. His voice was soft, Highland, precise.

'I've been employed by Mr Gibson for two months only.' When he moved forward into the light I noticed a familiar look about his eyes. 'I was formerly with Lord Brougham at Comrie.'

'Mr Strang was telling me his brother is none other than our Mr Strang.'

Of course. I nodded again. 'Your brother is a key part of our work. The farm is at the centre of the community.'

Mr Strang's face was still shadowed. 'He speaks well of the place. He was unsure…' There was a brief hesitation, 'initially. But now would work nowhere else.'

'Delighted to hear it,' I said.

'You have brought a weapon?' Sneddon's gun bag was propped against a chair near the back door. His game bag hung on the back.

'Yes,' I said. 'I left it in the car until I knew where we might be shooting.'

'Good forward planning, as always. Strang here has plans for us, though. Better tell Dr Fergusson too.'

Strang turned his cap round and round in his hands as he spoke.

'I thought that seeing as there is little time this afternoon, and you have no dogs, that you could walk up the inner fields, then up the hill to the Home Wood and back to the house along the Ban Burn. You've both shot here before I believe?'

'Often,' said Sneddon. 'Old hands. What do you have for us?'

'Thin, as you know, at this time. But you should be able to put up some partridge, there will be the stray pheasant and hare.'

'And the woods?'

'Plenty of pigeon.'

'And crow?' said Sneddon.

'Certainly. We're keen to thin them out during lambing. The farmers are grateful. If you can be bothered.'

'We're not above crow, are we?' He raised an eyebrow.

'I'll get my gun,' I said, 'if we are going to walk from the yard here.'

By the time I returned, Sneddon had his gun broken across his arm. The brass heads of the cartridges nestled snugly in the barrels.

'I'll be with you shortly,' said Strang.

'That won't be necessary,' said Sneddon. 'We know the land here well and Dr Fergusson and I use these afternoons for some informal business discussions.'

Strang looked perturbed. This wasn't the usual routine. Before he could say anything, Sneddon cut across him: 'Patients. Confidential. You understand?'

'As you wish,' said Strang. 'Sir.'

I was ready now. I noticed Sneddon had his older shotgun.

'No Holland and Holland today?'

'Ah. No. Keep that for special occasions. This is just a bit of rough shooting today. Over hill and dale, bumping through hedges and over walls. Not the place for the best weapon.'

At that Strang drew himself up a little. 'Gentlemen. Before you leave. And I know you are experienced shots, but I would ask you to take particular care, the ground is wet. And the going rough.'

I had seen Sneddon tear a strip off staff before. I tensed.

'I think you will find, Mr Strang, that my colleague and I have handled the odd rough shoot before. We were no strangers to heavier weapons than these in France.' He moved his arm so that the barrel of the broken gun came up to the general region of Strang's kneecap. But the keeper held his ground.

'I am aware of that, and I, too, served overseas,' he said. 'But an unfortunate event in my former employ showed that even the most experienced shot can have a moment of inattention. Sir.'

I waited for Sneddon to spoil the afternoon entirely. And spike my plan. But he smiled.

'Don't you worry Mr Strang. You won't have to report the loss of valuable customers.' He patted Strang on the arm as he made his way towards the door.

'Besides, we are physicians, we can patch the other up if the worst happens. Come along Dr Fergusson, the afternoon's wasting.'

He marched out. I caught Strang's eye. We nodded. I followed Sneddon. Our boots rang in the enclosed yard and then we were out under the ornate archway and clock and on a gravel roadway.

'Bolshie bastard,' said Sneddon. 'Two Strangs. What a coincidence.' He picked up the pace.

'Both in rural businesses, it's not so unusual,' I said.

We walked on, there was a gate ahead into the field, a stand of Scots pines shaded the road and the gate. The crowns of the trees were noisy, a crow city high above. Beyond the jumble of nests several crows hung in the breeze like black broken umbrellas.

'Let's ruin their day,' said Sneddon. He brought the stock of his gun up to close the breach, put the gun to his shoulder so it was pointing vertically and pulled the triggers so closely together that it was like a single blast. Twigs dropped through branches, a tattered, bloodied crow dropped heavily into bracken, another bird wheeled unsteadily until one wing stopped working and it fell away out of sight. Feathers and slimy egg fragments continued to fall as Sneddon broke the gun and dropped in two fresh cartridges.

'Your turn.'

I shook my head. Sneddon took a few steps into the group of trees, raised the weapon and let fly with both barrels again. There was more debris but no birds this time except for two mangled fledglings. They landed on the ground together, twitching. Sneddon stepped forward and brought his boot down on them. The gunpower smell lingered in the shelter of the trees.

'Good turn for Mr Gibson's neighbours. Don't you want a blast?'

I shook my head.

'Not sporting enough for you? Might be all we get today.' He didn't break his gun, but propped it against a pine. He reached into his checked tweed and pulled out his flask. He held it out to me, gripping it by the heavy stopper.

'Special reserve.'

I pointed towards the tree. 'Break the gun?'

He kept the flask thrust in my direction. 'I've shot both barrels, what do you think will happen?' There was the old sneer at Sneddon's mouth. At the corner of his lips. I took the flask. It was heavy, solid. I unscrewed and took a draw. Handed it back.

'Did you have much business to attend to?'

I wasn't surprised that he knew. But I liked the fact he was interested.

'I was meeting Miss Brown.'

We opened the gate and walked into the field. The metallic clicks as we closed the breeches of both shotguns were alien against the cries of the birds, the wind through the fresh leaves. Away from the trees there was more light. Wind blew patterns through the early growth grass. There was a smell of sap underfoot. Downwind the black dots of crows circled. Waiting.

'In her garden office,' I said.

'Smoking that ghastly pipe, I suppose?'

We had separated, walking ten feet or so apart.

'I'm glad of the fresh air,' I said into the wind.

'Dreadful affectation. Like an old time RSM. Cultured eccentricity.'

'Her work is invaluable.'

'We will review that against the evidence. She's not really a Miss you know.'

'She's unconventional.'

'No, not that aspect. She's been married.'

'Really?'

'During the war. Unsuitable type. Parents disowned her. Not a penny. Then he went down at Jutland. She had to come crawling back to her brother and he gave her a servant room on condition she never speak of it.'

'And she told you?'

'No. But I have my sources.'

'She makes a difference to the patients. She and the garden.'

'The garden will stay,' he said. 'But she will have to go. The garden men hate her and I'm afraid she will corrupt the nurses, too.'

'The gardeners did little or nothing for years, so I'm not surprised they are upset. And as for the nurses, I can't see the danger.'

'That's because you can be a little blind, John. Myopic. Where ladies are concerned.'

I let this drift past me on the stiff breeze. Too early, too early. We had reached the brow of the field. The horizon had become a viewpoint. The slope dropped away to a stone wall, another field beyond, a dark conifer plantation and beyond the blue smudge of hills under bruised clouds that went all the way to the Atlantic.

I hadn't risen to the fly he had cast for me. He went on.

'MacKenzie, too. I've spoken to Baird in Edinburgh. Told him we had an excellent prospect for promotion. Just the sort of ambitious doctor he is looking for. She's not a team player.'

Had she responded to the Italian paper? Had she asked too many questions?

'She's very insightful in her diagnoses.'

'She's not one of us, John.' He had to bark now the wind had whipped up. 'Not looking to the future. No interest in what we might be able to do if we escape from the old ways.'

I said, 'We can build on the old ways, too.'

A pheasant broke from a clump of stones and dead bracken, its bulk at odds with its speed. It rose to head height and turned straight back into the wind towards us. Sneddon put the gun to his shoulder and with the same movement brought the barrel round until I was looking straight into the twin black voids. I closed my eyes but I still saw the flash, felt the concussion. The pellets flew over my head.

'Sorry, old man,' said Sneddon. 'Lucky you've been closer to fire before.'

I said nothing. He walked back to where the pheasant had fallen. Wings outstretched, quivering. Sneddon bent over it, then walked back to me.

'Should have let it go,' he said. 'No eating there. I'll leave it for the foxes.'

We walked on, down the slope. The light seemed to fade with every step we took towards the lower ground.

'Your business with Miss Brown wouldn't have been about your new patient, would it?'

'In fact, it was.' I stepped around a clump of thistles, taking me a pace or two further away from Sneddon. 'She has had a number of very fruitful conversations with Miss Brown, and myself. I think we will be able to make good progress and have her back with her family soon.'

Sneddon stared down the field towards the trees.

'Back to her family. That's the way, isn't it? A bit of a chat, a bit of Dr Freud's folk-tales and all will be well.'

'She's not going to be part of your project.'

We were approaching the wall. The ground was rougher where beasts had churned the mud between the tufts of grass. There was no gate here, or stile. I broke my gun and handed it to Sneddon. He put it over his shoulder.

'She's perfect. As you well know.' His voice was even. A committee meeting voice. 'Intelligent, articulate. Not like the others. In good health too, according to Cunninghame's report. You've had time to...' He hesitated. My back was against the dyke. He loomed large, the wide field behind. 'Chat.' He smiled.

'No,' I said and scrambled over the wall. It was loose and mossy, but I was over. I wiped my hands on the seat of my trousers.

'I know how you enjoy your chats,' he said. 'With your female patients.'

'No,' I said again. We faced each other over the stone wall. 'Private patients have lawyers. Have you thought about that?'

He was still smiling, his hand patting the top of the wall. 'Lawyers don't understand what goes on in science, behind our walls. She will be able to report back from inside the experiment, from the shock of the chemicals.' His smile abruptly stopped. 'You read the Italians' paper. And you will help me. Out of gratitude.'

He placed my broken gun over the top of the wall and began to climb.

'Sneddon,' I said. He was half over the wall, both feet on the field side, balanced, one hand on the stone, the other holding his shotgun. 'Your gun.'

He looked down at it as if he hadn't noticed. Then he looked back at me.

'My word,' he said. 'Basic error.'

He grasped the barrels, swung the loaded, closed weapon on to his shoulder as if it were a spade, put a foot on the top of the wall and jumped down hard beside me. So close he bumped against me.

'There,' he said. 'No harm done.'

We stood there for a second, between two fields.

'Shall we?' He pointed with his shotgun, and we stared across the grass. Wet underfoot. 'All that business at Rainhill. I wasn't going to let an old comrade. An old student comrade, face a scandal.'

'There was no scandal.' I closed the breech of my gun. 'Only gossip. Unsubstantiated.'

'Apart from my notes.'

'Your notes?'

'Dr Byrne asked me to speak to her. He thought a third party, objective opinion would be helpful. I interviewed her. Took all the details down. In confidence. Don't pretend you don't know this, John.'

'Breaking patient confidences would be almost as bad as breaking our first rule. No harm. Remember? And who knows how a professional misconduct hearing might look at this?' I said.

We walked on. I would bide my time.

'Naturally,' he said, 'I wouldn't say a word in breach of confidence. Just make sure she was asked back in for an interview that would go on the record.'

We were across the barren field. A stile and the woods beyond. This was the place.

'That would be a challenge even for you. She took her life last week.'

Sneddon stopped. 'You did harm there, Doctor. And you know it.' He looked genuinely affronted, and not just thwarted. 'Perhaps the war, and everything else, has taken its toll.'

'Since we are speaking frankly, away from work,' I said, 'I should let you know that I have kept a detailed record of all your experiments. And I'll take them to the College.'

He slowly and precisely broke his shotgun. Took the live cartridge out and placed it in his belt.

'You'd kill your career just to finish me?'

'To stop you.' I tried not to sound too sanctimonious, I was enjoying the look in his eyes. A little of the fear I had seen in the patients' eyes as the drugs took hold. A little of the anxiety I felt at being complicit.

'Is this a trade?'

'Let the Raymond woman go home.'

'So you can fuck her?'

A deep flare of anger, like the flash from his shotgun through my closed eyelids.

'I will see she's safe.'

'Safe?' he barked, somewhere between a cough and laugh.

'It won't happen.'

'It will,' he said. 'Because it's not just me who knows all about drugs is it?' He reached into his jacket. Took the flask out, unscrewed the top and took a long pull. He didn't offer me. 'I had a patient once. Very difficult case. Unsuccessful. Unsurprisingly. He was one of the very few soldiers ever reprieved on the morning of execution.' He looked round the field. Far away the crows were returning to the site of the massacre. 'Imagine, the long wakeful night and then in the morning the King's pardon. Devastated him.'

The crows were tiny. Black ticks in the sky. But their sound carried clearly across the distance. I could smell the whisky from Sneddon.

'But that wasn't the most interesting thing we talked of. He had been sent to the guardhouse by truck from a few miles down the line. When they put him in a room, there was another soldier there. Waiting to meet the same firing squad. Different regiment. Strange one, my patient said. Gibbering like an ape. Worse and worse. Climbing the walls. My man told me that when he did get a word or two of sense from him, he told him the medic had given him something to calm him down. Seemed to have the opposite effect.'

I knew where this was going. I had plenty of time over the years to prepare how I might respond.

Sneddon went on: 'Then he said the other bloke went funny. Very funny, breathing hard and fast and not responding when spoken to and then.' Sneddon clicked his fingers. 'Sparked out. Still breathing fast till he stopped breathing at all. Blue in the face. That's what my patient told me.' Sneddon said all this in a casual conversational way. He might have been telling me the summary of the nutritional guidelines paper.

'My man then went a bit wild himself. Bashing on the door, screaming. He wasn't worried about being blamed for it. Nothing to lose. But spending your last night in a room with a corpse. Not a fun night out. Or in.' Sneddon took another pull on his flask. It was late now; the pale sky was still bright, but we were deep in shadow near the trees. There was a chill in the air.

'Anyway. My man had more to worry about than how he ended up with a stiff. "I imagine he was killed by fright," is what he said.' Sneddon drank again. 'But you know all this Fergusson, don't you? I was intrigued. I sniffed around. It is the sort of thing officers note when supervising a firing squad. No target. A dead man in the guardhouse. They were all in different sectors, of course. And not that many. We weren't butchers, despite what the bleeding hearts still say. But strangely, you always seemed to be in the vicinity.'

I looked at the ground. Let him talk. I was making my plans.

'There was plenty more to worry about, wasn't there? Who cared about some men dying of fright? Or adrenaline shock. Better than some opiate. That would have been suspicious. Condemned men don't sleep unto death. They don't sleep at all. Cowards in a blue funk? That's why they were there in the first place.' He looked away from me, across to the far away hills, still in light. 'Not exactly the Hippocratic oath though, is it?'

When all seems lost there is a strange calm that falls on you. I felt the same way when Emily confronted me. If it is over, it's over.

'I betrayed that oath when I certified men fit to stand trial. Fit to be killed. I was making it easier.'

'Oh John, of course. No one is more sympathetic than I am, but it remains that we can't have doctors killing people.'

'Like that girl last week? And the others?'

'Research is inexact. A tribunal of my peers will understand that.' He tipped the flask back. It was finished. 'Sorry old chap. Nothing left.'

He went over the stile. Jumped down with his gun in his hand, his boots crunching on the stones of the pathway through the woods. He didn't pause, but over his shoulder he said, 'I'll send a nurse for her at 11am. I expect you to assist.'

I realised then why I hated him so much. Not for what he knew about my past, but what he knew about me.

I brought the shotgun to my shoulder and clicked the safety. In the hush of the early dusk he heard it plainly and stopped but didn't turn round. He said, 'A tragic accident crossing the stile. My weeping children and wife. Such a glittering career brought short, and the talented but underachieving depute bereft. But you won't.'

With that he walked on into the twilight. And I brought the shotgun down, broke it and put the two cartridges back in my belt. I sat on the stile for a while. I watched the hills in the distance grow dark.

I passed few vehicles on the way home. On the darker stretches I wondered what it would be like to suddenly find a well-dressed woman walking the verge. How did other late-night travellers respond? The terrible dangers that a woman alone faced. Night walking was something I could no longer do. As a child in the country, I walked dark lanes all the time. A rush through the trees caused a physical reaction, the heart beating faster, skin on edge, of course. But back then, there it was only the wind. A faint gleam under roadside bushes was only the phosphorescence of some fungus. But I now knew that a rushing in the leaves was just like the pressure waves from a shell. A faint gleam– a gas canister beginning its work.

I concentrated on Lotte as I drove. I had failed her. The past had conspired against the future, as it always does. But

I would not let her down. She was driven out onto the dark roads by her own past. Outside the Asylum I could cure her. As I would have done with Hazel. That was gone now. But I could still help Lotte.

While the striped signposts loomed and slipped behind me, I saw visions of Sneddon's head vaporising in the twilight under the trees. Would I have got away with it? Of course, unless Strang had been close by. It was a secluded spot. But Sneddon was right. I couldn't have done it. Perhaps that's why I hated him so much. Because he had such knowledge of my weaknesses. All of them.

By the time I turned into the farm-track to the cottage my hands were tight at the top of the steering wheel. I switched off and listened to the stillness, the night noises. I sat in the dark as if to test myself. Then hurried indoors. Scrabbled for the switch. I hadn't expected to be this late. I would have left a light burning.

I realised I had hardly eaten all day. In the pantry there were three eggs and a piece of bread. I cut the bread, lit the grill and made toast while I put water in a pot to poach the eggs. I sat listening to the gas hiss, sniffed the faint smell of death that lighting the stove always created. I reached into my jacket, it was too cold in the house to take it off. I thought about a glass for a second but unscrewed the top and started to drink from the flask. It burned at my mouth and throat, but I drank and drank until there was only air. I gasped, inhaled the petrol reek. My sinuses singed.

When I had eaten, I settled at the table with a tumbler full of whisky and wrote all this down. As fresh and accurate a record as I could manage. I had no leverage on Sneddon. Never had. I couldn't get Lotte out of the Asylum. But I wasn't going to let her fall into the hands of Sneddon and his syringe.

9.

LOTTE

Thursday 3rd April 1920

'This?' said Peter.

Lotte took a step back. The dark blue scarf with diagonal red flashes was wound round his neck and the lower part of his face. With the round dark glasses only part of one cheek and the bridge of his nose was visible.

'Yes,' she said. 'Perfect.' She reached behind his neck and pushed a safety pin through the folds of silk cloth then through his collar to hold everything in place.

'It's not too bright? It doesn't draw attention?'

'No. And it's your regimental scarf. Your colours. You should wear it.' She put a hand on each of his arms and gently guided him back. The regimental colours were the only trace of his military life visible anywhere in the house. There was no trace of any of the letters. The first brusque postcard – Wounded in Action – the other two typed options, *Killed in Action, Missing in Action*, scored through in pencil. They'd gathered round the little buff oblong and agreed that it was the least worst of the options. It was followed by the letter from his officer, vague and foreboding. Margaret had carried around for weeks, folding and unfolding, conjuring hope from the space between the words. And then, long after Peter had been delivered, broken, to the railway station, his medals had arrived, the neat box, unopened at the back of a kitchen drawer.

'What's it like. Out. I heard wind all night.'

'Windy, dry, cool.'

'Bright?'

'Overcast.'

'Good,' he said. 'I'm less visible then. Less frightening.'

'No one is frightened.'

'Dogs? Small children?'

She adjusted the scarf.

'They see a hero.' They both almost laughed. It was one of their few jokes.

She looked round the room for his shoes. His drawings, his posters, his huge paintings based on Chinese figures were all still there. And his misty landscapes. He didn't paint now, but his current work sat on the dressing table, wrapped in a kitchen cloth. It was a clay model – a foot, a boot, lodged in waves of mud, two hands grasping, pulling – hands and leg all broken off abruptly. No one liked to say, but Peter's new work was much more dramatic and arresting than the old. Small knives and a spoon lay on the surface. There was a smell of still air and the half-closed curtains deepened the gloom in the corners of the room.

She found the shoes under the bed, rubbed her hands over the toes.

'You're not out enough,' she said. 'Stoor on your shoes.'

'I can't go with anyone else. I am not prepared to be

steered around by my mother or the aunts. I haven't given up that much.'

She tied the laces.

'You have no reason to hide.' She stood and took his jacket from the back of the door. 'I will come as often as you want me to. You can be out as often as you want.'

'You've got the shop.' He stood. 'And you've got Sam. Newlyweds. I'm sure you have better things to do'

'I promised,' she said. 'And it's no hardship.'

'She lied.'

'It really, really isn't.' She guided one arm then the next into his jacket. He felt for the buttons and did up two, pulled it down.

'How do I look? Escaped lunatic? Experiment gone wrong?'

'War hero,' she said.

She put his stick in her left hand. She had bought it. Silver band, black Malacca. A work of art. She went to Glasgow for it. Tried dozens, looking for one that would look good and feel interesting under his hands.

She pointed him out into the hallway.

'Straight on.'

'Yes. I get this bit.' His stick tapped the door. 'Jailer,' he said. 'The keys.'

The door was always locked. Had they discussed it? Not really. It was just agreed in the way that the aunts often did. If there was no dissent, then it happened. The dissent was all Peter's. And the response was always that he could be independent later, but currently he had to learn. Had to be accompanied, on the rare days when he could face it.

Lotte took the keys from her bag and unlocked the door. Peter stepped out onto the landing.

'Freedom,' he said.

Lotte stood on the edge of the silent flat for a moment. The aunts were all at the shop with Sam. She imagined how this stillness felt for Peter. Day after day. His hands in the clay. A long emptiness.

'Right,' she said. She put his hand on the banister. Their landing was the last. She had always, instinctively, taken the inside of the stairs. The black well, down four flights to the black and white tiles. He felt along, fingers over the brass studs until he felt the sudden angle, curving away to the left. Once on the first step he moved down the stairs quickly. Lotte followed, always anxious where the width of the tread narrowed on the corners. His hand guided his feet anticipating landings and descents as the banister curved and swooped all the way to the ground.

'Faster every time. I should just heave a leg over and slide.'

'That's what the studs are for.'

'Not that they'd do any material damage to me.'

'Step,' she called from behind. They were almost at the street. He paused.

'Over the top,' he said, and went out on to the pavement. They turned down hill, down toward town. People here were neighbours. They nodded silent greetings, forgetting, or preferring to forget, that only Lotte could see them. Others spoke. But from everyone, Lotte could pick up a note of pity and gratitude. Not mine, not me. We all have bad luck, but not that. We all suffered, but not that way.

'Who was that?' he would say when he thought they were out of range. As he never left the flat without covering up, the extent of his injuries was a matter of legend in the street. It wasn't something his mother or the aunts were prepared to discuss with neighbours or customers, so the imagined wounds were presumably graphic. But no matter, the vital detail was the loss of sight. 'And him with such promise.' They said, out of hearing. Within hearing some called him war hero. But he was unimpressed:

'Tragic work-shy war hero. Seems about right. But I was good at it. What I did. Blowing people up.'

But that was on positive days. On other days he would stay in his room when they were all at home. Lotte would visit in the evenings. The atmosphere round the kitchen table crushed by the firmly shut door across the passage. By his absolute silence. With Lotte and Marguerite both married, the three aunts were his keepers, their kindness and patience unlimited. Perhaps that was the problem. They absorbed his rages. Lotte would take the rubbish downstairs and hear the clatter of broken crockery and the rattle of smashed glasses as she emptied into the dustbins. She found Jessie carefully gluing two halves of a kitchen cupboard door together.

'Lucky it's easy to fix,' she said, squinting down at the join through her round glasses. 'Good solid wood.' Which was also a way of noting the force required to split it neatly down the centre.

'Let's not go down the street today,' Peter said.

'Shall we cut through to the Back Walk?'

'The Snowden. The cemetery.'

Through the gates, they were immediately surrounded by birdsong. Pale angels stood around under the drooping trees. There was a strong smell of earth.

'Ah, the reek of mortality.'

Lotte had his arm, although the smooth gravel paths were kind to him. She squeezed hard. 'Stop it,' she said.

'Why? The one thing I can say I have gained from the last

few years. The only thing. You're not afraid of this anymore.'
He waved his stick at the trees and the headstones.

A gardener swung his scythe in a steady rhythm, hacking
at long grass in the darkness under a tree.

'What's that?'

'It's a gardener cutting weeds.'

'Appropriate background sounds. A feast for the senses
here. As it should be.'

The man nodded at them out of the gloom. He squinted
at Peter and touched his cap.

'Would the Back Walk not be better?'

'It's fun to try to imagine the view again, but this suits me
here.'

'You tell me where you want to go, and I will take you
there.' Lotte steered him between great Victorian sarcophagi,
the solid furniture of death.

'That's the trouble, isn't it?' said Peter. He pulled a round
tin of cigarettes from his jacket pocket. He stopped, hung
the stick on his arm and felt for matches. She helped him to
adjust the scarf, created a slit between the cloth where his
mouth was. He held the cigarette in place with his fingers as
she lit and shielded the match.

He said, 'I need to get out here on my own. Make my
own mistakes. Not be led.'

'We don't want you to come to harm.'

'Harm? What other harm do you think I might come
to?'

'There's not much point in making things worse for
yourself. A broken leg wouldn't cheer you up.'

'How much do I have to lose?'

'Steps.' Three stone steps led upwards. He felt forward
with his stick, tapped the stone, then swung it back and

forward against the bottom step so hard that Lotte saw the stick flex, but not split.

She gripped his arm.

'Hoy,' she said, 'I went all the way to Glasgow for that and I won't tell you how much it cost.'

He was shaking.

'Shall we go back?'

'Please give me the key. One day. Just let me try this myself.'

'I can't.'

'You must.'

'No.'

'What do you all think will happen?'

Falling in the street wasn't their worry. Of course not. There were a hundred people who would take him home. His black moods were what worried them most.

'You all think that I'll sniff my way to the water, don't you?' She was leading him back through the township of the dead, back to the iron gates. 'All downhill, I'd find it eventually. Or listen for the trains, find the track. Get my head down on the lines so I can hear it coming?'

'Stop it.'

'Don't you think if I was going to do it, I'd have found a way by now? All the long days locked up.'

'You're not locked up. There's the Disabled Servicemen's club. Wingard's offered you a job.'

'Counting handbills? I think that would definitely finish me off.'

Lotte thought of the way that they had scoured the flat for pulley-ropes, drawstrings of blinds, knives, belts, balls of string. Short of someone being there every day, and they did try between them all to provide company, there was no way of being completely sure. But they wanted the comfort of having done their best. They had consulted physicians, expensively. All they had been offered was drugs to restrain, or the asylum. They shuddered at the last option. Better to risk everything than that.

'I'll speak to your mother, my mother. We can all speak about it.'

'No that will go round and round the garden again.'

'I can't.'

'No, you *won't.*' He stopped in the gravel. It was cool now. She smelled the tobacco, his scarf was loosening as he became more agitated, she glimpsed raw flesh and the smooth pink of the burn-tissue in the gaps between the scarf around his mouth. 'You promised me.'

'I promised to look after you. And I will.'

'Exactly that,' he said. 'And I'm asking you to help.'

'Let's all talk about it. Tonight.'

He walked away from her, across the wet grass, his head cocked, as if he were sniffing the air. There was a new grave, no headstone, but with a rectangle of turf a different shade from the rest, with a border of raw, excess earth. He knelt, sniffed again, felt along the grass till he reached the soil. Both hands delved. He pulled two fistfuls out, squeezed until the dark mud oozed between his fingers. With both hands he collected a heaped scoop of dirt, and methodically, thoroughly washed his hands in it, rubbing the soil into the palms, between his fingers, the backs, his wrists up inside his sleeves.

Lotte looked round. There was no sign of the gardener. She let Peter's ritual continue. Eventually she came up behind him and put a hand on his shoulder. He kept rubbing, soil dropping away, his pale skin showing through – the lines and creases of his hands like black roads through the fields.

'No one can understand this,' he said.

'Tell me.' She guided him to a bench. It looked out to the Ochils, the Wallace Monument, the sweep of the hills away to the Firth.

'My drawings were the best – angles, perspective, distance – easy for me. Usually, they sent an officer to do the spotting, identify the targets, the lads waiting for a signal, miles back. You were a bit exposed, it's true, but, being alone for a few hours, even if alone in hell, was almost a gift, so I often volunteered.'

'You told me –'

'I know, never volunteer. But there was a sort of peace out there in the dugout. But,' he shrugged deeper into his cowl, 'you had to get there first. On your belly. If it was only the mud, that would have been fine. You could wash it away, watch it darkening the water in a bucket. There was rarely anything organic that you could recognise – bones, teeth, maybe.'

Lotte winced. He'd never spoken with this intensity before. He spoke of the war as if it was a vague, humourless joke.

'There was an oily, greasy texture to the soil, organic, meaty, and a smell that stayed with you for days. Years. That night, I was looking for the wire. The densest tangles were like a bramble forest out of a storybook. It got thrown about by the high explosive, welded by the heat, torn, and then ripped again by shrapnel. In this sector, the wire had been left in peace for half a year. It was time to open it up. I crawled out through the stench and filth. With only my sketchpad, compass and Very pistol.'

'Just a pistol?' she said.

'A flare gun,' he said. 'The last resort, if things get desperate, I could still have done my duty by bringing down mayhem. A gun to my own head.' He was laughing, quietly.

'You don't see much out there at night, on your knees. All the features are gone, just the rolling mud at eye-level. I felt the ground sloping away under my hands. It might have been a grassy meadow full of wildflowers, once.'

Lotte faced the old hills, the Monument, the river, and tried to imagine.

'And then someone put a flare up. I was caught out in the light as if they'd turned a stone over. So, I wriggled on, like an insect, until I was safe under the shadow of the black wire. As I crawled down, I could tell I was in an old trench. As it deepened, I stood up, I had to put my hands out onto each wall. Feel my way. It was that dark.'

Peter seemed to have shrunk further into his scarves, into his memory.

'I felt along the wet walls until my hand went into a void. And when another hand grabbed it, I didn't even jump. The warmth of that hand in that horrible tunnel with its barbed roof was almost welcome. It didn't feel like a threat. Not even when I had a gun in my back. What was the worst that could happen? His voice wasn't continental, but he wasn't British either.

'After a while, we came to a fire, a tiny blue flame deep in the trench. First one, then more. And new smells, paraffin, food, life. Faces over the stoves. It was like all the unit huddles I'd ever come across. No one asked me who I was. No one was interested. It was ayeways like that. Frightened, tired men. If you weren't an immediate threat they didn't care.'

This was Peter, almost like the old, pre-war days. Telling a story.

'But what a gang that was. French uniforms with Prussian helmets. Boys with yokel Devon accents wearing field-grey jackets. White skins and dark skins, a gathering of all the clans, out there under that thick roof of wire. We'd heard tales, but no one believed it.'

'Deserters?' Lotte tried to imagine the small gas fires, the stranded souls.

'You could call them that. I gave them my last smokes, they gave me their booze.'

'Whisky?' She'd always loved this. Being part of his story-telling. Asking the question at the right moment. Picking up a strand and running off with it, so they both became the tale.

'Petrol more like. But I drank it down. You can't be unsociable.' Peter started to laugh. 'I was sociable all right.'

'You weren't tempted to stay?'

'They'd opted out. Given up on the madness. Both sides. Living out there, scavenging from the bodies. Hiding under the thickest section of wire. Friendly as you like.'

'But you didn't stay.'

'Oh no. And all the time I was sitting there, sipping their schnapps or tank fuel or whatever it was, I was thinking that this was the perfect place for a barrage. That our shells would do the most damage here. The best place to cut the line. So, I told them, thanks for the drink, but I had to go. They weren't quite so friendly then. I heard the rifles cocking in the dark all up the trench.'

Lotte held his arm. She could feel a tremor, a ripple of recalled fear and excitement. 'Oh Peter.' There wasn't much else to say. 'But you hadn't a gun.'

'Not really. But a flare shot at head height down a trench took their minds off me for a bit. I ran for it, back the way I'd come. By the time I was out in the mud the Hun trenches had opened up. There was machine gun fire, mortars, the whole fireworks. I couldn't lie down and be caught by the deserters, so I let loose the only other flare I had, the red one.

It was still hanging up there, right above that awful trench when our boys let a barrage drop.'

Sun was beginning to glitter on the wet landscape, the Ochils seemed to have come closer in the brightness.

'They were on song that night. As I got up to run I saw the flashes all along that line. Saw them all blown up through the wire – like cheese wire – cutting them into bits.' He hesitated there, the rhythm faltering now. 'But there's always a stray one. Just my luck it was right in front of me. The stretchers got to me at dusk the next day. Not that I could tell.'

The excitement in his voice was gone now. The tremor Lotte could feel in his arm had gone.

'And I see them still, hear their squeals too,' he said. 'All the time. Not just at night. The moment I don't think of anything else. Sometimes even when I'm making things, it's there. An endless film, playing.' He raised his dirty hand to his facecloth. 'It's worse than this. Much.'

'Peter, let me help.'

'How? It's not for you to help. You can't stop the film playing in the dark.' His hands were still rubbing. 'This soil is so clean.'

'People understand now,' said Lotte. 'The effect of the things you've seen. You can get better.'

'That's the thing. I've seen worse. Stuff I'd never tell you. And I've fired flares that brought down shelling that killed many more. On our own lads too – when we had to.' He stood now, pushing down on his stick. Stumbling over his own feet, he let her help him get his balance.

'Let's get back.'

He made no move. 'They were right. Braver than the rest of us. They'd found another way. And I put an end to it. Finished the hope.'

'They tried to kill you.'

'They'd no choice. It wasn't their fault I found them.'

'You couldn't stay.'

'No, I couldn't. I'm not sure why, but I couldn't.'

He shrugged her arm away and set off down the path, swinging his stick like a sabre. When the path curved left, he tripped on the neat verge and fell heavily on the wet grass. He made no attempt to cushion the fall with his hands.

When Lotte got to him his body throbbed and twitched with huge shuddering sobs.

The Journal of Dr John Fergusson

Saturday 22nd April 1933

'Doctor Fergusson. The very man. Assemble in my office in fifteen.'

I was caught out in the open, He stood, checked tweed suit, both thumbs in waistcoat pockets, his gold chain a double arc like a suspension bridge. I felt in my pocket for Lotte's glove.

'Doctor Sneddon.' I half bowed. 'I am, as always, at your convenience.' I stood in front of him, full square to his stance. 'Unless we can deal with whatever matter you have in mind right here.'

'Doctor,' he said, with that awful smirk. 'Come, come. Where are your professional ethics? What example would that be to set for our nursing colleagues? Discussing our patients in open outcry?'

'Upstanding professionals like ourselves?'

'What would Professor Deacon say?'

'He trained us like priests.'

'Tougher than priests.' Sneddon rocked back now on his heels. Teeth showing. 'Ten minutes, Doctor Fergusson.' He turned away.

'Please go through, Doctor,' said Mrs Nicholson.

Sneddon was standing over at the window. The lawns were a fresh green that was almost yellow. It was a colour brighter than you would expect from the weak sun. It would have been cheering had it not framed Sneddon's immovable bulk.

'You got home last night?' He went up on his toes. 'I mean you got home unscathed. I wasn't suggesting you had spent the night in your car.'

I said nothing. How was he going to play this? Directly or waste our limited time on this earth by going round the byways.

'Disappointing day. The brothers Strang are not an inspiring bunch.' He rocked again on his feet. 'Or competent even. Two crows and a pigmy pheasant do not a shoot make. Even at this time of the year.'

I was determined to force him out from cover. I said nothing but sat on the visitor's chair. He seemed equally determined not to have to look at me. He stared off towards the trees.

'Useful though, don't you think? For us to talk. Properly.'

I made a non-committal noise.

'Glad you're still with me Fergusson.' He looked over his shoulder, briefly.

'I think we sorted out the staffing issues very efficiently. Get a proper team together.'

There was a long pause that we were both quite comfortable with. Finally, I said: 'I'll start making arrangements. Just as you suggested.'

He turned round. Over to his desk: the files, the letter opener, his world set out there, the edges polished by his hands and elbows. He didn't sit down and I regretted having done so.

'And the other business, too. I'm glad we came to an agreement on that.'

I said, 'Did we?'

He sighed. Just a small one.

'But there is no need to go over it all again. At least I hope not.' He took the watch out of his waistcoat pocket, cupped it in his hand as if it weighed a great deal. Slipped it away again. 'It's the future, John, and you know it. She will be perfectly fine. You will be there.'

'As fine as the last one?'

He moved behind the desk now, sat down, clasped his hands in front of him as if he needed to keep them under control.

'You were there.' He paused for half a beat. 'You participated, so you know how hard we work to minimise risks.'

'I think we've established that.' I looked out the window. A party of men was walking across the far cricket pitch. Tiny figures in our huge estate. 'We've established how little choice I have.'

'Then better to take part a little more enthusiastically.'

I had no doubt that he believed it. That was the thing that made me most fearful.

'Is that everything?'

'If you could bring your patient to the usual treatment room at eleven tomorrow Thank you.'

'A nurse can do that.'

'I wish you to assist me, Doctor. And I also assumed you would like to be present. To ensure we meet all your safety criteria.'

As I closed his door behind me, Mrs Nicholson looked over her spectacles at me. A half-smile. I left her door open and made for the stairs. There was still time.

LOTTE

Monday 17ᵗʰ April 1933

They drove in silence until they got to the white hotel beside the Lake. As the car came to a halt, the keys rattled against the dashboard. Twenty keys or more, they hung there like a primitive weapon.

'I should have a set of keys, too,' Lotte said.

'More to lose,' Sam said.

'It's my shop too.'

Sam got out of the car without a word and led the way through the apparently deserted building. An older woman appeared without warning.

'We booked teas?'

The woman peered at Sam, then the two women and then Lily.

'Ah yes,' she said, as if a distant memory was now forming in her mind, perhaps something from her childhood.

'I phoned. Yesterday?' Sam sounded as if he could have come from anywhere in the country, until he got to that word – yesterday. Yester. Day. One bit of Birkenhead that gave the game away.

They were ushered through to the lounge. The cloud had thinned, and the lake reflected a pale sky. Between the lake and the sky, the islands were black, the ruins invisible among the trees. There was no one in sight. Tea and cakes were brought out. They huddled round the low table, held together by remarks about the freshness of the bread and the hue of the tea.

Lotte excused herself. She went to the toilet. It was lit by the late afternoon sun like a stage. Her dark eyes looked back from the long mirror. She adjusted her hat, tucked some stray jet-black curls underneath. She leaned in over the sink, closer to herself. She examined her face like a painting. Closer still, until she could pick the flecks of pure black in her dark brown eyes. Her pupils had narrowed in the brightness of the space. She rubbed at a frown line between her brows, ran a thumb along one brow then the other. She picked up her bag, left the toilet through the double swing doors and walked out into the car park. One more car had arrived after they had. She walked out onto the road. It was narrow, the solid girth of mature trees on both sides. Some cows stared in her direction from a field. Round a sharp bend she came to a boathouse and pier. The wood was bleached to pearl with an occasional plank of flaking black paint. Two open boats were tied to the pier. She walked onto the wood of the pier and looked into the boats. They were delicate and robust at the same time, spindly spars and seats across the breadth, coils of rope in the bottom. But their ribbed sides butted the rubber fenders of the pier like assertive animals testing a fence. The lake was almost flat calm.

'Can I help you? Madam.' The man, cap pushed back on his head, thick moustache, puffed pipe smoke into a haze around his head and shoulders. He was inside the dark of the boathouse. 'Nae trips till the start of May.'

'That's a shame.' She looked across the water. The reflections and distance made it hard to see where the shoreline of the island was. Was there a pier there too? A boathouse like this?

'Come back in a fortnight.' The bowl of the pipe glowed through the smoke. 'Bring all your friends.'

She tried to make out buildings. 'But not today?'

'No. We're not running. And too late in the day to see much anyway. I'm about to finish up and away home.'

She unclipped her bag and felt inside.

'And what's the usual fare?' she said. 'When you're running?'

'Shilling each. Sixpence bairns.'

'And for a pound?'

'You can take your whole street with you.'

'Or just me? Now?'

'It will be dark shortly, especially out on the island.'

'I don't want to be there for long.'

He puffed in his pipe. He wasn't old. Maybe in his forties. The pipe made him sage-like. She imagined he'd taken up the pipe as a young man, trying to put an end to the jokes from older boatmen.

'It doesn't seem worth it.'

Pound and shilling,' she said. 'A guinea.'

He smiled at that.

'You think we all have a price? Like beasts?'

She took a note from her bag.

'I'm a businesswoman,' she said. 'I make offers.'

He was moving now, tapping the residue from his pipe in a cascade of red pinpoints. They fell onto the darkened earth floor of the boathouse and flared for a second before going dark. He disappeared into the gloom and emerged with two long slim oars, paler than the palest wood on the boathouse or boats. He stepped down into the boat nearest to the open lake. The oars went into iron pegs and he positioned both carefully, so they lay inside the boat.

'Don't complain if you only have a few minutes ashore when you get out there.' He reached up. 'Careful, now.' She put a gloved hand in his. She noticed that every fingernail had a sharp black line underneath. 'Funeral letters,' her mother called them. He held her hand until he had guided her to the seat across the back of the boat, then swiftly slipped the ropes at both ends and with one smooth movement was seated with an oar in each hand. The blades cut into the still surface of the water. He had his back to the island and at no point made any effort to look in the direction they were going– he aimed the boat by instinct. The awkwardness of sitting facing him in such a small space was solved by both looking over each other's shoulder, she at the black smudge of the island, he at a retreating point somewhere on shore.

'Would you care for the Mary Queen of Scots story?'

She smiled. 'No thank you. I know it.'

'You're paying,' he said. 'I felt I should offer at least.'

'Thank you.' They sat in silence. Only the rhythmic sound of the oars in the water. She felt she was almost in a trance, the island growing over his shoulder. The water dripping into the still water as the blades came out. The pattern only changed when the island suddenly loomed closer; one oar at rest, the other pulling deeper, as the boat turned into a tiny bay. A short stone pier, no boathouse. Trees leaned down over the still water, the shadows made the shoreline as black as night, while the open lake seemed brighter than when they had set off. He let the boat nudge up against the pier, it rocked wildly as he stood.

'Sorry.'

He secured the boat then reached down to take her hand again. She stepped over the spars and seats; the bottom of the boat held dark pools of quivering water. She stood up onto the pier. He let her hand go. A path led into the darkness of the woods. The afternoon was fading now.

'Do you wish a quick look at the Priory before we have to get back? There isn't much light.'

'No,' she said, 'I'd like to be on my own.' For a moment she was aware of the vulnerability of her situation. Out here with a strange man in the near dark. But she felt only calm.

The boatman turned his back on her, stepped back on to the boat which rocked as he sat down on the stern seat she had just vacated. He took the pipe and his leather tobacco pouch from his pocket, set them on his lap, then looked up and said, 'As you wish madam. I will be here. Don't be more than quarter of an hour. And call if you require help. The island's small enough, I'll find you.'

She walked away from the pier, the miniature bay. The pathway was covered in last year's leaves and beech mast that crackled under her boots. The undergrowth between the trees was old growth. Bracken and grasses lay flat, bent over by rain and wind. On the trees the buds were not quite green, on the cusp of a new season. Away from the reflected light of the water it was gloomy, cool. She stumbled over roots; her toe caught on hollowed out bracken clumps.

The ruins appeared suddenly, pointed stone arches black against the fading sky. The grass and vegetation had been cut away from the remains; someone had brought a mower all this way to create small lawns around the space occupied by the building. But the stone litter and half walls still looked as if they had grown from the woods around. The bases of columns like the stumps of mighty trees. There was a deep silence here. Not even birdsong. It was easy for her to fill up the outlines sketched on the ground by these random stones with hooded monks, candles, the smell of cooking, leather on stone. A world of silence and separation from the world.

'Don't you believe it,' said Peter. He swung at the stone stump with his stick. Missed. 'I've been in the army, remember. Put a bunch of men in the one place. Seal them off from civilisation. Not a great outcome. Deceit, buggery and bullying.' He laughed. There was a smell of cigarettes.

'What happens next?' she said.

'Nothing.' He was walking away now, his back hunched over his stick. He was wearing civilian clothes – the clothes he wore at art school, a long shapeless coat, almost a cloak. 'Nothing. You did the right thing. Things will work for the best.'

'Are you sure?'

He paused on the edge of the trees, on the shadow. He turned round. There was no scarf, but she couldn't see his face.

'No.' Then he was gone.

She followed, his steps visible in the tired grass.

'Peter. You begged me for the key. What else could I do?' There was no sign of him now, but she kept walking. Walking, moving, this was the answer, this was her solution.

She was abruptly on the shoreline at the opposite side of the island from the small pier and the boat. Across the still water the hotel was doubled in the Lake, the white reflection as vivid as the real thing. Lights were on now. Two pinpoints, one upstairs and one downstairs in the room where she had been sitting. She walked to the edge of the water and stood on a low boulder. The Lake here was black under the shade of the trees. Her rippling reflection was indistinct, her dark coat hardly registered in the shadows, only her face floated pale in the water. She took off her right glove, knelt, reached down and put her fingers in the water. Icy. She felt its slight sliminess between her fingers, thought about the darkening depths here where the bed sloped away towards the hotel, the weeds, mud, hanging fish, a greater silence.

A tinkling of sound bounced across the flat expanse from the hotel. Voices. There were figures out on the lawn. There was Sam, and another dark male figure, in conversation. She couldn't make out their faces, they were turned towards each other. From behind a dark blot of bushes she saw the white speck of Lily, then Grace beside her. Grace kneeling now, the white speck became enfolded within her, so they became one dappled shape on the lawn.

The whole scene blurred. She put her wet hand back in the glove.

'What's to be done?'

'Never volunteer,' said Peter. 'Never jump.'

'Fine advice,' she said, 'from you.'

'Look where volunteering got me. Sing, play and walk.' He was behind her somewhere, in the trees. She could smell the smoke.

'And make the shop work?'

'Fuck yes. You better. They'd never forgive you.'

'What will they do? Haunt me?'

There was just the smell of smoke now and the darkening trees.

Over on the lawn there was more movement. Another man and woman had come from the hotel, there was pointing. Someone – was it Sam? – stared directly at her on the island. She remained stock still on her rock. How did the island look from where she was in the dwindling light? If she waved, would he see, would everything be alright? But then the figure moved away quickly.

'Madam.' The voice was muffled by the woodland. She turned on the boulder, careful with her footing, slipped her weight from one leg to the other. The image of the wall, with Peter, then a ridge high on a mountain flashed in her head. She stepped down on to the pebbles on the shore. They crunched under her boot – satisfying. All would be well.

'Coming,' she said.

She hugged Lily for a full quarter of an hour, while the manager, the waiter, the waitress, the barman, Sam and Grace stood around. She had given the boatman twice his fee. She had made it as clear as she could that she had persuaded him to take her, against his better judgement.

'Why didn't you tell us you had gone?' Their question asked in a dozen different ways, she answered in one way, 'Because if I had, I couldn't.' They couldn't understand and she couldn't explain.

She held Lily till she stopped sobbing. They went towards the car, with the emergency over and the staff preparing how they would present this story to the evening guests. Grace caught her eye. She saw something there which was more than the sadness and confusion she could see in Sam's. Disappointment? Betrayal?

The manager saw them out to the car. It was quite dark now, with a long drive home. Lily jumped into the back seat, and before Grace could gather her skirts, Lotte squeezed in. She and Lily snuggled together on the leather bench seat. Grace walked all the way round the front of the car and sat in the passenger seat.

They were quickly reliant on the short yellowy cones of the headlights. When lights came towards them Sam slowed even more.

'I hope no one is in a hurry to get home,' he said. 'This will take all night.'

After that, they sat for an hour and a half in silence.

When they got to town, they circled round the Castle rock and up to Baker Street to pick the boys up from the shop. Mrs Wilson had sat with them and their homework long after closing time. They climbed in the back beside their mother and sister. Their questions about the outing petered out in the silence of the car, and their own weariness.

At Snowdon Place, Sam left the car outside in the street.

'I'll take it to the garage in the morning, before I go to the shop.'

Grace made a supper which they ate together in the kitchen. When they had finished, Grace put her hand out to Lily. 'Come. It's the latest you've ever been. And for you boys too. School tomorrow.'

Lotte was ready to sit with Sam, to explain. But he had gone to his own room. She thought to follow him, to go back to the closeness. But it was too quick. He wouldn't understand. She didn't want to argue about the music lessons and the shop. All that would come. She could find a way.

Back in the kitchen, all was tidy. The door to Grace's room was firmly shut. There was a deep silence in the house, as deep as on the island. Lotte walked upstairs. She went into the sitting room. The curtains were open, the streetlight coated the room in a strange light. Against the wall the piano stood dark, the little pyramid of the metronome on top. The lid was down. She walked over and stroked the wood. Outside, the MG was a dark, solid presence in the street, like another tiny house.

'Don't think about it.' Peter was beside her, arm along the top of the piano, a finger tapping the metronome case. 'You or him. I told you. Act or it's you.'

Then he was gone again. Lotte moved over to the window. There was a half-moon above the Castle, clouds moving. She needed a little more time with Peter, then she would be resolved. It was late now, past midnight, and the house was as still as if she were the only one there. Out in the hall she placed her boots on the tiles lightly, automatically. It didn't make her feel furtive, this behaviour, it made her feel light, wraith-like, part of the ease with which she could move from the ordinary world to the world of outdoors and night.

She pulled her coat on, fished the gloves from her pocket, took the purse from her bag and slipped it in her pocket. She was ready to go.

Except the door was locked. She opened the drawer of the hall stand. Reached to the back of the drawer, pulled out the leather wallet that was kept there, loose change for hawkers and van-boys. She unbuttoned the change pouch. No key. She had a moment of panic. Her heart took off. She breathed in, out. Slowly. Think. She looked at the coats hanging on the five hooks behind the door. Someone will have a spare key. She went through every coat, Sam's, the boys', Grace's. Nothing. Sam locked the doors every night, like a ritual. His keys would be on his dressing table upstairs. She turned. Grace was standing, one hand on the banister, one foot on the bottom step.

'How could you.'

'Grace, please give me the key, or tell me where I can find it. I want to go out.'

'There are no keys. Not for you. Front or back doors.'

Lotte sighed. 'Please, Grace, don't turn against me.'

'Turn against you? It's the opposite I'm doing.' She took two steps towards her. 'How can you think of going out? Again. After last night? And what you did to us today?'

'I need to clear my head.' Lotte picked her hat off the table. 'Exactly because of last night, and today too'

'You can clear your head here.' Grace dabbed at her eye with the edge of her apron.

'Please Grace, it's important to me.' Lotte's hands were working together, her gloved fingers rubbing each other.

'And the rest of us aren't? Drive us all insane with worry out at that lake? Sam was nearly sick. And Lily.'

'I was completely safe.' They hissed at each other in whispers.

'No you weren't. You are not going out. I have all the keys downstairs. Sam asked me to look after them.'

They stood there in the hall, the checked tiles, the chandelier, the old dark wood of the door. Lotte took a breath, felt her heart again as something separate, a live thing within her.

'It isn't for you to tell me.'

'But it is,' said Grace. 'It is, I am your friend, Lotte, your sister. I will defy you to help you.'

'Grace.'

'Shh. Go to bed. You don't want to wake Sam, the boys, your baby?' Grace made as if to come to her, to hold her, but turned and walked back down the hallway. Lotte heard every one of her steps back down into the kitchen, then the soft closing of her door.

The Journal of Dr John Fergusson

Saturday 22nd April 1933

That night I lay awake in the tomb-like darkness staring at the ceiling. It made perfect sense for Sneddon to timetable his work for a Sunday. In practical terms it was like any other day. Staffing levels were similar. Sneddon himself, to the horror of his office staff who also had to turn up, regularly worked on a Sunday. But there was a difference in the atmosphere— a lack of hurry, almost a hush came with the distant church bells.

I'd had other sleepless nights, of course. Nights when I lay rehearsing a different task.

But tonight, thanks to Sneddon's games, I was back in that awful, wrecked village in France, in the February of the last year of the war, when I flexed such grim power.

'Medic come to see you,' said the Corporal. The condemned man made no acknowledgement.

'That will be all, Corporal.'

He seemed reluctant to leave, but the man looked beyond any last desperate resistance. I felt awkward standing.

'You've been fed?'

He looked up, nodded.

'It's been explained about the padre? He will come and sit with you if you want.'

He shook his head.

'Not a religious man?' I offered him my tin of cigarettes. He took one. 'No,' I said, 'keep them all.' As he lit up from the candle it flared briefly.

'Don't wanna be told about where I'm going,' he said. In these situations I found the joking felt like a reflex, rather than bravery. Life carrying on for a little longer.

'You don't have to believe to take comfort.'

'Rather be on me tod. Not sure I'd be best company. Be frightened what I'd say.' He paused. 'Why are you here?'

'I am here to ensure your fitness.'

He smiled at that.

'And,' I said, 'to do what I can for you.'

'What is that?'

'I can give you something that might make the time pass a little easier.'

'To knock me out?'

He was interested, but a native suspicion of doctors was still there.

'A bit, yes, I suppose.'

'Can't say I have much to lose.'

I undid the straps of my bag.

'Just let me take your pulse first.' Why did I always do that? To ensure they were alive at this point? It was more about going through a ritual. A professional ritual. For most private soldiers the army was their first experience of doctors and medicine. His heartbeat was unexpectedly normal. But when I looked up into his eyes, I could see the terror.

Men became so used to submerging their fear, holding it in. Everyone is terrified. Some are better at hiding it than others, that is all. He had been very good at it, only that brief moment of weakness, but that was enough. And he had chosen a particularly visible way of breaking, jumping out of the trench. There was no hope of a King's pardon here. A dispatch rider arriving just before dawn. That miracle did cross my mind on occasion – how it might make me feel if the reprieve came too late. But not this time.

'This will help.' I picked up my bag, put it on the table beside the candle.

'Please, Doctor.'

'At first though, it will make you very agitated, uneasy.'

'I am already quite uneasy Doctor.'

I smiled at that myself. 'Quite. This will feel extreme for a moment, like being strapped to the front of a fast train. Or under shell fire. But I promise that will not last long.'

'Please.' There was an edge now.

'Do I have your permission?' He nodded. It was such a pointless question. But it made me feel my vows had not been completely abandoned.

As I prepared the syringe, I caught his eye again. This was extremis. Face to face with the abyss. In an attack or being under a long bombardment, you could hope against hope while the fates rolled their dice overhead. This was the moment the dice stopped moving. Could I admit to a thrill? To a frisson from being in the presence of such an absolute experience? Of course. But I was also here to do good. To relieve harm.

'Roll up your sleeve, Private.' He was cold, his arm white and milky. There were no veins to speak of. 'This might hurt just a bit.' He was beyond any irony now. I rubbed his arm with a dab of antiseptic. A smaller vein would do, an artery would be too quick. I'd prefer to get back to my own shack before it acted. I could do without the guard running through the mud after me. I was careful with the needle though. Multiple punctures would look suspicious even to non-experts. But an officiating officer wasn't going to notice one tiny mark.

'I can't feel anything, Doctor.' He blinked.

'It will take time. Maybe an hour.' I looked at his other wrist, he did have a watch. I hoped it would make its way back to his family. 'Think about the ones you left behind, Private. They'd want to be in your thoughts.' He nodded. 'Read their letters. Have you pictures?'

'Yes,' he said. 'I feel a bit giddy.'

'That's to be expected. I will leave you now Private. Knock on the door if you need anything from the Corporal. He's a good man.' I packed everything away. He had a bundle of pictures, letters in front of him. A dark-haired girl stared up at the roof beams in the gloom.

'Thank you, Doctor.' He was looking at the picture not at me.

'You're a brave man,' I said.

Outside the Corporal was sitting on a large piece of rubble. Between his knees the letter E and the letter C were carved in the fragment. He stood up as I came out.

'Alright, sir?'

'Yes,' I said. 'Gave him something to sleep.'

'Sleep?' he said. 'That will be right. I hope he doesn't cry all night.'

'This isn't a pleasant job.'

'No kidding. And to think I volunteered. At least I can go when the party arrives.'

We both stood and thought about that for a moment.

'I'm afraid I don't have that option,' I said.

'Does it hurt much, do you think?'

'Bullet straight to the heart? Not much. The shock helps.'

'I caught one right here, back at Hammel.' He tapped his upper thigh. 'Hurt like fuck, but only after I was back at casualty clearing. Only hurt after the docs got hold of me.' He laughed. I laughed as well. But quietly. I didn't want the prisoner to hear.

'Shock's a wonderful thing, preserves us from much.' I turned back to the door for a moment. 'It's more the thought of it.'

We were both quiet then.

'I'll leave you to it, Corporal.' I saluted. I considered his long night outside the door. What he might find if he was diligent in his checks. But unless the prisoners called for help, wanted some human contact no matter how brusque and perfunctory, I was confident that he would only enter that horrible space when the light had fully returned.

'I shall see you in the morning, sir.' He casually touched the rim of his helmet.

'Indeed,' I said. I almost added, 'If we're spared.'

I caught a lift back to my billets. As the truck rose up a long slow incline, I looked out through the driver's window and got a brief glimpse of the straggle of ruins at the top of the hill. The Corporal and his lonely guard duty, and the man at the card table with the adrenalin surging in his blood, about to overrun his heart long before morning.

MARTIN

Saturday 22nd April 2017

I had to stop this nocturnal business. There's a narrow line between research and obsession. Or maybe being awake at this time was another way to explore Lotte's world. I certainly had some empathy with her need to be fully alive at night, to cut adrift from the daytime world of family and phones and things to do. Just you and your thoughts. It was a drug, compulsive and dangerous – the path to the asylum was a little clearer.

I looked down on the miniature landscape of my desk. The glowing keys of the laptop, the white screen, the lit oblong of the notebook – all unmarked. This table was inherited. In the family for some time, it had once been a proper table, in the corner of a living room in the 1950s, ready to be extended for visitors. At the top corner, nearest the window, the wrinkled cover of Dr Fergusson's testimony.

I looked up and out at the night. Streetlights flickered as the wind blew the trees around. My sense of the past seemed just as erratic and indistinct. It was easy to get angry, to judge the past and the people there. Who colluded in sending her there? No matter how desperate the scenes behind the doors of Snowdon Place they could not have been worse than what they imagined went on behind the asylum walls.

All the documents took me back to the NHS. I could hear in the rhythm and patterns of words in the carefully numbered paragraphs, the sound of an organisation folding in on itself – being open and transparent and learning lessons while doing the opposite. A rage at Fergusson's pompous justifications – in his head his reckless incompetence had become heroism – and at Sneddon's ruthless sadism. What were they all thinking of? And Lotte crushed between the town and the asylum. But as I raged and blamed, the fabric of the past became thin and tattered. Pity and blame were easy. Anger at the injustice of it all was superficial and performative. It took me no closer to the people.

I rubbed my finger over the part of the table where the dark veneer had chipped off all the way down to the light wood underneath. It would be nice to think that this was a result of a family argument in the table's heyday, a meaningful scar, the mark of history. Not my inept handling as I took it out the boot of the car when it moved in here. Imagination transforms but it also deceives.

When I felt that Lotte's family and her physicians lacked the capacity to find other solutions, to keep her far from the asylum, what I really meant was that I lacked the imagination to smell the smoky air of the 1930s. Shop-owners, not even ones with an MG and a grand address, were in no position to challenge physicians or Sheriffs. Everyone feared the gothic asylum, but by 1933 it was a place regulated by Commissions, its details recorded in official reports and guided by proper science – not just a holding compound for the dislocated and dispossessed.

Who was I to blame my grandfather for trusting professionals? What were the options? Not many. This wasn't cruelty or convenience or economic advantage. It was how it was. How things were. How life was lived then. Maybe they'd just run out of options and had to make a terrible decision that would haunt them for the rest of their lives.

When I wasn't walking rural roads by night, I was walking the daytime streets. The streets of Stirling. Walking past 5 Snowdon Place over and over, to the point where I wouldn't have been surprised to have a police car draw up with pointed questions. It's just the sort of neighbourhood where repeat appearances would be noted. I walked up and down Baker Street, past the shop, feeling the gradient under my shoes. In the 1970s when the centre of gravity moved down the hill in Stirling towards the novelty of a shopping centre. My father used the slogan in adverts in the local paper – 'It pays to climb the hill.' In my smart-ass teenage way, I thought this was a huge mistake. Why draw attention to the fact that the shop was a long haul from the new centre of town? But I knew nothing. My father had the visceral physical understanding of that place that I didn't have. It was, and still is, a place defined by steepness, gravity. The physicality of walking took me into the place. And that took me closer to the people – to Lotte walking all the way to her Aunt's house up these ancient precipitous streets, and to my father in the shop at the top of the hill as he tried to wrestle it into the late twentieth century. I walked back to the car park through the shopping centre and took a small vindictive satisfaction from the number of vacant units.

Gradually, as I walked the dark roads, I came closer to understanding, each thread braiding together to form more substantial insights into my father and how, as we all do, he had generated his own way of living in the world. I recognised his wariness around doctors and lawyers. His great calm when things went wrong. When bereavements barged into families, he was a still, calm point of certainty.

And with an abrupt twist of focus, I recalled clearly how much intensity he expressed through his music. When I was fourteen, he agreed to play the organ at a neighbour's wedding. They wanted Vidor's Toccata – a notoriously demanding piece. My father practiced on his piano to the point of obsession. It filled the house for weeks. The result was a triumph – precision and passion and drive in a few minutes of music that was both soaring and intricate. The austere Presbyterian kirk struggled to contain the grand roar of passion.

Music was an acceptable route he had found to tap something deep within. Otherwise, he stood back from his own feelings – even by the lukewarm standards of his generation – and he was equally distrustful of emotion in others. He could make my tears feel like an unnecessary luxury. But as I turned the pages of my notes, and remembered the smell of the asylum archive, I realised that emotions were not an indulgence for him, they were a threat. Too many intense feelings could take you behind the high walls, could take you to a terrible day when your mother was taken away and never came back. If I couldn't understand that, then I should have left the past where it belonged.

10.

I had to concentrate now. There was no room for errors of judgement. Or lack of resolve. In the corridor I looked for a suitable nurse. Two were coming down the main corridor towards me. Their shadows advanced towards me. I recognised one as the nurse who had assisted Sneddon last time. They stopped when I stopped.

'Nurse...?' I said.

'Sinclair,' she said.

'Yes, indeed. We met on Doctor Sneddon's research project.'

She said nothing. Waited for me to go on.

'I wonder if you could find Assistant Matron Kennedy and ask her to find Mrs Raymond, our new patient, and send her to the consultation room?' I had my hand in my jacket pocket. Lotte's glove.

'Now?' she hesitated. 'Sir?'

'Yes, Nurse. Now. It is urgent.'

She said something I didn't catch to her companion and turned on her heel and walked off. Her companion looked at me without expression and strode on past me. From these tiny moments the threat of anarchy begins to build. But it would not be my problem now.

I walked on. Shuffling patients, striding nurses. The smell that was both clean and filthy at the same time. I had time. I deliberately took a route that went by the treatment room. The door was open. As I drew level, I glanced in. No sign of Sneddon yet. Two nurses were bustling. One at a trolley, setting out a tray and sorting through a collection of bottles. All stage props for Sneddon. The other was passing long webbing belts under the mattress on the bed, she threaded them round the iron frame. A rubber sheet was folded over the end of the bed. I was too far away to pick up the inner-tube smell of the sheet.

I must have made a sound, or she sensed my eyes on her as she tucked and reached.

'If Doctor Sneddon appears,' I said, 'tell him I will be back shortly.'

Lotte was already in the room when I got there. It was a bright morning, but that only served to enhance the gloom in here. I could see the cobwebs in the corners, the yellowing paint that had once been a neutral white. The promise of sunshine outdoors chilled the closed air. She had her back to me, her narrow shoulders poised as if to take a step forward, but her hair looked dishevelled now rather than wild and untamed and her head was down. She was merely standing in the light, not attempting to see out from the high window.

'Lotte.' It felt bittersweet to use her name, at this moment.

She turned and I saw the same look in her eye as I had seen in the eye of the boy in the ruined school. Her face was white, blank. But her eyes – pupils wide and widening as she turned back into the dusky room – showed abject terror.

'Sit,' I said. 'Please.' I pulled out the chair. She slumped into it. I nearly brought the other chair round beside her, but I diligently took up my position opposite her across the table.

'What is happening?'

'Please don't worry,' I said. 'All will be well.'

'No. What is going on?' She passed a hand through her glorious hair, even here it shimmered under the bare bulb. 'Two different nurses came for me. In the day room. One to take me to Dr Sneddon, the other to take me here.' She stared straight at me, there was no genteel politeness about her now.

'Everything is going to be all right.' And I did hope it wasn't one of my lies.

'They argued. The nurses. One said Doctor Sneddon is the Superintendent so I should go with her. The other one, she said, Doctor Fergusson told me it was extremely urgent.'

'How did it resolve?'

'One said she'd report the other directly to Doctor Sneddon and went away. The other one brought me here.' She had been saved by Nurse Sinclair, by her willingness to get into trouble. She had been there in the treatment room before, had borne witness.

Lotte wasn't going to be distracted by my questions:

'Is this the experiment? Is this it?'

'Yes.'

Her eyes grew enormous. I reached across the table and took both of her hands. She wrestled, but I hung on. Her boots kicked at me under the table. But I held on, I held her.

'Lotte. Listen.' She tried to stand to kick over the chair. It shot backwards and she went on to her knees. She stood and to keep my grip on her hands I had to stand too. We grappled over the table, both of us breathing as if we were making love or fighting to the death. With huge effort we reached an impasse, rigid in our determination.

'Get me home. Get me home.' She said it over and over. Between breaths, through breaths.

'I will. But you must trust me,' I said.

Finally, she stopped pulling away. I kept my hands on her wrists and guided her back to the chair.

'Help me help you,' I said. Her eyes were still wide. In each deep black pupil, I saw a dark looming shape against the glare of the window.

'How? I have no one to help me here.'

'I will get you home.' And I meant it. My past was foolishness. I had stepped over a divide with Hazel, I had compromised the things I loved; my family, my career. I had placed myself at the mercy of Sneddon by letting my emotions run free. My imagination had led me into an iron trap. I was not going to make that mistake again. I would deliver Lotte to her family.

'Home,' I said, 'and we will continue your treatment in your own environment.' At that moment I believed this with absolute certainty. I would leave this place and all the others like it and establish myself in private practice. I would start with Lotte. As a patient. I would get to the bottom of her fixation with her cousin. Surely the source of her trouble.

'How? How?'

'First, you must allow the nurse to restrain you.'

'No.' She said this quietly, but with absolute conviction. 'No.'

'It is the only way. I cannot just tell Sneddon to halt his experiment. But I can demonstrate to him that you are too unwell to participate.'

She looked at me as if I had proposed an amputation

without anaesthetic. She shook her head. Her black curls swept across her face like a dark cloud.

'This will take only half an hour, I will give you something, after a period of excitement you will become unconscious,' I said.

'Is it dangerous?'

'The excitement it causes will make you seem ineligible to be a subject of the experiment. When you slip into unconsciousness, I can arrange for you to be taken to the Infirmary in town. The hospital here is a glorified first-aid post.'

'And then I will be brought back here again.'

'No, you won't be of interest to him then. And he won't pursue you there anyway. Not where there are other doctors, where he has no authority.'

I brought my chair round now, round to her side of the table. I sat down and felt in my pocket. I took out her gloves.

'Here,' I said. 'Here are your gloves. Your housekeeper brought them.'

'Grace? She was here?'

'Yes. She is concerned.'

'No one told me.'

'Your husband, your family. They're all concerned.'

Her eyes were wet, but I had never seen her cry. She took the gloves, bundled them into a tiny ball in the palm of her left hand. I gripped her forearms.

'I have no choice, do I?'

'Please trust me,' I said. I knew how empty these words sounded.

'Why the restraint?'

'For your safety.' She almost smiled at that. 'Honestly, and so Sneddon won't suspect anything amiss,' I said. 'You will only experience some excitement, mild…'

'Hysteria?' she said. 'That's what my doctor told me I had. When we talked about my insomnia.'

'Sneddon cannot proceed if you are having an episode. Not because of any great outbreak of kindness, but because it would invalidate his results.'

'Why can't you take me home now?'

'Because,' I said, and as I spoke I realised that there was no going back, that my time in these places really was over. 'I don't have the seniority for that. Doctor Sneddon has power to pursue you even if I took you away. No matter how far. But if he sees that you can't contribute to his work then he will leave you alone.' I could still see my face reflected in her eyes, like a pale shadow. 'Besides, you will be in a safe, public, place at the Infirmary. And then, after, I will help you to get better. That is my job.' I let her arms go. Her pulse, naturally, was racing.

She looked over at the bars on the window, up at the electric bulbs overhead. Finally, she looked back at me.

'Please get me home.'

I reached into my other pocket. I took out a sheathed, wrapped and prepared syringe. When I looked at the clear liquid in the syringe, I had a brief moment of hesitation. Professor Deacon used to say that these moments, the pause before administering a drug, before breaking the skin with the knife, were the moments that made a good physician. If you did not hesitate, if you hadn't contemplated the violence you were about to unleash upon an innocent, trusting civilian, then you didn't deserve to take the oath.

I could see her gloves balled, still, in her hand.

'Best put your gloves in your apron pocket. Keep them safe. You will need them when you are at home.' I tapped the air out of the syringe. It was a tiny proportion of the dose

I gave to the men in those sordid cells in France. I would have never embarked on this course of action had I not had that experience of being God already. In a funny way, all that seemed to have led directly to this moment.

I asked her for her left arm. It was smooth and white. For a second, I imagined what it might feel like under my lips, but no, no more of that. I found a vein right in the crook of her arm, where I knew from long experience a puncture would be less visible and if it bruised, then that was a consequence of the restraint.

'You are content for me to do this?'

She looked at me. There was a yearning there, but not for me. 'Yes,' she said.

Her eyes narrowed as I broke the skin, but she held my gaze as I pushed the liquid into her body. I had never felt as close to her as at that moment.

'You will be safe now,' I whispered.

LOTTE

Friday 21st January 1921

The locksmith had been there forever. A tiny frontage, just a door and a narrow window. Barely enough face to the street to fit the name – *Borrowman, Locksmith*. As Lotte entered, the door caught on the boards of the floor, the scrape enough to alert Mr Borrowman, who limped out of the dark at the rear of the shop. All through her childhood Lotte had been keen to run messages here. The magic wall of a thousand key blanks, from floor to ceiling, behind the counter, tinkling faintly in the draught from the door. Silver and gold, ranged by size from the smallest at the top left to the foot-long monsters at the bottom right, proof that the chaos of the world could be put into order.

'Yes?' said Mr Borrowman. The accent was eastern, exotic. No one knew about his background, so they had to make it up. In the community imagination he had been everything, from a white slave trader to a political refugee. What they did know for sure was that he was one of the first to volunteer in 1914. And one of the first to come back. Against the glittering wall of keys, he appeared an asymmetrical figure. His right side – a man in late middle age, smart, dark eyes, dark skin, alert. His left side – immobile, glass eye, a face stretched out of place and then imprecisely pushed back, the pinned empty sleeve.

Lotte handed him the two keys.

'One copy of each?'

'Please.' She watched as he assessed the two keys, one after the other, holding each one up to his right eye, feeling along the teeth, selecting a blank. And then the remarkable manipulation of the vice, the tools flashing, all with one hand. 'He'll never move to a bigger shop,' her mother said, 'just him on his own, taking a few pennies a day.' Yet he was a vital part of the street. So many kicked doors, lost keys.

Why had he signed up so quickly? They said he hated the Germans. Or the Turks or the Bulgars. There was revenge for something or other. People claimed to have asked him outright what had happened to his arm, his left side.

'It was lost,' he would say with a crooked smile. He seemed to have no life beyond his encounters with his customers. When he came back, broken, and reopened the shop, his windows were shattered twice. There was no rage or complaint. Sympathy was accepted but there was no more discussion. As if he knew those who sympathised were as likely to have thrown the stone.

He finished the keys and held them out to her, presented between his first, second and third fingers. In the poor light of the tiny shop the brass glinted like religious relics, something precious, passed from priest to believer and back again, taking on lustre from touching alone.

Lotte took the keys and paid.

'Is that everything that I can do for you today?'

'Yes,' she said, uncertainly.

'I wish you well.' As she opened the door to go back into the street there was the rustle of keys again, like delicate bells.

LOTTE

Tuesday 18th April 1933

Sleep only came in sporadic bursts, otherwise she would be wide awake, her mind racing through the darkness. Never longer than thirty minutes, but enough for her body and mind to keep functioning like a normal person. That is what Dr Campbell told her. 'You're a normal person, it is just that you see the world a little differently.' He had looked away as if the next bit had to be said but was a touch distasteful for King's Park. 'A little more intensely, that's all.'

She sat on her bed. It was warm enough now to lie there, fully clothed on top of the covers. Sometimes she went under her coat, especially on the nights when she didn't go out. It was a comfort. What pressed in on her now was the inescapable fact of harm done, of problems without resolve, of locked doors. She remembered the island, smelled the lake waters, the oily, faintly vegetable air from the stillness. She shivered, lying there on the counterpane as the apple trees brightened and she felt herself slip, the coldness of the water. When it reached her heart, it set free the familiar acceleration. The pounding hooves. 'Nothing,' said Dr Campbell, 'nothing to worry about. You are a young woman still. In your prime.'

She was, she had time, but it was running away from her faster than she could walk. Doors were closing. Locks turning over. The pools of shadow under the apple trees thinned as the sun rose. She heard all the noises of the house as everyone got up, the shoes on the stairs, the boys' voices, Sam's boom. Did she detect a hesitation, a subdued tone, no one shouting? Keeping quiet because she was ill, needed to sleep, needed peace, was part of how the house worked. In Castlehill there was none of that, the noises came from outside, through the walls, up the long stairwell, there was never quiet. Here, in mid-afternoon, if Grace took Lily out, there was a deep silence that was more profound than any night walk. Town and country were alive, stirring always, they rustled, groaned, the friction of life. But this house could manufacture silence, building up the layers like wool.

The sounds dispersed out into the street as the door thumped shut. Sam left first, then the boys. She heard Grace and Lily, the burble of their chatter as they went down to the kitchen. The silence crept up the stairs and into the bedroom. She would find a way. All of this she could work through.

'There's only one thing that cannot be sorted.' Peter sat on the other side of the bed. This was the widest bed in the house. Sam had chosen to sleep in the front room as he said it was noisiest, looking out over the street. The street with no traffic. But it was considerate of him. Kind.

'I can't sort this,' she said. The bed wobbled as Peter changed position. She didn't turn to look, but she was aware that he was sitting crooked, twisted in a way that wasn't physically possible. She didn't have to turn round further to know why.

'One thing. Trust me.'

'I've hurt people. It's hard to live with that.'

'It's hard to live. Full stop.' He breathed in. She felt a faint rattle when he did so. 'You had no choice in the vennel. And when you're ill, you're ill.'

'We always have choices,' she said.

'He gave you no option. You know that.'

'But I've hurt my family, Grace too. And I can't explain it to any of them. I can't talk to them.'

'Does that matter. Talking's overrated.'

'I've just you.'

'Not forever.'

'No.' She turned. He was perched on the bed, his shirt out of his trousers, shoeless, his head angled, turned straight down towards the floor, the bright red rug.

'You can't keep walking. And I can't stick with you for ever,' he said.

'No.'

'Yes.' He shifted on the bed slowly, and she turned away again. Outside the apple trees were bright, a slight breeze had picked up and the tiny new petals shimmered.

'I know I can keep going, but I need you to tell me that,' she said.

'No, you don't. You don't need to change the world to find what you are after. The shop, your music.' There was a muffled noise from deep in the house, it could have been crying or laughter, it was too far away to tell. 'The family. It is all there for you. There is only one thing you can do nothing about. I just hold you back. You don't need me now.'

She turned round, but there was only the bed, the cover slightly crumpled at the corner, and a sudden pounding on the front door. She started as if coming awake. She heard voices, men's voices, and Grace, the front door closing again. The cool of the brass doorknob in her palm. So smooth. Appreciate, appreciate what you have here, these little details. They will see you through. She looked down at her feet, the button up boots, they had seen her through those long nocturnal miles, they had taken her to her lunches, taken her on stage. Tight on her foot, the leather seemed an extension, part of her. They would carry her forward.

She stood in the doorway, the light falling from above on the stair, the bright white paint, the dark of the banister as it curved away out of sight. She heard Grace and Lily.

'Why?' said Lily. She couldn't hear Grace's reply as she walked below, downstairs to the kitchen.

'Why?'

The voices were quiet. And then Grace, by herself, her footfall on the tiles of the hallway, she was tucked away out of sight, but Lotte saw her shadow pass, reflected on the tiles. There was something in her pace, the click of her shoes, that told Lotte that the house was about to be picked up like a toy, rattled upside down, then thrown aside.

'Gentlemen,' said Grace. Boots on the mat, a scuffling, then the hard metallic clicking of metal on the tiles.

'Thank you, madam.' The voice was deep. 'Your assistance will be much appreciated.'

Lotte went to the banister and without thinking leant over. She could see nothing but the back of Grace's dress, the ties of her apron. Leaning further, she could see a leather bag on the hall table. So easy. So easy to lean further, for her feet to leave the ground.

She straightened herself and walked slowly down the stairs. As she turned the corner, Grace and three sets of male boots and legs came into view. Two policemen, huge against the light from the doorway, and in front, Dr Campbell. Why was he there? Did they expect her to faint?

As she reached the tiles, Grace turned, her head to one side.

'Lotte.' It felt like a question.

'Mrs…' Dr Campbell stepped forward.

Lotte put up her hand. 'No. No,' she said. 'Please do not get involved, Doctor. These men,' she nodded towards the uniformed men, 'are who I need to speak to.' The lighted window, high in the vennel. The only light, but there must have been a face there and then a story told across a police station desk.

Grace took her by the arm: 'Lotte. No. Don't say anything. Listen. Doctor Campbell has papers you need to see. The police are not here for you. He is here for you.'

Lotte's focus on one reality tumbled and changed, a new reality started to form. But it formed in her mind like a damaged kaleidoscope, the new pieces fell into position but had no pattern, no meaning.

'You need to listen to me,' said Dr Campbell. 'These men are here because of the law. Don't be afraid of them.' He stepped forward again. Lotte stepped back.

'Law? Which law?'

Grace was close now, her arm reached round. 'It's for your own good, Lotte.'

She shrugged the arm away. 'No. What is this about?'

'It can't go on,' said Grace. She stood now, hands in her apron pockets, four-square in front of Lotte, the doctor behind her, the policemen mute witnesses. 'We can't keep you a prisoner here.'

'Prisoner?' Lotte swung her arm, not at anyone, it was a gesture to take back her space, her hallway. Grace and the doctor moved back a pace. The two police, bareheaded, their helmets cradled in the crooks of their arms like babies, moved forward.

'Please, Lotte.' Grace's eyes were wet.

'Where is my husband? I'm not even going to talk to any of you until he is here.' She swung round on Grace. 'Phone Sam at the shop and tell him. Tell him to come now.'

No one moved. The silence welled up. Lotte took a half step towards Grace.

'Go and call him now. I can't be plainer.' Again, the silence, but within it the muffled sound of a child crying. Lotte turned towards the kitchen stairs. 'Where is my child? Grace, do as I tell you.'

As Lotte made to move, Grace gripped her forearm. 'No,' she said. Her hand bit deeper. Dr Campbell started forward. Grace warned him away with her eyes. 'Lily can't see this. You must go. Go with Doctor Campbell. You can get better and then come back to us.'

Lotte began to struggle, a fierce, focused, determined fight to break free. She struck at Grace with her free hand. The doctor raised his hand to stop the policemen moving forward. The two women gripped each other, feet shuffling on the shiny black and white tiles.

'Please,' said Lotte. 'Please.'

'You must go. We cannot help you anymore. This walking, this wandering. Look where it has ended already.' Lotte felt the strength waning from her arms, Grace was holding her up more than holding her back now. Her will was ebbing.

'My husband.'

'Sam knows,' said Grace. 'We've discussed it over and over.'

'Discussed it?' And Lotte's rage burned again, her heart pounded and she leapt at Grace. Dr Campbell put his hands on each shoulder and Lotte kicked him hard. She connected with his shin, he hopped back to collapse on the hall chair. The two policemen stepped forward and held her securely, an arm each. Lotte opened her mouth and Grace put two fingers to her lips.

'Shhh. Lotte. The child. Don't make it worse. The only good here is that she and the boys see nothing. Or hear nothing.'

Lotte stood between the two men. The solid, embarrassed officers. They now had a tale to tell, when they got home. Those big houses up the King's Park, they don't lead such great lives.

Dr Campbell was still sitting, rubbing his leg: 'I'd thank you not to do that again,' he said. 'I have all the papers here. You are required to read them. And you are required to come with us.' He stood and crossed to the table, opened his bag. A sudden sharp waft of ether. He had an envelope in his hand. He took out a single folded sheet and smoothed it on the table. Lotte ignored him, ignored them all. She was staring down the hallway, towards the kitchen stairs.

'Let's get your coat,' said Grace, busying.

'A bag,' said Lotte. 'A bag, I will need a bag.'

Dr Campbell looked over his glasses, the sheet of paper reflected the light back up into his chins, into the round lenses. 'Grace has packed a bag. Not that it will be required. They will supply everything you need when you get there. It's a good place,' he said. 'It has a very fine reputation. It is not the place you think it is. There are good people there. Professionals. They will help you. Can you read this now?' He presented the sheet to Lotte with both hands. She tried to move her arm to take it. The officer relaxed his grip. She took the paper, but the words – Authorised, Courts, Sheriff – registered without meaning.

'You understand what this means?' said the doctor.

She nodded. The house seemed to be drifting away from her already; the boys' bedrooms upstairs, Sam's room, her bedroom, the dining room, the living room and the piano, were suddenly less real. She smelt the outdoors, the street, on the police uniforms, the hard-wearing cloth. Grace was crying now. 'Please, Lotte, I can't leave Lily down there any longer.'

There was pressure on Lotte's right arm, a distinct squeeze. It was Peter.

'Just go, Lotte. You have to know when you're beat. Just go. You'll be back.'

'Come with me.'

'No, I can't.'

The squeeze was insistent now. The two officers started to walk her towards the door.

'Her coat,' said Grace. She had her coat over her arm, the fur collar glistened. Dr Campbell opened the door. His car was there and another vehicle, not marked as police.

'Can you let her put her coat on?' said Grace. 'It's cold outside.'

The officers looked at each other and at Dr Campbell who nodded. They let her arms free. Grace stepped behind her to help her into the coat. As she pulled it up on to her shoulders, she said: 'I will come for you.' She leaned over her shoulder and kissed Lotte awkwardly on her cheek.

'I can't do anything about the uniforms, I'm afraid,' said Dr Campbell, 'but I did ask them to use a car that would be a little more discreet.' He took the paper from Lotte and handed it to one of the officers. 'I would normally have asked you to come to my surgery and then discussed all this, in a civilised way. But there was too much urgency for that.' He glanced past Lotte at Grace. 'You are lucky to have so many people who care about you.'

They stood there for a moment, the five of them, silent but for the sound of a van in the street, the wind in the trees and Lily's far off sobs.

'Please just walk down and get in the back of the car.' The officer spoke for the first time. Lotte heard the voice of the Top of the Town. Her people. She put her hand on the railing, it felt cold and wet. She reached into her coat pockets. There were no gloves, or purse. She looked up over the roof of the mansion opposite, the church, to the castle where clouds moved behind the great bulk of the old stonework.

She walked alone down the steps and across the pavement. She didn't look back. She opened a rear door of the car, it was stiff, and the hinge squeaked. She perched on the scuffed leather bench seat. The door was slammed shut and the two officers climbed into the front. She stared straight ahead as they started the car and rattled off down Snowden Place.

11.

LOTTE

Monday 24th January 1921

If she hadn't gone back perhaps it would have been different. Things you don't see exist in the memory in a different way, the imagination does its work, for good or bad. She was on the great curve of Bow Street, the wind funnelling up between the walls, shop signs squeaking and the rattle of vans on the cobbles. The pull of the slope gave her a lightness, a sense of flight almost. Giving Peter the keys was a balanced risk, and she was the only one who could take that responsibility. Not his mother, or her mother or Jessie. And to have discussed it would have taken them where? Taken him where? To the Asylum? It was a quandary not amenable to the aunts' usual cunning and craft, the only thing that could not be solved around the kitchen table. In the bright afternoon light, she felt the exhilaration of decision. The wind caught at her coat, she nodded to neighbours, customers, at the turn of the street she saw the shop, the verticality of it, the way it stood at the corner of two hills, built on a double slope, as if it could slide in two directions at once, the delightful precariousness of it.

She heard the voice behind her. It had an edge, for a moment she hoped that it was an angry customer, a split seam, a colour run at the first washing. But there was also something about the restrained, polite urgency which triggered a coldness in her heart that worked its way to her fingertips. The urge was to keep walking, down the hill faster and faster, to keep going.

Mrs Miller, widowed, and then her son lost from a minesweeper somewhere in the vastness of the North Sea. Her headsquare was tightly tied under her chin, like a bandage. She came close to Lotte; on the slope she was almost eye to eye.

'Lassie, just come with me.'

Lotte nodded. She couldn't find a word that would do. She took a glance over her shoulder, felt her collar against her face, the touch of the ordinary.

'Come,' said Mrs Miller. She almost took Lotte's sleeve. But not quite. It wasn't what you did here. The fuss was worse than the deed. 'Come, before people gather.'

They went up the hill together. Neither spoke. What was there to say? Mrs Miller was fast on her feet, the drama of the moment gave her energy.

When they got to the dark mouth of the close a man Lotte did not recognise was blocking the way. He nodded at Mrs Miller:

'Davie's gone for the police. I've tried to keep people out.'

But there were three women on the first flight of the stairs – Mrs Connolly, Mrs Flett and Mrs Stevenson, who turned to catch her son as he ran down, turned him, and bustled him back up the stair. No one said a word. Mrs Miller looked directly at Lotte. She took her arm, her hand felt hard, unnegotiable. Mrs Miller was an expert in matters of the incontestable.

He was on his side, back to the light of the doorway, as if he might be about to push himself up onto his knees. But his head was in a position that wasn't right even for such an awkward pose, and it had changed shape.

'I'm a proper modernist portrait now.' She heard his voice whispering among the stone and ironwork. She pulled her coat open to kneel behind him. She put a hand down to his face. It was uncovered. She felt the tangles of scar tissue, the spirals and ridges. Her knees were wet through her skirt and stockings. She saw for the first time the pool of blackness in the gloom like a big round rug with him lying at the centre. Looking up she saw the stairs rising, narrowing all the way to the skylights above her floor, their floor, it seemed no distance. She saw the faces, leaning over, black against the light. A hand on her shoulder, Mrs Miller, then a commotion at the close entrance and she was in her mother's arms.

'I know,' she said into Lotte's curls. 'I know. The keys. We all knew.'

The Journal of Dr John Fergusson

Sunday 23rd April 1933

In order to calm my mind, I went back to my office, sat at my desk and made notes in the margin of the Italian paper.

I tried hard to keep my watch in my pocket. As I flicked through the plausible nonsense of the tables in front of me, the tiny numbers in precise columns, the claims for variations of doses, my thoughts slipped to the progress my own drug would be making through the delicate structures of Lotte's vascular and nervous systems.

Nurse Clark pushed the door open without knocking.

'Doctor Sneddon asks that you come right away to the treatment room.' She had clearly been hurrying. Her voice a little too loud for my small room. I was expecting the call from Sneddon, and I wondered what level of rage he had reached. I glanced down at the paper from the Italians – 'we can therefore conclude with some confidence…'

'Please tell Doctor Sneddon that I have not forgotten about his activity this morning and will join him when I am ready.'

I looked up. Nurse Clark's face was flushed, and her eyes were wide, there remained nothing of her pert manner.

'No, Doctor Fergusson.' She had taken a step into the room. Her hands were held together in front of the crisp white of her uniform apron. They were clasped together tightly, but I could still see the tremor. 'Please, come quickly.'

I followed her out into the corridor. This was unusual. A doctor trailing a nurse, especially a junior nurse. We had covered three corridors and two flights of stairs before I realised I hadn't put my jacket on. Let alone my coat. I could have put a stop to this picture of panic with a sharp word to Nurse Clark and a return to my office to collect my proper clothes and my composure. But the clip of Clark's shoes on the parquet drove me on in my shirt sleeves, with groups of nurses and auxiliaries staring at our backs as we swept by. Nearing the treatment room, I forced myself to walk more slowly, to control my breathing. Nurse Clark stopped abruptly at the door to let me enter first.

Inside, white backs were arranged around the bed. No one turned. Sneddon was bent over, his shoulders pumping rhythmically. The two nurses were alive with undirected energy, one was wringing a cloth noisily into a dish, the other was holding a stethoscope to Lotte's chest, moving the diaphragm rapidly around the skin.

'What did you give her, Doctor Fergusson?' Sneddon spoke through his teeth. He was bearing down on Lotte with both arms. The violence of his attempts had turned his face red.

'What did *you* give her, Doctor Sneddon?' The only, terrible, sounds were Sneddon's tortured breathing and the clatter as Nurse Clarke searched for something pointless in the equipment trolley.

In the middle of all this, Lotte was still as marble. Sneddon pounded between her small breasts, but her pale face was at rest, eyes closed. Her calm seemed to settle me. I took her cool hand. I was sharply conscious of time. Not in the conventional sense that it stood still or accelerated at moments of stress, or any of that nonsense. Suddenly and absolutely, I sensed the iron resolve of time having passed. There was no going back, no recovery. I squeezed Lotte's cool hand. Sneddon's pounding seemed to lose conviction. He looked up at me. All those years we had shared, from the anatomy hall until now, connections and repulsions, were in that stare. We saw our futures in separate but equally desolate ruin. The inquests, the hearings. This would not be an incident he could keep from the Board.

Sneddon turned to the nurse, but he had given up the resuscitation even before she shook her head. She bent over Lotte and buttoned the gown back up over her white chest.

'Total cardiac arrest, before we even started. Was that your modus operandi in France?' Sneddon whispered. His face was shiny with sweat.

'I'm not responsible for the patient,' I said. I still had her hand in mine. 'You are Superintendent.'

'You can let her go now, Dr Fergusson. You've done enough for her. Enough.'

12.

LOTTE

Wednesday 2nd March 1921.

They sat at the cardinal points. To the South, Aunt Margaret, with her long, straight back to the high window. Her mother, her back to the North and to the dark hall. Aunt Jessie by the range and the West. Lotte, with her chair pushed back almost against the dresser was East. A thick silence where there were normally so many words, clashing and sparking over the yellow oilcloth. Jessie picked up her teacup and the spoon ticked on the saucer. The best china used for everyday. Jessie's philosophy: 'No one wants to find unused best sets of china when you're dead. Use them up. If we can't afford to replace them then we will do without.'

Jessie moved the teaspoon before putting her cup back down. Margaret placed her hands in front of her on the oil cloth as if assessing the smoothness, the cleanliness of the surface. But Mary spoke first, her mother's tone offered no room for discussion: 'Marguerite will get a cash settlement.'

Lotte looked up. 'Is that fair?'

'There is going to be little that's fair here.' Margaret's right index finger made small circles on the oilcloth.

'Fair isn't the point.' Jessie was pointing at Lotte with the teaspoon. Her glasses caught the light and her eyes were obscured. 'It's what works that matters.'

'Sam wouldn't want to be part of something that was unfair.' Lotte could find no one to make eye contact with. They all looked down at the table. Margaret's face was shadowed by the blaze of white behind her, the light over the Forth and the hills and the distant sea.

'What is fair is that the business keeps going,' said Jessie, 'and you and Sam are the best qualified.'

'Nothing simpler than that.' Margaret looked up at Mary opposite and at Lotte. Her face had lost its alert intensity. There was only darkness now under her eyes. 'We do what's best for the business.'

Jessie tapped her teaspoon on the table. 'We didn't work this hard to let it all go.'

Lotte looked at her mother who was focussed on a patch of sun that had reflected off the dresser on to the table.

'You are all part of the business,' Lotte said. 'Everyone needs to get some benefit from it.'

With their three heads bowed, her mother and the aunts could have been praying.

Jessie looked up: 'We take what the business can afford. As we have always done. But you and Sam will be doing the work, so it's right you get the bulk.' There was a hard defiance in her look. 'Those of us who can work, can get jobs.' She pointed to the ceiling with her spoon. 'Margaret has here to rent.' Margaret raised her head for the first time, as if she had been waiting for her name to be called. She straightened her regal back, but her fire had gone out. Jessie went on. 'I can get a job. With that and my share of the sale I'll be fine.'

'It is your responsibility. You have to take this on,' said her mother. 'You have to take it forward. You owe us that.'

There was a long silence. It hung in the sunny air. Her responsibility.

'Nothing will get easier.' Her mother's eyes held Lotte's. It was as if she was a child again – home late and unable to explain herself. 'Nothing.' Her mother glanced at Aunt Margaret. 'It was fine in the war. Three women running a big shop like that.' She looked again at Margaret. No response. But Jessie was leaning forward now and she pointed at Lotte with the spoon.

'In fact, we did well out of that. A sympathetic ear for all those women, left alone and terrified.' Jessie leaned back and smiled. 'There's more to selling than selling.'

'She's right,' her mother said. 'We got the best of it. Now, once the rebuilding's over there will be less money to spend. And the men won't like the competition.'

Jessie struck the table with her spoon. 'So, you have to be smarter. Use Sam when necessary, when you need to send a man, when they won't speak to you. But you'll get the last laugh. If you can't go through them, go around them.'

'Jessie's right. You and Sam– you'll be a good team.' Her mother squeezed the back of Lotte's hand for emphasis.

'But Marguerite,' said Lotte.

'Has made her future, she's made her choice and it's not with someone who can run a business.' Her mother took her hand properly now. Lotte thought of Robert: one arm round her sister, the other in his jacket pocket, hat at an angle copied from the films, cigarette burning. A great man with motors. 'You can, and so can Sam. You can make it work.'

'You could make anything work. You could do it on your own.' Lotte tried to cut in, but her mother had more to say.

'Don't say anything. Fine I know that you could do it on your own. But like I said, sometimes it's easier if there's two of you. I want you to make the shop work well you can, for yourself and for us.'

Lotte said: 'But where will you go?'

'I'm not going far. A wee bungalow in Causewayhead. They are building there soon, so they say. I'll be fine there.'

Jessie was conducting them with her teaspoon now. 'And I've got the Council of Women, and the rebuilding plan for all this.' Jessie pointed out the window. Her plans for the town were ambitious. 'Plenty to do. Don't you worry about us.'

'We've had enough.' Her mother squeezed her hand again and stood up. She walked behind Jessie, took the kettle off the gas just before it started to squeal. As she spoke, she emptied the teapot at the sink, refreshed the pot and the air with the sharp tang of new tea. 'We've had enough.' She turned and half perched on the edge of the stove. 'You've seen us work seven days a week. The odd day away. The odd trip to Glasgow to the wholesalers. Ten o'clock, most nights.'

'But we know what you mean, the real reason, don't skirt on my account.' Aunt Margaret spoke for the first time. Her mother walked behind her, put a hand on her shoulder and then reached over to put the pot in the centre of the oilcloth.

'It's true though. We have all had enough. Exhausted.' Her mother spoke the words like plain facts.

'I, we, don't have the heart for it now,' said Margaret, so quietly that the silence that followed did not seem so abrupt. The silence was the space left in their lives. The space that Jessie and Mary would fill with a new existence in a different house; that Lotte would try to fill with Sam and a family. But Margaret would carry the emptiness with her always. Lotte felt a wave of guilt, a fierce burning that made her heart race.

Aunt Margaret turned to her. Were her feelings that obvious? They had all worked so hard to keep Peter from harm.

'Don't fret,' she said. 'We've spoken of this over and over. There was nothing for you to do. Nothing for any of us to do. We did our best for so long.' She caught her breath. There were no tears left for this anymore. 'He was always so determined. If you couldn't help him, none of the rest of us could.' Margaret hunched her shoulders, composed herself.

'I'm sorry,' said Lotte.

'I know,' said Margaret. Her mother reached for her sister's hand again. 'We know. But we have to keep moving. Me, especially.'

'What will you do?' said Lotte.

'I'm going to Canada. Our cousin Nellie. I'll keep this place, rent it out. That will be enough over there. To start anyway.'

'Canada,' said Lotte.

'Keep the name.' Margaret augured her finger into the table. 'Keep the name over the door that's all I ask. We have built something. It wasn't easy. But people trust us. That is something you can't buy. Don't throw that way.'

'Amen,' said Jessie. 'J. M and M. Don't lose that.'

They sat there, the three sisters, the aunts, Jessie, Mary and Margaret, high up above the twists of the river, in the silence of the kitchen and the silence of Peter's empty room, his unfinished clays, his drawings, they sat and Lotte imagined all the years of their struggle play like a newsreel; the money saved, the money borrowed and paid with interest, the thieves chased down the hill, the women comforted when they could no longer pay, the customers with the scarves hiding broken lips, the women who stood weeping over the counter, the War Office letter tucked in their apron, the chancers who never paid, and paupers who paid with all they had. She thought of the lives they'd built against the odds. And while they had done all this, the entire world had convulsed in war and depression until finally the pain and the fire had belatedly licked all the way up their own stairwell. And as these thoughts filled the silent room with silence, they slowly reached for each other's hands, the aunts and Lotte, until the compass points were joined.

The Journal of Dr Fergusson

Sunday 23rd April 1933

I stood holding her hand for some time. I was alone with Nurse Clark again. I could tell by the way she replaced the equipment in the trolley that she had made her judgement. I cared just enough about that to say: 'We can only do our best Nurse.'

'Shall I get help to get her ready for the mortuary?' There was no eye contact. She turned away and I looked down at Lotte.

'We take the oath; do no harm.' But Nurse Clark had gone by then. I tucked Lotte's hand back under the sheets and returned to my office. I didn't want to stay with her alone.

I set off back to my office with a sense of purpose. I wasn't sure yet where that purpose might take me, but I knew the time had come for decisive action. The corridors had that strange electricity about them that always followed an incident. I looked straight ahead. Lotte had gone, slipped away from me before I could begin to help her – before I even knew her. As I walked, I tried to calibrate my loss against what it would be like in that house in Snowdon Place when the letter from Sneddon arrived. Or perhaps he would stretch to a telegram for a private patient. That awful hour would only be the start.

When I got behind my desk, I took two sheets of headed notepaper from the top drawer. I addressed one to Dr Sneddon. I wrote the words – *I resign* – in the centre of the sheet and signed at the bottom. It was childish and pointless but satisfying. I took more time over the other letter, I addressed to the Chair of the Commissioners, advising a full investigation into Dr Sneddon's work, making clear my own complicity. I no longer cared to protect myself or my reputation. I dropped both envelopes in the out-tray – let the system I'd lived by for so long carry my wrath into the future.

All this was a way of not thinking about Lotte. And what I'd done. I was pushing away the reality of what had just happened. The guilt would only come later when the shock had worn off – the remorse of failure. A mistake I couldn't undo. But I knew who was to blame – Sneddon and his obsession. I picked up the ammonite from its place on top of my in-tray. I stood up and felt it's heft in my hand, the weight of all that time. I looked down at the delicate form of the creature set in the sandstone. It had left more of a trace than most of us. I fitted my thumb into its whorl, for grip, and I ground the rock against the desk. My intention, set in stone.

I put on my white coat and pushed my fist and the stone down into the pocket. All the corridors in my life seemed to have led into this one. The noisy University hallways with Sneddon, as we made our way to the anatomy theatre, with all of this still ahead of us. The trenches of France, and the high walkways of Rainhill, Craiglochart; they all seemed endless at the time, but now they were converging towards a destination.

I passed Dr MacKenzie's room. The door was open and she had her head down over her work. If she saw me from the corner of her eye, she didn't react. And I passed on. Dr Cunninghame's door was firmly closed. He'd clearly learned it is wise to be absent in a crisis. I turned into Sneddon's offices. Mrs Nicholson tensed as if to get up, but she registered something in my face and remained in her chair.

Sneddon was standing with his back towards me, looking out into the garden. It was lit by the first proper Spring sun of the year.

'Close the door, would you?' he said. 'You'd want to keep all this quiet, I'd imagine.' He turned, hands in pockets. 'And don't worry I will.' He paused and smiled. 'For your sake, I mean.'

'My sake?'

'I don't expect you to be grateful. But this work has to go on. It's bigger than you. And me.' He was leaning back against the window frame now. The brightness made it difficult for me to see his face.

'You killed a patient,' I said.

'No,' he said. 'I think you'll find it wasn't me who killed her.' He put his head to one side, as if talking to a child. 'What were you thinking of? If you felt that strongly you could have simply persuaded me to sign her papers. Or take her away with you one evening.'

'You'd have come after her – after us.'

'Don't flatter yourself, or her. Neither of you are that important.' I was never going to be able to see the thing I really wanted – that one moment of uncertainty, fear even, flicker across his eyes. He took his watch out, glanced down then replaced it in his waistcoat pocket.

'Did you just want to have one last go? One last reminder of what it felt like? We all yearn a bit for those days. The excitement.' He was totally relaxed now, thumb in the waistcoat pocket. He was talking to me as if I was a patient. 'The war affected all of us in different ways. We couldn't have gone through all that, even as doctors, even with our training, and not be disturbed in some way. I've always been able to tell you home truths. Does anyone know you better? Even your wife?' His face softened, there was something approaching warmth in his eyes. 'Stay with me here John. Help me with this work and I will protect you. This will be a place where you can be safe.'

I tightened my fingers on the rock to remind myself it was still there, a tangible reality in the face of Sneddon's fantasy. 'Don't try to twist the truth. My conduct here has been exemplary.' I noticed the beginnings of a smirk at the corner of his mouth. 'I took whatever risks necessary to save her from your cruelty.'

He took a step forward – a reaction finally. The moment of softness had gone. 'Cruel? Is it cruel to want to make people better? To send them home? Cured.'

'You wouldn't give me enough time.'

'Time? What did you think the alternative was for her? Stay here while you talked around in circles looking for the root of her problems? Meanwhile she'd become so infected by the dayroom and the bars on the windows that she'd never be fit for the world again.'

'I've had successes with patients. I could have treated her away from here.' I was tired of this endless debate, which was more about who we were than what we believed.

'Ah yes. Your attachments. The woman in Liverpool. Was this what you wanted again? For her to be dependent on you? That episode had such a fine outcome, didn't it? Isn't it better to search for a cure, no matter how difficult than get so close we forget our professional values? That's the real cruelty.'

'I don't believe you care about cures. It's about you, and getting your own way. It's an obsession.'

'We have great power.' There was no edge to his voice now. 'We are as the clergy once were. This place is where we make all the rules. We can exercise that power for good, or…' He leant back against the window frame and the detail of his face disappeared again into the brightness. 'Or we can use it for purposes of personal vanity.' He gestured vaguely towards his desk, the neat piles of paper. 'This is the way.' It was a lecture now – perhaps this *was* something that be believed in, that he would transform our profession. 'There's no mystery. The brain is just meat and chemicals. And electricity. All your talking, all that childhood stuff, it's important. It's nice for the patient, interesting for us, I understand that, but it only gets you so far.' He moved away from the window. I almost took a step forward, to close in on him, but there was still room enough between us.

'I've written to the Commissioners. It's in the system.'

Did he falter? Hardly. 'Mrs Nicholson will find it. I like her to keep an eye on the mails. That will save your embarrassment. The Commissioners know all about the work. They're on the side of progress. If I have to, I can find all sorts of delays, a sympathetic investigator if it comes to the bit. Don't worry, I'll square it.'

'My resignation. It's in the mail too.'

'That I can intercept too. If you want me to. We don't need to be hasty. It's been a difficult day, God knows. You can stay. We can run trials of your interventions alongside mine. Comparative studies. Proper analysis. There is no knowing what we are on the brink of here. Someday there will be surgery, the ability to cut the trauma right out. Safely, quickly. Think on that. In the meantime, we have the chemicals. And you're good with chemicals. Mostly.' He half smiled.

'You've forgotten they are people,' I said.

'And you think they're your friends. When you're not fucking them.' The smile had gone.

That didn't provoke me. The anger had gone by then. It all felt controlled and inevitable, like on the Front when a barrage began to find your range. There was nowhere to hide and the outcome was out of your hands.

Sneddon took a step away again, turned his back on me and looked out into the garden. 'You've always lacked ambition, commitment to your profession. Imagination too. It takes more than a gold medal.' He rocked back on his heels and his voice softened. I was a patient again. 'You're a kind person, John, I know that. You didn't have to do what you did, today, or all those times in France. We all want to intervene, do something. Sometimes we need to show off what we can do. In the name of kindness.' He paused. 'Well, whatever her future might have been, no matter how difficult for her and for her family, we will never know.' He made a small gesture towards the window, towards the sunlit garden, like flicking water off his fingers.

He and I were separated by the width of his office. It was no range at all. But I threw the rock at the back of his skull with all the force I had.

Did he sense the movement through the enclosed air? Was he expecting it? He turned his head and that was enough. The stone flew on, the glass shattered, jagged sheets fell back into the room and my ammonite embed itself in the neatly aerated lawn. My rage, my resentment, my righteousness went out through the window too. There was nothing left. Sneddon's face looked calm, but his hands were out of his pockets and I saw them shake. 'Mrs Nicholson.' There was a tremble in his voice too. 'Call Madden, tell him I need him up here immediately.' She was in the doorway already but quickly stepped away when she saw me make towards the door. As I did there was a sudden expansion, like a benign airburst, and the room inflated with cold Spring air, smelling of earth. All the papers which had been on Sneddon's desk rose over my head, flying and fluttering until they fell like shot doves on the carpet at my feet.

INQUEST INTO THE DEATH OF MRS CHARLOTTE RAYMOND Presented to the General Board of Control of Scotland.

14/11/39

Background

Mrs Charlotte Raymond, a private patient at Stirling Asylum, died on 23rd of April 1933. The cause of death was heart failure due to an underlying long-term arrhythmic heart condition. She was admitted seven days earlier after a period of deteriorating mental health. The fatality occurred before a full assessment of her mental condition could be made by physicians at the Asylum, but her doctor, Dr Campbell of Stirling, reported that she had given her family cause for great concern, neglecting her children, subject to occasional hysterical episodes and obsessive nocturnal walking. The latter behaviour placing her at great risk, her husband asked Dr Campbell to initiate a formal request for emergency admission to the Asylum. She was admitted at 2.00pm on 16th April 1933.

Context

Two points should be clarified at this stage of this report.

1. Considerable time has elapsed since the events under question took place. At the family's request, Dr Sneddon, Medical Superintendent at the time led an initial investigation. This report was not available to the present enquiry. A number of files were discarded after becoming severely water damaged in the winter of 1936. It is understood that this report confirmed the cause of death but did not explore the circumstances further.

2. The elapse of time has presented complexities in contacting potential contributors to the enquiry. The present international emergency has also made communications more difficult. However, the current crisis has also given this enquiry added impetus. The Asylum is presently being re-structured to meet an anticipated need for residential accommodation for future casualties. Men suffering both physical and mental injuries will soon be our patients. In this circumstance it is imperative to clear outstanding questions and to focus on future demands.

Testimony

The enquiry sought evidence from:
Dr Sneddon, Medical Superintendent
Dr Fergusson, Depute Medical Superintendent
Dr MacKenzie
Dr Harris
Dr Cunninghame
Miss Brown
Mr Alan Strang
Mr Samuel Raymond
Mrs Grace Semple

It is no reflection on the efforts of the staff involved that testimony, written or verbal, was only obtained from:
Dr Harris
Dr Cunninghame
Mr Strang
Mr Raymond (letter appendix 1)

The circumstances of the other potential witnesses are as follows:
Dr Sneddon was approached in his position as

Director of Mental Health for the Commonwealth of Massachusetts. He is, as the Board will be aware, at the forefront of research in our profession involving the use of electric therapy for the most severely afflicted patients. His work there continues to reflect positively on Stirling Asylum where many of his research interests were formed. A note was received from his secretary that his schedule did not allow him to devote time to events of six years previously. Moreover, he had himself thoroughly investigated the events in question and did not consider that there was any warrant for an enquiry at this date. We ensured that the best wishes of the Board were passed to Dr Sneddon and we wished him continued success in his vital work.

After a period in private practice Dr Fergusson re-enlisted in the Royal Army Medical Corps. We approached his commanding officer, who reported that Dr Fergusson had considerable skills and experience. This had facilitated the unusual step of a medical officer of his age being assigned to an active service unit. He was currently with his unit and likely to be deployed in France. Again, we took the decision not to pursue a physician and an officer who is serving his country. We also wrote to his wife but received no reply.

We were keen to interview Mrs Grace Semple. We believed that she would have important information about the deceased patient's mental condition before arriving at the hospital. Dr Campbell's clinical notes show that it was she who had first approached him with concerns about Mrs Raymond's behaviour and had initiated meetings between Mr Raymond, Dr Campbell and herself. Our search was unsuccessful. Mr Raymond reported that she had been dismissed from his service shortly after the death. It is understood that she went back into service with a family in a larger rural property in England, but had subsequently taken up munitions work. We did not have the resources to follow this up.

Miss Brown, who volunteered with the Asylum at the time and had contact with the patient, is now the proprietor of an independent facility offering non-mainstream treatments which concentrate on the relationship between patients and the natural environment. Board members will be aware of recent attempts to investigate the efficacy of her programme of treatment. On that occasion Board Inspectors were physically assaulted by Miss Brown when an unscheduled visit to her facility was made. We did not expect or receive a reply to our request for information. Given these circumstances, we set no great store by the trustworthiness of Miss Brown's testimony and her absence is no loss to the enquiry.

Dr Harris, now in retirement, was interviewed. He indicated that there was some friction between Drs Sneddon and Fergusson. This, in his opinion was a natural, and healthy, difference of opinion around approaches to treatment, given added edge by the fact that the doctors had studied together and so there was some scope for personal and professional rivalry.

There is further evidence of friction between Drs Sneddon and Fergusson. It came from Mr Allan Strang, Asylum Farm Manager. He stated that his brother, a gamekeeper at the time, witnessed an

altercation between the physicians during a shoot
at his place of work. He told his brother that
voices were raised, and he had been alarmed. Both
men had been drinking and firearms were involved.
We could not verify this as Mr Strang's brother
lost his life in a shotgun accident two years ago.
However, as a vital part of the Asylum community,
we have no reason to doubt Mr Alan Strang's report.

Findings

1. We conclude that the death was a natural
   medical episode. The Asylum is designed to
   specifically treat mental health conditions.
   We are very proud of our reputation for
   careful and considerate care of our patients.
   We cannot be cut off from the rest of humanity
   and our patients suffer from the same range of
   ailments as the rest of the general population.

2. We place an emphasis on diagnosing possible
   physical health conditions during the
   patient's time with us. The nature of their
   mental health conditions can make this a
   difficult task. But we are especially vigilant
   concerning the admission examinations and we
   carefully consider any medical notes which
   accompany new arrivals.

3. Dr Campbell's notes accompanying this patient
   concerned themselves solely with matters
   of mental health. There was no mention of
   underlying heart conditions. A history of
   heart palpitations and weakness was verified
   by Dr Campbell in a letter to the Asylum
   following the death.

4. Nevertheless, we would expect even a brief
   admission examination to note the presence of

arrhythmic cardiomyopathy. The examination was carried out by Dr Gerald Cunninghame. Although the most junior doctor in the Asylum at the time, it is poor professional practice to fail to note a serious condition. We try to provide a stress-free environment for our patients. This is not always possible, and a heart condition of this type is potentially dangerous in our community. Drug therapies would have been available.

5. Accordingly, we found that Dr Cunninghame did not meet the high clinical standards we set in the Asylum and he was dismissed from our employment on 31st October 1939.

6. Dr Cunninghame subsequently joined the Royal Air Force and is currently undergoing basic flight training.

Action

1. We ask the Board to note the findings of the enquiry.

2. We ask the Board to resist any attempt to re-open the matter. It is not good use of resources in a time of national crisis.

3. Improved admission examination procedures have been in place for some time to ensure that there is no repetition of this oversight.

Conclusion and Notes

The enquiry has been properly carried out, findings established and action taken.

Dr MacKenzie, although a member or staff at the Asylum at the time, and known to all those involved, had no personal contact with the case,

and as author of the enquiry report, could not,
in any event, give evidence.

Thanks   are   due   to   Senior   Nurse   Clark   who
compiled most of the evidence for this enquiry.
As a footnote it should be recorded that highly
trained professional nurses now make a substantial
contribution to the running of medical aspects
of the Asylum. Their work is invaluable.

Signed
Dr Agnes MacKenzie. MD RMPA
Medical Superintendent.

Appendix 1:

> 5 Snowdon Place
> Stirling
> 5 May 1938

Dear Chairman,
Five years have passed since my wife Charlotte died while
under your care. Five bitter, hard years for the entire family.
For her children especially, there has been no light in their
lives since she went through your gates. While Charlotte's
mother has been dead for over ten years, her sister Marguerite has also lived under the pressure of the sudden loss and
has faced her own difficulties as a result.

I was persuaded that the only way for her to overcome her
troubles was by entrusting her to the treatments available in

Stirling Asylum. I overcame my huge anxieties and believed that modern medicine had challenged the dark perceptions we all hold of these places.

Your records will show that I have suggested an enquiry several times and have been provided with a range of reasons why this was not possible. My dealings with the Medical Superintendent at the time were difficult and unproductive. Furthermore, I have had promises, but no assurances, from the current Medical Superintendent that a proper investigation will be initiated.

While the current situation is peaceful, I fear that the international situation will deteriorate and the matter will become lost in great events.

My children grow older. My oldest son has recently won a scholarship to study music, and my daughter, though still very young, is something of a musical prodigy. I cannot stress enough how they have suffered from the loss of their mother.

I am not without means. I have a number of retail and residential properties. My instinct has been to put the matter in the hands of lawyers. But Charlotte's aunt, a member of various local committees, has persuaded me that a final appeal to yourself, as Chair of the National Board, should be attempted before legal redress.

I trust I will not be disappointed again.

Yours faithfully

Samuel Raymond Esq.

MARTIN

Saturday 7th November 2020

'I told him. Don't say anything.'

'Mikkel?'

'Yes. He had no right. It wasn't his family to uncover. No! Come here right now. Now I meant!' The dog was usually much more obedient for my daughter than for me, but the lure of the unspeakable, somewhere deep in the bracken, was too much.

'It's not his fault,' I said. 'If he hadn't told me I'd never have known. I'd have no story to tell. I liked Mikkel.'

'Whether you liked him or not isn't the point. That was my decision. The point is he should have shut up. He had no right.'

'The dead have difficulty getting through to their lawyers. They've no rights at all. It was all on an open access site, anyone could find the basic details.' I could tell I wasn't going to be able to convince her. She strode off into the bush to retrieve the dog. They reappeared, the dog now on the lead and looking very pleased with herself.

My daughter looked less delighted. 'Look at that dog! Filthy.' The dog didn't care much, she wagged her tail and as soon as she was off the lead again, ran off up the track. 'OK, but you'd still never have known. I don't remember you ever being the least bit interested in your ancestors.'

'I'd have lost out then. It was a bit missing, like pages torn out a book that you need to make sense of the ending.' I said. My daughter marched along, a step or two in front. The roadway was scarred by the heavy timber trucks that had been taking cut wood from the forest all summer. The cold hovered between autumnal and wintry. No gloves but you regretted the decision to leave them in the car. The wind rustled frost-shrivelled leaves on a few scrawny deciduous trees. The big commercial Sitka spruces were unmoved.

'Still better if you'd discovered it yourself. Or if I had told you.'

'Your telling me wouldn't have made a difference. Families aren't sealed units. It's not the Mafia.' I sensed she was about to cut in, so added quickly: 'Even if it seems that way sometimes.'

The forest road here skirted what had once been tall swaying trees. Now all that was left was the debris that had no commercial value. Already it was bleaching white in the rain and the wind. For reasons that weren't clear – to deter deer? – the contractor's digger had piled smashed branches round the perimeter of the old plantation. Spiked and tangled, it reminded me of photographs of the Western Front. If you looked over this wall into the acres of devastation you could see tiny green seedlings pushing through the chaos, the next forest.

'You can't deny information,' I said. 'It's out there, things happened in the past even if you didn't know about it. And this way she wasn't lost. Her story told and all that.' I was trying not to breathe too heavily. It was a punishing slope and my daughter set a tough pace. 'I don't blame anyone for the silence. There was so much shame attached to it that I can understand that no one would talk about it.'

My daughter stopped and picked up a broad brown and white feather. What was that? A buzzard? As she spoke, she smoothed the ragged edge of the feather so the barbs knitted together and it formed its proper shape. 'I'm not sure it was just shame. It might also be shock. Losing a parent must be tough, but in these circumstances it must have been traumatic. It's not even like it was an ordinary hospital.' She tucked the repaired feather into the bunched needles of a spruce.

'You're right,' I said. 'Shock can silence you for generations. My grandfather was an amazing person in many ways, but he wouldn't have been especially warm and comforting to these children. If he hadn't spoken about it at the time, and maybe he thought that was for the best, then that would be that. You can mean well and do harm.'

'Your grandfather didn't quite do it all on his own though. There was a whole other family. These sisters.' She pinged the feather with her finger and it fluttered away into the dried-out grass. 'Did it make you feel closer to your dad? Knowing?'

I stopped, I was looking at the view that had appeared as we reached the crest of the road, down across the Forth to the flares of one of the last industrial sites in the country – the petrochemical works. That too would pass, and quickly.

'No. It wasn't something I could grasp. The awfulness of it all. So, in some ways I felt even more distant.' Banks of cloud were heaping up, miles away, off towards the low Borders' hills. 'But I did get a better idea of the gap that had always been there. The holding back. I knew why he didn't want to get too close. I think he was protecting me. In case he went suddenly. Or something that might happen and change everything in a moment.'

'Well. That's not as if you could ever have discussed with him, is it?' She stopped now too. 'Don't you try any of that protecting stuff with me. I'll take my chances thank you very much.'

'I tried to get a grip on it all as best I could. When you don't know all the facts sometimes you have to do what you can.' I wasn't so sure about this bit, so I shut up. I punched my daughter's arm lightly. In fiction, I'd have hugged her at this moment, high above the Forth in the November winds. Families, generations, and so on. But the dog ran up and, rich with fox shit, put her paws all over my shiny down jacket.

Later when Yvonne was back to the city, back to her real life, and the dog was cleaned and fed and was curled up with her head and all four paws on the radiator, Molly and I sat down across the kitchen table.

'Well?' she said. 'Did you find what you were looking for?'

'I wasn't sure what I was looking for.' I was playing with one of the placemats Yvonne had woven for her Higher Art. 'It would have helped if I'd had a proper quest. A proper mystery to solve.' There was a different figure on each mat. It had been the work of decades to try to sort out what they represented.

'But you worked out what happened to her? Who was to blame.'

I turned the mat upside down. 'I'm less sure about that. The more I found the less I was sure.'

'Great,' said Molly. She leaned back. 'All those hours. Days. You'd have been better taking up landscape painting.' She tapped her placemat. 'Something arty. Or,' she paused to let this sink in, 'golf.'

'I did learn that if you create a silence it will grow. The unspoken is contagious. Down through the years. Nearly a century. Until now. I'm still not sure if it was a good idea or not. I think it was a silence to protect everyone. Not to hide.'

'But you understand more?'

'About my father and me, yes. About the distance. Not a stand-off, nothing hostile although we disagreed on lots. But emotions never got as far as words. And about my grandfather. I realised why he was so pugnacious. And difficult. But I don't judge them. They all had their reasons. They all meant well.'

'It's too late to ask them about it.'

'I'm not sure I'd ask them even if I could. I'd respect their right not to talk about it.'

'What about your grandmother? That was supposed to be what it was all about. At least you rescued her story, pulled her out of the past. And if you hadn't done it, just think, someone else might have found her in the archive.'

'I couldn't tell her story. Only she could do that. Or at a push the people who were around at the time. But they chose not to. Or maybe they really didn't know what was going on. They didn't have the documents.'

'The unverified documents.'

'That's true but it was all I had. The Asylum report and my grandfather's letter all looked authentic enough. Doctor Fergusson was a strange man. So strange that he was probably the real thing.'

'I see.' Molly got up. 'This is more your story then. Not hers. Typical.' She was heading upstairs. 'All about you.'

The dog growled in her sleep, paws twitching.

'Of course it had to be about me, my version. It's all you can do, unverified documents or not,' I said, trying to convince myself as much as Molly. 'You can't reach back. Not properly. They were good people, I think. Trying to do their best.' I was faltering. 'You can just possibly understand the past, I'm not sure you can know it.'

But by the time I finished Molly had gone. She'd heard this sort of thing before. Her bare feet padded on the wooden stairs, then creaked overhead. The dog settled and the house was silent.

EPILOGUE

Lotte was the name they used in the family. Or didn't use. I might have heard it used once, maybe twice in my childhood. That's how people disappear into the past, with all their traits and skills and that thing they said to a patronising neighbour. All that is lost.

What is worse is that it was no great loss to me. It didn't leave a gaping hole in my growing up. I just had the usual bunch of crushing insecurities and frustrations. Otherwise, it was what they used to call idyllic. I didn't know what I didn't have until I went looking for the few traces that marked the edges of her story.

I have seen a photograph of Lotte. She is sitting at the Collard and Collard piano. That model of piano sold at £71 in 1936. In the same period an MG Sports Tourer cost £160 and a family house could be bought for £300. Sam is standing behind her. Their clothes are immaculate. It is the late 1920s. She would have been in her early thirties – beautiful, dark, her eyes intense, but showing no trace of any internal storms. Or at least that's how I remember it. It's said that every photograph foreshadows a loss. In this case the photograph foretells a greater absence, a disappearance. I couldn't change that absence, but I could attempt to fill the silence with a story.

I told her story as best I could, from what I had. And from what was in Dr Fergusson's unverified journal. There is always imagination involved in organising the material, always choices to be made. Had I rescued her from the past, from the decisions that had been made for her? Or was I just another well-meaning man, still making decisions on her behalf? I'd given her a voice, but it was my voice not hers. The only consolation was that I'd taken possession of her story; at least I had appropriated it and not a stranger.

The past still remains out there somewhere. I understood, I think, the pressures on everyone involved in the story. Although that in itself sounds very 21st century, alien to the period. What I tried to acknowledge was that life then, like life now, was complex and nuanced. Absolutes crumble when you put them under any sort of scrutiny. I understood more and judged less. I understood my father's reticence, my grandfather's confident carapace, all the things unsaid took form in their won tortured logic. It was a silence designed to protect, not to remove Lotte from history. I had no idea if that was a good thing or not. Easy judgements are easy. My thoughts were satisfyingly conflicted.

But the past was still just beyond the trees. I understood but I didn't know. Words on the page had filled the silence of all those decades and I had got closer to a part of my own history. And I'd replaced the old family origin myths with a new narrative – of Lotte and her astonishing Aunts.

I could light her up in the dusky interior of my head. Lotte singing in the Holy Rude church. I could pick her out in the streets of Stirling in her meticulously researched coat and hat and shoes. I could place her among the news of the period, both local and domestic. I could understand her dislocation, and her yearnings and her frustrations and her sense of betrayal. I could feel all that in my imagination. But, because I had heard no one tell their stories of her, she would always remain just out of reach. I had only one version of her story – my own. And that was not reliable.

On the dark roads it was different. When I was out in the night winds it went beyond understanding, out there were things I did know. I knew in my bones the intensity of her craving for a different destiny and I knew the space she'd left in the lives of her family – all of them now part of the circling darkness.

ACKNOWLEDGEMENTS

Damien Mosley, for insightful editing and belief,
Kika Hendry, for marketing smarts,
Kevin MacNeil and Liam Bell and colleagues in the Creative
Writing Department at the University of Stirling, for sending
me back to another draft,
Sarah Bromage and staff in Archives and Collections, also at
the University of Stirling, for factual inspiration,
my alarmingly grown-up children for encouraging this
project with a minimum of eye-rolling,
Kipper for listening thoughtfully to my early ideas and for
dragging me away from the screen,
and M, for everything else.

THE ROCK 'N' ROLL
OF INDIE PUBLISHING

We're Indie Novella and we were founded by a group of friends with one mission, to make publishing more accessible to everyone.

We love literary fiction, but we don't love the snobbery that gets associated with it. Great literary fiction comprises of stories that capture our imagination and resonate with us. Stories that shed light on modern issues, which use relatable and understandable language, which are about characters who speak for the communities we live in.

That's why we're publishing novels which make literary fiction less elitist and get readers as passionate about books as we are. We're also revolutionising publishing by doing something so few others are. Levelling the playing field. Our writing course is funded by the Arts Council and has been designed in collaboration with leading literary agencies such as Watson Little, David Godwin Associates and Georgina Capel and is completely free.

When it comes to writing and storytelling we believe there are so many voices that go unheard. Therefore we made a vow: We won't sit down. We won't shut up. We will commit to being our authentic selves. Just like our authors.

Stories of identity, community, belonging, and being proud of who we are. Our authors write the stories that represent what they stand for, in a truly authentic voice.

If that's not Rock 'n' Roll, I don't know what is.

ABOUT THE AUTHOR

Martin Raymond is an unrepentant late starter. After working in communications for the NHS, teaching in schools and universities, plus some broadcasting with BBC Radio Scotland, he studied creative writing at Stirling University. His work has been longlisted for the Watson, Little x Indie Novella Prize and shortlisted for the VS Pritchett Short Story Prize. His short stories have appeared in the New Writing Scotland annual collection in 2019, 2020 and 2023. *Lotte* is his first novel.